Daisy in Chains

Also by Sharon Bolton
(previously published as S. J. Bolton)

Sacrifice
Awakening
Blood Harvest
Now You See Me
Dead Scared
Lost
A Dark and Twisted Tide
Little Black Lies

Daisy in Chains

SHARON BOLTON

Minotaur Books
New York

DAISY IN CHAINS. Copyright © 2016 by Sharon Bolton. All rights reserved. Printed in the United States of America. For information, address St. Martin's Press, 175 Fifth Avenue, New York, N.Y. 10010.

www.minotaurbooks.com

The Library of Congress has cataloged the hardcover edition as follows:

Names: Bolton, S. J., author.
Title: Daisy in chains / Sharon Bolton.
Description: First U.S. Edition. | New York : Minotaur Books, 2016.
Identifiers: LCCN 2016016831| ISBN 9781250103420 (hardcover) | ISBN 9781250103437 (e-book)
Subjects: | BISAC: FICTION / Suspense. | GSAFD: Suspense fiction.
Classification: LCC PR6102.O49 D35 2016 | DDC 823/.92—dc23
LC record available at https://lccn.loc.gov/2016016831

ISBN 978-1-250-13006-8 (trade paperback)

Our books may be purchased in bulk for promotional, educational, or business use. Please contact your local bookseller or the Macmillan Corporate and Premium Sales Department at 1-800-221-7945, extension 5442, or by e-mail at MacmillanSpecialMarkets@macmillan.com.

First published in Great Britain by Bantam Press, an imprint of Transworld Publishers, a Random House Group company

First Minotaur Books Paperback Edition: June 2017

10 9 8 7 6 5 4 3 2

For the ladies of the Blue Socks Book Club,
who have cheered me on from the very beginning.

Prologue

HMP Isle of Wight – Parkhurst
Clissold Road
Newport

My love,

When I think of the moments that have given me greatest pleasure: scaling an impossible rock face, watching the moon over the ocean on Christmas morning, the first time my dog saw snow – all of them pale beside the second I looked into your eyes and knew that you loved me.

You come into this dismal place like a rainbow. Your colours glow, scaring away shadows, softening the cold, hard lines of my prison. Your presence changes everything.

When I first came here, I thought no fate could be more cruel. How wrong I was. These bars are nothing. Being apart from you, living every moment of my day without you, is the torture that will break me.

I yearn for you.

Hamish

PROPERTY OF AVON AND SOMERSET POLICE. Ref: 544/45.2
Hamish Wolfe.

1

HMP Isle of Wight – Parkhurst
Clissold Road
Newport

Maggie Rose
c/o Ellipsis Literary Agency
Bute Street
London WC3

Monday, 2 November 2015

Dear Miss Rose,

I am not a killer.

I know the lawyer in you will be saying: evidence, give me evidence. And believe me, I can, lots of it. But for now, I make one simple appeal to the seeker of truth that I know you to be. I am an innocent man. Please help me.

Sincerely yours,

Hamish Wolfe

Anne Louise Moorcroft
Ellipsis Literary Agency
Bute Street
London WC3

Mr Hamish Wolfe
c/o HMP Isle of Wight

18 November 2015

Dear Mr Wolfe

Re: Maggie Rose

My client regrets that her answer to you must remain the same. Her
current projects will keep her entirely occupied for the foreseeable
future and consequently she must decline, once again, your request
that she consult regarding your case.

She has asked that I refrain from forwarding any future correspondence
from you. It would be better if you did not contact us again.

Yours faithfully

Anne Louise Moorcroft

Chapter 1

ON THE SOMERSET COAST of the Bristol Channel, roughly equidistant from Minehead and Weston-super-Mare, is a large storm-water drain.

No one likes it.

A blackened pipe, four feet in diameter, the drain carries excess water from the arable farmland of the Mendip Hills and outflows into the Channel a hundred metres from the sea wall. At high tide, seawater moans and roars inside it, whilst rocks and driftwood crash against the concrete sides with a startling ferocity.

As hikers, dog walkers and fishermen pass by the access manhole they quicken their steps. A square of steel railings keeps them at a distance, but the tall, cage-like structure merely serves the illusion that something menacing is moving below ground. And no one relishes the fetid, oily droplets that shoot through the meshed steel cover with every strong wave. Organic matter gets trapped inside and rots. Indeed, the drain captures and concentrates everything about the sea that is dark and dreadful. Maggie Rose has always been unnerved by the drain. In a few more minutes she will be afraid that she is about to die in it.

Most days, when Maggie reaches the seafront she takes the cliff path. This morning she is distracted by a small Raggedy Ann doll that lies, discarded, on the sea wall. She bends to pick it up, puzzled, because children don't come to this beach. There is no sand to play in and the large smooth pebbles are awkward underfoot. Maggie has never seen a child here and wouldn't expect to in the middle of winter.

With the doll in her hand, she looks around, at the angry water, at the gulls that are high and sly amidst the lowering clouds. In the field behind, she sees sheep, limp and miserable in their frosted coats.

The beach is almost empty. She doesn't see a child. Just two people who may have lost one. Up to their knees in water, at the point where the storm drain outflows, are a thin woman with short fair hair and a man dressed for fishing. The woman seems to be trying to get into the drain, but the breaking waves, and the fisherman, are holding her back.

'What's happening?' Maggie isn't sure they will hear, because the wind is snatching up and stealing all sounds but those of its own making. Another wave hits the couple and the man falls.

The water is icy cold when Maggie steps into it. The churning pebbles make wading dangerous and she can't see the seabed through the grey, silty water. Slightly out of breath, she reaches the couple as the fisherman staggers to his feet.

'I'm going in,' the woman says. 'It will kill my son if anything happens to her.'

The rag doll, now tucked in Maggie's coat pocket? A grandchild? A child of six years old or younger could stand upright in the drain, would see only the adventure the mysterious tunnel offered, not think about the danger of the returning tide.

'When did you last see her?' Maggie has to shout in the woman's ear.

'A minute ago, maybe two.' The woman's voice is almost gone from the strain of yelling. 'She was running further in, away from the waves.'

Well, that was something, at least.

'You can't go in this way,' Maggie says. 'It'll be completely full in a few minutes. You'll both drown.'

Minutes might be optimistic. The tide is already high, is nipping at Maggie's thighs. The water level in the pipe will rise with each new wave, until there is simply nowhere for the little girl to go.

'We might be able to get her out higher up.' Maggie turns to the fisherman. 'Can you stay here for as long as it's safe, just in case she gets washed out?' To the woman she says, 'Come with me, I'll need help.'

Holding hands, the two women wade back through the water, their clothes sodden before they reach the shore. As they clamber back over the sea wall, Maggie, the younger by over twenty years, runs ahead. She walks this way every day. She has seen workmen access the drain from above.

'What is it?' The woman catches up as Maggie reaches the metal fence surrounding the access manhole.

'Ssshh!'

Both listen to the rumbling, sucking and moaning beneath their feet. Something sizeable is crashing around beneath them.

'Those are waves you can hear.' Maggie points through the railings. 'When the tide's fully up, it sprays out through the grille in that manhole cover. It's not doing that yet, so the drain beneath us is still dry, at least some of the time. Give me a leg-up.'

On the other side of the fence, Maggie drops flat and puts her face against the grille. 'Hello! Can you hear me? Come this way!'

'Daisy,' says the woman, her voice heavy and hoarse. 'Her name's Daisy.'

Maggie yells again as she tugs at the manhole cover. 'Daisy, if you can hear me, come this way.' She tugs again but the cover doesn't move.

'Will this help?' The fisherman has arrived and is holding something out to her. 'It's a Leatherman. Try one of the spanners.'

To the sound of the grandmother's whimpering, Maggie takes the all-purpose tool and finds a spanner the right size. 'Hold on, Daisy, we're coming.' She twists the lock again and feels it give.

'Come on, lass,' says the fisherman. 'You can do it.'

The lock is released. The hatch clangs back on to concrete and Maggie is staring into darkness below. Before she can change her mind, she swings her legs round and jumps. Crouched in the tunnel, she can see nothing, hear nothing, but the sound of water getting closer. Holding on to the sides for balance, bent over almost double, she begins to move forward, calling encouragement to the child.

'Daisy! Don't be scared. Just come towards me.'

Fewer than a dozen steps into the drain and water is covering her ankles, surging higher with every wave. The grandmother and the fisherman are still yelling for the child, which is good, because Maggie doesn't want to open her mouth in here again if she can help it. A dozen steps more. The water is almost at her knees. Her back is starting to ache and the muscles of her thighs can't hold her in this position for much longer.

'Daisy?'

A big wave strikes, hitting her full in the face. The child is gone. This is hopeless. She turns back, just as another wave throws her off balance. As she stumbles to her knees, Maggie hears a scraping noise behind, followed by a strangled cry and then heavy breathing. A shivering body is pushing against her. She turns to see terrified eyes looking into hers, hears a desperate, grateful yipping.

Daisy is a dog.

She can curse her own idiocy later. Maggie grabs hold of the dog's collar, just as another wave tries to pull the animal back out to sea. As the wave recedes, the dog kicks back against Maggie's body and scampers towards the hatch.

Another wave, a bigger one. For a second Maggie is beneath the surface, feeling herself sliding along the concrete base of the drain. There is nothing in the smooth, circular pipe to catch hold of. Another wave, she slides back again. The waves are giving her no time to recover before the next strikes. She is being dragged deeper into the tunnel.

Some yards away, Daisy, unable to leap to safety, is barking. The woman and the fisherman are still yelling. Almost too cold to keep moving, hardly able to get her breath, Maggie crawls forward.

She is going to die saving a dog. How completely ridiculous.

Then the dog is on top of her, its sharp claws digging through her jacket, using her as a stepping stone. Claws scrape against stone and then the dog, at least, is safe.

Maggie plants her feet, holds on tight to the sides of the manhole and jumps. Safely on dry land, she falls to the ground beside the exhausted Daisy.

'Oh, good girl, clever girl, well done.'

Unsure whether the woman's praise is for her, or the creature she's just rescued, Maggie runs her hand down the flank of the wet, trembling dog. Big, brown eyes stare up at her from a sweet canine face. The white, smooth body is peppered with black spots. Daisy is a Dalmatian.

'Hey, beautiful.' Nudging the dog out of the way, Maggie lowers the hatch again just as a wave – the one that could have killed them both – comes racing up the pipe. She hears something metallic clanking against the grille and knows instinctively what it is. A quick check in her pocket confirms it. She has left her car keys in the tunnel.

'I'm Sandra,' says the woman as she starts her car engine and waves goodbye to the fisherman. 'I'll have you home in no time.'

8

'Thank you.' Maggie watches her own car getting smaller in the wing mirror. She will have to cycle back to collect it. Or call a cab.

'I think there's another rug in the back.'

Maggie already has a travel rug around her shoulders and the heating has been cranked up to maximum but she can't stop shaking. 'You're sure you can get into your house? Because I'll take you back to ours, run you a bath there. I'm Sandra, by the way.'

'I keep a key hidden in the garden.' Maggie would prefer to take the two-mile journey in silence.

'I can phone my husband. Get him to turn up the heating, make you some hot chocolate? My clothes would probably drown you, but they'll be warm and dry.'

'Thank you, but I left the heating on.'

'Do you have dogs?' Sandra isn't an attractive woman. Her face is too thin, her lips almost non-existent, her jaw too prominent. Probably almost as cold as Maggie, her skin is mottled, the tip of her nose bright red. She needs to get home too.

'It would be with me, don't you think, if I had a dog?' Maggie turns to look at the Dalmatian, fast asleep on the back seat. The Raggedy Ann doll, sniffed out and claimed by the dog before the two of them had even got back over the fence, is just visible beneath its head. 'I'm glad Daisy is OK.'

Sandra pulls over to let another car pass. 'I came here today to talk to you,' she says. 'I didn't want to come to your house, I didn't want to intrude, so I thought I'd wait for you at the beach. And then Daisy ran off just before you arrived. It all nearly went so horribly wrong.'

Maggie fixes her gaze straight ahead. 'The road's clear,' she says.

'I drove over this morning,' Sandra says before she's even changed gear. 'And yesterday morning too. I watched your car pull out of your drive. I guessed you were coming here. And that you come at high tide.'

To have made that guess, the woman must have been watching her for more than two days, has probably followed her here before now.

'What did you want to talk to me about?' They are almost at the main road. She can walk from here, if necessary.

'I've read all your books.' Sandra is breathing heavily, as though walking at speed, not driving a car along a country lane. 'Someone sent

9

me three of them, about six months ago. A well-wisher, I never did find out who. I bought the others.'

'Thank you.' It will take between ten and fifteen minutes to get home from this point. Longer if she is forced to walk.

'I enjoyed them. Is enjoyed the right word? I'm not sure. I found them interesting. You make a good argument. They were readable. Not too much technical stuff. And you go easy on the gore, and the violence.'

'Readers usually choose crime fiction for the gratuitous violence,' Maggie says.

'Are you working on another one?'

'Always.'

'I don't suppose you're allowed to say what it's about? I mean, who it's about?'

'I'm allowed to do whatever I like. But I choose not to talk about work in progress, I'm afraid.'

'You're obviously wondering why I'm going on like this.'

'Actually, I'm wondering how you found out where I live.'

Sandra slows to take a corner. When she is back on the straight she glances over. 'I'm Sandra Wolfe,' she says.

For a second, the two women stare at each other. 'Hamish's mother,' Sandra adds, unnecessarily.

'This is Hamish's dog.' Maggie looks round at the motionless animal. 'Of course. I remember a photograph of the two of them together. It was used a lot while the trial was ongoing.'

'His defence team thought it would be the most sympathetic. Hamish with his beloved dog. Not that it made any difference.'

'Her name is Daisy?'

'My son wrote to you. Four times. I know you saw the letters. He showed me your replies.'

'How did you get my address?'

Sandra's chin has the stubborn set of someone who knows she's in the wrong but won't back down. 'Someone found it for me. I promised I wouldn't say who exactly. Please don't worry. I wouldn't dream of invading your privacy. That's why I waited to talk to you at the beach.'

'One could argue this is a greater invasion. At home I could close the door on you. All I can do now is wait until you drive me home.'

They've reached the main road. Sandra applies the handbrake.

'Miss Rose, my son is innocent. He isn't a killer. I know him.'

Maggie wraps her arms around herself. The cold is starting to hurt. 'I'm sure you believe that, but do you imagine any mother of a convicted killer says anything different? The traffic is usually heavy here at this time of day. You need to be careful.'

They pull out into the path of a yellow car.

'He was with me the night Zoe Sykes was killed.' Sandra ignores the angry horn. 'We had dinner, I drove him home. He couldn't have killed her, so it follows he didn't kill the others, doesn't it? All four women were killed by the same man, so if Hamish didn't kill one of them, he couldn't have killed the others.'

They cross the village boundary. Less than five minutes to Maggie's house. 'I'm afraid I know very little about the case.'

'The police didn't believe me. They thought I was lying. The restaurant couldn't help. There was no CCTV footage. The staff couldn't remember, but I know he was with me. He didn't kill that Sykes woman.'

'And yet a jury believed that he did.'

'Have you ever been in a prison, Miss Rose?'

'Yes, many times.'

'Then you know what it's like. Decent people, people like Hamish, they can't survive in prison. The stench and the violence and the endless noise. He's not known a moment of silence since he was convicted.'

'Then the best thing you can do for him is keep him well supplied with ear plugs.'

Sandra flinches. 'There was a fight on his corridor just yesterday. They pick on him all the time. Every day he's in fear for his life.'

'Why me?'

'I'm sorry?'

'Why is it so important to your son that I take up his case? Turn right here, please, on to the High Street.'

'It isn't just me. There's a whole bunch of people who support Hamish. People who've read about the case. Who know there was a miscarriage of justice. Miss Rose. I wish you'd meet them. They have a website. You can google it.'

'Mrs Wolfe.'

'Sandra, please.'

'As I wrote to your son directly, my work schedule is full for the foreseeable future. I simply don't have the time. Just before the pub, on the right. Thank you for bringing me home.'

'I can drive you back to collect your car. When you've changed.'

'I'll get a cab. And now, if you'll excuse my being blunt, I don't expect to see you waiting for me at the beach again.'

'Wait!'

Maggie is half out of the car. She turns back to see that Sandra is holding something out to her. A small, square cardboard box. 'He asked me to give you this. He makes them himself.'

Maggie starts to shake her head. On the back seat, Daisy opens her eyes.

'Please, Maggie, what harm can it do?'

Maggie takes the yellow box tied with white ribbon, closes the car door and sets off along her drive. Only when she has turned the corner and she can no longer be seen does she open it.

Inside is a flower, fashioned from paper. The petals are white, the stalk and leaves a bright emerald green. It is beautiful, perfect.

A convicted murderer has sent her a rose.

Chapter 2

The Times Online, Monday, 8 September 2014

CONTROVERSY IN COURT AS WOLFE TRIAL OPENS

Accused surgeon, Hamish Wolfe, refused to enter a plea on the first day of his trial at the Old Bailey today. In accordance with English law, he will now be tried as if he had pleaded not guilty.

Dressed in a dark grey suit, white shirt and blue tie, Wolfe appeared to be paying close attention to proceedings, but when asked to speak, he remained silent, in spite of the judge, Mr Justice Peters, on three occasions, advising him that it was not in his interests to do so.

Up until the time of his arrest, Wolfe was a leading cancer surgeon, one of the most highly regarded young doctors in the south-west. He was an active sportsman, a rugby and hockey player, experienced and talented at both climbing rock faces and crawling beneath them. He held a pilot's licence. Generally considered a very handsome man, he seemed blessed with a loving family and a wide circle of friends. He had just announced his engagement to celebrity model Claire Cole. Today, he faces four counts of abduction and murder. If convicted, he is likely to spend the rest of his life in prison.

The disappearances of four young women between June 2012 and November 2013 sparked one of the biggest police investigations ever conducted by Avon and Somerset police, but it was a lucky break on the part of Detective Constable Peter Weston that led to Wolfe's arrest in December 2013.

Refusal to plead is rare but usually indicates a desire, on the part of the accused, to decline to recognize the authority of the court. Interestingly, three separate psychiatric reports commissioned by the Crown Prosecution Service were submitted incompletely, giving rise to speculation that Wolfe may be unfit to plead and to stand trial. The detective who arrested him, though, emphatically disagreed when the suggestion was put to him.

'Absolute rubbish,' commented Weston, since promoted to Detective Sergeant. 'Wolfe understands perfectly well what's going on and is more than capable of entering a plea. He's playing games with us. It's what he does.'

The case of the Crown *v.* Hamish Wolfe will continue tomorrow.

(*Maggie Rose: case file 004/TT8914 Hamish Wolfe*)

Chapter 3

'I'VE REALLY GOT to go. Why don't you discuss it with Tim?'

'There is no fucking way—'

The line goes dead. Detective Sergeant Pete Weston starts to count. *One, two, three* – no, he isn't going to make it to double figures. Not this time.

His eyes slide to the passenger seat where a gold wristwatch lies like tossed litter. He picks it up, wondering at the ability of gold to retain its warmth, even on days like this, and looks at it for a second or two.

Well, it's never going to fit him.

He gets out of the car, still livid, and pops open the boot, hardly noticing the minuscule ice shards that stab his exposed skin. The wheel wrench is cold in the way that gold never is. He drops the watch to the pavement and strikes it once with the wrench.

He gathers three pieces, doesn't bother collecting all the shattered bits of the face, and drops them into an evidence bag from the glove compartment. His hands are stiffening with cold by this point, but he takes up his phone.

Found your watch, he types. *Must have got caught on the seat runner. Might be repairable. I'll give it to Tim.*

Domestic arrangements sorted, he can get on with the job.

He pushes open the iron gate and crunches his way up the path, through an avenue of frozen laurel bushes. The garden is long and narrow. Tall trees grow behind the early Georgian rectory, curving around it, sheltering it like a protective parent. There are large windows to either side of the front door and Weston feels as though he can describe, without seeing them, the elegant, spacious rooms beyond with their high, carved ceilings and limewashed walls.

There is neither bell nor knocker on the red-varnished door, just an old-fashioned brass bell that he swings to produce a deep, sonorous clanging. He waits, for thirty seconds, maybe a minute, until he hears the sound of a chain being removed, of a lock being turned.

Warm air wafts out as the door opens and a woman is standing directly in front of him, the raised step bringing her face on to a level with his.

'Miss Rose? Maggie Rose?'

He feels that momentary loss of control at being taken by surprise. Every copper in the land has heard of Maggie Rose: defence barrister, true-crime author, pain-in-the-police-force's-collective-arse, but few have met her. She doesn't do interviews, has never released a photograph.

She is probably the right side of forty and slim enough to look fragile, even in the oversized white woollen sweater that reaches almost to her thighs. She has small features in a sharp, very pale face. Her eyes are blue.

So is her hair.

'What can I do for you, Detective?' she says.

Not just the blue rinse of a genteel elderly lady. Not just the half-hearted blue streaks that are sometimes seen amongst the crowds at the Glastonbury Festival. This is bright, turquoise-blue, waving gently to a little below her chin.

He has no idea how she knows that he's with the police.

'Detective Sergeant Pete Weston.' He holds up his warrant card. 'I was hoping to have a few minutes of your time.'

'Come inside for a moment.'

He follows her down a pale green corridor, past panelled doors that are firmly closed. The kitchen they enter is large, painted shades of cream and pale gold.

While he's been looking round – he's a copper, he can't help himself – Rose has curled into an armchair close to an Aga. Her slippers are enormous, furry boots. Blue, like her hair.

'Have a seat.'

He sneaks a glance at the laptop on the central table as he pulls out a chair, but the screensaver has kicked in to show constantly changing scenes of Arctic wastelands: massive snowdrifts, ice formations, blue ice.

'Can I just confirm that you are Maggie Rose?'

'I am. Will this take long? And does politeness demand that I offer you coffee?'

'That's your call, Miss Rose. I'm here because I understand you had a visit from Sandra Wolfe yesterday.'

She nods her head as she speaks. 'She came here first, from what I understand, but didn't make herself known. By her own admission she followed me to the beach and spoke to me there.'

Maggie Rose has a measured way of speaking, of choosing each word carefully, as though addressing an audience.

'Can I ask what was the nature of the conversation?'

'I expect you can guess.'

'Indulge me.'

'She wants me to take on her son's case, to get her beloved child – in whose innocence she genuinely believes, by the way – out of prison.'

'What did you tell her?'

Rose blinks. Her eyelashes are dark, but he can't see the clogging gloop of mascara. 'May I ask you a question first?'

'Shoot.'

'How did you know she and I had met?'

'We monitor the website she and a few of her friends run. There's a chat room that's publicly accessible. She – Sandra Wolfe, I'm talking about now – was telling another member of the group that she'd met you.'

'Then you probably already know the answer I gave her.'

Well, she had him there. 'She'll try again,' he says. 'Sandra Wolfe is not a woman who gives up easily. Next time, she might not bother waiting on the beach, she might knock on your door. She might bring some of her friends with her. She's a woman grieving, Miss Rose. She believes her son has been stitched up and women like that aren't always stable.'

Rose wriggles in the armchair, pulling her heels back against her bottom. 'So you're here out of concern for me?'

'I'm here because while this group of people – who, frankly, I'd like to refer to as nutters and misfits, but that's a bit judgemental and not very PC so I'll just call them misguided individuals – can do whatever they like in their own time, I don't want them bothering or even frightening ordinary members of the public.'

17

She holds eye contact. 'I wasn't frightened.'

'No, I don't expect you were.'

'And you're lying to me.'

He gives an exaggerated start. 'Come again?'

'You're not here out of concern. You're here because you don't want me to take on Hamish Wolfe. You don't want me digging up old details, finding your mistakes, holding you to account. Putting Hamish Wolfe away was the greatest success of your career – it was you, wasn't it? I remember your name in the newspapers – and you can't bear the thought of someone overturning that conviction.'

Pete feels his heartbeat starting to race. 'We didn't make mistakes. Hamish Wolfe is guilty.'

'Everyone makes mistakes. Even Hamish Wolfe. That's why you caught him. And for what it's worth, I agree with you. I have no plans to take on his case.'

She moves again, lowering her feet to the floor. 'But let me be very clear, Detective,' she says. 'If I were to decide to do so, no amount of pressure on your part would put me off.'

He stands before she has a chance to. 'Would you mind if I used your toilet? Cold day, too much coffee, I'm afraid.'

She nods towards a door behind him. 'That will take you into the rear hall. The door immediately opposite is the downstairs cloakroom.'

'Thanks.' He leaves the room, conscious of her eyes following him. To his right is the back door of the house and through its glass he can see a double garage. The downstairs loo is a small room, plain and functional. To his left is another door.

The sound of voices, low-pitched but unmistakable, comes from the kitchen he's just left.

When he returns to the kitchen, Maggie Rose is leaning over the table, staring at her laptop. She is alone. She closes down the screen, but not before he's spotted his own name on it.

'Thank you,' he says. 'I suppose I've taken enough of your time.'

She says nothing, but slips back into the armchair, this time tucking her legs inside the sweater. There is something very childlike about the way she sits. Were it not for the tiny lines on her face, she might even look like a child.

18

He takes one step towards the door. 'I'm sorry Sandra Wolfe approached you. I'm sorry you've been pestered with letters from Wolfe himself. We found that out on the website as well. I wish I could offer to do something about the inconvenience and disturbance that must have caused, but I can't, I'm afraid. These people are free to do what they like within the law.'

'I understand the law well enough, thank you.'

'But what I can do is advise. And I advise you to have nothing to do with Sandra Wolfe, or the Wolfe Pack, or whatever that bunch of idiots are calling themselves this week. And I certainly advise you to have nothing to do – ever – with Hamish Wolfe.'

'If you're advising me, Detective, why am I feeling threatened?'

She hasn't moved. She's still curled up like a cat in the large armchair. He can't imagine anyone looking less threatened.

On a sudden whim, Pete moves to the window. The garden is huge and the few colours visible through the frost are dull and muted. The lawn that stretches out from the back door is the opaque white of chalk and the high brick walls, the line of mature trees, the dense shrubs all seem to conspire to keep out sunlight.

'Do you live here alone, Miss Rose?'

There is movement in the glass's reflection as Maggie Rose gets to her feet behind him. Her weird hair and pale face materialize behind his shoulder.

'That feeling of being threatened has not gone away,' she says.

'I apologize. Really not my intention.' He turns to face her. 'Before her son was arrested, Sandra Wolfe was probably a perfectly nice, middle-class Somerset lady, working part-time, having friends round for dinner, eating at the golf club on Saturday evenings. But we all know what female animals are capable of when their young are threatened.'

'I just thought her very unhappy, but I'll bear in mind what you say.'

She turns and he has little choice but to follow her from the room. In the hall, he looks around for signs of someone else in the house, but the doors are all still closed.

'The pressure group are another story,' he says. 'None of them were ever normal, in my view. Several have either a minor criminal record or a history of psychiatric problems. Most are unemployed, or under

19

employed. They have very little in their lives so, to fill the gap, they give themselves a cause. And having got one, they're pursuing it with a great deal of conviction. Individually, they might not be too much of a problem, but they wind each other up and egg each other on.'

At the front door she turns to face him. 'I'm familiar with the idea. It's called group-think.'

'Yeah, well it's at work here. So, I'd advise you to review your security arrangements. Make sure the locks are solid, fit a few security lights, if you haven't got them already, and keep a chain on your door. These people know where you live.'

There is a softening in her face that makes him think, for a second, that she might be about to smile. 'I'll bear that in mind.'

He takes the opportunity to glance up the stairs. No one on the landing. 'Please do,' he says. 'But above all, don't be tempted to have anything to do with Hamish Wolfe. I've looked into that man's eyes, and trust me, there isn't anything human there. Wolfe isn't a man, Miss Rose. He's a monster.'

She smiles. Properly this time. Her mouth is wider than he'd realized, her pale lips fuller. She has neat, small white teeth. 'I've heard he's quite the ladies' man.'

'They often are. That's why they manage to kill so many.'

'Do you know what, that does interest me. Not the fact that he was popular before he was arrested. He's a good-looking man, there's nothing remarkable in that. What fascinates me is the number of women who, by all accounts, write to him in prison. Why would they do that, do you think?'

'All notorious killers have a fan club,' he says.

'Fascinating.' She's still smiling as she reaches for the lock. 'That would, actually, make a very interesting book. If I had the time, which I don't.'

'Wolfe wouldn't be interested in you, I'm afraid,' Pete says.

They swap places in the doorway and he catches a whiff of the odd, chemical smell of her hair.

'Why's that?'

He makes a point of looking her up and down. 'You're about four stone short of his preferred body weight. Thank you for your time.'

The door closes before he's taken three steps down the path. He doesn't look back, doesn't pause, even though his phone starts ringing when he reaches the gate. He climbs into his car, shuts out the cold, and checks his phone. It is one of his detective constables, thirty-four-year-old Liz Nuttall. He presses Accept. 'Talk to me, Nutty.'

'You made it out, then?' she says. 'How'd it go?'

'She's not what I was expecting, that's for sure. Seems to be pretty cool on the Wolfe front. No real interest in engaging with Sandra Wolfe further.'

'Could she be faking it? By the way, Latimer's been asking for you. I told him you were at a meeting at County Hall about the schools' drugs outreach programme.'

'Nice one.' Their boss, DCI Latimer, will expect no feedback from a meeting at County Hall. He makes no secret of the fact that bureaucracy bores him.

'Listen, Nuts, do me a favour, will you? Run a check on The Rectory.' He glances sideways at the big old house he's just left. 'Electoral roll, utilities, you know the sort of thing. Rose was talking to someone while I was in there but did a good job of keeping whoever it was out of sight. As though she really didn't want me to know she wasn't on her own.'

'I'm not getting anything,' says Liz, after a few moments. 'No record of her having a partner or a lodger. No, nothing.'

Pete is still looking at the house. The windows are blank and empty. 'There's someone else in there,' he says. 'I'm sure of it.'

Chapter 4

www.CommonplaceSexism.com

HOW FAT BECAME A MATTER OF LIFE AND DEATH

Posted 5 October 2014, by Beth Tweedy, regular contributor and self-confessed 'bigger-than-average girl'

Zoe Sykes, Jessie Tout, Chloe Wood and Myrtle Reid were killed because they were fat. That is a fact.

Zoe, Jessie, Chloe and Myrtle were targeted on the strength of their dress size and then murdered. We still don't know exactly how, but you can bet your life it wasn't pleasant. Their bodies were dumped in wet, dark, underground places, from which they were never supposed to be recovered. Zoe's still hasn't been. This happened to these women because we've become a society in which body size is the last remaining bastion of prejudice. Because fatness has become so despised, we can tolerate the annihilation of it.

Hostility towards those who don't conform to our body-image ideal has been growing steadily in the last couple of decades. Oh, I know, girls in plus-sized school tunics have always been catcalled in the street. Fatties, fat women in particular, have long been the (big) butt of comedians' jokes, but in recent years, this fat-ism has taken a much darker turn.

We've seen larger women attacked in pubs and on the streets, by assailants of both sexes. Dental hygienist Tracey Keith, 22 stone, was left shaken and badly bruised by the verbal and physical attack launched upon her as she travelled home by train one night last June. Her offence? Taking up too much room on the seats. Many women tell similar tales. Fat women get refused entry into nightclubs, they're abused in doctor's surgeries, because, of course, their ailments have to be directly related to their body size and conse-quently their own fault. Fat people don't get jobs, they don't get interviews for jobs, they can't even get cabs, half the time, as though their excess body weight might prove too much for the seat springs.

And all this is being condoned by those in authority.

It's OK now, for influential bullies, like the vile Ron Carter writing for *The Spectator*, to talk about the 'horribly fat woman' in the Tesco queue, accompanied by her 'wobbly kids' and to joke about sending them all to starvation boot camp. When educated, intelligent opinion-formers talk in such ways, what hope is there for the jabbering Twitter underclass?

As a nation, we pride ourselves on being diverse. And yet there is almost zero tolerance of anyone of size. Women of my size and larger cannot walk the streets without being verbally or physically assaulted. The normal rules about behaviour, respect and common courtesy don't apply to us.

And now the most fundamental of the Ten Commandments doesn't seem to apply to us either. Hamish Wolfe swore to preserve life wherever possible but allowed himself to become so enraged by what he saw as the drain on the NHS by overweight people that he took matters into his own hands. Even those who outwardly condemn his actions are secretly relieved he didn't kill anyone of worth. He chose to kill large, unattractive women, so that's not so bad then. He may even have done us all a big favour, by reducing the financial demand on the NHS in future years. Think I'm exaggerating? Search Hamish + fat people on social media and see what you find.

By his actions, Wolfe has legitimized the ill treatment and abuse of people of size. He has set us back decades.

Hamish Wolfe will never come out of prison alive. But the threat to women roams our streets continually.

COMMENTS:

SuziePearShape writes . . .

I'm a larger than average but perfectly healthy woman and so far, today, I've been called Tubs, Nelly the Elephant and Fat Cow. It's not even the middle of the afternoon. I've lost count of the number of times I've been pushed, shoved, or abused by perfect strangers in the street, simply because of the way I look. In the queue at Asda, other shoppers look into my basket and sneer. A man asked me once if I was planning to eat it all myself. I have three kids, thanks very much, dickhead. You're right, Beth, bigger women just don't matter as much.

MellSouth writes . . .

A darker side of fat-shaming is to assume that fat women are easy. Because they look the way they do, they will sleep with anyone, they are grateful for the attention. They aren't allowed to be particular, they have to take what they can get (and frequently do). Inappropriately touching a fat woman in a bar, grabbing her breasts or her bottom, will be viewed by all around as humorous. Either she was asking for it in the first place, or she should be grateful anyone wants to touch her at all. Fat women simply aren't afforded the same protection by the law as their skinnier sisters.

GazboGoon writes . . .

Fat cows like you make me sick. Just stop eating so much and your problems will all vanish, daft bitch.

Jezzer writes . . .

Ever shagged a fat bird? Talk about fart and give us a clue. LOL.

'Never read below the comments line.'
     'You're right.' Maggie closes the screen.
     'Do you think people buy this idea of the killings being a vendetta against fat women?'
     'No. Most of the stuff in the national press was a lot more sensible.'
     'Where?'

24

Maggie flicks through her bookmarked articles. 'This one. In the *Telegraph*.'

Telegraph Online, Wednesday, 15 October 2014

FAT WAS NEVER THE ISSUE

Dismayed by the hysterical outpourings surrounding Hamish Wolfe's conviction last month, Sally Kelsey argues that the victims' size was largely irrelevant.

Since Hamish Wolfe started his prison sentence barely a day has gone by without an article decrying our habit of 'fat-shaming'. 'Justice for Fat Girls Too', screamed one well-known blogger's headline last week, as though Wolfe hadn't just been handed a whole life tariff, effectively locking him away for the rest of his days. If justice can strike a heavier blow than that, I'm not aware of it.

The police have been criticized for not catching him quickly enough, for not realizing when Zoe Sykes vanished back in June 2012, that there was a fat-slayer at work. Never mind that Zoe still hasn't been found, that for days, weeks, even months after she was last seen she was still just listed as a missing person, the police should have known back then that something was up. They should have warned fat girls that they were in danger.

The media have been accused of not taking the serial killer seriously enough, because he 'only killed fat girls'. We've been accused of condoning the behaviour of the social media 'low-lifes' who trolled the victims' Facebook pages and Twitter accounts, posting hateful comments about how they deserved what they got.

These commentators, on both official and unofficial channels, are seriously missing the point.

Hamish Wolfe wasn't running a one-man campaign against fat women. He was too intelligent for that sort of nonsense. He was a killer and, like every other serial killer of our time, he had a victim type. Zoe, Jessie, Chloe and Myrtle rocked his boat. He liked them. Unfortunately for them he had a very warped way of showing it.

There's a lot of evidence, and much of it came up at his trial, that Hamish Wolfe had always had a bit of a thing for chubsters. Our size-obsessed society found it hard to believe, given his own Greek-god looks, but like them he did. (Don't be fooled by press photographs of him with his reed-thin fiancée – some men are remarkably good at using their partners as smokescreens.) Wolfe dated quite a few larger ladies at college and there was even a rather seedy video found, allegedly, of him having sex with a Rubenesque young lady.

What he did was dreadful. Shocking. But it says nothing more about our society than occasionally we produce something that is twisted and broken. There is a great deal wrong with Hamish Wolfe, but no serious commentator has ever suggested there was anything wrong with his victims.

Eat up, ladies. You're as safe as any of us.

Comments . . .

'No. No comments. Stop right there.'

Maggie shuts down the site. 'I'm done.'

'What did you make of Detective Sergeant Weston then?'

She tries, and fails, to stifle a yawn. 'Haven't really thought about it. Seemed sensible enough.'

'Think there's anything in this idea that Wolfe's supporters might come and bother you here?'

'I doubt it. Why?'

'Oh, I'm just wondering how long you're going to ignore the crunching on the gravel, the knocked-over flowerpot and the sound of several door handles being tried. How long before you admit that, for the past half-hour, someone's been wandering round outside?'

At first, there is nothing outside that Maggie can see. The night is too dark. Nor can she hear anything, except the click and rattle of the central heating system as it cools. Then a pinpoint of light appears from around the side of the house as a solitary figure heads towards the road.

Maggie watches as, not once looking back, her midnight visitor walks away down the street.

Chapter 5

People of Our Time magazine, December 2014

HUNGRY LIKE THE WOLFE?

Silvia Pattinson braves Parkhurst Prison to meet the infamous Mr Wolfe.

Hamish Wolfe receives over a hundred letters a month, over 90 per cent of them from women. Most of his correspondents, he tells me when I meet him at HMP Isle of Wight (Parkhurst), believe him to be the victim of a miscarriage of justice.

'Sometimes the truth is obvious,' he says. 'Only those with a vested interest of their own remain blind to it.'

When I question the extent to which we should rely on the opinions of people who've never met Wolfe personally, who've never studied the case and its evidence in detail, who might be – I'm sure I blush as I say this – more influenced by his good looks than by any real sense of justice or truth, he denies that his personal attributes are the issue at stake.

'When a body of people believe something to be true, it's usually because it is. I'm the victim of a narrowly focused, cost-pinching investigation that went for an easy and obvious solution.'

When I ask why, then, he hasn't appealed against the verdict, he tells me that he fully intends to. 'Sometimes the dust needs to settle. I'm thinking carefully about who I'd like to work with in the future. I want my lawyer to be the best and I can wait. My liberty is too important to throw away on a rushed appeal.'

While he waits, he has no shortage of women only too happy to help him pass the time. Women send him money, write letters of support, suggest escape plans and even propose marriage. Each assumes that she is the only person who has taken an interest in him, that he must be lonely, longing for her letters.

I suggest that giving this interview might let the cat out of the bag on that one, but he just shrugs. I get the feeling he is unmoved by the adoration of women he will probably never meet. He responds to very few, he says, only the ones who strike him as being intelligent and sensible, and then usually just to thank them for their good wishes. Many of his letters he gives to fellow inmates, particularly the lewder ones.

When I question the morality of doing so, he looks at me sharply. His green eyes narrow and for the first time I remember that I'm in the presence of a convicted killer.

'If a man sent you his boxer shorts,' he says, 'along with a note telling you he'd worn them two days in a row and then masturbated in them, what would you do?'

'Bin them,' I respond. 'Throw them out.' I'm a little unnerved by this stage. Wolfe and I are alone in a windowless room. He is cuffed to the table but he is a powerfully built man and very close to me.

'I did that,' he tells me. 'The guys started fishing them out, so now I just save them the trouble.'

I ask him if most of the letters he receives are sexual in nature. 'A lot are,' he admits. 'Some of them want to know what I'm supposed to have done to the victims. Those are the most disturbing, if I'm honest. These women don't care whether I'm guilty or not. They're actually hoping I am and that I can give them salacious details. Others ask if Parkhurst permits conjugal visits. It doesn't, by the way. Mostly, the women who write to me are lonely, even if they already have families. They're desperate to reach out to someone, to have that special connection. They see me as a bit of a soft touch. I'm not going anywhere.'

At this point, Wolfe smiles at me, and I'm suddenly far more afraid of him than I was when he was being less than charming.

'Not immediately, anyway,' he concludes.

(*Maggie Rose: case file 00326/5 Hamish Wolfe*)

Chapter 6

HMP Isle of Wight – Parkhurst
Clissold Rd
Newport

My darling girl,

I woke in the night from a dream of you; so vivid that, for a few sleep-drugged seconds, I thought you were there beside me. I opened my eyes before the disappointment could bite too hard and found the room filled with a pale, eerie light.

I got up and walked to the window, remembering how oddly excited my dog would become on certain nights. I'd follow her downstairs, through a house filled with a strange, silver glow, and out into the garden to discover no hovering alien spaceship, just the full moon. She never had any pressing need to go out (I won't lower the tone by reference to canine bodily functions), she just wanted to lie in the light of the moon and watch the stars. So the two of us did it together.

I stood at my window last night, watching the moon, thinking of the dog that I love, and the woman I love, and was filled with a sense of time stretching out endlessly, that this small cell-room will be my world for all eternity, that even when I die, my hell will take this form, and the shit-stained walls and phlegm-polluted food will go on, and the remembrance of you will become like a dying star, just a memory of light that makes the darkness unbearable.

Hamish

PROPERTY OF AVON AND SOMERSET POLICE. Ref: 544/45.2
Hamish Wolfe.

Chapter 7

THE CID ROOM at Portishead police station is unusually quiet for a weekday morning, thanks to an armed hold-up and two muggings in Bristol city centre last night. For now, only Pete, Liz Nuttall and Sunday Sadik, a rotund, disgustingly cheerful man, are in the room.

Liz is staring at her computer screen. 'Shane Ridley drowned his wife in the bath,' she says, 'before hacking her body into pieces to dispose of it. The jury took less than an hour to convict him. Maggie Rose, however, has supposedly found evidence that Lara Ridley was having an affair – or affairs – with person or persons unknown. She's arguing that one of the lovers killed her.'

From directly behind Liz's chair, Pete can see the photograph of Ridley's wife, Lara. Mid twenties, blonde, beautiful.

'So, not only was she murdered, the world is being told she was a whore,' Liz goes on. 'Ridley's appeal is coming up in two months and is expected to be successful. Lara's father had a stress-related heart attack last month and her mother is on antidepressants.'

Sunday, who will never stand up if he can avoid it, glides over on his wheeled office chair, catching himself inches before he collides with Pete's legs.

'Steve Lampton beat up and strangled three women he met on internet dating sites.' Liz has opened another screen. 'Except he didn't, according to Maggie Rose, who got him off in 2007. He received nearly half a million in compensation and, rumour has it, his lawyer got 40 per cent of that.'

'Gwent police never looked for anyone else in connection with those murders,' Pete adds.

'Nigel Upton was her second big success.' Liz is on a roll now. 'He got out in 2008. His claim for compensation was settled out of court but it was believed to be big.' She looks back over her shoulder. 'So, if anyone was wondering how she can afford that big, fuck-off house of hers, there's your answer.'

Sunday's desk phone rings. He shoves his chair in its direction and picks it up.

'She's a vampire,' Liz says.

'She's in reception,' Sunday says. 'Want me to go get her?'

Pete stands upright. 'I'll do it. I'll let Latimer know first.' As he steps away from Liz's desk, he knocks over her bag, spilling some of its contents. He bends down, but Sunday has jumped out of his chair ahead of him.

'Something you want to tell us, Liz?' Sunday is holding up a copy of *Brides* magazine.

Liz blushes scarlet and can't look at Pete. 'It's for a friend,' she says. 'Like I'd be that dumb again.'

Pete pulls open the chief's door. 'Maggie Rose is here,' he says. 'She's down in reception.'

DCI Tim Latimer closes the file he's been reading and puts it away in the pulled-out drawer. He switches his phone to answer-machine mode and adjusts the angle between the only other objects on the desk. Two photographs. Getting to his feet, he lifts his jacket from the back of the chair and shakes out imaginary creases.

'Better bring her up,' he says at last. 'Brenda's already in MR 3, I take it?'

'She is. With the FLO.'

Latimer is several inches taller than Pete and has a habit of standing just a little too close, of looking down his nose. 'Don't forget your jacket,' he says.

There is a small, square mirror on the back of the door of the DCI's office. It isn't standard issue and the previous incumbent didn't have one, but Latimer never leaves his office without glancing at it. Satisfied that not a short silver hair is out of place, he strides ahead of Pete through the main office. As he walks, his head darts from side to side. In spite of his instruction that he doesn't want to see any decorations until Friday the eleventh, two weeks before the big day, paper chains and tinsel have started to creep in, like weeds in the outer corners of a neglected garden.

Liz is waiting by the door with Pete's jacket. Her short, corn-coloured hair – rarely flat on her head after ten o'clock in the morning – has the look of a fight in a hay barn. She shakes his jacket, matador style and he pulls a face.

'Don't rock the boat.' She steps behind him so that she can more easily pull the jacket up over his shoulders. As their bodies touch briefly, he can smell her perfume. And her sweat. 'Good luck,' she tells him.

In the corridor the two men go separate ways: Latimer to the meeting room, Pete downstairs to reception.

Maggie Rose, in a woollen coat the colour of her name, looks up when he is just a couple of feet away. Away from home, dressed to be among people, she looks different. Her lipstick is the same colour as her coat, giving her mouth a fullness he didn't notice before, and she's used a softer shade of the same colour on her eyelids, a hint of pink on her cheeks too. The pink contrasts sharply with the blue of her hair and eyes, with the pallor of her skin. She looks like a character from one of his daughter's storybooks.

'It was good of you to come.' They are shaking hands.

'No it wasn't.' Even beneath a leather glove her hand feels cold.

'Excuse me?'

She takes her hand back, but stays close. 'I came partly because it's never a good idea to get on the wrong side of the police, partly because I wasn't particularly polite to you last time we met and I've been feeling a little guilty, and partly because I expect something in return.'

'Ah, yes, you mentioned. Do you want to talk now?'

She glances round, takes in that the reception area is quiet. 'OK. Here it is. I've got a pretty good idea what this is all about, and I know I'm not going to like it, so you owe me. Agreed?'

'In principle,' says Pete, cautiously.

'Next time I need to talk to a detective, next time I need information, you will take my call.'

He pretends to consider. 'OK. But once only. Then we're quits.'

'We'll see.' She pulls back the sleeve of her coat to look at her watch. 'We're late. Are you planning on blaming me?'

Pete thinks of Latimer, kicking his heels in MR 3 upstairs. 'Oh, trust me, taking the blame on this one will be my very great pleasure.'

'Miss Rose, DCI Tim Latimer. Very good of you to come in. I'm a big fan.'

She tilts back her head and looks at him curiously. 'Of what?'

Pete hovers in the doorway, watching the two of them. Maggie is tiny

32

in front of Latimer but, somehow, the physical presence that normally gives the boss such an advantage pales beside hers. It isn't just her wacky colouring, either. It is her stillness. Her calm.

'Of yours,' Latimer says.

She's getting the benefit of his vigorous two-handed shake now, of the gentle politician-style double-pat on the back of her hand, the one that says, *I'm pleased and gratified to be in your presence, but I'm in charge here, let's not forget that.* She still hasn't removed her gloves.

'I've read all your books,' Latimer is still talking. 'Excellent stuff.'

In six months, Pete has yet to see the boss reading a book.

Latimer finally drags his eyes away from Maggie. 'Come in, Pete, I assume you're joining us. And can we sort out some coffee?'

'Not for me, thank you. Where would you like me to sit?' Maggie's eyes, a gleam in them now, are making their way around the conference table. They pause on the taut figure of Brenda Sykes, skip over the family liaison officer sitting next to her and fix on Latimer.

'Why don't you sit at the end?' he says.

Pete pulls his chair out noisily and sits opposite Brenda and the FLO. 'Miss Rose,' he says, 'this is Mrs Brenda Sykes, the mother of Zoe Sykes, the first of Hamish Wolfe's victims.'

'I know.' Maggie gives Brenda a gentle smile. 'I've seen your photograph in the papers. I'm very sorry about what happened to your daughter.'

Brenda's eyes fill. She mutters something that might have been 'thank you'. The FLO reaches out and pats her hand.

'I'm not sure how much you know about Zoe's murder, Maggie,' Latimer begins, 'but—'

'I know that Zoe's body was never found, but that there were enough similarities between her case and those of the three murdered women for the Crown Prosecution Service to charge Hamish Wolfe with her murder too. Unsuccessfully.'

'Since Wolfe was sentenced, Brenda has been petitioning him to admit where Zoe's remains are,' Latimer says. 'It will make no difference to him, he can't be given a worse sentence than a whole life tariff, and it will bring some much-needed closure to Brenda and her family.'

'It's probably worth adding that the area around Cheddar Gorge has been searched as much as we possibly can,' says Pete. 'We believe she's somewhere in the cave system, as the other women were, but there are miles of underground tunnels and caverns in that part of Somerset and Wolfe knew them as well as anyone. We have all the climbing and caving clubs on alert for anything unusual but, barring a lucky accident, we cannot hope to find her unless Wolfe gives us a clue.'

'I understand that.' Maggie turns her startling blue eyes to Pete. 'But I am neither caver nor climber, so what does it have to do with me?'

'Brenda has had a letter from Hamish Wolfe,' Latimer tells her.

'Join the club.' Maggie's expression is still friendly. 'I've had four.'

'We have a copy here.' Latimer straightens the A4 sheet in front of him. 'Shall I read it?'

He waits for a response from Maggie that doesn't come.

'*Dear Mrs Sykes.*' Latimer gives up waiting. '*I liked your daughter. As you may know, she was referred to me for investigation into some cervical cysts that turned out to be harmless. I talked to her at some length about her health. There were a number of issues she was happy to discuss, others she was more reticent about. You might question my discussing her medical history, even with you, and strictly I should not, but I somehow doubt I can ever be in worse trouble with the GMC.*

'*I am far from certain that I can help you find her remains, but I promise to do my best, if you can persuade Maggie Rose to visit me here at Parkhurst Prison. She need only visit once, but she must come with an open mind and a willingness to listen. Yours sincerely, Hamish Wolfe.*'

'May I see it?' Maggie's hand has stretched out across the table.

Latimer gives her a few seconds to look it over. 'Obviously, finding Zoe is our top priority and if Wolfe is willing to cooperate, then we have to give this due consideration. But another issue for us is that this note could constitute the first sign that Wolfe is changing his plea. In effect, admitting his guilt.'

'He isn't.' Maggie's eyes haven't left the note.

'Excuse me?'

'He isn't admitting his guilt. "I am far from certain that I can help you find her remains, but I promise to do my best". That could mean nothing other than he'll look at a map and suggest a few caves you might search based on his previous caving experience.'

'Even so, we have to try.'

'Maybe. But I don't.'

There is a sharp intake of breath from Brenda and a nervous sideways glance from the FLO.

'I understand that—'

Maggie isn't cutting Latimer any slack. 'Hamish Wolfe has no intention of cooperating with you. He can't without admitting his guilt, and that he'll never do. He'll never throw away the chance of getting his whole life tariff overturned one day and he certainly won't do anything to jeopardize the appeal that I know he will be planning.'

'Miss Rose, can I ask you something?' Brenda Sykes's Somerset burr takes them all by surprise.

'Of course.' Her face says something other than her words. Maggie does not want to engage with Brenda Sykes if she can help it. She wants to wrap this up and get out of here.

'Do you have any children?'

Maggie's lips press closer together for a second before she speaks. 'I'm not a mother.'

'Then you can't know what it's like, when something happens to your child.'

Zoe was twenty-four years old, hardly a child, but no one points it out. Brenda is talking to Latimer now. 'What about you? Any kids of your own?'

Latimer's eyes fall to the tabletop. 'There is a small child in my life,' he says. 'A four-year-old girl. She's becoming very important to me, so yes, I—'

'I have a daughter.' Pete hadn't intended it to come out quite that loud. 'A four-year-old. If anyone's interested.'

'Go on, Brenda,' the FLO says. 'You have something to say. You should say it.'

'I knew something had happened, that Friday night when she didn't come home.'

'I'm sure it must have been a very dreadful time.' Latimer speaks the placating words, but Brenda ignores him, her attention fixed on Maggie.

'I spent all night imagining what was happening to my baby.

35

I pictured her crying out for her mum, because they all do, when they're frightened or in pain, they still want their mums, and I couldn't do nothing. I couldn't help her.'

She stops to take a breath, to receive another pat on the hand from the FLO.

'I still hear her. Every night. I wake up and I can hear her screaming. And now, I'm not sure I can face another Christmas without her.'

Maggie's body language indicates how close she is to getting up and walking out. 'I'm very sorry for what you're going through, Brenda, but I can't help you.'

'Yes, you can. You can go and see him. You can make him tell you where she is.'

'He won't. I know this is hard for you to hear, but this isn't about you. He's using you. He's playing a game. But he's playing it with me.'

'You? Who the hell are you that you're so imp—'

Latimer cuts Brenda off. 'You could be right, Maggie. But you're more than capable of dealing with Hamish Wolfe. Isn't it worth a try?'

Maggie snaps her eyes away from Brenda to Latimer. 'Let me tell you the worst thing about prison for a man like Hamish Wolfe. It won't be the cramped, filthy conditions, or the dreadful food or the ongoing threat of violence. It will be the boredom. He has no access to computers, or the internet, he'll have read everything in the prison library twice over already, the TV is restricted and will be permanently tuned to what he will consider mindless drivel. He's been in prison just over fourteen months with several months on remand before that, and he will be going out of his mind with boredom. The chance to play a few games with us, to wind us up, will be an absolute gift to him.'

She turns back to the woman on her left. 'Nothing will bring Zoe back, Brenda. I know you think finding her body and being able to bury her will bring you some closure and, it will, to a point, but the pain and the anger will still be with you. If you're strong enough, you'll find a way to deal with them. But letting Hamish Wolfe mess with your head will only prolong the agony for as long as you choose to let it. He's got all the time in the world. You don't. You have a life to be getting on with.'

'You're a heartless bitch, you know that?'

Maggie gets to her feet. 'Ignore him. Forget about him.' She looks round, talking to them all now. 'That's the most effective way you can punish him. I'm sorry I can't help.'

Pete catches up with her at the top of the stairs and she allows him to fall in step beside her. 'You're not angry with me, are you?' She glances sideways at him. 'The others are, but not you. You don't want me to see Wolfe.'

'No, I don't.'

'Why? Because you think I might get him off?'

He forces a laugh. 'Wolfe's conviction is solid. I don't want you to see him because I agree with you. He's playing with you, and us, for his own entertainment. I don't want to give him the satisfaction.'

'Even if there's an outside chance we might find Zoe?'

Others are coming up the steps, so he falls in behind her, talking to the back of her head. 'I don't believe he'll tell us where Zoe is,' he says. 'And, frankly, we don't need to know. Brenda thinks she does, but we don't. Zoe's dead, he killed her, and he's serving time. Finding her body will make no real difference.'

She reaches the bottom of the stairs. 'My thoughts exactly. So what's the male equivalent of a heartless bitch?'

He grins. 'Probably just a man. Have you heard from him again?'

'No.'

'Let's hope he gives up now.'

It is on the tip of his tongue to ask her about the voices he heard at her house. Before he can open his mouth, Maggie stops a few feet short of the outside door. 'Why do you and DCI Latimer dislike each other?'

'Is it that obvious?'

'He's been at this station, what, less than a year? He played no part in putting Hamish Wolfe away but it's the sexiest case Avon and Somerset police are likely to deal with this decade, so obviously, he's going to muscle in every time something comes up. You resent that. It's your case, you want to call the shots.'

'Yeah, that must be it.' He takes a step back, then another, away from the door, away from her. 'Thanks for coming in. I won't forget. I owe you.'

'The four-year-old girl.' Maggie stands her ground, even raises her

37

voice. 'The one who's becoming important to Latimer. She's yours, isn't she? Which must mean he's—'

This is not a conversation to have at volume. 'Shacked up with my ex-wife. In my ex-house. They met at a police conference. While I was attending lectures, they were finding other ways to pass the time. It was a bit easier to deal with before he got promoted and transferred here.'

'I'm sorry. That must be very difficult.'

He shrugs, tries to make the *it's no big deal* face. 'We're being civilized.'

'Meaning, you're being civilized, and they're getting away with it.'

He doesn't want her feeling sorry for him. He walks to the door and pulls it open. 'Why don't you let me know if you hear from Wolfe? Or his gang of crazies.'

'You're genuinely worried about Hamish Wolfe and I getting together, aren't you? That case of yours must be leakier than a sieve.'

'That case is watertight. To be honest, it's you I'm worried about. Wolfe is insane. If he'd tried for an insanity plea, he'd have got it, in my view, but that would have meant pleading guilty and he wasn't going to do that. I've spent time with this bloke, Maggie, and I know what I'm talking about.'

She smiles suddenly. He might just have told her a joke. 'Two thoughts for you, Peter, although I'm sure we'll speak again before too long. The first: she'll always love you the most, as long as you let her.'

'My daughter?'

'Yes. Your wife's probably a lost cause. DCI Latimer is very good-looking and quite the charmer.'

'Thanks. And the second?'

'If your case against Wolfe is as watertight as you say, then there's another reason why you're so edgy about him. Have you considered that, on some level, you actually think he's innocent?'

Chapter 8

DRAFT

THE BIG, BAD WOLFE?

Note: almost certainly too corny but worth keeping as a working title.

By Maggie Rose

CHAPTER 1, THE VANISHING OF ZOE SYKES

Zoe Sykes is one of our missing. Her death has been assumed, her supposed murderer caught, tried and sentenced, but we do not, and possibly never will, know what happened to her on that Friday night in June, three years ago.

Zoe was twenty-four years old and unmarried, living with her mother, Brenda (forty-nine) and younger sister, Kimberly (sixteen) in Keynsham. She worked at a tanning and beauty salon in the town centre and had a boyfriend, Kevin, of four years' standing. As anyone would expect, Kevin was the initial principal suspect in Zoe's murder. For good reasons, as we'll learn.

Note: actually nothing concrete on Kevin at this stage. Will need to dig something up.

One treads carefully with a physical description of a victim, especially when it comes to the clothes she was wearing, but when serial killers are involved, the victims nearly always conform to a type, making consideration of an individual's 'fit' important. In other words, the need to examine Zoe's physical presence outweighs the sensibilities of the easily offended.

Zoe Sykes was fat. I'm not going to pander to political correctness or feminist sensitivities by calling her large, sizeable, or plus sized. She weighed, by my best estimate, around thirteen stone, giving her a body mass index (BMI) of 32 and putting her in the obese category.

On the last night of her life that we know about, Zoe met up with four friends at a town centre flat. She was wearing a black leather jacket, a red-and-black floral print dress, black tights and red cowboy boots.

The women shared three bottles of wine before heading out, arriving at the Trout Tavern on Temple Street, Keynsham, at around half past nine.

The pub became busy and the group of five began to talk about going on to one of the town's nightclubs. Zoe took no real part in the discussion, but that wasn't exactly unusual. Often, Kevin would meet Zoe in the pub and walk or drive her home.

Zoe's friends, to a woman, were unanimous in their disapproval of Kevin. He was controlling, too inclined to dictate what she wore, where she went, even how she behaved.

'Zoe always seemed anxious,' one friend told police. 'As though she was looking over her shoulder all the time.'

Kevin claimed not to have met Zoe on the night of Friday, 8 June, to have been in a different pub, in a different town, until well after midnight. He and a friend then went back to the friend's house where, they claim, Kevin spent the night. At this point, the alibi becomes flimsier. The friend was drunk and fell asleep soon after arriving home. He cannot vouch for Kevin's movements from midnight onwards.

Zoe was captured on three separate street cameras that night and we can therefore assume she left the pub between eleven o'clock and eleven twenty, some time before her friends. Police were unable to ascertain why Zoe left earlier and alone, and why she failed to tell any of her friends where she was going.

She was last seen at 11.45 p.m. walking in the direction of the railway station. There is, though, no evidence that she ever entered the station, bought a ticket or caught a train. We have to assume she did not.

We now enter the dead hours. The time between a disappearance taking place and it being noticed. Zoe vanished shortly before midnight. Her mother, Brenda, began looking for her at ten o'clock the next morning. We have no idea what happened to her during those ten hours.

The police version of events is that Hamish Wolfe, with murderous thoughts in mind, happened upon Zoe as she staggered in the direction of the station's taxi rank. The two had more than a passing acquaintance already. Wolfe's mother, Sandra, frequented the salon where Zoe worked and, more significantly, Zoe had become a patient of Wolfe's some months earlier. Had Hamish offered her a lift, the police argue, she almost certainly would have accepted.

This is speculation, pure and simple. There is no evidence putting Hamish, or his car, in the vicinity of Keynsham railway station that night. On the contrary, he and his mother both claim they had dinner together that night, that she drove him home afterwards. However, as no one in the restaurant can confirm this (they were especially busy that night and weren't even asked about it until over a year later), the alibi has largely been discounted.

Should it have been? It is a fundamental principle of British law that people are assumed to be telling the truth, until evidence suggests otherwise.

According to the police and prosecution, Hamish happened upon Zoe - tired, drunk, cold - and offered her a lift. He didn't drive her home. He took her somewhere else and murdered her. The time frame remains indeterminate partly because Zoe's body has never been found and partly because the remains of the other three murdered women were in a state of such advanced decomposition as to make a forensic examination practically worthless. We have no idea what happened to them in the final hours of their lives.

The search for Zoe

At ten o'clock on Saturday morning, Zoe's sister, Kimberly, mentioned to her mother that Zoe hadn't come home the previous night. Brenda got in touch with Kevin, who told her that not only had he not seen Zoe but that, to the best of his knowledge, she hadn't spent the night at his flat.

A detective constable visited the Sykes's home within two hours of Brenda reporting her daughter missing. Zoe had her purse and mobile phone with her. It was a smartphone, with a tracing application, but when the police activated it, they found it was listing the last-known location as the Trout Tavern on Friday evening. For some reason, Zoe had turned off her phone in the pub.

The hunt steps up
The next few days were spent interviewing Zoe's friends, colleagues and acquaintances. Her boss at the salon described her as a conscientious and reliable employee. Kevin Walker was interviewed at length but maintained consistently that he had no idea of Zoe's whereabouts.

The search was widened to the whole of Avon and Somerset constabulary by Monday evening. The local TV news programme carried a small piece. Nothing happened for several days.

The red boot
On Thursday, 14 June, a red cowboy boot was found on the roadside just outside the village of Cheddar in Somerset, a mere two hundred metres from the cave where Myrtle Reid's remains were to be discovered, nearly two years later. The boot was identified by Zoe's mother. Small bloodstains inside it suggested she'd been harmed.

At this point, the police search went national. All police forces in England and Wales were sent copies of Zoe's photograph. Her disappearance made the national news and Brenda Sykes took part in a televised appeal for information.

Two weeks after the finding of the boot, three weeks after Zoe was last seen, the blood was confirmed as being hers. Kevin Walker was taken in for questioning, his house and garden were searched, as was Zoe's family home.

Nothing. Zoe had pulled off as effective a vanishing trick as anyone had known. After time, as is largely inevitable, the police search was scaled back and Zoe joined the ranks of the missing. Arguably, that's how she should have remained. There is not a jot of evidence that Hamish Wolfe, or anyone else for that matter, killed her.

Maggie saves the draft. It is all she has found on Zoe Sykes. Without access to the police files, it is as far as she can go for now.

'So, you've decided, then?'

She closes Word and opens up her email. 'Nope.'

'Lot of work for a case you might never take on.'

'Just organizing my thoughts.'

'If I were a gambler . . .'

'You're not.'

'I'd be placing my bets right now. Ten to one, Hamish Wolfe will be your client before the year's end.'

Chapter 9

THREE HUNDRED FEET above sea level, above the hills, the quarries and the rivers, above the woods and meadows of the Somerset country-side, stands a painted-steel observation tower. Those who ascend to its octagonal platform can look directly down into the jagged cleft that is the Cheddar Gorge and watch it winding its way through the limestone mass of the Mendips.

The rusty old watchtower creaks and grumbles. Not with the wind, because today is quite still, but with impatience at the man who climbs its steps so often, but who never comes to look. The man who stands as still as the tower itself, with his eyes tight shut.

Detective Pete has stood here many times.

In spring, he can almost smell the world waking up; the rich sweet-ness of the soil as the worms churn it, as the buried bulbs send up their shoots. In the summer months, when the wind races across the levels, it brings with it the bitter tang of the ocean. In autumn, the trees of the nearby forest give off their own scent, a muskiness that reminds him of the scent of his ex-wife's hair. Today, though, the air seems too cold to move and he can smell nothing but his own breath.

If Pete were wise, he'd wear gloves and a decent coat when he makes this pilgrimage to the tower in winter, but he never seems quite dressed for the time he spends here. Maybe he thinks suffering will bring him closer to Zoe, make it easier for him to sense where she is. Because Pete comes to this tower to find Zoe.

Every time he comes here, he stands with his eyes shut, telling him-self that, when he opens them, he'll be looking directly at the place where Zoe lies.

In his coat pocket, his phone trembles, letting him know a message has arrived. Taking it as a signal, Pete opens his eyes. No good. He is staring at the north cliff, at the area around Rill Cavern where Myrtle was found, and that area has been thoroughly searched.

Where are you, Zoe?

He turns, tucking his hands deep within his pockets, and looks north-east towards another limestone gorge called Burrington Combe and the cave known as Sidcot Swallet that became Jessie Tout's grave.

No one has ever been able to explain quite how Hamish Wolfe got the body of Jessie Tout into the bottleneck hole that is Sidcot Swallet and he has yet to enlighten the world, but somehow he did it, because that's where she was found, nearly four months after she vanished.

Not far at all from where Jessie lay is Goatchurch Cavern, a popular cave with those new to the sport. Boys from a grammar school in the north-east were exploring it in January, nearly five months after Chloe Wood vanished. A small group left the main route to explore one of the narrower passages and found a whole lot more than they'd bargained for.

Rill Cavern, Goatchurch Cavern, Sidcot Swallet. Pete's team have spent hours staring at road maps, Ordnance Survey maps, cave maps and Google Earth, looking for patterns, for the fourth point that might indicate where Zoe is. They looked after Chloe was found, after Myrtle was found, and they looked again when Latimer arrived and imagined he was the first to have the idea.

There is no discernible pattern. Nothing to indicate where Zoe is. And sometimes Pete feels that, if he doesn't find her, he might spend the rest of his life looking.

So Pete comes here and hopes that one day the idea will come. That one day, from his vantage point on the tower, he'll follow the track of a lone walker – like that one just now, in the white coat and blue hat, the one climbing over shingle falls to reach the northern cliff – and realize, in a eureka moment, where Zoe is.

The climber in the white coat pauses for breath and pulls off her hat. She sweeps her hair back, twisting it into a loose knot at the back of her neck, before tugging the woollen hat back on.

Pete moves quickly. He cannot run down the forty-seven metal steps of the watchtower and he certainly can't run down the two hundred cut into the rock face that will take him back to the road. But he will make his way down into the gorge and back up the other side again as quickly as he can because the hair he just watched being tucked into a hat was blue.

Maggie Rose is climbing the northern cliff, heading for Rill Cavern.

Chapter 10

DRAFT

THE BIG, BAD WOLFE?

By Maggie Rose

CHAPTER 2, THE SHAMING OF JESSIE TOUT

At first glance, Jessica (Jessie) Tout, the second victim, could not have been more different to quiet, unassuming Zoe. Jessie was an attention seeker, a blogger and a small-time journalist, her main subject being body size. Jessie, if we are to believe what she wrote, was not ashamed of being fat.

Jessie had a day job, handling claims for an insurance company in Bristol but dreamed of making it big with her writing, of being taken on by one of the nationals. In the meantime, she wrote a column for her local newspaper, called 'Confessions of a Fat Bird'. It was popular, by all accounts. She had over ten thousand followers on Twitter.

In her relatively small way, Jessie was becoming known. She wasn't afraid to pitch into those she described as 'fat-shamers'. She was controversial, combative, her blogs attracting huge, not always calm and reflective, comment streams. Her tweets were inevitably met with a torrent of abuse, hate and threats. Rarely a day went by without a spat of some sort playing out. This all happened online, of course. There is no suggestion that Jessie's online enemies ever brought the fight into the real world.

She had a family (parents, two siblings) and a wide circle of friends. She lived alone, in a small top-floor flat in one of the older houses on the outskirts of Clifton.

Note: some potential here? An obsessive Twitter troll taking matters too far? Discovering a taste for stalking and killing fat women?

Jessie dressed for attention. She dyed her hair jet-black, was always well made-up and wore stylish, attention-grabbing clothes. Big and beautiful seems to have been her mantra.

The stealing away of Jessie Tout
Around the middle of the morning on Saturday, 6 July 2013, Jessie texted three of her friends to say that she had a 'big' lunch date. Reluctant to give too much information, she did admit that this man was a stranger, that it was, in effect, a blind date. She assured them that both she, and he, were being entirely sensible. They were meeting in a city-centre park and then walking to a restaurant close by. She would be surrounded by people at all times and completely safe. This was all at his suggestion, she added and, also, that although she hadn't met him before, they'd been in touch for several months.

As far as Jessie's friends were aware, she'd gone to meet the man as planned, and the date had gone well. Her best friend received three further texts during Saturday afternoon.

3.15 p.m.: Just finished lunch. Amazeballs. Off to beach. Going really well.

5.47 p.m.: I think I'm in love!

7.18 p.m.: And he can cook!!!

That is the last we hear of Jessie.

Enter DC Pete Weston, stage left

Jessie wasn't properly missed until Monday, when her mother, Linda Tout, phoned Jessie at work to learn that she hadn't shown up. Using her own key, Linda let herself into Jessie's flat, to find no sign of her. She and her husband both went in person to report their daughter's disappearance. The detective who took their statement was Detective Constable Peter Weston.

Something about this new case set DC Weston's spider-sense a-tingling. It's unclear when he made the connection between Jessie and Zoe, but we do know that his attempts to convince his bosses of a connection between the two cases went unheard for quite some time.

There was no sign of a struggle at Jessie's flat. In fact, no sign that anyone had been in it since she'd left it on Saturday lunchtime. Her computer was removed to the station and investigated. What detectives found on it proved crucial to the investigation. It was on Jessie's computer that the police met Harry Wilson.

Who is Harry?

Jessie's contact with the man called Harry began with a private message on Facebook in which he congratulated her on her latest blog. As a doctor, he wrote, he'd long felt the health risks of being a certain percentage overweight were being seriously exaggerated. If people eat a good diet, exercise moderately and don't take recreational drugs including alcohol, he wrote, they can be as healthy as anyone. Current preferences for ultra-slim women were no more than societal taste and an excuse for pack-mentality bullying.

Exactly what Jessie wanted to hear!

Harry seemed determined to be helpful and supportive. He attached a link to a piece of research. The tone of his message was respectful, professional and non-intrusive. The language he used, the technical terms he included, suggested that he was indeed what he claimed to be – a medical doctor. On the other hand, anyone with half a brain and the time to do a bit of research could probably have written the same thing.

Jessie replied to him. Of course she did. She was a young woman, uncomfortable in her own skin, whatever she might have claimed to the contrary, and here was an intelligent man telling her she was right, praising her point of view and her writing skills.

The conversation continued on the private message facility of Facebook. It was carried in full by one of the weekend broadsheets after Wolfe's trial and what follows is a short extract:

Jessie: What frustrates me particularly is the idea that there must always be a reason behind weight gain. The woman must be suffering low self-esteem, is unsure of her place in the world. Eating is always seen as compensatory, a defence mechanism. Have you ever had people make assumptions about you, purely on the basis of how you look?

(She is trying to find out what he looks like. His Facebook profile picture shows only an extremely cute Husky puppy.)

Harry: I had weight issues growing up. My mum was an amazing cook and mealtimes were always a big thing in our house. At secondary school I started playing rugby and that turned most of the excess pounds to muscle. I do remember, though, how quickly the pack that is a group of teenage boys can turn on anyone who deviates from the norm. Good luck with the Bristol Post *pitch. Let me know if you have any success.*

(He's sympathizing, but at the same time letting her know he's a bit of a hunk. He signs off, as he always does, with an invitation for her to respond. In low-key, unthreatening ways, he keeps the conversation open.)

Unfortunately, the Facebook exchanges told the police nothing more than that Jessie was stalked. The Harry Wilson page was fake, set up using a computer with an IP address that has never been traced. The profile and cover pictures were all taken from the internet. He had a small number of 'friends', just twenty-four, and all of them, subsequently contacted by police, had no idea who he was. As often happens on Facebook, they'd accepted 'friendship' requests indiscriminately.

Harry and Jessie spoke on Facebook for several months before she suggested that they exchange email addresses. Jessie then created an email folder called, simply, Harry. In it she stored all his messages, flagged in various colours. The police were unable to work out the significance of the flags and I can only imagine they didn't ask a needy young woman. The different flags refer to how encouraging, on a romantic level, Jessie considered the messages to be.

Still it remained professional. He helped her with her research (although one gets the impression

51

she was making excuses to contact him – most of what she asked she could have got herself from Google). He proofread blog pieces and articles, always getting a good balance between helpful criticism and praise. He encouraged her to submit pieces to the nationals.

Towards the end of May, her desperation to take the relationship further was becoming apparent. She initiated a conversation about the homosexual community. She was trying to find out if he was gay. He mentioned a past girlfriend.

The meeting on that last Saturday was documented on email. Red flag.

Harry: I'd love to meet you. I'd have suggested it long before now but a) I didn't want to alarm you and b) working as a medical professional, I really do have to be careful about how I'm perceived. It sounds terribly old-fashioned to worry about 'reputation', I know, but in my line of business, a loss of reputation can be ruinous.

Jessie: Where shall we meet?

Harry: Don't give me your address yet. I don't want you to feel any level of anxiety. What about The Downs, near the children's playground? We could walk to Al Bacio on the Queen's Road.

Jessie: Sounds great. I can't get away before 12.45, will that be OK?

The date

Jessie arrived on time wearing a bright apple-green dress and was noticed by several people in the park. Three of them remember her talking to a man, although the descriptions given of him are vague and contradictory. One witness claims she saw Jessie leaning on the railings, by the children's play area, talking to a woman.

The Italian restaurant mentioned in the email conversation had no memory of Jessie and a companion dining there that lunchtime. They'd had no bookings in the name of either Harry Wilson or Jessie Tout, nor did they have any 'no-shows'.

In court, the prosecuting barrister made much of the idea that whoever was luring these smart young women away would need to be possessed of a great deal of charm, most likely physical good looks. Few women would get into the car of a creepy-looking stranger, but if (turns dramatically to look at Hamish in the dock) confronted with a man with movie-star good looks, how much more forgiving can we be?

We associate good looks with goodness. No arguments. We just do.

The search for Jessie went on although, at this stage, no one was publicly linking her disappearance with that of Zoe. Only DC Pete Weston actively pursued this theory, spending much of his own time trying to establish links between the two women, to find someone who knew them both.

And then Jessie was found. On 22 October 2013, a caving expedition came across human remains fifty feet underground in a cave near Burrington Combe, around four miles north of Cheddar Gorge. The corpse had been the focus of much insect activity and had lain in water. Decomposition was very advanced. Jessie might have entered the cave as one of Somerset's larger women, she didn't leave it as such.

The body was unclothed which, whilst not conclusive evidence of a sex crime, would point towards it. There was no obvious cause of death. Some of the bones, including the skull, showed signs of trauma damage, but it proved impossible to tell whether they'd been inflicted before death or post-mortem.

The police investigation had one bit of luck. A small piece of Sellotape, just short of an inch long, was found clinging to Jessie's hair. Speculation is that it was lying on the floor of the killer's home. Jessie's hair was long and thick. The killer didn't see it.

It held carpet fibres and two short, white hairs that were subsequently found to be canine. The fibres were identified and the police now knew they were looking for someone with a white dog and a BMW 6 series.

Chapter 11

MAGGIE STANDS at the mouth of Rill Cavern, listening to the sound of running water and the steady drip, drip of a stalactite forming. It is cold here, at the cave entrance, because the December sun is low in the sky. Already shadows are lengthening, and the pale, weak beams can no longer reach the north cliff. It will be warmer inside.

There is plant life in this cave, strange though it may seem. Spongy clumps cling to vertical rock faces, fungus-like ferns peek out through cracks, the damper walls have the green sheen of algae. Some light squeezes in here, through cracks in the rock, through chimneys that lead right up to the world outside, allowing these alien, distorted growths to survive.

Another step and her foot slides. She pushes the switch on her torch and lets the beam move around the walls. There is something disturbingly, flesh-crawlingly organic about the limestone mass around her. A curve of rock to her left could be the haunch of an animal. To her right hang formations that have the appearance of drying skins. Directly ahead, the roof of the cave lowers and she will have to bend low if she is to reach the chamber she knows to be beyond.

Maggie steps into the narrow, low passageway, conscious of the massive press of rock above her, but turning around in this cramped space will feel worse than going straight on and so she makes herself take the final few paces.

Suddenly, the low rock ceiling is gone and in its place is a vast emptiness. Maggie shines her torch up and around, but its beam is hardly strong enough to reach the highest or furthest points. This chamber is huge, as though the entire cliff is hollow, and still the rocks around her have the appearance of living flesh. She might almost imagine herself in the belly of some giant creature, that were she to reach out and touch the walls they would be warm, would yield to her fingers, be pulsating with blood.

A fluttering sounds high above her head and instinctively she lowers her torch because disturbing the resident bats is against the law. She moves towards the river, past a raised pool on a rock shelf, with limestone fingers reaching down into its depths. The rocks below the water's surface gleam in jewel colours and patterns.

The underground watercourse is flowing in an easterly direction, linking this chamber with others near by, creating a network of caves and passageways. Eventually, it will make its way out from the Mendip hills and flow across the Somerset levels to the Bristol Channel.

A sound behind, louder than the trickling and dripping and scuttling that is the noise of the caves. Without thinking, Maggie switches off her torch and the cave is plunged into darkness.

She waits, hearing the gentle murmur of the water, the constant dripping. In the darkness of this cave, she can hide for ever. Whoever is coming will never find her.

'Maggie?'

A light appears and she stands up quickly, ashamed of the instinct that made her fearful. With her torch back on, she sees feet, a pair of legs in dark suit trousers and a head, with short brown hair. He reaches the end of the overhang and stands upright. His light is much weaker than hers, just the beam from a mobile phone.

'This can't be coincidence,' she says.

Pete shakes his head, a little like a dog trying to dislodge drops of water. 'I saw you come in. And I couldn't help but wonder why.'

She feels guilty, and not just at being caught trespassing. He will know she's here out of interest in the Wolfe case and Pete Weston does not want her to become involved in the Wolfe case.

'Curiosity, I suppose,' she says. 'Wolfe has been forced on to my radar screen. When that happens, I just have to dig a bit deeper.'

'Did you find anything?' He's looking around, into blackness that his tiny torch beam can't penetrate.

'What would you expect me to find? I assume you've checked already. You'd know if Zoe were here.'

'She isn't.' He steps carefully past her. 'Police divers, assisted by very experienced local cavers, searched every inch of it. We even had divers search the river. Or as much of it as we could access.'

Maggie joins him at the water's edge. 'She could have been swept out of reach.' She shines her torch to where the water disappears below rock. 'Be stuck on something.'

'Quite likely she is. Either in this cave or one of the dozen others in the area. But until Wolfe tells us where to look, we haven't a hope of finding her.'

'Where was Myrtle?' she asks him.

He nods towards where a narrow strip of rubble pretends to be a beach. 'Half in, half out of the water,' he tells her. 'Probably washed up, because this cave gets a lot of visits and if she'd been there since she went missing, she'd have been found a lot sooner. So, Maggie, are you staying down here long, or would you like to get a coffee?'

Maggie opens her mouth to say that she has to get home, that she has a dozen things to do. Instead, she finds herself taking one last look around. 'I'm done here,' she says. 'Coffee sounds good.'

Chapter 12

DRAFT

THE BIG, BAD WOLFE?

By Maggie Rose

CHAPTER 3, THE FOOLING OF CHLOE WOOD

Chloe Wood became the third plus-sized woman to go missing, on Wednesday, 11 September 2013. Her disappearance took the investigation into a new league – that of the hunt for a serial killer.

Chloe was thirty-two, a self-employed jewellery designer, running a moderately successful small business from her home on the outskirts of Glastonbury.

She lived with her boyfriend of eight years, Jeremy, a barrister. By all accounts, the couple were happy and Jeremy was never a serious suspect.

Not quite as large as the other three, Chloe had long auburn hair and very good skin. The photograph used most often in the police hunt shows her in a floaty, teal-coloured dress. Her listed hobbies included power walking and yoga. She was also a vegetarian. She seemed living proof of the much-repeated adage that it is possible to be big and healthy.

For some months before her disappearance Chloe had been 'talking', first of all via her website and later, by email, with a woman called Isabelle Warner, managing director of JustOffMainstreet.com, a jewellery distribution company that wanted to mass-produce and distribute Chloe's jewellery around major stores and high-street retail out-lets, starting in the south-west, but with a potential roll-out nationwide. Had it been real, this would have been a big deal for Chloe's small business.

The two women arranged to meet on Wednesday, 11 September at the public library in Cheddar. This may seem an odd choice of meeting venue, but accord-ing to Chloe's boyfriend, there were plans to go on from there to the company headquarters.

Her boyfriend reported her missing that even-ing. The desk sergeant knew of DC Weston's interest in the possibly linked cases of Zoe Sykes and Jessie Tout and his antennae pricked up. He phoned Weston immediately and the hunt for Chloe went into top gear.

At this point, remember, neither Zoe's nor Jessie's bodies had been found. They were still just missing persons.

Chloe's computer was taken away, and it became the work of minutes for the police to establish that the emails to Chloe from 'Isabelle Warner' had been sent from the same computer that hosted 'Harry Wilson's' Facebook page. The two women had fallen foul of the same predator.

Chloe's body was found in January 2014, in Goatchurch Cavern, a well-known Mendip cave.

Chapter 13

THEY FIND A TABLE in a café that has a river running beneath its re-inforced glass floor.

'Same river?' Maggie is watching the play of water over stones as Pete takes his double espresso and her flat white off the tray. They'd had a brief argument about who would pay for the coffee. He liked that she hadn't taken his willingness to pay for granted. And also that she'd let him win.

'Possibly a different branch.' He shrugs off his coat. 'Only way to know for certain is for you to go back to the cave and send a toy boat down. I'll wait here for it to come through.'

He waits for her to smile. Her sapphire eyes are startling against the pallor of the rest of her face.

'Are you from Somerset?' She breaks the uncomfortable silence.

He nods, gulping down his coffee too quickly. 'Born and bred. Grew up in Weston-super-Mare. Whereas your accent suggests the north to me. Just occasionally. The odd word.'

'My father was a Yorkshireman, but we never lived there. He was in the army. We lived abroad for much of my childhood.'

'So what brought you here?'

'I was a bit New Age, when I was younger. The idea of Glastonbury fascinated me. The convergence of the ley lines, that sort of stuff.'

'I'd never have guessed. You look so conventional now.'

There's a smile bubbling beneath that icy composure. She's just remarkably good at keeping the lid on it.

'I pestered my parents for months to let me go to the music festival when I was seventeen,' she says. 'They finally gave in and I never dared tell them I hated it. I liked the place, though.'

'Have you heard anything from Hamish Wolfe or his fan club?'

A tip of pink tongue licks coffee froth from her upper lip. 'A couple of emails from the group. They're meeting tonight in Minehead. They've asked me to go along.'

'I strongly advise you not to. But if you do, don't go alone.'

'I've met people like them before, you know.'

He does know. She goes into prisons, talks to some of the worst offenders there are. She doesn't need him to look out for her.

'Can I ask you something?' he says.

'You can ask me whatever you like.'

'You told me you live on your own.'

She looks at him over the cup rim. 'No, I didn't.'

'When I came to your house, when we were talking about the Wolfe fan club, I asked—'

'And I took it as a veiled threat. I didn't answer your question.'

'True.' He starts again. 'So, I had someone check. Turns out, you do live alone.'

Two perfectly shaped eyebrows rise.

'When I was out of the room, I heard you talking to someone.'

Smiling doesn't seem to be in this woman's repertoire, but she has a way of softening her eyes that lets you know she's amused. 'Maybe I was on the phone.'

He shakes his head. 'Didn't hear a phone ring.'

'I made the call.'

'While a nosy copper is in your downstairs loo? And, you know what, it really didn't sound like someone on the phone. The pitch of a voice is completely different. Raised. Clearer. Designed to carry. You were talking to someone in the room.'

'And if I was?'

He gives up. 'Whatever. I have no right to ask. It's in the job description to pry.'

'How about I tell you when I know you better? Does that sound fair?'

'OK.'

'Now it's my turn. I've been doing some reading about the case. Not because I've decided to take it on – I'm still pretty certain I won't – but it does interest me, I'll admit. There was something I found a reference to. Twice. But it wasn't explained. I wondered whether you might fill me in.'

'Try me.'

'What's "*Daisy in Chains*"?'

He feels the stiffening in his spine and hopes she hasn't seen it. 'Where'd you hear about that?'

'There was a reference in a book about Wolfe. Trashy piece of work, so I'm not sure how seriously to take it. But you've obviously heard of it too, so go on, what was it?'

'To be honest, we don't know. It was only ever a rumoured piece of evidence. We never found it.'

'Found what though?'

'When Wolfe was on remand and we were building our case, we spoke to people who'd known him when he was younger.'

Maggie has leaned forward across the table, removing her gloves to reveal small, pale hands and pink painted nails.

'We were trying to get an idea of his character. Some signs that he had a history of violence. Or, at any rate, disturbed behaviour.'

'Torturing animals, that sort of thing?'

'Exactly. Or girlfriends presenting at A & E rather too frequently for comfort.'

'Did you find anything?'

He shakes his head. 'Nothing in terms of violence. What we did uncover was a lot of talk about his – how shall I put it – sexual preferences.'

'Is this about his fondness for plus-sized females?'

'There was a club, when he was at university, allegedly. Called themselves the Fat Club. A group of four or five male students who dated fat women and – this is the interesting part – made sex tapes with them.'

Her black eyelashes tighten. 'With the women's knowledge?'

Pete shakes his head. 'No. The sessions were filmed secretly. Trouble is, the men who supposedly were involved, the so-called Fat Club themselves, have stayed tight-lipped about it. We had them in countless times. Nothing. It was a couple of people on the periphery who told us about it. A bloke on the same course, one of the women who supposedly was one of the victims. Trouble was, it was all just hearsay. No proof.'

'What was the hearsay?'

'That these five guys deliberately targeted large women, quite often plying them with drink, maybe recreational drugs too, getting them into a state where their inhibitions were pretty relaxed, and then taping the sexual encounters.

'Charming.'

'Exactly. But it gets worse. Because these tapes weren't intended just for private viewing. Rumour has it they were sold, via some backstreet distribution channel, under the brand name Fat Girls Get Fucked. According to hearsay, they sold a lot of copies, made a lot of money.'

'And there's no proof of any of this?'

'It was almost twenty years ago. Backstreet video outlets closed down long ago. And something happened. We don't know exactly what, but my guess is that some of the women found out about it and complained to the university. Maybe some parents got involved. Anyway, the game came to an end and the footage was destroyed. There's no trace of it left. Just rumour and supposition.'

'And *Daisy in Chains* was one of the videos?'

'By all accounts. One of the dodgier ones.'

'How so?'

'It starred Hamish and a young student called Daisy, who apparently had very ample charms.'

'And chains?'

'Yeah, they figured too. Allegedly. Some people claimed it was heavy-duty S & M stuff, that Daisy got hurt. One guy even went further and speculated it was an actual snuff movie; that Daisy ended up dead. This was all very unreliable evidence because it was so long ago, the boys were always drunk when they watched the tapes, and it was never clear whether they'd actually seen it or just talked to someone else who had. What we do know is that the Daisy in question – sorry, can't remember her last name – left the university when this all kicked off and no one knows where she went. She vanished.'

Maggie appears to think for a second. 'You think she could have been his first victim?'

'Who knows?' Pete says. 'Ask me, I think something went wrong during the making of the *Daisy in Chains* video. Maybe there was an accident, maybe he got carried away. I think Daisy ended up dead and he managed to cover it up. With or without the help of his friends. I think, initially, he was mortified by what he'd done, vowed never to do it again, tried to put it behind him and concentrate on building a career as a brilliant surgeon.'

'But his true nature couldn't be suppressed?'

'Can it ever?'

Her eyes widen. 'His dog is called Daisy.'

'I know. And that really turns my blood cold. Because he got that dog just before he started killing again.'

Chapter 14

DRAFT

THE BIG, BAD WOLFE?

By Maggie Rose

CHAPTER 4, MYRTLE REID'S FAIRYTALE TURNS DARK

Myrtle Reid was twenty-three years old, the youngest and also the largest of the four victims. Living at home with her mother, her four siblings, her fifth stepfather (although I'm not sure her mother ever actually married) it seems fair to say her life wasn't especially happy or fulfilled.

Not particularly bright at school, with no obvious talents, Myrtle was never going to be one of life's high achievers. Leaving school at sixteen, she did a string of minimum-wage jobs, not managing to hold down any of them for more than a few months.

Myrtle's best feature was probably her thick, long dark hair. Whether it made up for poor skin, heavy, black-rimmed spectacles and crooked teeth is another matter. As she'd never had a boyfriend that we know of, the chances are it didn't.

Myrtle's one great passion, verging on obsession, was Disney. Her Facebook page featured little else. Her Tumblr blog consisted of daily, short, misspelt postings about films she'd watched, news items she'd read about the theme parks and her thoughts on characters, their costumes, even their relationships.

Her profile picture on Facebook, taken a few years earlier, showed Myrtle at Disneyland Paris, wearing Mickey Mouse ears, and standing next to Mickey and Minnie. The cover picture showed her bedroom at home, practically a museum of Disney memorabilia.

Myrtle spent all her spare money on Disney toys, clothes, posters and pictures. It was an obsession that was to cost her her life.

She had few friends in real life and few real friends on Facebook. Most of the people she interacted with were those who shared her interest, whom she'd encountered on the various Disney-related pages on the site. One of these 'friends' claimed to be a seventy-two-year-old grandmother called Anita Radcliffe. If Myrtle had been as smart as she was passionate about all things Disney, she might have spotted that Anita Radcliffe is the name of a character in *101 Dalmatians*.

Anita Radcliffe was yet another fake identity. The police discovered very quickly that 'her' posts all came from the same computer that had hosted Harry Wilson's and Isabelle Warner's email accounts. Harry Wilson and Anita Radcliffe were even Facebook 'friends' – how twisted is that?

On 12 February 2013, Myrtle spotted a posting on her page from Anita Radcliffe. Anita had been browsing through Myrtle's photographs and had been struck by a picture of Myrtle in a Snow White costume.

'My oldest granddaughter looks about your size,' Anita wrote, 'and she's desperately looking for a Snow White costume for a party. Do you mind me asking where you got yours?'

The two women began chatting. With the benefit of hindsight, it's easy to see how easily Myrtle was played. On Myrtle's birthday, Anita posted a Disney-themed card on her page, writing:

'Wishing a wonderful day to my new friend in Disney. Lots of joy, my sweet young friend.'

When Myrtle posted a rather obvious comment about the relationship between Marlin and his son, in *Finding Nemo*, Anita complimented her on her insight.

'*Watching Find Nemo for the millionth time, LOL. Wanting to scream at Marrlin to let the kid grow up, ffs.*'

'*That's quite insightful of you, Myrtle. Over-nurturing our children leads to co-dependency that becomes hard to break in later life. I sense, from your maturity and strength, that you come from a large family, in which everyone was encouraged to stand on their own feet from an early age. Am I right?*'

'*Dead right, clever lady. Five of us at home, + mum and garry. never a moments piece.*'

Anita began laying her trap. Every few days, she'd post a photograph of a piece of Disney memorabilia, supposedly that she'd bought years earlier for her grandchildren. She started to hint that it was all languishing in the loft, gathering dust and taking up space. Some of the pieces she showed were quite rare, selling for over £100 on eBay. Myrtle's covetous nature was awoken.

At the same time, Anita's interest in her, her willingness to talk and ask her opinion, spoke to the self-esteem of a young woman who had little in her life.

Of all the victims, Myrtle was probably the easiest prey.

On 19 October, Anita sent Myrtle a message.

'Dearest Myrtle, I feel we have become friends and, even if what I am about to say is unacceptable to you, I hope and pray that you won't take offence, my clever, funny young friend. I have decided, after much soul-searching, to leave my house and move into somewhere smaller.

'The reason for writing is to ask if you would like my Disney collection? My grandchildren have no use for it any more. Of course, I know I could sell it and probably get quite a lot of money for it, but I have no need of money. I'm not boasting, I know you know that, I'm just telling the truth because I want you to understand my wish that the collection goes to someone who will treasure it.'

It hardly seems necessary to record Myrtle's reply. Of course she wanted the Disney collection. Anita kept her waiting for a few more weeks, but eventually, on 4 November, they agreed to meet. Anita offered to collect Myrtle at a bus stop on the outskirts of town.

And another young woman steps off our pages.

A few days after Myrtle's disappearance, the police had their first piece of luck in the case. The cashier at an Esso-owned petrol station on the Bridgwater Road (A38), a few miles north of Cheddar, had spotted something unusual in the forecourt. The owner of a black BMW had stopped to check his tyre pressure and the cashier happened to notice him opening the boot. The cashier describes what happened next as a 'sort of scuffle'.

We may never know what might have been if he'd checked the footage immediately and called the police. He didn't. The station was busy, he wasn't entirely sure of what he'd seen, and he didn't at that stage know about Myrtle's disappearance.

Three days later, he saw a piece on the news and was alarmed enough to mention it to a police officer he knew – DC Pete Weston again.

What Weston and the cashier saw when they watched the footage was a figure dressed in dark clothes open the boot of the car carefully, then dart forward and close it again. The interior of the boot is too dark to be seen, but as the car was driven away, something that looked like fabric could be seen dangling from the boot.

A search of the grounds around the petrol station unearthed a discarded 'pop-sock'. It was later to be linked, via DNA and skin particles, to Myrtle.

DC Weston immediately traced the black BMW to a Mr Hamish Wolfe, consultant surgeon. Wolfe was arrested.

His computer was seized. Had detectives been hoping to find a familiar IP address, they were disappointed. Wolfe had, though, made one big mistake. He'd posted, just once, on Jessie Tout's Facebook page using the Harry Wilson account. It was the other crucial piece of evidence that was to seal his fate.

Chapter 15

ACCORDING TO ITS WEBSITE, Minehead Caravan Park is one of Somerset's most popular holiday destinations. Photographs on the website show the 'homes' painted the white of fresh milk, with picket fences and neat gardens. They show families making their way along reed-lined paths to the 'miles of sandy beaches' just a seashell's throw from the closest caravans.

None of these photographs were taken in early December, at 6.30 in the evening, when the world is dark and the wind aspires to be gale force.

Maggie waits, her car engine ticking over, at the park entrance. The barrier shudders and lifts and, for a second, the ghostly movement unnerves her. Then she sees the security camera on top of the hut. Someone knows she's here and that should be reassuring but somehow isn't. She drives forward and the barrier closes behind her.

The road through the holiday village follows the line of the sea before curving inland towards the administration facility and social hall. In the near distance she can see the Ferris wheel and the helter-skelter of the fairground.

The edges of the road are blurred by sand. Sand lies on window ledges, weighs down roofs, gathers in corners. After a minute or two, she sees the few, low lights that indicate the admin building. In the summer neon signs offering *Dancing, Music, Licensed Bar* can be seen from the other side of the Channel, but none of them are lit tonight.

The foyer smells of stale beer, cooking fat and damp carpet. There are stacks of metal-framed chairs against one wall. Crumpled crisp packets and sweets lie amongst balls of dust in the corners. A wide-headed brush has been abandoned on its side, its bristles encrusted with dirt and human hair.

The ballroom is almost in darkness but emergency lights lend a green glow to the walls as Maggie heads for where she can now hear voices. Directly ahead of her is a stage, curtained with heavy red velvet.

For the first time, she is beginning to regret not taking Pete up on his offer to come with her.

She would not have been welcome here with Pete.

The voices have fallen silent and she has a sense of people, just around the corner in the bar area, listening to her approach. She gets closer and can see shoulders, backs of heads. Moving as one, the heads turn to face her.

She can see them all now. Around a dozen, most seated, some standing by a bar in which every optic is empty. She spots Sandra Wolfe in one of the seats, sitting next to a young woman with very long black hair.

'Maggie?'

A man is coming towards her. He is small and skinny, with an angry-looking patch of eczema around his neck and several shaving cuts.

'I'm Mike Shiven.' He's holding out a small hand towards her. She fights back a shiver when it lies, flat and dead, in her own. Up close, she can see a crusting around his eyelashes and, when he releases her hand, she feels as though he has left skin behind.

'It was good of you to come,' he says. 'We're all very grateful.'

Everyone is staring at her, not even trying to soften their curiosity. One woman looks quite elderly, a couple barely more than teenagers. Most are women. All of them, she sees now that she's closer, are wearing paper flowers as buttonholes.

'This is Andy Bear.' Shiven is indicating a huge man who's followed him over from the bar. 'He's the manager of the holiday village. It's thanks to him we can meet here.'

Bracing herself, Maggie holds out her hand to Bear, whose hairy stomach is hanging below the rim of his sweatshirt. He is wearing oversized sweatpants, but the elastic in the fabric has gone in the knees and the thread is looking thin around the crotch. His hand is cold and clammy and she drops it quickly.

'Shall we sit down?' With one hand in the small of her back, Shiven steers her towards the waiting circle of chairs. 'I'm sure we'd all like to welcome Maggie Rose here tonight.' There is a half-hearted smattering of applause. 'Maggie, thank you for coming. We're here for you. What would you like to say to us?'

'Can I suggest we start by you introducing yourselves to me,'

Maggie says. 'We'll go round in a circle. Tell me who you are, whether or not you know Wolfe personally, and why you believe him to be innocent.'

'His name is Hamish.' The woman on Sandra Wolfe's immediate left, with long black hair and hard black eyes is staring at Maggie.

Maggie returns the look. 'Why don't you go first?' she says.

Black eyes mutters something.

'Sirocco, I wish you'd stop saying that.' Sandra's voice cuts across the cold air like a colder wind. 'That's the sort of nonsense that just embarrasses Hamish.'

'Give me your name again?' Maggie asks.

'Sirocco.' The woman sits upright on her chair, like a cat about to lick her paws. Her clothes are black, flowing and shapeless.

'Like the car?' Maggie says.

The woman shakes her long hair. 'Like the wind. I'm Sirocco Silverwood. Hamish and I are soulmates.'

It is difficult to guess Silverwood's age. Her dress, hair, make-up suggest early to mid twenties but there is a coarseness to her skin that typically only occurs after the age of thirty. She looks thin, but is dressed in such loose, shapeless clothes that it is impossible to be sure.

'Does he know?' Maggie asks.

A narrow-eyed glare. 'Of course.'

Sandra practically jumps in her seat in frustration. 'They've never met. Sirocco talks nonsense.'

The black-haired woman's body tenses, as though she might leap at Hamish's mother. 'We write to each other all the time. The only reason I don't see him is because you take all the visits.'

Sandra doesn't seem remotely intimidated. 'He wants to see family, not some stupid girl who's living in a dream world.'

Maggie turns away from the quarrelling women. 'Mike, why don't you start with the introductions. We'll go anticlockwise.'

They begin again and this time get round the circle without interruptions. Fewer than a third have met Wolfe. The women talk about being moved by his photograph, about feeling him calling out to them, of an instinctive belief in his innocence. All of them claim to write to him on a regular basis.

To Maggie's immediate right is a man in a crimson corduroy jacket and a bowler hat. On his other side, barely visible, is a small, plump woman. The two of them belong together, it is obvious from their eccentric clothing, from the badges and pins that adorn their jackets and hats, from the mud on their boots and the faint smell of unwashed clothes and bodies coming from them both. They are travellers.

The woman is called Odi.

'I met Hamish when I had pneumonia.' Odi speaks so quietly that everyone in the circle, Maggie included, has to lean towards her. 'I was rushed into the Bristol General and he was the doctor on call. I'll always remember how kind he was. He knew I was a traveller, and it didn't make any difference to how well he treated me. I just don't believe someone that kind can kill women.'

Having said her piece, Odi shrinks down further into her seat. Maggie has yet to catch a glimpse of anything more than her colourful, shabby clothing.

'I'm Broon.' The man in the corduroy jacket is holding tightly to Odi's hand. 'I don't know the guy. I'm here for him because my lady is.'

A man called Rowland, with the trembling hands of a drinker, speaks more about himself than Hamish. He is a crime writer, with four novels to his name. Researching his latest book, he's become interested in Hamish's case. He doesn't want to tread on Maggie's toes, of course, but he thinks the story will make a good docu-drama and is already working on the screenplay.

'Do you think him guilty?' Maggie asks.

By the side of Rowland's chair leg is a lager can. Rowland reaches down but lets his hand dangle. 'No,' he says. 'Too many discrepancies in the evidence.'

'What discrepancies?'

Rowland, in some discomfort, looks around the group.

Shiven jumps to his feet. 'Why don't I do this bit?' He turns to Maggie. 'Of course we've formed a collective view in the time we've been meeting. Shall we share that?'

'By all means.'

'You might want to take notes.'

When Maggie makes no move to take either pad or pen from her bag, Shiven steps into the centre of the group. 'The first problem we have with the Crown case against Hamish is that the prosecution never explained how he supposedly got his victims into the caves? Am I right?'

Nods all around the group.

'The feat Hamish supposedly pulled off is considered practically impossible, even for a fit and strong caver who knew the underground system.' He spins on his heels to point a finger at Maggie. 'The prosecution argued that Hamish knew the caves well. That as a doctor he had access to sedative drugs, and that he was familiar with ropes and pulleys. If anyone could do it, they claimed, Hamish Wolfe could. The question remains, could anyone have done it?'

The question hangs in the air. Shiven closes his eyes, raises his head, as if listening to an inner voice.

'The next thing that makes no sense to us,' Shiven's eyes snap open again, 'and we're grateful to Rowland for pointing this out, is the inconsistency in the placing of the bodies. He concealed Zoe's body very effectively, but Jessie, Chloe and Myrtle were found relatively quickly, because all three had been left in locations regularly visited by caving groups. This argues against Hamish. If he'd wanted those bodies never to be found, he could have weighted them down and dropped them into a sump. He could have thrown them into cavities that are never explored. Am I right?'

Everyone seems to think he is.

'I've had the same thought,' says Maggie. 'It's possible there was a deliberate placing of the latter three victims to ensure their early discovery and to disguise a possible personal connection between the killer and the first victim. If so, wouldn't this rather point to Hamish? Zoe was the only victim he knew personally.'

'He was with me when she disappeared.' All heads turn to Sandra. 'Why does no one believe me?'

Shiven clears his throat. 'OK, next point. From where, exactly, did the killer supposedly cyber-stalk Jessie, Chloe and Myrtle? This killer, who I will not call Hamish, thank you very much.' His hands open wide in front of his body. 'Does anyone here want me to call him Hamish? No? Thank you. This killer managed to create three entirely fake

74

identities: Harry the doctor, Isabelle the jewellery tycoon and Anita the Disney-loving grandmother.'

As Shiven calls out each alias he counts them off on his fingers. 'The computer he used to do this has never been found. In the last five years, there is no record of Hamish Wolfe having bought a computer that the police were unable to trace. Hamish didn't cyber-stalk these women.'

'And yet one posting on Jessie Tout's Facebook page was definitely sent by Hamish,' says Maggie. 'It was traced to his home computer. One posting is enough to establish a connection.'

Another argument breaks out and Maggie hears the words *fake, set-up*. If they are going down the path of conspiracy theories, she'll be home earlier than she's planned.

'Rowland has also pointed out the next problem with the case,' says Shiven. 'Rowland, would you like to step in at this point?'

Rowland suppresses a belch and shakes his head.

'OK.' Shiven is only too happy to carry on speaking. 'We know that during February and March of 2013, the killer was "grooming" his next three victims. Thanks to Rowland and his in-depth knowledge of serial killer pattern behaviour, we know that this simultaneous victim selection is entirely untypical. Stalking three at once has a 'kid in the candy store' feel about it which is out of character with everything we know about this sort of killer.'

Actually, that is a good point.

'So what do you think, Maggie? Have we convinced you?'

The faces around her have an unquestioning belief in the rightness of their cause.

'Far from it,' Maggie says. 'You haven't come up with a single good reason for doubting Wolfe's conviction. The jury heard all about Sandra's alibi for the night of Zoe's disappearance. They heard the speculation about the difficulties of getting women into the caves but concluded, quite rightly, that Hamish was as likely a candidate as any other. And, whilst I can understand that these might seem like discrepancies to you, they are balanced against some iron-clad evidence, namely the hair and carpet fibres found on Jessie's body, the Facebook posting from Hamish's computer and the sighting of his car at the petrol station on the night Myrtle Reid disappeared. I've heard nothing new here and before I can even think of taking on this case, I will need something new.'

'We have something new.'

Broon is speaking so quietly that only Maggie can have heard him. 'What?'

There seems to be some sort of unspoken conversation taking place between Broon and Odi. She is shaking her head firmly and Maggie catches a glimpse of a puffy, pale face, framed by short grey hair.

Around the circle, others look mystified.

'What is it, Broon?' asks Shiven. 'Do you and Odi know something you haven't shared with us? Because absolute honesty was a founding principle of our group.'

'Broon?' Sandra looks about to get out of her seat. 'Odi, what is it?'

Broon seems to make up his mind. 'Hamish was arrested on 4 December 2013. Before the bodies of Chloe Wood and Myrtle Reid were found.'

'Broon, no!'

Maggie ignores Odi's outburst. 'That's right. They were found some months later. They'd decomposed quite considerably.'

'We saw someone going into Rill Cavern the following April. Odi and me. We saw somebody going in carrying something heavy.'

'Only me, Broon. You were asleep.'

Maggie's heart is beating faster, she simply can't help it. She leans forward to get a good look at the woman. Odi is older than she'd first thought. Her short, straight hair is completely grey. Just the plumpness of her face smooths out the wrinkles, giving her a younger look. 'You saw someone carrying the body of Myrtle Reid into Rill Cavern?'

'No, no, it wasn't a body.' Odi can't look up from the floor. 'It was dark, we were a long way away. I just saw someone, with a small light. You know, like one of those miner's lamps? On their heads? Nothing really, just a dark figure, with a light.'

'I know,' Maggie says. 'People buy them for camping. Sometimes for running.'

'Well, Odi saw someone wearing one of those,' says Broon, 'and carrying something, going into the cave.'

'What time?' Maggie ignores Broon, keeping her eyes fixed on Odi.

'After dark.' The other woman shrugs. 'Maybe around eleven o'clock. Possibly midnight.'

'Male or female? Young? Old?'

'I couldn't tell. They were too far away.'

'Did you tell the police this?'

Silence. Odi is still looking at her feet. Broon is watching his girlfriend.

'Odi!' Sandra can't keep quiet. 'I can't believe you haven't told us this before. I can't believe you didn't tell the police. Hamish has been in prison for nearly two years.'

'Now don't you be having a go at my lady. We joined this group. We did what we could for Hamish.'

Sandra is furious. 'You did nothing! You had evidence that could have helped him and you didn't even tell us.'

Odi risks glancing up at Sandra. She has tears in her eyes. 'We have enough hassle from the police as it is. They'd have said we were too far away, that it could have been anyone exploring the cave, of course they'd be carrying equipment. It wasn't necessarily anything to do with Myrtle.'

'And another thing – when Odi saw what she did, we had no idea it would mean anything.' Broon has raised his voice. 'I'm not sure we even knew about the missing women. Or Hamish's arrest. We don't take *The Times* every day. This was weeks before Myrtle's body was found.'

'And by the time you knew it could be significant, more time had passed, your memory wasn't that clear anyway.' Maggie looks across at Sandra. 'You mustn't blame Odi. The chances are a good prosecution barrister would have made mincemeat of her on the witness stand. If the defence even thought she was credible enough to put up in the first place.'

'But—'

Maggie turns away from Sandra, cutting her off. 'Where were you, Odi? When you saw this person?'

'We were higher up the gorge. In Gossam Cave. We often sleep in it if the weather isn't too bad. Lots of travellers use the caves in summer. I just thought it was someone spending the night.'

Maggie gives the other woman what she hopes is a reassuring smile. 'Most likely it was.'

'But—' Sandra is barely able to keep her seat.

'On the other hand, if it was Myrtle whom you saw, then the person carrying her couldn't have been Hamish, because he'd already been remanded in custody.'

'Exactly.' Sandra is standing, Daisy whimpering at her side. 'Odi, we're going to the police. We're going now. I'll drive you.'

'No.' Odi jumps to her feet, Broon copying her a second later. He follows his girlfriend from the room.

'So what do you think?' Shiven asks again. 'Will you take the case on?'

Maggie looks round at the group. At the people who are here out of a sense of drama, at those who are looking for a cause – any cause. At those who come because it is something to do once a month, because it lets them kid themselves they have friends.

'I'm sorry,' she says. 'I can't help you. There is nothing here for me to work with. I'll let you get on with your meeting.'

Maggie reverses away from the building, slowly, because the area is dark and she can't quite remember what is behind her. As she switches gear, the passenger door opens, letting cold, wet air fly into the car. The wild-haired, dark-eyed woman, Sirocco, climbs in and pulls the door shut.

Close up, there is an intensity to her face that is unnerving, and yet in spite of the coarse skin, the heavy make-up, she has a beauty that Maggie hadn't noticed in the clubhouse. Her dark eyes are wide and clear, her cheekbones high, her jawline clean. She stares straight at Maggie. 'I'm sorry about having a go at you. I know you're only trying to help.'

Maggie pulls on the handbrake. 'Actually, I'm not. I would only ever have got involved if I thought it was worth my while. You have no need to apologize to me.'

'People say if anyone can get him out, you can. You have to try. He can't stay in there. He needs people on his side.'

Maggie glances back over her shoulder. 'He seems to have quite a few people on his side.'

78

Sirocco makes a dismissive gesture. 'You think that lot know, or care, whether he did it or not? Sandra doesn't care how many women he's killed, she just wants her baby out of prison. The rest don't give a monkey's, they go along with it all because it gives some meaning to their sad little lives. If Hamish walked through the door at one of these stupid meetings, they'd probably all run screaming like kids frightened of a bogeyman.'

In spite of her annoyance, there is something about the image that tickles Maggie. 'If the rest of them are here for the glamour, what's motivating you?'

'I told you, I love him. He loves me. Hamish and I are soulmates, born to be together.'

'Even though you've never met?' The woman is a fruitcake. Hopefully, given that they are alone, a harmless one.

'You don't know that. You only know what Sandra told you.'

'Sirocco, this is all very well, but it's getting late, and I have another appointment to get to. So, unless you have something of substance to tell me, I'm going to have to ask you to get out of my car.'

'Give me a lift to Minehead town centre, we can talk on the way.'

'Certainly not. Please get out of my car.'

Sirocco sits back in the passenger seat, arms folded, her body language saying she is going nowhere. Maggie can see the other woman's face in the dark mirror of the windscreen. Their eyes meet in the reflection. Oh, what the hell? Maggie starts the engine.

'Actually, I live a few miles the other side of Minehead, where are you heading for?'

'Minehead town centre, and you get out without argument or I call the police.' The barrier is up and Maggie drives out of the park, narrowly avoiding two people who are walking, hand in hand, down the road. Both are carrying large backpacks. She takes her foot off the accelerator.

'Those two weirdos will stink your car out.' Sirocco has seen them too, is looking back through the rear window.

The two travellers draw closer and Maggie opens the passenger window.

'Can I give you a lift into Minehead?' she asks.

'That's very dece—' Broon is interrupted by a tugging on his arm. He turns his back, there is a mumble of conversation, and then he bends down.

'Thank you, but we prefer to walk. Have a good evening.'

The main road into Minehead is quiet, the weather keeping most people indoors. 'Sirocco, you seem like an intelligent woman,' Maggie says. 'Why are you spending time with these people? Why are you fixating on a man who is likely to spend the rest of his life in prison? And, please, don't give me any soulmate nonsense. Did you even know Hamish before he was arrested?'

'We don't choose who we love, Maggie. Have you ever been in love?'

'You can't love a man you've never met, a man you never will meet, because he's never getting out of Parkhurst.'

'Hamish won't be in prison much longer. He has a plan.'

'A plan? What is he doing, digging a tunnel?'

'He hasn't told me the whole plan. It's not that he doesn't trust me, it's just that he can't be too careful. One thing I do know, though. You're part of it.'

Chapter 16

Sunday Telegraph, Sunday, 9 November 2014

WOMEN WHO LOVE MONSTERS

Fiona Vermeer asks why women fall in love with the worst possible men.

Every other Saturday, Helen Rayner gets up at four thirty in the morning to catch an early train from her home in the north-east. Her destination is Wandsworth prison, her purpose to visit her husband of two years, Stephen Rayner, known to most of us as the Stevenage Strangler.

Between 1998 and 2001, Rayner raped and strangled three women in their homes in the Stevenage area. The prosecuting barrister at his trial described his crimes as some of the most violent and sadistic murders he had ever encountered. Rayner is serving a whole life tariff, which means he is extremely unlikely, ever, to get out of prison, and yet he is a married man, with a wife who claims she loves her husband very much.

Helen started writing to Rayner eighteen months after he was sentenced. He wrote back. She was later to say, of that first letter, 'It changed something in me. I knew this was the man I was destined to spend my life with.'

A decision, I imagine, that must have proven tricky to explain to her husband of thirteen years and her teenage sons, but explain it she must have done, because she started visiting Rayner in prison shortly after that first exchange of letters. She and her husband divorced in 2003 and she married Rayner three months later.

The marriage has never been consummated. Wandsworth does not allow conjugal visits and the couple have never been alone. On the face of it, it is difficult to see what she's gained in return for such a cataclysmic life change. Helen's two sons are estranged from their mother, many of her family and former friends no longer want anything to do with her. The

81

marriage has put Helen's life on hold. It is likely to remain so for many years to come.

Helen is by no means unique. It is believed that several hundred convicted killers in British prisons are married to women whom they've met since they were sent to prison. A far greater number than this will be in long-term, romantic relationships. In the United States the number is far higher.

Death-row romances are relatively common in the US, where the threat of an imminent execution brings even more glamour and excitement to a prison relationship. In spite of their horrific, murderous rampages, both Richard Ramirez and Ted Bundy attracted gangs of admiring groupies right up to the time of their deaths.

Tempting though it might be to dismiss these women as poorly educated and easily impressed, the evidence might suggest otherwise. Convicted prisoners have married their lawyers, their psychiatrists, police officers and prison guards. Women whom, you would think, should know better.

It isn't hard to understand the appeal of a relationship to a man serving time. A wife, or long-term girlfriend, will be an advocate for his cause, driving forward any appeal process. A steady relationship, and its accompanying permanent address, is considered a big advantage when the possibility of parole comes up. A regular visitor will bring money, food and other desirables. Letters and phone calls provide a much-needed break from the monotony of prison life. A prisoner with a woman, especially a good-looking one, gains automatic status within the prison, and there is always the erotic frisson of stolen sexual encounters during visits.

How though, does one explain the appeal for the woman? Why would any woman commit emotionally, and legally, to a man with whom she cannot possibly build a future? Why should she dedicate herself to a man who will never fall asleep beside her, will never be there at Christmas and holidays, who cannot give her children? Esteemed psychologist Emma Barton explains it as the modern equivalent of medieval courtly love. 'Courtly love isn't real love,' she says. 'It's a romantic ideal. The perfect suitor adores his lady, gives her unconditional love and devotion, and expects nothing in return.'

This absence of expectation appears to be the key. A woman need not cook, wash or clean for a man in prison. He won't fart in bed, roll home drunk in the early hours or cheat on her. He'll never mistreat her, because the guards won't let him close enough. She doesn't have sex, but she has sexual tension in abundance and, for many women, it is the thrill of expectation, rather than the act itself, which is so very delicious. Desire is never replaced by duty-sex.

The particular case of Hamish Wolfe, recently convicted serial killer, serves a different need, according to Barton. 'Wolfe is the ultimate bad-boy celebrity,' she says. 'The hordes of teenage girls and young women who allegedly send him love letters and explicit photographs are succumbing to the age-old teenage need to rebel with the unsuitable boyfriend. Girls who dote on Hamish can shock their parents in the knowledge that, barring a breakout at Parkhurst, they are perfectly safe. Older women who fall for his charms see the essential evil in him as a vulnerability. He's broken; they can fix him.'

Unrealistic narcissism lies at the heart of a woman's relationship with an evil man. It matters not how many others he's mistreated; in her twisted mind, she will be different.

Sue Van Morke doubts that a longing for a lost romantic ideal can entirely explain the fascination of killers. For her, the motivation is often much darker. In her book, *Darkest Love*, she argues that many of these women are addicted to violence. She writes: '. . . many prison brides have a history of violent relationships. Becoming involved with a convicted killer allows them to feed this addiction, while remaining relatively safe.'

Association with a notorious killer can bring a twisted sort of status to women with low self-esteem. A man who kills is powerful. By becoming his woman, the female in question is absorbing some of this power.

Which rather begs the next question: How innocent are these women themselves? A hybristophiliac is someone who is sexually excited by violent outrages performed on others. Some of the women drawn to violent men may not just be passive observers. They may be offenders themselves, or potential offenders.

Like attracts like, says Van Morke. 'You show me a woman attracted to a violent man, I'll show you someone with a potential for violence as great. These women are to be treated with extreme caution. Possibly avoided altogether.'

(*Maggie Rose: case file 00357/4 Hamish Wolfe*)

Chapter 17

PETE SITS AT the mullioned window that chills the room down faster
than the open door of a freezer might. The heavy-lined curtains keep
out a lot of the cold but for some reason, tonight, he wants to look out at
the night. He is keeping one eye on his phone, trying to pluck up cour-
age to make the call he's been planning all day. He dials.

'Maggie Rose.'

Poor reception. 'How was it?' he asks.

'How was what?'

He can barely hear her. He presses the receiver closer to his ear.
'Your first encounter with the Wolfe Pack.'

'What, you have a trace on me now?'

'Course not,' he says, although he has. He had a patrol car sit just
down the road from the caravan park with instructions to let him know
when Maggie drove her car out of it. 'I just figured you wouldn't be able
to resist. So, go on, how was it?'

She gives a soft laugh. 'They're all completely bonkers. But you
knew that, didn't you?'

'Tried to warn you.'

'I've dealt with worse. Actually, there were a couple of things that
came up. Have you got a minute?'

'Sorry, you're breaking up. Say that again.'

'I need to ask you something. Perhaps I can call you when I get home?'

'I can barely hear a word. What are you up to? Have you eaten yet?'

A second of silence. 'Are you asking me out?'

'I live above the Crown in the square in Wells. I'm about to go down
and get some dinner. Why don't you come and join me?'

'Reception seems to have improved, have you noticed?'

'You're probably on top of a hill. You'll lose it again in a minute.
They do a very good fish pie. And great burgers. Also, an early turkey
dinner with all the trimmings if you're up for it.'

'What if I'm vegetarian?'

'They'll rustle you up some beans on toast. But you're not.'

'How would you know about my eating habits? And, you know what, I can hear you perfectly.'

'There was chicken defrosting in your kitchen when I came round. What? Did you say something? I'm getting really bad static.'

'I'll be with you in twenty minutes, Detective. Order me the fish pie.'

She is late, as he'd known she would be. He knows that road in all weathers, all traffic conditions. When she walks in, blue hair windswept, cheeks bright pink with the cold, the conversation in the bar lulls. Condensation has formed on the wine glass he has waiting for her. She gives it a quizzical look.

'Recycling bins just outside the cloakroom,' he tells her. 'You seem to favour Sauvignon Blanc.'

'I don't drink when I'm driving.'

'That's 125 millilitres. Even someone of your size will stay under the limit. Trust me, I used to be a traffic cop.'

She sits. Her coat stays on. She lifts the glass. When she puts it down again, the level has significantly reduced. 'Thanks, I needed that.'

'Thought you might. Food will be five minutes. So, let's get the work stuff out of the way: what did you want to ask me?'

'Have you come across someone called Sirocco Silverwood? Almost certainly not her real name.'

He pulls a face. 'Can't say I have, but anyone cautioned or charged would have to give their real name, not the one they use when they're doing the turn at kids' parties.'

'I'm not sure you'd want this lady anywhere near young children. She's either an habitual fantasist or borderline psychotic.'

Pete sips his pint while Maggie fills him in on her short, but weird, conversation with the woman claiming to be Hamish Wolfe's true love.

'She's not the only one,' he says when she's done. 'Wolfe gets more mail than the rest of Parkhurst put together. Anything else?'

'Yes, a possible sighting of the real killer, carrying a body into Rill Cavern after Hamish had been arrested.'

85

He puts his glass down.

'And now I have your full attention.' She's watching him, bright blue eyes combing his face for anything he might give away. He says nothing, but finds Google Earth on his iPad and sets it to show the relevant area around Cheddar. He takes his time, does a couple of mental calculations, then shakes his head at her.

'It's fifty metres from Gossam Cave, where Odi and Broon were camping, out to Rill Cavern where they allegedly saw someone carrying Myrtle's body.'

'It's too far, isn't it?'

'Almost certainly. In the dark, only one witness, the other asleep. And I know those two.'

'Odi and Broon?'

He reaches out for his pint. 'Yeah, they sleep rough in the square here sometimes. They drink to keep out the cold. Can't blame them, but it doesn't make them reliable witnesses.'

'Will you talk to them?'

'Of course,' he says. 'Yes,' he adds, when the look on her face says she's not sure she believes him.

The food arrives, the bustle of the waiter interrupts their conversation for a few minutes. Pete nods at the food. 'I'd eat it while it's hot.'

She doesn't need telling twice, tucking in with enthusiasm. 'I've been reading up on the Wolfe case,' she says.

He becomes conscious of a tightening in his chest. 'Why am I not surprised?'

'When did you know you had him?'

Pete has answered this question many times. 'We had the means of identifying our killer when we found hair and carpet fibres on Jessie Tout's body. The hairs especially. Canine DNA is as unique as its human equivalent. At some time close to the point of her death, Jessie came into contact with Wolfe's Dalmatian, Daisy.'

'But at the time, you didn't know which dog?'

'No, it was the sighting of Wolfe's car at the petrol station that really did for him. Once Ahmed the cashier put two and two together and checked the CCTV footage, it was all over.'

'No trace of Myrtle in the car though?'

'He'd had time to clean it.' Pete finishes his food and puts his fork down. 'So, are you his new lawyer? Do you and I have to become sworn enemies?'

'I'm sure that wouldn't be necessary, but no. That weird and wonderful bunch have nothing. I doubt I'll hear from any of them again.'

Chapter 18

THE LETTER IS WAITING for Maggie when she gets back. This one, for the first time, has been directly addressed, rather than sent via her agent. This one looks different. The stamp, HMP Isle of Wight, for one, isn't quite the same as on his previous correspondence. The paper is different too. So is the handwriting. It was posted two days ago.

> HMP Isle of Wight – Parkhurst
> Clissold Rd
> Newport
>
> Friday, 4 December 2015

Dear Maggie,

You are owed an apology. This is the first letter you have ever received from me. The rest were written and posted by my mother, without my knowledge. She also wrote to Brenda Sykes, similarly pretending to be me. I hope you can forgive her. She is a good woman, a little over-fond, perhaps, but I've always considered that an advantage in a mother. She is suffering terribly, at what she believes to be a great injustice to her son.

I made no offer to Brenda Sykes concerning the whereabouts of her daughter's body. I have no idea where Zoe is and, as such, nothing can be gained by your visiting me. My mother is desperate for you to see me, believing you only need talk to me once to be convinced of my innocence. She has always had an unrealistic view of my charm, I'm afraid.

One thing I do want to thank you for, though, and that is saving my dog. Daisy means everything to me. My heart hurts every time I think of her, sad and missing me. Had she died in that dreadful pipe, I don't think I would have been able to bear it. My mother tells me you were quick-thinking and brave, and that Daisy would have died without you.

For that, you will always have my gratitude. I wish you well, I wish you success in your future endeavours. I am sorry we never had the chance to meet.

Yours sincerely,

Hamish Wolfe

Chapter 19

THE LAVATORIES AND SLOPPING-OUT ROOMS in older prisons can be miserable places and Parkhurst, on the Isle of Wight, has its moments. On bad days, the sinks, the urinals, even the lavatories get blocked and overflow, sending a stream of evil-smelling swill across the already filthy tiled floor.

Most guys hold their breath and get done as quickly as possible, which isn't easy, because there are always hordes of other guys trying to do exactly the same thing.

Not today, though. Today, Hamish Wolfe is alone. And afraid.

This should not have taken him by surprise. His first mistake. None of the officers on the corridor just now looked him in the eye. He should have known then. He should have realized when every other occupant of the room slipped out. Too late. The bloke in the doorway, a massive hulk of tattooed flesh, is blocking his way out and he hasn't come alone. Behind him, Wolfe can see two other figures. In the corridor, silence. The sound of waiting.

Sex offenders rarely stay healthy and whole in mainstream prison. First to be picked off by the pack are the delicate, precious bits – the eyes, ears, genitals. Then they go for the essentials – kidneys, gut, brain. A lucky nonce doesn't survive the first major attack on him in a mainstream prison, because if he lives through it he's likely to be blind, toothless and pissing through a tube for the rest of his life.

Technically, Wolfe isn't a sex offender. If he were, he'd be 'on the numbers', safe in a segregated wing. Nothing has been proven about how his supposed victims died, or what happened to them in the hours leading up to their deaths, but kill three, possibly four women and you're going to get labelled a sadistic, sexual predator. That's just the way it goes.

'Don't want any trouble, guys.' Eyes down, palms held outwards, Wolfe takes a couple of steps backwards. There might still be a chance – slim – that he can make it out of this, but if that isn't happening, he has a plan:

One – let them think it's going to be easy.

Make yourself look small, easily threatened, cowardly. Don't square up. Don't make eye contact. Let them expect a walk in the park.

'Murdering scumbag,' says the murdering scumbag walking towards him. He's big and strong but he'll be slow. A fighter who likes to crush. Wolfe backs up further. His eyes still down, he can see just three pairs of legs approaching. A fourth, feet facing the other way, stands guarding the door.

Two – keep calm, keep breathing.

The biggest danger to an inexperienced fighter is that fear takes over. First hint of trouble, you feel anxiety, followed quickly by panic. You stop thinking, hold your breath. You quickly lose energy, you're a dead man in minutes. So the air has to keep coming in and going out.

Three – assess the situation.

Wolfe has done this already. No windows. One door and that's being guarded. Three open lavatory cubicles behind him. They'll want him in one of those, where the chances of avoiding blows will be non-existent. Prison staff will prefer it too – easier to wash away the blood.

Wolfe is two large paces from the edge of the cubicles. No further. This is where he makes his stand. Directly in front, a row of metal washbasins that could work in his favour; and a line of steel mirrors, in which he can see the three men coming for him. Crusher is first, followed by a man of similar size who is wringing and flexing his hands. Bringing up the rear is a younger, slimmer bloke.

Wolfe keeps his eyes on the mirrors. If he doesn't look directly at his attackers, he can't give anything away.

Four – don't let your body betray you.

Most fights are lost because of telegraphing, unconsciously signalling to your opponent the exact move you're about to make. He'll see the leap in your eyes when you're about to throw a punch, the sharply indrawn breath, the backward pull of the shoulder. He'll see the bounce of a leg before a kick. Be very conscious of what your body is doing and of what his is doing, because he's going to be telegraphing too.

91

Right now, Crusher is squared on to Wolfe, keeping his distance, too far away to throw a punch, which is good because:

Five – use your fists as little as possible.

There is a reason why boxers wear padded gloves. Fists are delicate pieces of machinery. Twenty-seven small, fragile bones bound together in a complex structure that, in a street fight, you're expecting to make contact with the hardest bone in the human body and do some serious damage. It rarely happens. Pit the skull against the fist and the odds are stacked against the fist. Break a fist in the first punch and the fight is over.

Six – stay on your feet.

Most street fights end up on the ground, and Crusher will want him down as soon as possible, because once Wolfe is on the urine-soaked floor, Crusher can bang his head repeatedly down, kick him in the face, stamp on his hands, bring the full force of his weight on to Wolfe's rib-cage. His buddies, Wringer and Slim, can weigh in with their boots. They might only have minutes before the guards feel obliged to step in, but minutes will be enough.

Seven – be ready.

Wolfe can hear the indrawn breath. Crusher has mild asthma. Any second now.

Crusher launches himself at Wolfe. Wolfe hurls himself at Crusher. Crusher must weigh seventeen stone but Wolfe is no lightweight and he's a hell of a lot fitter. He has speed on his side and, at the point of impact, it is Crusher, not Wolfe, who is driven backwards. They crash into the sinks and from the grunt of pain Wolfe knows he calculated right and that the metal rim has just done significant damage to Crusher's kidneys.

No fists. The elbow. A sharp, upward stab, right on to the centre of the mandible, sending a shock sensor up into the cerebellum. Done right, this move can cause immediate unconsciousness, but Wolfe doesn't quite have the momentum. Though Crusher is stunned, he stays upright. Wolfe slams his left hand, side on, into Crusher's laryngeal prominence, his Adam's apple. Now the big man is suffering serious pain and he can hardly breathe.

Shin kick. Groin kick.

Seven and a half – never take off your boots. Never.

Wringer and Slim are coming in fast. Wolfe grabs Crusher by both ears, yanking hard.

Eight – go for soft targets.

There are no rules in street fighting. Wolfe swings the big man round by his ears and into the path of the next. Crusher hits Wringer and they both stagger back. Slim is wary now, knowing what he's up against. He's also younger, lighter, fitter than the other two. He throws a punch, another, another. Wolfe dodges, skips from one foot to the other, staying just out of reach. A minute of this and Slim will tire – throwing failed punches takes a huge amount of energy – but he doesn't have a minute. Crusher and Wringer are getting up. This isn't the movies and the bad guys don't wait their turn. *Come on, come on, you can't punch me, you have to – yes!*

Nine – get the other guy to kick you.

Kicking is bad news. For the kicker. Kicking throws fighters off balance. Kicking is easy to predict and avoid.

Wolfe grabs Slim's leg and pulls. Slim loses balance, begins hopping around in a desperate attempt to stay on his feet and it is the easiest thing in the world now to go for his groin. Wolfe kicks hard and Slim is out of the fight.

Ten – it's not over till it's over.

Crusher has sneaked around behind and Wolfe finds himself grabbed in a headlock. Wringer is running in. Wolfe jumps, kicking backwards with both feet, and this is his second mistake. Both men pitch forward. They're going down and Wolfe will be the one underneath. Once a fight goes to the ground, the heavier man nearly always wins.

Hitting the floor almost ends it. Crusher is flat out on top of him. Wolfe can't draw breath but Crusher has to shift to strike his next blow. He leans away, pulls Wolfe up and turns him over so that he can get at his face. That is his last mistake.

Mountain climbers are always stronger than their build would suggest, they have to be, to haul their own body weight up vertical cliff faces, and much of that strength is in their core. Wolfe's abdominal muscles are second to none.

Wolfe grabs Crusher's ears, already sore, and pulls down, simultaneously tensing his oblique muscles and crunching up. His aim is perfect. The ridge of the frontal bone, just below his hairline, strikes down exactly on the bridge of Crusher's nose. One of the strongest bones in the human body striking two of the most delicate. Blood spatters across Wolfe's face as Crusher's nasal bones fracture. Now, at the end of the fight, he risks his fist. A sharp punch to the point just above Crusher's ear, where the parietal bone meets the temporal bone. This is one of the weaker points of the skull and a recognized pressure point. Crusher slumps. Wolfe rolls and now he is the one on top.

He grabs Crusher by one ear, raises his fist with the other hand and looks at Wringer. 'One step closer and your boss is picking teeth out of his shit.'

Wringer gets the message. He doesn't care that much anyway about a couple of fat birds. He steps back, holds up both hands in a surrender gesture. He's done.

Wolfe grabs both ears again and bangs Crusher's head down hard.

'You so much as look me in the eye again and I will cut off your dick and feed it to you. Do you understand, fat boy?'

No response. Another sharp slam of the head. More blood drips on to the tiles.

'Do you understand?'

A grunt of assent. Wolfe jumps to his feet, looks from Wringer to Slim. The younger man is on his hands and knees now, bleeding from the lip. 'Same goes for you two. And you, dickhead in the doorway. Have you got it?'

Eyes down. Grudging nods. It's the best he can hope for. He turns back to Wringer, the only one relatively unscathed.

'Give me five minutes, then bring them round. Gavin's lip is going to need two stitches and I can probably set Terry's nose for him. It'll be quicker than waiting to go to hospital. And I can give you all something for the pain.'

Wringer gives a brief nod. 'Thanks, Doc. I'll bring them.'

'And clean this fucking mess up.' Wolfe leaves the room and heads back to his cell. Nobody stands in his way.

Some say street fights are won with the right attitude. An ability to put aside fear and weigh straight in. Some say they are won by those in the best physical condition. Wolfe knows better. He knows that street fights – specifically those taking place within the close confines of prison walls – are won by a superior knowledge of human anatomy.

Chapter 20

Independent on Sunday, Sunday, 12 October 2008

LOVE'S LABOURS LOSING?

Sandy East goes to meet one of England's most notorious married couples.

At first glance, Nigel and Carly Upton look like any other recently married pair. She is slender, with sleek, dark hair and an elfin face. He is larger, a strongly built man, albeit unaccustomed to physical exercise in recent years. They sit close together on the sofa, holding hands as they talk to me. Clearly in love, still at the stage where physical contact is regular and important, but mature enough to be self-conscious about being openly and demonstrably affectionate, they could be any couple that have found a fresh lease on love in their middle years.

Until you remember that Nigel Upton has served seven years of a life sentence for the murder of two teenagers. And that the two met, fell in love and married while he was a convicted prisoner in Strangeways.

Upton was arrested in 2001, following the discovery of the bodies of Sam George and Esther Fletcher in their car in a well-known 'lovers' lane' just outside Buxton in Derbyshire. Prior to the double murder, police had received numerous reports of a man loitering in the area, watching the 'courting' couples. Investigators believed that Sam and Esther surprised and recognized their Peeping Tom and didn't live to report him to the police.

Carly Upton, née Gleeson, was an unmarried forty-one-year-old primary school teacher who became interested in Upton's case, started writing to him, then visiting and eventually campaigning for his release. Her efforts mainly took the form of letters to newspapers and Members of Parliament and minor fundraising until she had the great stroke of luck to secure the interest, and then the support, of Maggie Rose, a lawyer, author and campaigner who first came into the public eye last year when she secured the release of triple murderer Steve Lampton.

Rose spotted three significant discrepancies in the case against Upton. First, that the primary crime scene, where the two bodies were found, was contaminated by bystanders and the first police officers to attend. Second, that the initial search of Upton's house was incomplete, necessitating a second search and opening up the possibility of evidence being planted between the two. And third, that crucial evidence suggesting Upton could have been several miles away on the night in question was withheld by police at the original trial.

'Having Nigel home still feels like a dream,' Carly tells us. 'All we want now is to find out who really killed those teenagers and be left in peace.'

Such a happy ending is unlikely to happen any time soon as Derbyshire police are not looking for anyone else in connection with the crime. A source close to the investigating team told us, 'Upton is guilty as sin. Maggie Rose doesn't care about justice, just about proving to the world how clever she is. Thanks to her, a killer is back on the streets and he will kill again.'

At their home in Macclesfield, already subjected to vandalism and acts of graffiti, Carly is obstinate in the face of public threats. I ask her how long she would have carried on supporting Upton, had Rose not come to their aid. 'As long as it took,' she tells me. 'Nigel is my lover, my best friend, my husband. If I'd had to spend the rest of my days as a prison wife, I would have done.'

Chapter 21

SNOW CLOUDS. They've been gathering all morning, thundering in from the west. They are above Pete Weston now, pregnant with a thick, cold purpose, layer upon layer of damp air in which ice crystals are forming. With every minute that passes, the textured density of the sky seems to be getting closer. It has to break soon, or the world will drown in the freezing mass that is above him.

'Pete, the boss wants a word.'

Pete takes a long, slow drag and holds out his fag. Sunday is trying to give up but takes it anyway.

'Any idea what about? And give me that back. I thought you'd quit.'

Sunday nicks a second puff before handing it back. 'He's just heard Maggie Rose has requested a visiting order for Hamish Wolfe.'

'I saw her last night,' Pete says. 'She said nothing about going to see him. In fact she said the opposite.' He takes another drag, wondering how he feels about the news. The warm, stale air of the station hits him as he goes back inside and he still doesn't know.

'You saw her last night?' Sunday is following close behind.

Pete lets him catch up. 'Are we sure? How does Latimer know?'

'Contact at Parkhurst. Lets him know everyone who visits Wolfe. So, you saw her last night?'

'We had dinner. Followed by a walk around the Bishop's Palace in the moonlight. Her suggestion.' He looks down at Sunday's expectant face. 'She drove herself home at eleven.'

'Goodnight kiss?'

'What are we, twelve-year-old girls?'

Like he'd dare try to kiss Maggie Rose. If she didn't slap him, his lips would freeze on her face. There had been something there, last night, though, he was sure of it. Not a melting, exactly. More like, a softening. The way snow loses some of its crispness when the sun shines on it.

Latimer is at his desk. When Pete opens the door without knocking he looks up, frowning. 'Pete. Come in. Shut the door.'

Pete gives Sunday a tight-lipped smile of apology and slips inside the boss's office.

Latimer sniffs. 'You been smoking?'

'You sound like Annabelle.'

Latimer sighs. 'Save it, Pete, I'm not in the mood right now. Have you read this?'

Pete pulls out a chair and sits down, picking up the press cutting Latimer has just pushed in his direction. He sees the headline, *Love's Labours Losing?*

'Yep,' he says, shoving it back across the desk.

'Maggie Rose doesn't care about justice.' Latimer stabs his forefinger down on a line of text. 'Just in proving how fucking clever she is.'

'I'm sure the *Independent on Sunday* didn't say "fucking".'

'I want to know every single loophole in the Wolfe case,' Latimer says.

'Don't you mean flaw? Shortcoming, perhaps? Chink, maybe?'

'Don't get clever, Pete, you're on thin ice right now.'

'There are no problems with the case against Wolfe. It's solid.'

'So why has Maggie Rose taken it on?'

'Who says she has?'

'She's going to see him. Why else would she do that? She's been spending time with his mother, with that pack of mad bastards who call themselves the Wool Pack or something. Why would she do that, if she wasn't taking him on as a client?'

'Maggie has told me repeatedly that she wants nothing to do with Wolfe. I spent the evening with her last night and she said nothing to make me think she's changed her mind.'

Latimer's expression changes, into that of a fox that has just caught the scent of a mouse. 'You saw her last night?'

'That's right. Will that be all?' He pushes himself up and notices the books piled on Latimer's desk. Four of them, all written by Maggie. Latimer is watching him.

'Have you read these, Pete?'

'No. I get my fill of violent crime coming to this place every day.'

'Maggie Rose has written seven books.' Latimer reaches out and picks up the top of the pile. He looks at it curiously. 'Two of her cases have had the guilty verdict overturned on appeal. Three more are pending review. If she wins those, that'll make five out of seven.'

'Thanks, I can do the maths.'

'Five out of seven will make her fucking invincible.'

'No offence, but how is that anything to do with us?'

'Back to what I asked you at the outset. Where are the weaknesses? If I'm going to defend your work against the likes of Maggie Rose, I need to know what I'm up against. If I'm going to cover your fuck-ups, I have to know what they are.'

Would he just lose his job if he landed Latimer one right now, or face criminal charges? One would probably be worth it. The other . . .?

'No fuck-ups,' Pete says. 'No weaknesses, chinks, flaws or loopholes. Wolfe did it. We have physical evidence, a technology trail and witness statements. Not to mention motive and opportunity.'

Latimer, too, gets to his feet. 'Exactly. There's only one way the physical evidence can be bogus, and that's if it was planted.'

'Excuse me?'

'Oh, come on. You wouldn't be the first. Noble cause corruption. We all know of coppers who've bent the evidence trail to convict someone they know to be guilty.'

Maybe a short spell in prison wouldn't be too bad. He'd have a very nice memory to console him: that of Latimer, blood spurting from his broken nose, falling back against the partition wall and crumbling to the ground.

'I think I'd like legal representation if this conversation is to continue.'

Latimer's eyes narrow. 'Got something to hide, Weston?'

'Oh, use your fucking brain, Latimer. That's if my wife hasn't shagged it out of you.'

'Hang on a—'

'We found the dog hairs and the carpet fibres on Jessie *before* Hamish Wolfe was a suspect. No one had even mentioned him in connection with the case until he was spotted on the CCTV camera weeks later.'

'His car was spotted. Not him.'

'And at what point did I sneak into his house, guess the passwords for his computer and post on Jessie Tout's Facebook page?'

Latimer is holding up both hands. 'Keep your voice down, Pete. Half the department are poised to rush in here and stop you thumping me.'

Pete spins round to see several heads turn quickly away. 'Trust me, they wouldn't exactly rush.'

Latimer gives a quick, sharp exhale of breath. 'Possibly not. But personal animosities aside, that's the route Maggie Rose will go if she takes this case on. The evidence is strong. She can only discredit it by claiming it was planted. That someone framed Wolfe.'

'Wolfe had no enemies that we found.'

'From what I know of that woman, she'll find one. And we know she's already working on the case. She's been phoning around, asking questions. And now this visiting order request.'

'It's what she does. She told me last night while we were walking round the Bishop's Palace beneath the stars. Cases spark an interest and she learns more about them. She has umpteen books that never got more than a third of the way written. I'm sure the one she's started on Wolfe, if she's even started it, will end up the same way.'

'I need to know if there's anything you wouldn't want to see held up to scrutiny.'

'Nothing. And the killings stopped, remember? No women have been killed in even remotely similar circumstances since Wolfe was put away.'

'Won't be enough. She doesn't have to find the real killer, she just has to throw enough doubt on your investigation for his conviction to be overturned. If she gets Wolfe out, she ruins you.'

Latimer is right. He's a git, but he's right.

'Has it occurred to you that this personal interest she's showing might be a ruse to get closer to the investigation?'

'Yes, that has occurred to me.'

'And?'

There is a knock on the door.

'Sorry, sir, Sarge.' Liz's voice. 'I thought you'd want to know there was a disturbance reported at Maggie Rose's house last night.'

Pete watches Latimer think for a second or two, before nodding at Liz to go on.

'She didn't report it herself,' Liz says. 'It was a neighbour, by all accounts, who saw someone hanging round in the garden and called the police. Uniform attended, looked round a bit, spoke to Miss Rose and went away again.'

'What do you think?' Latimer says to Pete.

Still Pete doesn't turn round to look at Liz. 'I think I'd better go and find out what's going on,' he says.

They wait until the door closes behind Liz.

'Will that be all?'

Latimer, distracted, nods briefly. Pete turns to leave.

'Pete.' Latimer calls him back just as he is about to step out. 'Something I've been meaning to mention. Have you considered taking your inspector's exam?'

'Not sure I've done the time.'

'If you were successful, I'd be happy to recommend you for promotion. As long as Wolfe stays safely inside, I can't see any reason why it couldn't happen.'

And a promotion to Detective Inspector will almost inevitably mean a transfer away from Portishead station. He and Latimer will no longer have to see each other every day. It has to be worth thinking about.

It can also be seen as a veiled threat. If anything goes wrong with the case that made him, promotion might be beyond his reach for ever.

Chapter 22

PSYCHIATRIC REPORT INTO HAMISH WOLFE

PREPARED BY SONIA OKONJO

NB: As is my normal practice, I recorded my interview with Hamish Wolfe and, subsequently, arranged for the tape to be transcribed. The reader can therefore be confident that where I quote snippets of conversation, they accurately reflect the exchange that took place between us.

Introduction

I was briefed about the case against Hamish Wolfe in March 2014 and the interview took place nearly five weeks later. By the time I met Hamish Wolfe, I'd had the opportunity to read the formal charge documents, the witness statements, the interview transcripts, the accused's statement, his school, university and medical reports, the summary of the investigation prepared by Detective Constable Weston and the post-mortem reports, and view the crime scene photographs. I was as well prepared as it is possible to be.

Preliminaries

Upon being shown into the interview room where Hamish Wolfe was waiting, alone, I introduced myself and explained that I'd been appointed by the Crown Court to carry out an interview with him. The purpose, I went on to say, was to enable me to form a view of the state of his mental health, both at the present time and at the time of the alleged offences, and to prepare a report for the Court. In particular,

I would be considering whether or not, in my view, he was fit to stand trial.

I then went on to say that I would use his preferred mode of address, whether it be his Christian name, Hamish, the more formal Mr Wolfe or even Dr Wolfe. I asked him how he would prefer to be addressed. He made no response. I repeated the question. Again, no response.

Erring on the side of caution, I stated that I would call him Mr Wolfe and asked if he understood the basis and purpose of the interview. Mr Wolfe made no response. He made no response when I repeated the question. (At this point, I had a sense that the interview was going to prove a difficult one.)

The interview

Nevertheless, I commenced in the customary fashion. I asked Mr Wolfe how he was feeling, how he was coping with being remanded in custody and whether he was worried about the upcoming trial. I asked if he was missing his family, his friends, his fiancée. Mr Wolfe gave no indication of having heard any of my questions.

I then went on to attempt to form a picture of his early life. I asked about his childhood, relationships with parents, siblings, even family pets. I continued the interview along these customary lines, as the attached transcript will show, but at no point did Mr Wolfe make any response.

Hamish Wolfe's demeanour

For the first few minutes of the interview, Mr Wolfe kept his eyes fixed on an A4-sized sheet of black paper on the table in between us. (More about this later.) When I started asking him direct questions, he lifted the sheet and began to fold it. Of course I asked him what he was doing. He didn't reply.

I explained that it was very much in his interest to cooperate with me; that a court needed a professional opinion about his mental capacity in order to ensure him a fair trial.

I might as well not have spoken. It was becoming increasingly obvious that the interview was wasting both of our times.

At this point, I think it useful to insert an extract from the attached transcript, as it will indicate, better than any summary of mine could, the nature of the interaction between us.

Transcript begins . . .

DR OKONJO: Mr Wolfe, unless you're going to engage with me, there doesn't seem any point in continuing. Please say so now if you have any objections to our bringing the interview to a close.

HAMISH WOLFE: (No response.)

DR OKONJO: From your lack of response, I'm assuming you agree to closing the interview now. Thank you for your time, Mr Wolfe.

HAMISH WOLFE: I made this for you.

(I was already at the door by this point. I turned round. Hamish Wolfe was holding out the black paper he'd been fiddling with.)

HAMISH WOLFE: I'd say about a hundred and seventy-five pounds. Body mass index of around twenty-nine – would that be right?

DR OKONJO: Excuse me?

HAMISH WOLFE: Why would the CPS send a woman of your size to interview a man whom they believe has abducted and murdered four fat women? Was I supposed to get an immediate hard-on and tell you everything?

DR OKONJO: Personal attacks on me will have no impact, I promise you. I'm sorry you didn't feel able to talk to me before now when it might have done you some good. Good luck with the trial.

104

HAMISH WOLFE: I'm getting very bored with this mindset that I'm turned on by fat women. I promise you, I'm not in the slightest.

DR OKONJO: Good for you. Goodbye.

HAMISH WOLFE: Lose forty pounds, Sonia. You know better than anyone the risk of diabetes, heart disease, stroke, cancer. That's before we get on to the strain on the NHS of people who can't control what they put in their mouths. Set a bit of an example.

DR OKONJO: An example? Like you did?

HAMISH WOLFE: You forgot your present.

(The folded paper shape was on his outstretched hand and I could see it perfectly now. It was a farm animal. A pig.)

Conclusion

This is a thorough and accurate representation of the only meeting I had with Hamish Wolfe.

The particular circumstances of this interview lead me to do something that I would normally avoid, namely to speculate. I have never been a fanciful woman. I deal in facts and demonstrable conclusions, not gut-reaction opinions. I have had cause to interview many people accused of many crimes and can say, with some confidence, that I have met people whose moral compass seems entirely absent. I have never, though, met anyone so completely lacking in human empathy as was Hamish Wolfe. I do not use the term 'evil' lightly, but when I looked into Hamish Wolfe's eyes I felt something essentially human was missing.

I do not envy my colleague who takes on his case.

PROPERTY OF AVON AND SOMERSET POLICE. Ref: 544/45.2 Hamish Wolfe.

Chapter 23

THE WORLD SEEMS to be slowly choking on snow cloud by the time Pete pulls up outside Maggie's house. The taller rooftops seem blurred. Chimneys and aerials have all but disappeared. The sky is the colour of unwashed bed sheets.

Two hours have passed since his meeting with Latimer. Not wanting to arrive ill-briefed, he'd found the report on the system.

Mrs Hubble of 78 High Street, directly across the road from Maggie's house, had spotted a dark-clad figure moving around in Maggie's garden. She wasn't entirely certain, but thought perhaps the time was around 10.50 p.m., which would be around the time he'd put Maggie back in her car in Market Square, Wells and told her to drive safely.

At about the time he was having one last cigarette (the pub didn't allow him to smoke indoors) the dark figure had completed an entire circuit of the house and Mrs Hubble had assumed it was probably Maggie herself. The arrival of Maggie's car twenty minutes later had convinced her otherwise, but she hadn't done anything about it.

Only at two in the morning, when all the lights had suddenly gone on in Maggie's house, waking Mrs Hubble up, because she was a light sleeper and her bedroom faced the road, did she think to call the police. She reported seeing someone dressed in dark clothes slipping away down the street.

The attending constable had spoken to Maggie on the front doorstep. She'd assured him that nothing had disturbed her, and that all the doors were locked and bolted. She declined his offer to come in and look around but had promised to double-check everything herself before going back to bed. The officer had wished her goodnight, taken a brief look around outside, and driven away.

Pete walks past the gate and up the drive. The back garden is still in the grip of a hard frost. There are lots of tall, thick shrubs, box hedging, misshapen yew trees. Lots of hiding places. Even in daylight.

She appears a few seconds after he's knocked on the back door. Slim blue jeans, those big, fluffy slippers, an oversized, knitted sweater, white with black snowflakes. No make-up. Hair in a high ponytail, eyes bluer than he's seen them yet. Also a bit damp, and pink around the edges.

'I was wondering when you'd show up,' she tells him, as she heads inside.

Pete tugs off his coat and hangs it over the back of the first chair he comes to in the kitchen. 'Are you spending time with me to pump me about the Wolfe case?' he asks.

She practically springs into her usual chair. 'You make it sound like we're dating. We had dinner. I paid for my own food.'

'You insisted.'

'We're not dating.'

'What happened here last night?'

'Which are you worried about – me or your career?'

He leans against the table. He's not ready to sit down yet. He doesn't want to look relaxed. 'You. My career can look after itself.'

She blinks. 'And I can't?'

'What happened? And do I have to make my own coffee? It's frigging freezing out.'

She glares, but gets up anyway, crossing to the kettle and filling it. 'My neighbour, who has form when it comes to calling the police out unnecessarily, had a bad dream, saw my lights on and was on the phone before she'd woken up properly. I imagine she feels silly right now. Or maybe not; people have a remarkable ability for self-justification.'

'You were up at two in the morning?'

'Often. I don't sleep well.'

The smell of roast coffee beans fills the room.

'Anything out of the ordinary that you saw?'

'Not a thing.'

'Anything disturbed? Missing?'

'Nothing.'

'Anything left behind?'

Blue eyes narrow. 'Like what?'

He turns to the bookshelf behind her chair that mainly holds cookery and gardening books. 'Like an origami rose, for example?' He points to the small, paper rose he'd spotted the moment he walked in. 'That thing's got Wolfe written all over it.'

She turns her back on him, completely forgetting he can see her reflection in the window. 'Now you're being fanciful.'

'I've seen him make them. He even made me one once. Told me it was a pansy.'

'Maybe I made it myself.'

'Fine.' By the side of her chair is a notepad. 'May I?' Without waiting for permission, he tears out a page. She turns at the sound. He holds it out. 'Make me a pansy.'

She doesn't move.

'Daffodil? Tulip? Something simple?'

She turns her back again. When she picks up both mugs her hands are shaking. He says nothing but, using a pen, he pushes the paper rose around on the shelf to look at it properly. Pink. Perfectly formed. A little creased, where it might have been squeezed in someone's pocket. A smear of dirt on one of the petals.

A rose. For Maggie Rose.

'The rose was in my kitchen this morning,' she says. 'I'd already received one via his mother, so obviously I thought of him when I found this.'

He waits.

'I was working last night, after I got back. I thought I heard someone come in. I hadn't locked the back door at that point.'

'Maggie, if you're going to associate with—'

'I know, I know. I searched the house, pretty freaked out, I don't mind admitting, but there was no one here. I locked the door and went to bed. It was probably some time after midnight, not as late as 1 a.m.'

'Mrs Nosy across the road called the police at 2 a.m.,' Pete says. 'Claiming to have seen someone leaving your garden.'

'She may well have done. Something woke me up then and I noticed the security lights were on. I told the officer who knocked on the door that I was fine, but first thing this morning I noticed something.'

'The rose?'

Her eyes go briefly to the rose then back to him. 'No. I noticed that the chairs around this table weren't pushed right under. They always are, every time I leave the room. They were last night before I went to bed. This morning they'd been moved. And the back door was unlocked.'

Pete looks at the back door, then back at the table as though measuring the distance. 'So where was the rose?'

She bends down, indicating that he should do the same. They face each other beneath the table. 'This is going to look weird,' she warns him, before squeezing herself into the narrow space between the table-top and the chair seats. Pushed together, the seats form a platform. She lies on it, curled in a foetal position, looking at him.

'I think I'm supposed to turn my back and count to ten first,' he says.

'This is where he hid. This is where he was while I was searching the house. I might have glanced under the table. I didn't look here. He came in, while I was still working and hid here. Sometime later, probably at around 2 a.m. when Mrs Hubble claims to have seen someone, he left the house.'

She pushes herself backwards, drops to the floor and stands up again. The exertion has made her face pinker than normal. 'The rose was on the floor underneath one of the chairs,' she says.

He gives an audible sigh of annoyance. 'Why am I only hearing this now?'

'It's a paper rose, Pete, and I need the police to take me seriously. It's difficult enough persuading you guys to cooperate as it is. I'm sure you'd love to be able to write me off as a loon.'

Well, she has a point. 'Got a freezer bag?'

She brings him the bag, he uses it to pick up and contain the rose. When it's safely in his pocket, he asks her: 'Maggie, are you telling me everything?'

Chapter 24

Email

From: Denise Prince, consulting psychiatrist
To: HM Director of Public Prosecutions, FAO Stephen Bachelor
Cc: DC Pete Weston, Avon and Somerset Police
Date: 12.6.2014

I regret that, following my recent meeting with Hamish Wolfe at Wandsworth Prison, where he is currently being held on remand, I am unable to proceed further with this assignment.

I have prepared no report. The exchange between us, such as it was, simply didn't lend itself to any formal record.

If I might be allowed a recommendation: any further attempt to draw a psychiatric profile of Hamish Wolfe should probably be attempted by a man.

PROPERTY OF AVON AND SOMERSET POLICE. Ref: 544/45.2 Hamish Wolfe.

Chapter 25

THE A39 IS BLOCKED by a white van that has skidded on ice and over-turned and Pete has to take the back road past the Avalon Marshes. The day has been darkening since he left Maggie's house, the clouds falling lower, fooling the wildlife that dusk is coming sooner than usual. As Pete nears the reed beds where hundreds of thousands of starlings bed down for the night, a dense cloud looms in the sky ahead of him. Darker than the snow clouds, its particles dancing like a giant dust storm, this is a Hitchcockian scene of beautiful menace. The daily murmuration of the starlings.

'Has she told you everything, do you think?' Latimer's voice over the phone startles him. For a second, Pete had forgotten he'd just called his boss.

'Hard to know for sure. She wasn't keen on me looking round. I think she's got someone else living there and doesn't want to admit it, for some reason.'

The dark cloud shoots up high above him and Pete half expects the heavens to open up and admit the river of birds.

Latimer says, 'What's happening about the intruder last night?'

'Well, that's another thing. She admitted it's not the first time some-one's been on her property at night. She saw someone hanging around a few nights ago. Presumably that time, they couldn't get in.'

'Well, she works with some dodgy people. If you play with fire . . .'

'I've arranged for the crime scene team to stop by, but a trespass with nothing stolen isn't a high priority. Maggie promised me she'd change the locks today and be extra careful about security in future.'

'So, she's going to go and see him, you think? Wolfe, I'm talking about now.'

'She is. She seems to think that, if she meets him once, finds nothing to even get the ball rolling, then that will be the end of it. She'll have done all his little support team can ask for and they'll leave her alone.'

'They don't just want her to meet him, though,' Latimer says, 'they want her to get him out of prison.'

The road straightens and Pete is able to pick up some speed. 'As she says herself, Wolfe hasn't asked her to take his case. She's only had one letter from him, and all he did in that was thank her for saving his dog.'

'Come again?'

'Long story. Look, you're getting very faint. Ley lines must be getting in the way. I'll see you later.'

Chapter 26

PSYCHIATRIC REPORT INTO HAMISH WOLFE

PREPARED BY RICHARD RIDELL

Introduction

I was appointed to carry out a psychiatric assessment on Hamish Wolfe in August 2014, some three weeks before his trial was due to start. To say I felt a little underprepared would be an understatement – I'd barely had a chance to read the case file – but I had confidence in my ability to judge whether or not Hamish Wolfe was fit to stand trial.

Appearance and demeanour

Having heard a great deal about Hamish Wolfe's good looks, I was curious to see if the man in real life lived up to the legend that was rapidly growing up around him in the traditional and social media. My first impression was that being remanded in custody for several months hasn't improved his appearance. He is a tall man, but he had the look of someone who'd lost a lot of weight, quite quickly. His skin had a pallor that would have concerned me, had I been his GP; his eyes were blood-shot and his hands were showing a propensity to shake when he wasn't actively controlling them. There was a swelling under his right eye and around his mouth, and he moved very carefully, as though in some pain.

I began, as is customary, by explaining the parameters and purpose of the interview. He made no verbal response, but immediately began work on his new origami shape (I'd been prepared for this by reading Dr Okonjo's report). Again following the normal practice, I began by asking him questions about his family situation and early years. Much to my surprise (I was mentally preparing myself for the same silent treatment that Dr Okonjo had been subjected to) he spoke immediately, if not courteously. He told me that I could acquire all the information I needed from the files and that he had no intention of talking about his childhood.

(At this point, I'd like to borrow a trick from Dr Okonjo and insert an extract of the transcript.)

Start of transcript:

HAMISH WOLFE: I'd like you to apologize to Dr Okonjo for me, would you mind doing that?

DR RIDELL: Of course. But might I ask why you feel the need to apologize to Dr Okonjo?

HAMISH WOLFE: I was very rude to her. She didn't deserve that. Tell her I regret it, please.

DR RIDELL: Why do you think you were rude to her?

HAMISH WOLFE: I was angry. I took it out on her. I shouldn't have done.

DR RIDELL: Why were you angry?

HAMISH WOLFE: Have a look at my situation, Dick. I'm sure you can work it out.

(For the record, I had not given Hamish Wolfe permission to address me by my Christian name, nor a derivative of it, but I chose to let that pass.)

DR RIDELL: Do you often lash out, verbally, when you're angry?

HAMISH WOLFE: Don't we all?

DR RIDELL: Have you ever hurt someone physically, when you've been angry?

HAMISH WOLFE: (grinning) How do you think I got these bruises?

DR RIDELL: What makes you angry?

HAMISH WOLFE: Twats. Stupid questions.

DR RIDELL: Are you angry now?

HAMISH WOLFE: (lifting his wrists to show me the chains tethering him to the table) Don't worry, Dick. I can't reach you from here. And the muppets outside will come charging in if I so much as flutter my eyelashes too vigorously.

DR RIDELL: What is that you're making? (By this time, the origami figure was taking shape, but it was difficult to see what it was supposed to depict.)

HAMISH WOLFE: A weasel.

DR RIDELL: Have you ever hurt anyone who didn't deserve it?

HAMISH WOLFE: Yes.

(I think it worth pointing out that Wolfe's demeanour changed at this point. I saw what appeared to be genuine regret on his face.)

DR RIDELL: Can you tell me about it?

HAMISH WOLFE: No.

DR RIDELL: How do you feel when people ask you about the four victims? Do you think they deserve what happened to them?

HAMISH WOLFE: Apart from the fact that they led to my being here, I don't think about them at all. They don't come on to my radar screen.

DR RIDELL: You're saying you don't think of them as people?

HAMISH WOLFE: I'm saying I only think of them in terms of

115

how they affect me. And, yes, I do appreciate that I've just described a classic symptom of psychopathy.

DR RIDELL: Would you describe yourself as a psychopath?

HAMISH WOLFE: Dick, I'm going to save you some time. I am not, at this moment in time, nor have I ever in the past, suffered from any form of mental illness. I'm sure you've checked my medical records already. If you haven't, fucking shame on you, you don't deserve the grossly overinflated fee that you guys charge for the pieces of piss you call psychiatric assessments. Nor am I psychotic. I don't hear voices. There is no chip in my head. I have never been abducted by aliens. I was not sexually abused as a child, nor did I torture small animals. I fully understand the concepts of right and wrong and know only too well that if I fuck around with the law of the land, the law of the land is likely to jump up and bite me on the arse. Now, take your weasel, and fuck off out of here.

End of transcript.

Conclusion

It would be dishonest of me to say that I was satisfied with the outcome of my interview with Hamish Wolfe. I found him uncooperative, angry and aggressive. What I can say with some confidence is that he understands well the concept of being fit to stand trial and has, in his own words, declared himself to be so. I have nothing to add.

PROPERTY OF AVON AND SOMERSET POLICE. Ref: 544/45.2 Hamish Wolfe.

Chapter 27

IT IS STILL ONLY the second week in December and yet cell 43, corridor 2, H wing of Parkhurst Prison is as festive as the Christmas aisle in Poundland, and every bit as tacky. Paper chains run from the central light fitting to the four corners of the room and drape the window bars like a climbing vine. More chains festoon the length of the two bunks and paper baubles dangle from the ceiling. A man called Phil James is perched in the corner, folding and sticking narrow strips of red and green paper.

'OK, Mr Sahid.' Wolfe is on his feet, looking down at the Pakistani man on his bed. 'I need to have a look at your backside.'

The whites of Sahid's eyes have turned yellow, his skin has the look of ageing leather. He is in his mid fifties, could be a decade older. He has been in this place for five years. He is unlikely, ever, to leave.

'You better not try anything.' Sahid doesn't move. His two henchmen, their bodies as solid as the door they're guarding, don't take their eyes off him for a second.

'I'll try to restrain myself.' Wolfe takes the single step that will bring him to the washbasin and soaps his hands. When he turns back, Sahid hasn't moved.

'It's entirely up to you, Mr Sahid. I'm sure you'll get an appointment with Dr Evans next week.'

'What do you think it is?'

'I don't speculate, Mr S., I diagnose. I've got others waiting if you've changed your mind. How many out there, Phil?'

Wolfe's cellmate looks up from his chain-making. 'Seven, last time I checked, Doc. Kids on C wing have been spliff-banging again.'

Wolfe shakes his head. 'Give me strength.' Spliff-banging is the latest craze to hit the prison. Youngsters film themselves punching each other, in a sick, ritualistic fashion, with the violence tolerated because it will be rewarded later by cannabis. They bring the broken noses, the split lips, to Wolfe to fix up.

'If you're not going to show me your bottom, Mr S., I'll wish you good morning. When you see Dr Evans, tell him I'm not happy about the yellowing in your scleras. If you were a drinker, I'd worry about liver damage. As it is, gallstones would be my best guess.'

These daily surgeries annoy the hell out of the prison doctor.

The small, slim man, who is probably the most powerful and feared in Parkhurst Prison, glares. 'No one comes in.' He barks the order at his bodyguards, who turn their backs and swell to fill the entire doorway.

Phil turns round too – he has a healthy respect for Sahid and his gang of 'Muslim Boys' – to look out of the small window at the leaden greyness beyond. Wolfe, caught off guard, does the same and feels the sharp stab of panic that hits him every time he sees the sky.

'Trousers down, lean over.' He concentrates on the patient, because even here, this is normal, this is who he is.

'Try anything and you're a dead man.'

'You're really not my type, Mr Sahid.' Wolfe adjusts the angle-lamp and crouches, trying not to breathe too deeply. An arsehole is just an arsehole. Though the smell intensifies somewhat when showers are rationed.

'Any noticeable change in bowel habits, other than the blood you mentioned?' There is hardly any flesh left on Sahid's backside. The brown skin is fading to a dull beige, dry and flaking. This is more than poor diet and five years without sunshine. 'Going to the toilet more often? Passing looser stools? Pain when you go to the toilet?'

'Not particu— What in the name of God are you doing?'

'Keep still, please, try to relax. I'm checking for swelling just inside the anus. OK, we're done. You can get dressed.'

Phil has filled the sink again, adding hot water that he's had to bring from the kitchen. Water from the taps is never hot after eight o'clock in the morning.

'Thank you, nurse,' Wolfe says, as he sometimes does.

'Suck my dick,' Phil replies, and passes him a towel. Wolfe joins Sahid, who is dressed again, on the bunk.

'You look like you've lost weight, to me.'

Sahid gives a flat smile. 'My bathroom scales are broke. It's hard to tell.'

118

'Trousers feel looser?'

A grudging nod. 'A bit.'

'Any itching?'

A shrug. It means little, anyway. With hygiene so poor, itching of the genitalia is more or less the norm. Some cons seem never to take their hands out of their trousers. The constant movement down there could be scratching; few like to enquire.

'How's your appetite?'

'How's anyone's in this place, the shit they serve us.'

Wolfe thinks of the porridge he was given in his first week, with actual shit in it. He'd taken a mouthful before realizing where the smell was coming from. 'If you're lucky, Mr Sahid, you've got haemorrhoids. I can't see anything, and I don't have the equipment for an internal examination, but it's quite possible you've got enlarged blood vessels inside your rectum. They'll be causing the bleeding you talked about, any itching you might have experienced, and can also cause discomfort, particularly when passing stools.'

Sahid looks at his guards. 'You two, outside.' He doesn't bother looking at Phil, just raises his voice a fraction. 'You too.'

They obey him. It wouldn't occur to them not to. The door closes.

'And if I'm unlucky?'

No point not giving it to him straight.

'The symptoms you described to me just now can be indicative of bowel cancer.'

Wolfe gives him a second or two. No one wants to hear that word. And if word gets around that Sahid is seriously ill, his position as head of the Muslim Boys, the most powerful gang in Parkhurst, will be undermined. And there is always another gang just waiting for the opportunity to strike.

'This is not a diagnosis, mind you. You need to see Dr Evans, have him carry out tests. If he refuses to refer you, remind him that under the Prison Act you have the right to prompt medical attention.'

'Is there anything I can do in the meantime?'

The man is scared. There really is no leveller like cancer. 'Assume it's haemorrhoids. Tell everyone it's haemorrhoids. Increase the fibre in your diet, if at all possible, and drink plenty of fluids, especially water. Avoid painkillers that contain codeine, it can make constipation worse.'

Sahid gets to his feet. 'Thank you, Doctor.' He glances back, at the supplies that, of course, Wolfe isn't allowed to have, but that are tolerated because these informal daily surgeries help to keep the peace in the block. And go some way towards repairing the damage when peace doesn't hold out.

'I'm sorry about what happened this morning,' Sahid says. 'In the lavatories, I mean. I hope you know it was nothing to do with my people.'

'No harm done,' says Wolfe, even though he's still sweating when he thinks about it.

'Anything you need?'

Sahid and his contacts are among Wolfe's main suppliers. When drugs, money and phones are smuggled into prison, a packet of aspirin or a roll of medical plaster often slips its way in too.

Wolfe and Phil have already been through the stock. 'We're getting low on paracetamol, as always. Ibuprofen would be good too. Bandages and plasters always needed. Any donations gratefully received. Ideally not smuggled in up someone's arse.'

'I'll make enquiries if Superdrug can deliver.'

'And that map I asked you about?'

'That's in hand.' The other man nods as he gets to his feet.

The door opens. There is a blast of noise and stale disinfectant from the corridor. Something is kicking off somewhere close. In the next cell, music begins, full volume. Sahid's Muslim Boys have largely put a stop to non-Islamic music on the wing, but when disguising the sound of a fight, it's tolerated.

Wolfe turns to the window. He shouldn't, it never ends well, but sometimes the temptation to look at the outside world, even a tiny square of it, is irresistible. The smell of tobacco and stale feet tells him that Phil is back.

'Who's next?'

'Stan from H. Wanker's been cutting himself again. I told him you wouldn't see him unless he hands over his tool.'

Wolfe clenches his eyes shut and tells himself that this is a normal

120

day, he's had a hard morning at the Bristol General, spent several hours in surgery. This afternoon will be bad too, consultations and meetings, a late finish, but then he can drive home and take his dog for a run in the forest.

He looks up at the green canopy, watches the light dance through. He can hear twigs breaking beneath his feet, the dry leaves scratching in tree hollows. Behind him is the soft padding of his dog's paws.

And Daisy. He tries not to think of Daisy during the daytime, but sometimes she creeps in, is upon him before he can steel himself to keep her out. The glint in her eyes, the cold curve of her smile. Daisy, after all this time, the woman who will never leave him.

He takes a deep breath. And another. The panic is fading. He can go on. One more day. He nods at Phil, who is used to him by now. 'Show him in.'

Chapter 28

HMP Isle of Wight – Parkhurst
Clissold Road
Newport

My love,

In the eyes of the world I am a monster, the unspeakable,
unnameable thing. I am that which must be buried in unholy
ground, against which women veil their faces and children are
pulled in terror. I am creation warped and twisted, the evil that
walks amongst human kind.

I have been told these things so often, by voices so loud and
so many, that I was on the verge of believing them.

And then you came into my life. You look at me with those
clear, bright eyes and I can see no trace of fear. There is no
hint of dissemblance behind your smile. You talk, touch my
hand, tell me what must be so and why, and I feel normal once
more. You remind me that I am a man. You remind me of one,
undeniable truth.

I cannot be a monster, if I am loved by you.

Hamish

PROPERTY OF AVON AND SOMERSET POLICE. Ref: 544/45.2
Hamish Wolfe.

Chapter 29

My darling Hamish,

*I was sleeping when we met. I've been sleeping my whole life.
You woke me. Not with a kiss - oh, if only! - but with the
knowledge that there is another in the world like me. You are
the shadow that never leaves me, even when the light fades
completely, I sense your presence. You are the other half of me.
Together we make a whole.*

*I feel as though I've waited years to say these things to you.
To say I love you, and hear you say it back. I will rescue you,
my handsome prince. I will pull you from the grip of those
prison walls and then never let you go again.*

*I yearn too. But I know we will be together, and that day
is coming soon.*

Yours, always,
Me

PROPERTY OF AVON AND SOMERSET POLICE. Ref: 544/45.2
Hamish Wolfe. Letter found in Wolfe's cell at HMP Parkhurst. (NB:
Of hundreds of letters received by Wolfe during his time at Parkhurst,
this was one of fewer than a dozen that he kept. Most of that number
were from the same anonymous author.)

Chapter 30

THIS IS THE THIRD LOCKDOWN this month. Everyone is on edge, like dogs kept in a kennel that is too small. The slightest grievance, real or otherwise, gets blown out of all proportion. This one kicked off in the showers, as they often do, when they don't start in the dining room, or the games room, or the exercise yard, or even chapel. Someone with a score to settle. A fist shooting out. A well-aimed boot kick. Two bodies thud together and crash to the ground. A second later, pandemonium.

Wolfe sits on his bunk, folding and refolding a small, thin rectangle of paper.

'Like Santa's frigging grotto in 'ere.' Sedge, a Scot in his early twenties, has been dragged into the cell by Phil because if you spend too long on the corridor during a lockdown, you're likely to find yourself swept up with the reprisals. Participant or bystander, it makes little difference when the batons start swinging. He looks over at Wolfe. 'Fuck's he doing?'

'Ornithology.' Phil can never remember the term origami, and Wolfe has given up reminding him. Ornithology isn't way off beam. Often he makes bird shapes. Not today, though. Nor is he making yet another Christmas bauble. There are more than enough of those hanging from the ceiling.

'He makes things out of coloured paper. Look.' Like a proud parent, Phil is directing their visitor's attention towards the narrow, metal window ledge. 'It's like having a window box.'

Most often, Wolfe makes flowers. Their simple, regular form makes them amongst the easiest of shapes to create and he is a relative newcomer to origami. Using the coloured paper his mother sends he's fashioned roses, tulips, chrysanthemums and lilies, that to his mind seem to emphasize the drab squalor of the room, but which nevertheless delight Phil. Other inmates on the block have started to copy their Christmas decorations, fashioning their own chains, which are relatively simple, begging lessons in how to make the baubles, which are not. There have been rumours that the Governor is getting concerned about the fire hazard, is threatening to have the home-made decorations taken down. This worries Wolfe. His chains and baubles are important to him and Phil.

'What are these about?' Sedge can't keep still. He stands below Wolfe's bookshelf, looking up at the row of paperbacks, seven of them by the same author. '*Throw the Key Far.*' Sedge spells out the words slowly. '*A true-life tale of harsh justice*, by Maggie Rose.' He pulls the book from the shelf, oblivious to Wolfe's glare of annoyance, and opens it at a page marked with a yellow Post-it note. 'Part . . ., part . . .' he tries.

'Participle.' The tone of Wolfe's voice makes Phil frown, nervously. 'She uses the participle *sunk*, when she really needs the past tense, *sank*. It's a common mistake.'

Sedge flicks through the other Post-it notes peering out of the top of the book. 'So you've, like, gone through the whole book, looking for mistakes?'

'It passes the time,' says Wolfe.

In the corridor someone is hurting, although not so badly that he doesn't have the strength to swear and threaten the officers who are trying to contain him. Then he falls silent, and maybe he is hurting that badly now.

'Can't get my fuckin' 'ead round it.' Sedge has grown bored with the books and has found Wolfe's pile of mail on the narrow desk. He's flicking through the latest batch of coloured, even scented, paper and photographs. 'Are these bints mental, or what?'

Wolfe is fairly certain that Sedge's reading ability is limited to the more basic of the graphic novels. Not that he'd care. He feels no need to protect the confidentiality of women he will never meet. 'You could describe it as a mental disorder,' he says. 'But it's pretty much common to every woman in the world.'

'You what?' Sedge says.

'All women are drawn to the alpha male.' Wolfe goes back to his folding and twisting. 'They can't help themselves. The cleverer ones, the feminists, will deny it, but the evidence is against them.' He glances up at Sedge, sees no sign of light dawning. 'It's instinctive,' he tries again. 'The bigger, stronger, smarter men are going to be better at protecting the women and their children. They'll bring home more food. A man who is capable of killing is the ultimate protector.'

125

'Aye, but, like . . .' Sedge has an idea in his head, is struggling to get it out. 'You can't protect any of 'em. You can't even bring 'em home a takeaway pizza, you're banged up in here, so how does that work?'

'It works even better. It makes me a fantasy figure. They can dream about how dark and dangerous I am, with no chance of real life getting in the way. They'll never find out that, like most blokes, I can be a bit of a twat.'

Phil looks up. This is something he and Wolfe have discussed before. Phil is yet to be convinced. 'Yeah, but like, my missus, she won't take shit from no one, especially not me. I just don't get what you say about birds secretly wanting to be bossed about. It's the other way round at our gaff.'

'Jezz, this one is well fit!' Sedge has pulled a photograph from the pile. Wolfe glances over. It is a selfie, taken in a bedroom. The girl is naked from the waist up.

'She looks fifteen.' Wolfe takes it and drops it in the bin. 'If I could be bothered, I'd send it home to her parents. And we're talking fantasy here, mate. Just about every erotic film or book going is about a young, innocent woman being dominated by a dangerous man. All women secretly long to be dominated.' He grins to himself. 'Especially by a bloke who's fit and handsome. That's why I get the letters, you Scotch pillock, and you don't.'

'Frigging Nora, look at the tits on this one!' Sedge probably isn't listening. He hands another photograph over to Phil who nods, appreciatively. 'Hamish, mate, why don't you get some of 'em to visit?'

'That's what I keep saying,' Phil pipes up. 'He should find one he likes the look of, write to her a few times and get a relationship going. Has to be better than just getting visits from his mum.'

'Yeah, why not, mate? Don't you want a woman?'

Hamish smiles to himself and glances up at the calendar on the wall. 'Maybe I'm waiting for the right woman.'

The flower is finished. Wolfe twirls it between forefinger and thumb.

'Nice one.' Phil has given up watching the action on the corridor and comes back to admire the flower. 'Want me to put it on the ledge?'

'No thanks, mate. I'm keeping hold of this one.'

'What is it?'

Wolfe looks down at a dozen, slim white petals, the yellow centre, and raises it to his lips. 'It's a daisy.'

Chapter 31

'WHY IS YOUR HAIR BLUE?'

The child before Maggie is a girl of about six years old.

'It's my favourite colour,' Maggie tells her.

'Mine's pink.'

'Kelsey, don't bovver the lady.'

Kelsey doesn't even glance at her mother.

'I like pink too,' says Maggie. 'I nearly wore my pink coat today.'

'Why didn't you?'

'I don't know, it just felt like a white coat sort of day. Do you ever have days when only one coat or one dress will do?'

Kelsey stares.

'It won't stay white for long in this place.' The woman, several seats away, is in her mid thirties. Her blonde hair looks freshly dyed and her make-up better suited to a nightclub than a prison. On her lap is a baby of about eighteen months old. 'Not seen you 'ere before. First time?'

Maggie nods. If she accepts Hamish Wolfe as a client, she'll be entitled to legal visits, which will be more flexible, and conducted in private. Until then, she is a visitor like any other.

'We come every fortnight. Costs a frigging fortune: B and B in Southampton, three of us on the ferry. Not so bad in summer, the kids get to go to the beach, but this weather it's a bloody pain.'

'Are you visiting your husband?'

The woman wrinkles her nose. 'Well, not my husband, exactly. We're not married yet. We will, when he gets out. Kids are his, both of them. We're a proper family.'

'Is he due home soon?'

'Five years. If he behaves.'

'That sounds like a long time to me. It must be difficult.'

The woman pulls up the hem of her skirt and scratches the inside of her knee. 'Well, it's not what you sign up for, is it? I miss the money, obviously, although it were never that regular, and I never really knew where it were coming from. Mainly, though, it's the sex I miss. Having someone there at night. It's hard for him, too, if you know what I mean.'

Maggie glances uneasily at the six-year-old girl. Her pale blue eyes are flicking from one woman to the other.

'I'd move closer but I stink.'

The room smells of cleaning fluids and stale smoke. Maggie can smell perfume, instant coffee, cheap white bread. She can't smell the woman sitting a few seats away.

'I don't wash when I come here. Not for four days. Five if I can stand it. My Jason likes to smell me. The real me, he says, not perfumed me.'

There is no answer to this that Maggie can think of.

'Who you here to see, anyway?'

'Hamish Wolfe,' Maggie says.

Is she imagining it, or has the buzz of conversation noticeably dropped? Are more heads turning her way?

'You 'is girlfriend?'

'Lawyer.'

Kelsey's mother opens her mouth, but a grating sound catches their attention. The door into the main body of the prison has opened and an officer is in the doorway, beckoning them forward. It is time.

The prisoners are seated at tables in a large hall that smells of sweat and the stale oil of an antiquated heating system. Maggie is one of the last to enter. The others have rushed forward, have found the man they are visiting. Some children are in their fathers' arms, whimpering at the unfamiliar contact, others hang back, warily. Most people are already seated, deep in conversation. More than one couple appear to be quarrelling.

Maggie stands, just inside the doorway, taking stock, trying to find the man she has come to visit.

Someone is watching her. This is not so very unusual in itself, a woman can't look the way she does and not expect to be stared at, but this is different. This feels intense, even slightly predatory. She scans the room, the prickle of scrutiny stirring up the tiny hairs on her neck, knowing that somewhere in this mass of people, Wolfe has got her in his sights.

128

There he is. Directly beneath a window, its dust-clouded light softening the darkness of his hair. As their eyes meet, he remains as still as the walls that imprison him, and yet she has a sense of tremendous movement going on inside his head. He is processing her, absorbing information, preparing himself. She has to do the same, but it is as though a barrier has come down. All her usual powers of perception have deserted her. All she can see is the obvious.

She already knows that he's tall, but he sits so upright, so straight in his chair as to give the impression of being even taller. She knows he is handsome, but she hadn't expected the reaction just seeing him has provoked. He is brighter somehow, more colourful, the lines of his body sharper, than his surroundings.

Holding eye contact across the body-filled, stale-smelling room is like standing on the edge of a great lake, catching a glimpse of the far shore and being overcome with an urge to reach it. Swim, sail, float, whatever it takes. Or, like standing on a clifftop, looking down into the most perfect valley – lush and green, and wanting more than anything to get to it, but knowing the only way is to leap.

Maggie starts making her way towards him, weaving around tables, avoiding small children. She can see the detail of his eyes. The irises are green, maybe hazel. She sees his eyebrows lift, one corner of his mouth stretch out in a cautious smile. He is on his feet now, is smiling properly, his teeth white and perfect. His skin is so pale, has barely seen sunshine in two years. Physical contact is allowed, she remembers, at the start and end of these sessions. If he stretches out his hand, she'll have to take it.

He doesn't. He waits until she's at the table and then his eyes dart across her face, her hair, her body. On the tabletop is an origami shape.

'Hi.'

His voice is deeper than she expects, as though prison life has roughened and toughened it. He is wearing blue jeans and an oversized blue sweatshirt.

'Hello, Hamish. How are you?'

How cool, how calm her voice is. It doesn't sound as though her hands, were she to lift them from her sides, would be shaking.

'Please.' He's indicating the chair. She sits. He does too, and now

129

they seem only inches apart. The origami shape is made from silvery-white paper but she doesn't want to look at it. His shoulders are wide beneath the sweatshirt. He is a powerfully built man.

'Can I get you something?' she says. 'Tea? Coffee? Something to eat?' Even here, in this dreadful place, social norms prove strong.

'No, thank you.' He isn't cuffed, although she'd half expected that he would be. There is a graze on his right hand.

'Did you have a good journey?' he asks her.

She'd driven through snow in the pre-dawn darkness, the Solent had been rough, the ferry cold and uncomfortable. 'Yes, thank you,' she says, and thinks how polite they are being, the murderer and the – what, exactly?

He smiles again, suddenly, as though overcome by a moment of joy and she sees that his incisors are longer than his other teeth. They spoil the perfect symmetry of his mouth. 'Why is your hair that colour?' he asks her.

The question she never answers truthfully has an oddly relaxing effect. And she has her answer prepared. 'When I was thirteen, my school went to see a performance of *A Midsummer Night's Dream* at Stratford on Avon. Titania had blue hair. I thought it was just beautiful, but of course there was no way my mother would agree to my dyeing my hair blue, so I had to wait.'

He says nothing, but holds eye contact and a faint smile plays on his face. He is interested in the blue hair story.

'It didn't seem quite the form with the legal profession when I was starting out. Goodness me, those people take themselves seriously, so I had to wait a bit longer. And then I had a stroke of luck.'

'You became a maverick celebrity and they're allowed to be quirky?'

'I went prematurely grey. Not a lovely, snowy-white, sadly, but a rather coarse, iron grey. I had to change it. The blue moment had come.'

'I can't call you Titania.'

'Maggie will do.'

'Can I get straight to the point, Maggie?'

'Please do.'

'Do you believe me guilty?'

'Yes.'

130

She sees a twitch around the eyes that might be annoyance. 'Then why are you here?' he asks her.

She looks down, at the origami shape on the table. 'Is that for me?' It is a fox, she sees now. An Arctic fox.

'If you'd like it.'

She traces its outline gently with her index finger. 'I'll put it with the others you sent.'

His eyebrows lift but he doesn't rise. Does she push it? Maybe not yet. Around them, she can sense people watching surreptitiously, straining to hear what she and Wolfe are saying to each other. Her voice, always low-pitched, falls even lower, forcing her to lean fractionally closer to him. 'What is it you want from me?' she asks.

'Honestly?' He leans back, and something treacherous inside her misses his closeness.

'Of course.' She doesn't expect honesty. But she will know if she doesn't get it.

'I wanted to meet you.'

Actually, that does feel like honesty. 'Why?'

His head lolls to one side. 'Oh, come on. You wanted to meet me too.'

'You killed four women. Why would any woman want to meet you?'

He takes in a deep breath and lets it out noisily. 'It sometimes feels like every woman in Britain wants to meet me. God knows enough of them write to me.' Then he sits up straighter, his face alive again, as though a sudden thought has struck him. 'And it's three women. You can't count Zoe. She may not even be dead.'

'I wanted to talk to you about Zoe in particular.'

His confidence falters. 'I didn't write that letter to her mother.'

'I know. But her mother is suffering terribly. It can make no difference to you, and lots to her, if she can find and bury her daughter properly. I promised the police I'd ask you.'

He frowns. 'Ask me what?'

'To tell them where she is.'

The frank and honest smile is gone now. In its place is a smirk of pure cunning. 'And what will they give me in return?'

'They didn't send me in here with an offer. You'd have to ask them.'

'Will you pass on my terms?' He is deadly serious. Her heartbeat, already in overdrive, picks up a notch.

'If you want me to.'

'I'll show them where Zoe is, in return for two hours on a beach. With you.'

For a second, she doesn't trust herself to speak. 'You know the police will never agree to that. And you're a murderer. Why would I want to spend any time with you?'

'It will help Zoe's mum, whom you pretend to care about. And it has to be fine. If it's raining, we cancel and go another day. And it has to be just the two of us. The police and guards stay out of earshot.'

'The beach isn't happening. But are you admitting to having killed those women? Do you know where Zoe is?'

He runs his hands over the back of his head, exhales loudly. 'Of course I'm not. I have no idea where Zoe is. But I could run the boys in blue a merry chase through Cheddar's caves. I could even escape. I know those caves very well.'

'You'd live on the run for the rest of your life.'

He gives a quick, dismissive look round and more than one pair of eyes drops. 'Has to be better than spending my life in here. And maybe I'd prove my innocence. Become a free man again. If I do, maybe you and I can meet normally.'

The conversation is spinning out of control. She needs to slow it down. 'Let me explain a little about how I work. I monitor every high-profile or controversial conviction for murder or serious violence that takes place in this jurisdiction. I do some research, a bit of digging, into all those that catch my interest. I make notes and they form the first draft of a book. Currently, I have around two dozen books in progress. Most of them will never go beyond two or three chapters because I take on very few cases.'

'How many chapters does mine have?'

His directness, his presumption, is bothering her. 'Half a dozen,' she says, although it has more.

'I'm encouraged. But please tell me the title isn't some lame reference to my name.'

She feels her face glow a shade warmer. 'I think we've seen enough

132

lupine puns over the past two years. The point I'm leading to is that, unless I become convinced there's been some serious miscarriage of justice, I won't get involved. More than that, and more important to me than justice, is a belief that I can win. I don't flog dead horses.'

'That's why it has to be you.'

There is something in the simple sentence that feels too intimate. 'It would be very foolish to pin hopes on me.'

'You must have wondered why I haven't appealed. Others did. And concluded, wrongly, that it's because I accepted the justice of the sentence. Nothing could be further from the truth. I've been waiting for the right time.'

He reaches forward. He's going to touch her. She waits for someone to step in. Physical contact is only allowed at the start and end of visits, not now, not—

No one does. Her hands stay, flat, on the tabletop, as though they are nailed in place. His fingertips rest lightly on hers.

'I've been waiting for you.'

Chapter 32

PETE STANDS IN THE DOORWAY of Maggie's kitchen, watching the crime scene processing team. One is taking photographs. Another is dusting for prints. The photographer pauses for a second. 'We've got access to the whole of the house and the garages, but not the cellar. She says it's permanently locked and only one way in. No one's been in it for years, she says, and the stairs aren't safe.'

Just the sort of place Pete wants to see. 'Did she leave a key?'

'Not that we've found.'

'OK if I take a look upstairs?'

'Yeah, we're done up there.'

As he walks through the hall, Pete checks his watch. Visiting time at Parkhurst began half an hour ago. Barring an act of God, Maggie and Wolfe are together.

The stairs are a tall, straight flight, ending in a wide landing. White orchids, as pale and fragile as Maggie herself, stand on narrow tables along its length. Five doors. Gambling on her bedroom overlooking the front of the house, he turns left and passes an open door. A technician is inside it, sitting at Maggie's desk. He doesn't even look up. Pulling on latex gloves, Pete pushes gently on the next door.

He'd no idea how many shades of white there are in the world.

The walls are the colour that snow assumes on forest floors, the painted woodwork around the windows and doors a brighter shade, like sun on snow. The curtains and bedding are in the palest shades of grey. The bed is silver, the wooden furniture stripped birch. This has to be her room. Guest rooms are never this fancy. And yet, apart from the endless variety of white, he can see nothing in it that is essentially Maggie.

Almost without realizing what he is doing, he slips off his shoes to find the carpet is thick and soft beneath his feet. He checks the bedside cabinets, the dressing table.

The wardrobes line one wall. She favours trousers and sweaters, but there are a few slim, tailored dresses, all with long sleeves and low hemlines. She is a size eight. There are several woollen coats, including the fondant pink with black buttons that she'd worn to the station. Everything in the wardrobe is in bright, jewel colours or shades of white and cream. Nothing green, brown or beige.

Nothing that will fit a man.

A sound startles him and he opens the door of the en suite bathroom to see a male backside sticking out from beneath the bath.

'Found anything?' he asks.

Sunday shuffles out and sits back on his heels. 'Plumbing needs some attention. Apart from that, nothing yet.'

As Sunday half disappears again beneath the bath, Pete pulls open the bathroom cabinet. Make-up, contact lenses, all the usual 'lady products'. In a cupboard below the washbasin are toilet rolls, cleaning fluids and industrial-sized bottles of cream peroxide.

He turns to leave and gets halfway across the bedroom when he hears Sunday in the bathroom.

'Whoa!'

Pete stops. 'What've you found?'

'Not sure. Give me a minute. I'll catch up.'

Leaving Sunday behind, Pete makes his way along the landing. He finds a spare bedroom with empty cupboards and an unmade bed, a smaller room that is used as a furniture and box store.

The room at the end of the corridor has a plain wooden floor, and is almost devoid of furniture. There is a single leather chair, old, easy, comfortable, and a small coffee table holding seven hardback books. They are Maggie's; her bestselling, true-crime books, one for each of the convicted killers she has represented. There is nothing else in the room at all, apart from what has been pinned to the walls.

'Like a museum exhibit, isn't it?'

Liz is behind him, is looking over his shoulder at the photographs, the newspaper cuttings, the internet screenshots and the case documents that have been arranged around the walls of the room.

'Not one you'd take your kids to,' Pete says. He still hasn't moved from the doorway.

Huge cork noticeboards have been hung around the room, each one dedicated to one of Maggie's clients.

'It's like an incident room,' Pete says. 'Except, it's a bit, I don't know . . .'

'Gleeful?' suggests Liz, who slips in and stands in front of the board dedicated to Shane Ridley. Maggie, as Ridley's lawyer, had access to police files, and several of the key documents, including crime scene photographs, are here. Only three pieces of Lara Ridley's body were ever found; one of them, her head, by a troop of scouts in woodland. Liz is looking at a photograph of that head now, empty eye sockets staring up at the camera from a pile of autumn leaves.

'She's really proud of her work, isn't she?' Liz says.

'She's very good at it.' Pete has stepped closer to the portrait photograph of Ridley, taken on the couple's honeymoon. His hair is windswept and damp, there is sand on the side of his face. His shoulders are bare.

Next around the wall is a board dedicated to Maggie's first major success. Triple murderer Steve Lampton was released in 2007 after serving five years of a life sentence. He, too, is looking down at Pete now, surrounded by grisly photographs of the young women he killed.

Next is Nigel Upton who killed two teenagers in a well-known lovers' lane near Buxton in Derbyshire. Upton, too, was released after Maggie's intervention.

To one side of the big, uncurtained window is Niall Caldwell, who bludgeoned his mother to death to get his inheritance faster than he might otherwise have done. On the other side of the window, Russell Mulligan, who shot a village postmistress in an armed robbery that went disastrously wrong. Then Bill Fryer. Arguably, Bill Fryer is the worst of them. He was the only one who went after kids.

'She has pictures of dead children on her wall.' Pete can't help it. He's seen some things in his time, but . . .

The final board in the room is dedicated to Hamish Wolfe. His picture is staring down at them.

'She's really odd, Pete.' Liz is staying close to his side. 'I know you think I'm biased against her. I know she has a job to do, but look at the table.'

Of all the things to capture attention in this room, Pete wouldn't have bet on the coffee table, but he does what he's told. It's a mess, stained by several rings left by coffee mugs and glasses. The leather in the chair is old and worn and there is a glass beside the pile of books. He picks it up and smells Scotch.

'She sits here, drinking coffee and Scotch and looking at innocent people who've been killed horribly and the monsters who she's helping,' says Liz. 'What kind of woman does that?'

Pete can think of nothing to say. He turns to leave. Liz, though, seems reluctant to follow him. 'You know what really freaks me out, though?' she says.

Pete stops in the doorway. 'What?'

'Look at these blokes. Look at Ridley, Caldwell, not quite so much Mulligan but Fryer. And especially Hamish. Just look at them.'

Pete does, and sees exactly what she's getting at.

'If she's only concerned with justice,' says Liz, 'how come she only gets involved with the good-looking ones?'

'Pete!' Someone's voice calling from downstairs. 'You need to see this!'

Leaving Maggie's box room, he and Liz make their way back downstairs into the kitchen, where he almost falls over a pair of legs. One of the SOCOs is flat on his back, looking up at the underside of the table. The chairs have all been pushed away.

'What?'

'Come and see for yourself.'

Pete gets down, the floor tiles cold beneath him, and rolls over on to his back. The SOCO is shining a torch upwards.

'Christ.'

'Yeah. Think she's seen it?'

Pete thinks. 'She'd have said something, I'm sure. What is it, it's not—'

'Blood? No we don't think so. Although almost certainly intended to give that impression. Probably just a thick red marker pen. We need to get some shots.'

The SOCO slides out, leaving Pete staring up at the writing on the underside of Maggie's kitchen table. Just three words.

HE LOVES ME.

Chapter 33

THE NOISE LEVELS IN THE VISITING HALL have picked up and Maggie and Wolfe have had to lean closer to hear each other.

It has to be her.

She wishes she had something to drink. 'OK, then, give me something to work with. Tell me who might have killed those women.'

Wolfe shakes his head. 'I have no more idea than you.'

'Explain the trace evidence, your car being used to transport Myrtle Reid's body, the Facebook posting from your computer.'

His bruised hands lift from the table. 'Someone got into my house. Accept that one, simple fact, and all else becomes easy to explain.'

Someone got into his house. Took his car keys, maybe had another set made. Picked up a few dog hairs. Used his computer.

'Who had keys, apart from you?'

'My mother, cleaner, fiancée. Personally, I don't suspect any of them, but by all means check them out.'

'Did any of them report their keys missing at any time? Did you lose yours for any period?'

'Afraid not. I do keep a spare set in the house, but I don't remember them ever going missing. Not that I would check them every day.'

'This intruder, if he or she exists, also accessed your computer. Presumably it's password protected?'

He pulls a face. 'It is, but I was never that careful about logging out when I went to work in the morning. I'd quite often come home to find it still on. Once in the house, accessing the computer would have been easy.'

'OK, I admit it's possible. But who would go to such lengths to frame you for murder?'

She's struck a chord. 'Exactly. It has to be about me. If the killer simply wanted a scapegoat, he wouldn't choose me. He'd pick someone much less able to fight back. Someone not too bright, maybe educationally subnormal. Someone with a troubled background.'

She lets her face betray just a hint of scepticism. 'Someone wanted to hurt you, specifically?'

'That's right.'

'Do you have any enemies?'

'Thousands. Do you see the stuff posted about me on Twitter?'

'I mean before. Patients who felt let down? Medical secretaries or nurses you've had fired?'

He shakes his head. 'I've never had a malpractice lawsuit filed. Never had to formally reprimand a junior colleague. People usually cooperate pretty well with me.'

'Does the name Sirocco Silverwood mean anything to you?'

His brow lifts. 'Is she a character in a young adult novel?'

'She's real. She claims you and she have a bond.'

His face says he's unimpressed. 'A lot of women write to me, quite a few of them seem to think we're in some sort of relationship. I don't keep their letters, I'm afraid.' He stops, still thinking. 'Actually, I think Mum might have mentioned someone of that name. Is she a member of that support group?'

'She is. Have you met her?'

He shakes his head. 'Nope.'

'Tell me about Fat Club.'

His head is suddenly very still. 'I have no idea what you're talking about.'

'A woman scorned has a long memory. Rumour has it you've done some unspeakable things in your time.'

His eyes have a way of turning dull when he's angry. 'Luring a woman to a cave and slitting her throat is unspeakable. Letting her bleed out in the pitch-dark on a cold, stone floor is unspeakable. I've heard those rumours too, and let me tell you, having consensual sex with a fellow student is pretty much OK in my book. Whatever her dress size happens to be.'

His assurance annoys her. She didn't want to find him desperate, pathetic even, but his calm feels wrong too. 'You made video recordings. Without the girls' knowledge.' She waits for him to deny it. The porn business was only ever rumoured. His stare remains impassive.

'You and your mates pretended to like those girls, you probably plied them with cheap wine to make the job a bit easier. You thought this was funny. You passed the tapes around your mates, so that you could all gawp at women's bodies and laugh at how hideously ugly they were.'

Wolfe slaps one hand down on the table. Not loud, but sharply enough to draw a few extra glances. Some of their neighbours have given up all pretence of having a conversation of their own.

'Point of order, Maggie,' he says. 'Don't suggest I got women drunk in order to have sex with them. Students drink. They drink and they have sex and rape doesn't come into it. And, you know what, even if these sad old rumours were true – and I'm not saying they are – it's a big leap from behaving like a twat at medical school to murdering four women.'

Maggie waits. It's good that he's angry. When people get angry they let things slip.

'Ten minutes, ladies and gentlemen. Start to wrap it up, please.'

Wolfe seems to droop a little. 'I guess it's make-your-mind-up-time, Lawyer Rose. Can you and I do business together?'

Maggie holds up her hands. It is a gesture of hopelessness. 'You've given me nothing. Someone broke into your house and stole your car. Not impossible in itself but impossible to prove. Someone was trying to frame you for the murders but you have no idea who . . .'

He leans forward. 'Has it occurred to you yet that Detective Sergeant Weston's conversation with the attendant at that particular station was a remarkable stroke of luck?'

'Sorry, what?'

'Wouldn't you think, Maggie, that a man with murder on his mind, a man with a woman tied up and terrified in the boot of his car, would check his tyre pressure before he left his house?'

Of course. She'd thought exactly the same thing. 'Accidents happen. Things go wrong. Maybe you drove your car over a piece of glass that night.'

'Or maybe whoever was driving my car needed to be seen. Needed to be caught on camera somewhere and had previously checked out that petrol station because it was in the right area and it had an air pump somewhat removed from the main building. We don't even know for

140

certain that Myrtle was in the car, just that her sock was found in the bushes some time later. Does it not have a staged feeling about it?'

A guard is making his way around the tables, encouraging stragglers to get up and head out.

'The murders finished,' Maggie says. 'Once you were taken off the streets, the killings stopped.'

'I told you it was all about me.'

She shakes her head. 'No. An opportunistic framing, I might accept, but the idea that someone killed four women just to get you into trouble? That's nuts.'

The guard is very close now and she stands up. Hamish doesn't move. 'Maggie, if this case were easy, I wouldn't need you.'

Chapter 34

'THERE IS A PATROL car parked outside my house.'

'Ah, you're home. I'll be ten minutes.'

'No, I don't think— Oh, for God's sake.'

Maggie is listening to dead air. Ten minutes? Weston can't drive from Wells in ten minutes, he has to be lurking somewhere close. Damn. She wants a bath, to curl up in bed, she needs time to get her head in order. Spending time with Wolfe has exhausted her.

'So, you don't need Detective Pete any more?'

'I never did.'

'You were starting to like him.'

Maggie locks the back door. 'It's gone nine o'clock. I'm cold. I'm hungry. And I know he's only coming to ask me about today.'

The kitchen smells of intruders. It smells of their bodies, of the food they brought in their packed lunches, the cigarettes they smoked outside her back door. It smells of their curiosity, their prying into her cupboards and drawers. It smells of the comments they exchanged about her, of their snide observances and their disrespectful banter.

She hears the doorbell as she is getting out of the shower, again as she is pulling on clothes. It is being clanged for the third time when she reaches the bottom of the stairs. It has started snowing again, there are flakes in Pete's hair, on the shoulders of his coat.

'Any chance we can do this quickly?' she says.

'Depends how fast you eat?'

Balanced on one arm Pete holds a white carrier bag. She catches the scent of garlic, ginger, warm food. She should be cross at the presumption, resentful of the interruption. All she can feel is hunger. She opens the door a little wider, silently giving him permission to come in. 'Chinese?' she asks.

'Thai.' He steps inside, bringing the dark chill of the night with him.

She closes the door quickly, although not quickly enough. She can still see the cold air, lurking in corners of her hallway.

'Cutlery in the drawer by the sink,' she tells him, when they're both in the warmth of the kitchen. 'I may even have chopsticks. Don't bother setting a place for the elephant.'

This makes him smile. He avoids the chopsticks, finding knives and forks instead, not commenting on the fact that none of them match. She rinses plates under the hot tap and finds half a bottle of white wine in the fridge.

'So go on,' he says. 'Did you and Wolfe hit it off?'

'You'd have to ask him what he thinks of me. For my part, I thought him polite. Intelligent. In good shape, physically and mentally.'

Pete lifts his eyebrows.

'In good health, I should say. Prison life hasn't beaten him down yet. It will, though. It gets them all in the end.'

'He wields a lot of power on the wing. He doles out medical advice. The big men look after him, offer him protection, of sorts. And he's a pretty physical bloke too. He can handle himself.'

'I also found him calm.'

'Calm?'

'Yes. And not a medicated calm, either. He isn't taking anything, I'm sure of it. There was none of the anxiety, the urgency I normally expect when I see people who believe they're suffering a miscarriage of justice. He wasn't even particularly angry. Strange as it may seem, he's remarkably relaxed about being in prison.'

'Does that suggest innocence to you?'

She turns back to the fridge. 'No. No, it doesn't.'

Pete straightens the knives and forks.

'Did you ever consider the possibility that Wolfe was framed?' She throws the question back over her shoulder and sees from his face that he'd known that one was coming.

'Of course,' he says. 'It was his first and only defence. The trouble is, he never put forward a single candidate. By his own admission, and as we found out, he had no enemies.'

'And you were prepared to believe this nice guy capable of killing four women?'

143

'I can name you some very charming mass murderers.'

She pours wine, the friendly gurgling softening the mood. He takes lids off food containers. They sit down and she feels a moment of regret that she and Pete Weston will never be friends.

'Will you admit, though, that it's possible?' she says. 'Let's say his cleaning lady works with headphones, listening to music. If she's upstairs, hoovering, there's every chance someone could come in down-stairs, find a spare set of keys, get them copied, and return them the following week.'

'It's also possible his mother, being a domineering, jealous type with serious control issues, decided he'd be easier to keep tabs on if he was behind bars. Possible, just not that likely.'

'Tell me how the conversation between you and the pump attendant came up?'

He fixes her with a stare, just long enough to let her know he's reg-istered the abrupt change of direction, knows he's being interrogated. 'I use that place a lot. I usually exchange a few pleasantries with Ahmed. He asked me how the case was going, I told him we were pursuing sev-eral lines of enquiry. He said, Tell me sumfink, Pete, that girl what went missin', was she wearing a blue coat, like? I said, Might have been, why? He said, Wait here a minute, and disappeared out back. Would you prefer beef or chicken? Or a bit of both?'

'Both, I think. Thank you, this looks very nice. So, go on. The coat?'

'He'd noticed the BMW with the oddly behaving driver and then, when Myrtle's disappearance was on the news, he checked the CCTV footage. He was umming and aahing about whether to call it in or not, when I turned up for my tankful of unleaded.'

'And that was the lead that took you straight to Hamish. The dog DNA and the carpet fibres established a link between him and Jessie. Case just about closed.'

He has a mouthful of food, but he nods his agreement.

'Did it never strike you as being rather too much of a lucky break? I mean, the case is going nowhere – no offence – and then, out of the blue, the killer is caught on camera, in your favourite petrol station.'

He is hungrier than she, piling food into his mouth, talking between mouthfuls. 'Pure luck caught the Yorkshire Ripper.'

'There is no dedicated parking at Hamish Wolfe's house. No drives, no garages along that whole road. Everyone parks in the street, but there's a lot of competition for spaces. He regularly had to park some distance from his house.'

'Yeah, he mentioned that.'

'So, someone with a copy of his car keys could borrow the car for the night and fill the tyres up with air in a petrol station they'd already established was frequented by the lead detective on the case. You have no proof that the hooded figure seen on film is actually Hamish Wolfe.'

'Other than that he was driving Hamish's car, you're right, we don't. But we also don't have anyone else who might have done it.'

'You never found the computer that most of the Facebook postings were sent from, did you?'

Pete's plate is empty. He picks up the beef carton. 'No. Facebook were cooperative, but when we got on to BT to link the IP address to an actual location, we drew a blank.'

'Because whoever owned that computer had put enough technical blocks in place to prevent it being traced?'

'I seem to remember routing through Eastern Europe being mentioned at some point. It didn't matter. We figured one posting from Wolfe's own computer was enough.'

She pushes food around on her plate and sips at her wine. 'So.' She looks round her kitchen. 'Find anything interesting today?'

He did. She can tell from the way the light leaps in his eyes. He found something in her house. Her fork clatters against her plate.

'What did you find?'

He picks up his phone and turns it to show her a photograph. Wooden boards. Words, written in red ink, chalked angrily, in harsh capital letters.

HE LOVES ME.

It means nothing. This has nothing to do with her, with her house. Then.

'Oh!' She pushes back the chair and falls to her knees.

'Can I assume it's not your work?' He's crouched down, peering under the table at her.

She reaches up and rubs. The wood is rough on the underside, unsanded, and will fill her hands with splinters, but she spits on her fingers and tries again.

'Hang on.' Pete is moving closer.

She can scratch the offending words away, peel away the fibres of the wood with her nails.

'Oh no, you don't.' Pete's hands are under her shoulders, pulling her out. 'There's sandpaper in my coat pocket. I had a feeling you'd want to get rid of it. The crime scene guys have everything they need and I can do it before I go.'

'Thank you.' She lets him help her to her feet. 'I'm OK, thank you. I'm sorry, finish your food.'

Pete sits and picks up his fork without taking his eyes from her.

'What does it mean?' he asks her.

'I don't know.'

'You're pretty upset for something that has no meaning.'

Distress makes her snap at him. 'They could have written a recipe for chocolate brownies and I'd be upset. Someone did this while I was asleep. Where else did they go?'

'Impossible to say. No fingerprints in the house other than yours. You have a very good cleaning lady.'

'I don't have a cleaner of either sex.'

'Tell me the truth now: when you saw it, who was the first person that came into your head?'

She shakes her head. 'It's stupid.'

'Go on.'

'Sirocco. You know, that woman I was telling you about? She kept going on about how she and Hamish were soulmates. I thought she was harmless enough, but possibly a bit unhinged. And as you pointed out yourself, that lot know where I live.'

'Anyone else?'

'No, they were all odd, but she was the only one claiming he loved her. And she could have got that paper rose from Sandra. Did you find prints on it?'

'Nothing conclusive. A few partials that could be Wolfe's, but paper is very difficult to get clear prints off. Another that definitely isn't Wolfe's or yours, but didn't come up on our system.'

146

'I mentioned it today, when I met him. I should have pressed.'

He picks up his fork, holds it in mid-air. 'You were telling me the truth when you said you live here alone.'

'Of course I was.'

'Do we know each other well enough, yet?'

For a second, she has no idea what he means. Then she remembers. He wants to know whom she talks to, when she thinks she's alone. She says, 'You'll think me nuts.'

He has a nice smile, she decides. Kinder, less complicated than that of Wolfe. 'You have blue hair,' he says. 'I thought you were nuts the second I laid eyes on you.'

What difference can it make? 'I had a twin. A sister. She died.'

His smile fades. 'I'm sorry.'

'It was a long time ago. I never knew her, not really. Except I do. I know her as well as I know myself and I feel her loss every day. There are times when, without her, I feel like half a person.'

'And you talk to her? Use her to work out stuff you'd normally discuss with a mate?'

She wouldn't have expected him to understand so quickly. 'I talk to her and she talks back. I hear her voice, as clearly as I hear yours.'

His eyebrows draw closer together. 'Any other voices you hear in your head?'

She smiles. 'No. Just hers.'

'Have you thought about getting a pet?'

She has a sudden image of a dog. A Dalmatian, chasing sticks into the sea, barking at waves, giddy with delight.

'Do you talk to anyone who isn't there?' she asks.

'Yeah. I talk to my daughter. I know what it's like to miss someone.'

She is calmer now. Pete drains his glass. 'So what do you plan to do about the Hamish Wolfe case, if I may ask?'

She feels an illogical and unexpected urge to please this man. 'Nothing,' she says. 'Wolfe is guilty. He can stay where he is.'

Maggie walks slowly up the stairs once Pete has left. She needs to sleep now, sleep and not think, for hours.

'Twin sister? Seriously?'

'First thing that came into my head.' In her bedroom, Maggie looks around for her dressing gown.

'What if he checks?'

'He won't.' She smiles a tight, brief, smile. 'I think he's a bit smitten.'

She pulls off clothes and goes into the bathroom. Her eyes are sore from wearing contact lenses for too long. She takes them out, cleans her teeth and steps on the bathroom scales.

'Someone's messing with you.'

Before leaving, Pete had been as good as his word, sanding down the underside of her table so that the intruder's mysterious graffiti could no longer be seen.

'I know.' She has lost weight again.

'That woman from the Wolfe Pack? Sirocco?'

'Seems most likely. The question is, why?'

Chapter 35

WOLFE FEELS EVERY PUNCH thrown at fight club. The two fighters slam into the metal lockers and he feels the blow in his kidneys. He feels skin peeling off knuckles as a fist slams into the side of a jaw.

He closes his eyes, tries to picture Maggie's pale skin, her slim, gently tapering fingers edged in fondant pink. He tries to remember the scent she'd brought into the prison with her, an odd mixture of warm wool and cold chemicals. He tries, but can't quite take himself out of the stark, cold violence of the here and now.

He can almost feel the blood start to flow, its warm stickiness trickling down his face. Maybe it's because he knows, on a precise and detailed level, the physical damage these two are doing to each other, or perhaps it's because his will be the job of fixing them up later. Fight club injuries are rarely seen by the prison doctor, because all injuries, however small, have to be reported to the authorities, and if the prison authorities get wind of fight club, steps will be taken to shut it down. So guards are bribed, inmates close enough to hear what's going on are threatened into silence and the CCTV cameras in the gym are blacked out.

The yelling is inside Wolfe's head like a migraine. The crunch of bone hitting bone is a sound he feels, deep in his gut. He looks down, at the scuffed, worn gym floor and tries to remember the sound of Maggie's voice. Light but low-pitched. Measured, as though she tests each word out in her head before speaking it. He tries to imagine her saying something nice. Something nice and nonsensical. Instead he hears grunts and curses.

Around the gym, eyes are fixed on the reeling pair in the middle. The Muslim boy is winning. He's smaller but faster, aiming his blows just beneath his opponent's ribcage. One accurately delivered body-punch in that spot can stop a fighter. Repeated body-punches will wear any fighter down. His opponent, white, heavier, tattooed, is struggling to do anything other than fend off the blows.

In the corner of the gym, tucked away behind some five-a-side goal-posts that won't be needed again until spring, is a canvas equipment bag the exact colour of Maggie's hair. Blue hair? He hadn't expected that. He hadn't expected her to be quite so beautiful.

A gossamer light spray of red mist forms in the air above the fighters. The Muslim boy staggers. The spectators yelp like hyenas circling prey and the fighters crash into the goalposts. Wolfe looks around, nervously.

The noise level builds. Inmates in their cells who can see nothing of what's going on yell encouragement all the same. Many will have a bet on the outcome, even if they can't afford the premium to watch. At the end of the corridor, those guards on weekend night duty stare at TV screens and turn up the volume. Wolfe looks at his watch. Three minutes and twelve seconds. Longer than many fights. These two are evenly matched. It could go on for some time longer. The injuries could be beyond his ability to patch up.

Maggie had been one of the last of the visitors to leave the visiting hall. He'd sat and watched her walk away, her shoulders tense, conscious of being observed but never once looking back. She'd disappeared, a flicker of white in the doorway, and he'd been overwhelmed by a feeling that he'd never see her again. That one visit would sate her curiosity.

The Muslim is back on top. He's holding the white boy by the hair, hammering punches up into his chin. White boy kicks out and misses. The flesh of his face is bouncing in time with the blows. Already it looks red, swollen, as though its insides are bursting through the skin.

The crowd senses victory is close. The bookmaker's eyes have narrowed. White boy is down on the stained tiles. He holds up his hand. It's over. He gets one last kick from his opponent, a torrent of abuse from those who have lost money on him, and then people start to slink away back to their cells.

The winner staggers to a corner where his supporters look after him. Wolfe kneels down by the loser. The boy, younger than he realized, has lost consciousness. Wolfe checks his breathing, his pulse.

'Tyler.' Wolfe finds an unmarked spot on the boy's cheek and slaps it. 'Talk to me, Tyler, can you hear me?'

'Stand back, Doc, we need to get him out of here.'

150

'I don't know how badly he's hurt. You can't move him.'

But they can, and they do. Three men hoist him up and carry him out. Wolfe and Phil follow, bringing their towels, their buckets, their bandages.

Behind them, the gym door closes and is locked. Neither looks back, because it doesn't do to know the guards who are in on this, who allow fight club to happen.

The corridor is empty. Tyler and his supporters have vanished into one of the cells. Finding them won't be hard. All Wolfe and Phil need to do is follow the blood.

Chapter 36

From the office of

MAGGIE ROSE

The Rectory, Norton Stown, Somerset

Friday, 11 December 2015

Dear Mr Wolfe,

There is nothing I can do for you. The case against you is as sound as any I've seen and you gave me nothing yesterday that hasn't already been speculated upon endlessly and fruitlessly by those who campaign for your release.

That effort, I'm sure you know, is driven by your own personal charisma rather than any conviction as to your innocence. People want to believe in you because you are handsome and capable of being charming; and what people want to believe in, they usually do.

I can't believe this will come as a surprise to you. I had no sense, yesterday, of your taking our meeting seriously. I was a diversion for you, a brief entertainment. I don't blame you for that, but I have neither the time nor inclination to indulge you further, I'm afraid.

Yours sincerely,

Maggie Rose

Chapter 37

HMP Isle of Wight - Parkhurst
Clissold Road
Newport

Saturday, 12 December 2015

Dear Maggie,

Two years ago, without warning, my life was ripped from me. I lost everyone and everything I care about. I am surrounded by those who would kill me in a heartbeat; and in the world outside, those who do not hate me as a monster despise me as a freak.

If you have ever wondered what hell is like, let me tell you. It is knowing that one final blow will destroy you, and that you will spend the rest of your existence waiting for that blow to strike.

Is it any wonder I've learned to put up barriers?

What you saw on Thursday was the mask I wear to protect myself from that last blow. I know you are capable of delivering it. For a while, after I received your letter, I thought you had.

I'm sorry if you feel I wasted your time, if you think I was playing games with you.

Come and visit me one more time, armed with ten questions. I will answer them instantly and honestly. I will have ten for you. That's fair, don't you think? If I'm to trust you with the rest of my life, I should know you a little better than I do already?

One last chance, Maggie? A real one?

Yours,

Hamish

Chapter 38

'SHE'S GOING AGAIN.'

Glass trembles in the door frame as Latimer doesn't break stride, bears down upon Pete and slaps paper on to his desk. Liz, who's been perched on its edge, slides off and backs away.

Pete picks up the printed email from a member of the Isle of Wight prison management team letting Latimer know that Hamish Wolfe has sent out another visiting order to Maggie Rose.

'Doesn't mean she'll accept it.' Pete catches Liz's eye across the room.

'She already has.' Latimer scrunches the email, throws it and misses the waste bin. 'Pick that up, someone.'

'One visit, you said.' Latimer is talking to Pete as though it is his personal responsibility. 'Tick the box, you said.'

Pete lifts up both hands. 'What can I say? She told me she thinks he's guilty. That he can stay where he is. And this was after she met him.'

'Well, he's got to her somehow. Which means we have to up our game. All of us.' Latimer looks around the room, then back at Pete. 'Go through that file again. Think how she thinks. Second-guess what she's going to do. In fact, put your own application in. Go and see him.'

'Why me? Liz is his liaison officer.'

'You know why you. You know the guy.' Latimer turns and heads for the door. 'Step it up, people. I am not losing this conviction.'

Across the room, Liz is wearing a small, tight smile. 'Sir,' she calls out. 'When is she due to see him?'

'Today. She's probably with the bastard now.'

Chapter 39

MAGGIE IS MORE NERVOUS this time. Her breathing is too fast, her mouth too dry, and her stomach is trying to churn contents it doesn't have, because she hasn't eaten in hours. This time, she sees him the second she steps into the visiting hall. He smiles. She doesn't.

'How are you?' he says when there is nothing more substantial than a piece of re-formed wood between them.

'I'm good. You?' She sees the raised pores around his jawline that say he has shaved within the last hour. 'Can I get you something?' She glances back at the serving hatch, at the weak beverages and cheap confectionery. 'Coffee? Something to eat?'

'No, thank you. You've had a long trip – please . . .' He gestures that she should sit down. He will take nothing from her, and his gallantry is flying in the face of prison visit convention. Every other inmate she has ever visited has been eager to stuff himself with cakes and chocolate.

She sits, checking the chair first. She isn't wearing white this time, has chosen instead a masculine-cut trouser suit in navy blue. Today, blue hair aside, she looks like a lawyer and the thought helps her pull herself together.

'You got my letter?' she says. 'And you agree to my condition? I assume you must, because the visiting order arrived so quickly.'

'I agree,' he sits slowly. 'For five of our ten questions we can ask the other to elaborate or explain the answer.'

'I wasn't coming all this way to get ten one-word replies.'

'Nor was I.' He smiles again and, once more, she looks for the game behind the smile. 'And I only came down one flight of stairs.'

'So who's going to start?'

His hands make a *go-ahead* gesture. 'Ladies first.'

'What happened to your sister?' she says, and notes with satisfaction, and a small level of guilt, that she has surprised and hurt him. He was not expecting to talk about his sister.

'She died,' he says.

'Explain.'

His face tightens, his eyes close briefly, but this is his game and he will play by the rules. 'We were on a family holiday in Wales. Dad, Sophie and I booked a climbing day at an outdoor activity centre. Sophie and I were similar weights so we climbed together, Dad went with another bloke, but they were close by. We got to the top easily enough, it wasn't a difficult climb, and then Sophie abseiled down first.'

He stops, takes a breath, swallows. 'There shouldn't have been any problem at all. Except she'd picked up the wrong rope. An easy mistake, it was very similar to hers, but it was twenty feet shorter.'

Maggie has no real experience of climbing. 'Meaning?'

'Meaning it didn't reach the bottom of the pitch. And there was no knot in it. She went spinning off the end. I was at the top, watching.'

The image he's conjured is vivid and horrible, but it is too late to apologize. 'Did she fall far?'

'Less than fifteen feet but she landed badly. She broke her neck.'

'I'm sorry. Your poor parents.'

'They've lost both their children. Dad has just about given up and Mum is . . . well, you've seen how Mum is. She was very different when we were kids.' He gives himself a shake. 'My turn. What made you change your mind and come visit me?'

Hesitation is against the rules. Hesitation allows time for invention. 'I came as soon as you asked me to,' she says.

His eyes narrow. 'Explain.'

She smiles at the memory of the half-dozen, clearly fake letters that arrived before his. She'd known, the day she met his mother, that the grieving, unbalanced woman was their most likely author. 'I've received lots of letters from inmates in prison,' she says. 'I can tell when they aren't genuine. I knew you hadn't written those early ones. They were decent fakes, I don't imagine most people would have spotted the difference, but I did.'

Now the smile looks real. 'So all I had to do was ask. Not a question, by the way.'

'As you said yourself, I wanted to meet you. Thousands of women secretly want to meet you. The charismatic killer fascinates us. Don't

156

over-rely on its effect, though. Curiosity got me here first time. Then you appealed to my better nature. You'll have to work hard for a third visit. Is it my turn again?'

He nods.

'What do you miss most?' she asks him.

His eyes fall. She is about to remind him of the immediacy rule when he answers. 'My dog.' He looks up and his eyes are a little brighter. 'Just about everything else I can replicate to some extent. I still see my parents. I have company, of sorts. I can read. I can shut my eyes and go to all sorts of places in my head. I can dream that I'm climbing, running, flying my plane, but I will probably never see my dog again.'

'Why is she called Daisy?'

He doesn't hesitate. 'Because she's sweet, and faithful and beautiful. And because she adores me. And you've jumped your turn. Where did you do your law degree?'

So far he is being easy on her. 'I didn't. My first degree was in a science subject. I did a Graduate Diploma in Law and then my Bar Professional Training Course at City University. Pupillage with Gray's Inn.'

'But you never appear in court?'

'Is that your third question?' she asks.

'No. My third question is why don't you appear in court? Why do you avoid the limelight?'

Another prisoner passes close by their table, forcing her to lift her bag from the floor, giving her a few extra seconds. 'Bestselling authors are anonymous celebrities,' she says. 'That's how I like it. My privacy is important and appearing in high-profile court cases would jeopardize that.'

He leans forward. 'What are you trying to hide?'

She mirrors him. 'Do you really believe the only people who value privacy have something to hide?'

'Is that your fifth question?'

'No, nor is it my fourth.' She glances down and finds the folded sheet of paper she'd brought with her. It is a copy. The original magazine article is in her files at home. She puts it on the table and turns it to face him. 'My fourth is, how do you feel when you see this?'

Chapter 40

Hello! magazine, September 2015 issue

CLAIRE AND TOM CELEBRATE THEIR HAPPY NEWS

Claire Cole was beaming with health and happiness as she showed off the Chelsea home she shares with her fiancé Tom Flannigan. Just days after announcing Claire's pregnancy, they welcome *Hello!* staff to their stylish penthouse apartment on Chelsea Embankment, with its stunning views over the river.

The baby (the couple are keeping mum about the sex) is due in March, and the parents-to-be are hoping for a straightforward, uneventful delivery at the Lindo Wing of St Mary's Hospital in Paddington, ideally not on a match day.

'March is mid season for Tom,' Claire says, one hand holding tight to the man she clearly adores, the other resting lightly on her barely discernible bump. 'So we just have to keep our fingers crossed the baby doesn't arrive during a big game. I'm not sure how José will feel about losing his star striker at a moment's notice.'

The supermodel's new-found happiness is in marked contrast to the difficult time that surrounded the break-up of her previous engagement, to eminent surgeon Hamish Wolfe. 'Hamish's betrayal nearly broke me,' she has previously admitted. 'After two years together, it was heartbreaking to find out I had no idea who he really was.'

Those dark days are behind her now. Tom's eyes seldom leave his beautiful fiancée. The future of this young family looks assured.

(*Maggie Rose: case file 062/118 Hamish Wolfe*)

Chapter 41

MAGGIE ESTIMATES it will take Hamish two minutes to read the article. He looks up after several seconds.

'Fourteen women and two gay blokes sent me this cutting,' he says. 'One woman sends me every clip on Claire and Flannigan that she can find.'

'So how do you feel about it?'

He shrugs. 'Glad she's OK. Not sure about the *future being assured* business. I met that twat. He must have had a fistful of coke up his nose.'

'Explain. Not about Tom Flannigan taking cocaine. About why you can be so relaxed about the woman you planned to marry moving on. About her not standing by you.'

His eyebrows almost meet in an incredulous frown. 'It never occurred to me that she would. She came to visit me once, on remand. You'd have thought she was being asked to walk through Belsen. Back when it was open for business.'

'Her fiancé was in prison. Of course she found it hard.'

He actually laughs. 'Oh, trust me, the wrongly accused fiancé she could have dealt with. Just as long as she had fast-track through the queues, her own personal security and a private lounge to meet me in. It was mingling with the great unwashed that Claire couldn't handle.'

'And this was the woman you were going to spend your life with?'

He sighs, as though having to explain something to a difficult child. 'Maggie, men get married for all sorts of reasons, not always good ones. Claire was the one pushing. And my mum was desperate for grandkids. Granddaughters in particular.'

'You got engaged to please your mother?'

The laughter is gone now. 'It really didn't matter how many people told me Sophie's death wasn't my fault. I was there. I was at the top when she fell. Maybe I felt grandkids were my way of making amends. Possibly they would have been. A little Sophie? Yeah, that would have been nice.'

She pauses to take stock. Five questions left. He has the same.

'Could you kill someone?' she asks him.

His face clouds, as though a grim memory is passing through his head. 'I probably will if I spend much longer in this place. So, yes.'

There is something very dark behind his eyes now, but whether memory or prediction, it is impossible to tell.

'What's your favourite colour?' he asks her.

'White,' she says, then backtracks. 'No, I mean blue. Of course I mean blue. What else would it be, I mean, look at me.' She lifts the ends of her hair.

The corner of his mouth twitches. 'White isn't even a colour.'

'No, it isn't. Where is Zoe Sykes?'

'I have no idea. Are your parents still alive?'

'I lost my mother over a decade ago,' she says. 'My father five years after that.'

'Any close family? Siblings? Secret husband?'

'No, to all three. What happened to Daisy Baron?'

She sees a start of surprise in his face, but he recovers quickly. 'I don't know. She vanished towards the end of the Trinity term.'

'What was she to you?'

'Fellow student. Friend. Girlfriend, for much of that first year.'

'Was her leaving something to do with you?'

His eyes narrow. 'I never got a chance to ask her.'

Around them, people are getting up and saying goodbye. She waits for Hamish to say something more. He doesn't.

She is the only visitor still seated. The rest are heading for the door. 'People believe Daisy is dead. That she was your first victim. Was she?'

'You've had your ten questions, Maggie. More than.'

She waits. He takes a moment before replying. 'She wasn't. And I really hope she isn't. Something warm will slip out of my world if I lose the possibility of ever seeing Daisy again.'

'Time please, miss. Come on, Hamish, you know the rules.'

They ignore the guard. 'What do you regret most?' she asks him.

He grins as she gets to her feet. 'Getting caught,' he tells her.

Chapter 42

HMP Isle of Wight – Parkhurst
Clissold Road
Newport

Thursday, 15 December 2015

Dear Maggie,

When I said my biggest regret was getting caught, I wasn't talking about Detective Sergeant Pete Weston. All else being equal, that bozo is no match for me.

I was talking about Daisy!

Good to see you again today. If you request a legal visit, you can come again as soon as you like.

Best wishes,

Hamish

Chapter 43

IN ONE OF THE POORER ESTATES in the Bristol area, the Sykes's family home is neat and orderly. The single row of paving stones leading to the front door has been kept clean of winter slime. The patch of brown lawn is short. The bins stand to attention on one side of the door. Just behind the still-white net curtains, Maggie can see a row of china ornaments: female figures, in period costume; six of them, each perfectly spaced, each facing at exactly the same angle into the room within.

The sound of her knocking has barely time to fade before the front door opens. Brenda stands facing her. 'When's it going to be? When's he going to show us where Zoe is?'

'Brenda, I really don't think you should get your hopes up. Hamish is still claiming he didn't kill Zoe.'

She follows the older woman to the kitchen. It is a small room, dated, but immaculately tidy.

'He said, though. He said if you went to see him, he'd show us. Kimberly, make Miss Rose a cup of tea.'

'I'm afraid he didn't. That letter was from his mother.'

The muscles around Brenda's mouth twitch. 'Effing cow. Kim, use the PG Tips, not that cheap stuff from Lidl. And make sure the cups are clean.'

Maggie looks in a corner of the room to see a thin girl intent upon her mobile phone. Her long fair hair hides her face.

Maggie turns back to the mother. 'Brenda, do you think Zoe could have had another boyfriend?'

When Brenda shakes her head, she purses up her mouth and chin and the lines of a habitual smoker fan out from her lips like a child's drawing of a sun. 'I'd have known. We didn't have no secrets. Did he tell you anything? About what he did to her? Where he took her? Kim! I won't tell you again.'

Making no sound, moving so slowly that Maggie can almost imagine the air doesn't move around her, Kimberly gets up from her chair and crosses to the sink. Her shape is still the skinny, angular one of a child. Her clothes are childish too: plain jeans, a fleece sweatshirt.

'Zoe's actions on that last night suggest she was planning to meet someone,' says Maggie.

'Do you think they might let me have her boot back? Kim, sniff that milk before you use it, make sure it's fresh.'

'I'm sorry, what did you just say?'

'Her boot. The red cowboy boot, what she were wearing when she was taken. They've never let me have it back.'

The cowboy boot, found on the roadside in the gorge, with bloodstains that were matched to Zoe. Her mother wants it back, as though her pain isn't sharp enough without a tangible reminder of what her daughter went through.

'I imagine it will be classed as evidence. The police probably need to keep it.'

'She loved them boots. They were her favourites. She always wore them. They were a present from me. Cost a bloody fortune. I'd really like it back.'

A once expensive, now worthless, item. It is odd, the things that grieving people obsess over. On the kitchen counter, a mobile phone starts ringing. Brenda turns away and reaches for it.

'Yeah, oh, hiya, Mand, all right?' As though she's forgotten Maggie, she wanders out into the hallway just as the teenager turns round, a mug in each hand. She has the trace of an old bruise on her right cheek, just below her eye. Her hands are shaking.

'I put sugar in.' She stares at Maggie with wide, pale grey eyes.

'Thank you.'

'Not everyone takes sugar. Mum and me both do. It's habit. I can make you another cup.'

'It's fine, thank you. I can drink it with or without sugar.'

Kimberly reaches out, spilling some of the tea on her hand. She puts both mugs down clumsily and turns back to the sink.

'Cold water,' says Maggie, unnecessarily. The girl is already holding her scalded hand beneath the tap. 'It would be really useful for me to see Zoe's bedroom. Would you mind showing me?'

163

The girl's shoulders stiffen. 'You want to see Zoe's room,' she says to the kitchen window.

In the hallway, conversation stops. The door bursts open again and Kimberly flinches.

'Can I ask you something?' Brenda's eyes drop to the mugs on the table. 'Oh, for God's sake, why do you make such a mess all the time?'

'Actually that was me,' Maggie says. 'I wasn't expecting the mugs to be quite so hot. Let me clean it up.'

'Kim will do it.' Brenda glares at the girl, who is staring down into the sink.

'What did you want to ask me?'

'Huh?'

'You said you wanted to ask me something. Just now, when you came back into the room.'

Reminded, Brenda stands square on to Maggie. 'Why are you here? If you're going to be that animal's frigging lawyer, what do you want with me?'

'Hamish Wolfe isn't my client and may never be. For what it's worth, I'm still inclined to think he's guilty. I'm here because there are details about Zoe's disappearance that don't make a lot of sense to me. If you help, I promise to try one more time to get him to tell us where Zoe is.'

'What if he doesn't know?' says Kimberly.

Brenda's head shoots round to her daughter. 'What the hell are you talking about? Course he knows.'

Kimberly has a way of drooping, of dropping her head so that her hair falls and covers her face, of letting her shoulders slump so that she seems diminished.

Maggie fakes a loud cough. 'Brenda, can I please see Zoe's room? Does it still have all her things in it? And if you have any family photographs, that would be useful too. Perhaps Kimberly could show me?'

Brenda glances dismissively at her daughter. 'I'll take you.'

The room Zoe shared with her sister is a double bedroom, with twin beds. One of them unmade but recently slept in, the other devoid of linen, just a bare mattress.

'Kim!' The shout makes Maggie jump. 'Get up here and make your bed. What have I told you?'

164

Although shared by a teenager and her twenty-something sister, the room has a childish feel to it. The furniture is white MDF, the sort you might see adorned with Hello Kitty and One Direction posters in young girls' bedrooms. The pink curtains have faded from years of sunlight. There is a photograph on the dressing table of Brenda and three young women, two of them Kimberly and Zoe. From their formal clothes, Maggie guesses it was taken at a family wedding. Zoe, the largest of the three young women, has been pushed slightly to the back of the group. Another photograph of the same three girls stands on the window ledge. This one shows them on a park bench. Kimberly and the oldest girl sit on the bench. Zoe leans over them from behind it. Kimberly and the older girl look very similar.

In the corner of the room is a small fibre-optic Christmas tree. It is the first decoration that Maggie has seen in the house.

'What did you want to see?' Brenda asks.

'I just want to get a feel for her. Do you still have her clothes?'

'Of course,' Brenda nods towards the built-in wardrobes along one wall.

'May I?' Maggie slides the door to one side. The wardrobe smells like the back room of a second-hand shop but the clothes are neatly hung. On the far left of the rail hang several outfits that look new. Gently, conscious of Brenda's barely tolerant stare on her shoulders, Maggie pulls them towards her. Several still have labels attached. She pulls out a red dress. Size 14. She moves quickly to the middle of the rail. The rest of the clothes are sizes 16 and 18.

Behind her, Brenda breathes out an impatient sigh.

'Are these Kimberly's?' It seems unlikely. No way is Kimberly a size 14.

'They were Zoe's. She was on a diet. I always think it's good to have an incentive.'

Several pairs of shoes, boots and trainers sit neatly on the carpeted floor of the wardrobe. Maggie crouches.

'I bought her those cowboy boots. They were a birthday present. I don't want it back for myself, it wouldn't fit me, or Kimberly, and what good would one boot be anyway? She just wore them so much. Loved them, really. It's not right it's just stashed away in a police cupboard somewhere.'

165

'I'll mention it to DS Weston. It's possible it's just been forgotten about.'

Maggie picks up a court shoe, in purple patent leather. Size six. She upturns a trainer. Size six and a half. She stands, closing the door behind her and notices that Kimberly has appeared in the doorway.

'Do you have another daughter, Brenda?' She looks towards the wedding photograph on the dressing table. There had been no mention of a third child in any of the police reports and yet the family resemblance is strong. 'An older girl?'

'That's Stacey. She lives in Aberdeen. Works for an insurance firm up there.'

'Thank you. I won't take up any more of your time.'

The phone rings as Maggie is sitting in her car outside the Sykes's home. It is Pete.

'I've done a bit of digging on this Sirocco Silverwood,' he says, as she tucks away the photographs she's been studying for several minutes. 'Real name Sarah Smith. Bright lady, once upon a time, dropped out of Dundee University in her second year. Studying English literature. Significantly, she was working in Magaluf for nearly nine months in the run-up to Wolfe's arrest. The chances of her having met him are slim.'

'So I can just write her off as another fruitcake obsessive?'

'Looks like it. So what are you up to? Anywhere close to the station? Fancy a coffee? Lunch?'

'I'm miles away. Thanks, Pete, I'll be in touch.'

166

Chapter 44

From the office of
MAGGIE ROSE
The Rectory, Norton Stown, Somerset

Wednesday, 16 December 2015

Dear Hamish,

OK, I'll admit that I'm intrigued. Not by you – all you've given me are impossible-to-prove conspiracy theories – but there are discrepancies surrounding your case and one of them is Zoe Sykes.
   I visited her family home today. It was interesting.
   Let's be clear, I am making no promises. For what it's worth, I still believe you to be guilty. I'm just curious to dig a little deeper. If you can go along with that, I'll try to clear my diary so that I can visit you on Friday.

Best wishes,

Maggie

Chapter 45

Email

From: Anne Louise Moorcroft, Ellipsis Literary Agency
To: Maggie Rose
Date: 17.12.2015
Subject: Hamish Wolfe

Dear Maggie,

I've had over a dozen emails and phone calls from journalists wanting to know if Hamish Wolfe is now your client. They've all requested interviews, or failing that a comment at least. And social media's going nuts.

Anything you can share?

Anne Louise

From: Maggie Rose
To: Anne Louise Moorcroft, Ellipsis Literary Agency
Date: 17.12.2015
Subject: Hamish Wolfe

Dear Anne Louise,

He is not my client, although I am having my third meeting with him tomorrow and that could change. I'll give you the nod and you can send out the usual press statement.

Maggie

Chapter 46

DAYLIGHT DOES NO FAVOURS for the Grey Mare at Bishopstone. It is a night-time pub, meant for live bands and overflowing pint glasses, for cigarette smoke creeping in from the smokers' area out back. It is a pub that needs crowds pressed together, shouting into each other's ears, coughing with the effort of making any audible sound. It is a pub for sports, on the huge wide-screen TV, for noise, for broken glass, for soon-forgotten fights in the doorways and furtive shags in the ladies' loo. It is a pub where drugs are sold, if you're lucky, dropped into an unguarded drink if you aren't. It is a pub where smart women take their mai tais into the toilets with them.

In the daylight, every stain on the paisley patterned carpet is visible, and tangible. Every surface seems covered with a thin film of grime. With eight days to go before Christmas, even the festive decorations look shop-soiled.

Steve Lampton leads the way from the bar, carrying his own drink, and Maggie's. He insisted on paying for them. He always does.

'I'm loving your local.' Maggie brushes crisp crumbs off the fake Tudor chair seat and sits, thinking of yet another dry-cleaning bill.

He grins and she sees his teeth have improved since the last time they met. He's had them professionally cleaned and whitened, private dentistry he can now afford, making up for years of prison neglect.

'It's a bit of a dive,' he admits. 'But I only have an hour off work and I can't lose my bonus, not this time of year.'

Since his release in 2007, Lampton has been forced to take one temporary contract after another. His jobs usually only last until one of his co-workers finds out who he is.

'You actually his lawyer, then? That Wolfe bloke?' Steve pulls out a chair and sits before gulping down most of his double Scotch. He always drinks quickly and, whilst he never really shows it in other ways, Maggie wonders if she makes him nervous.

'Not yet. I'm thinking about it.'

He pulls a face that is half smile, half sneer. 'You will.'

'What makes you say that?'

'You can't resist a challenge. And Wolfe's even prettier than me.'

She doesn't argue. Lampton might be very easy on the eye, especially now he's eating properly and working out regularly. He looks younger than his forty-five years, as though prison somehow pickled him. Wolfe, on the other hand, is in a league of his own.

'Are those highlights in your hair?' she says, because she doesn't really want to talk about one of her men, with another of them. In prison, Lampton's hair was always a dark, dirty blond. Now, even in the dim lights of the pub she can see the lighter streaks.

'You can talk,' he tells her.

'What happened on the thirtieth of October, Steve? In this pub, if my memory serves.'

His face clouds. 'Misunderstanding.' His eyes, that haven't left hers since she arrived, drop to the greasy tabletop.

'You were cautioned. A woman made a complaint.'

He looks up again, bravado restored. 'I misread signals. It happens. No harm done.'

'I disagree. If you get arrested again, I can't help you. I won't even try.'

The knuckles of his hand whiten as he tosses back his head and makes a show of polishing off the drink. When he puts the glass down, he's smiling again. 'I got something for you,' he says. 'Christmas present.'

'Will I like it?'

He lets his head fall to one side, looking at her appraisingly. 'I like it.'

She makes a point of peering around the table to look at the carpet beneath his feet, although she already knows he brought nothing into the pub with him. 'It must be very small. And you must be doing very well if you can afford jewellery for someone whom you don't even need to keep on side any more.'

'I didn't bring it with me. It's not the sort of thing you open in public.'

'I'm not giving you my address, Steve.'

He leans forward. 'Now, you see, that makes no sense to me, Mags. If you think I'm innocent, what reason do you got to be afraid of me?'

She laughs. 'Remind me, exactly, when I said I thought you were innocent?'

He tries to laugh too, but doesn't quite make it. He has never, quite, been able to reconcile her refusal to pretend with her willingness to work on his behalf.

He gets to his feet and looks down at her almost-empty glass. 'Top-up?' he offers. 'Or are you racing back?'

She hands him her glass. 'Thank you,' she says. 'I'd love another drink.'

Chapter 47

'I WANT TO TALK ABOUT JESSIE, Chloe and Myrtle. How do you know how they died?' Maggie watches Wolfe's face carefully. Normally, she can spot lies in an instant. It's nothing to do with the eyes, accomplished liars get very good at controlling their eyes when they're spinning yarns, but every liar she's ever known has taken a deeper than average breath before the lie comes out.

'I don't.' He holds her stare. 'How could I? I didn't kill them.'

No lie that she can see, but she's only just got started. 'My first visit, you were very specific about how they met their deaths. You talked about them being lured into a cave, having their throats slit, being left alone in the cold and the dark, to bleed out. But by the time the three bodies were found, they were largely bone. The post-mortems didn't come to any conclusions about how the victims died. So, back to my question, how do you know?'

He smiles, a careful, tight smile that doesn't reveal his teeth. Only his guile. His breathing hasn't changed. 'I guessed.'

'You guessed?'

He lets his forearms rest on the table. 'Yeah, it's easy. Let's try it again. Whoever took them into the caves – and I'm not saying it was me – lured them with some sort of story. Maybe tales of a remarkable rock feature. Personally, I'd have plumped for the romantic angle. Perhaps he offered to show them the place where Arthur and Guinevere's wedding rings are encased in limestone.'

'Arthur and Guinevere?'

He's still smiling, everything about his body language is upbeat. 'Perfectly plausible. Glastonbury is generally agreed to be the site of Camelot. I can see that appealing to young impressionable women, especially the jeweller. So he leads them to where he wants them to be and he says, "Over there, just where I'm shining my torch, there's a bit of a slope, so you have to watch your step, lean over a bit" – can you see what he's doing, Maggie? He's getting them off balance – then he comes in behind, maybe puts one hand on a shoulder, as though to steady them. He's being super gallant. He gives them the torch, to free up his other hand. Maybe he wraps that hand around their hair, he figures he can step up the romance factor, and women like that, don't they? It's an intimate, alpha-male gesture, reminiscent of cavemen. He makes sure he's got a nice firm grip then, just as she says, "Where, Hamish, I can't see anything?" he bangs her head hard against the rock.'

Maggie pushes back against her chair, feels it slide along the floor an inch. Her eyes flick to the nearest officer on duty. He's on a raised platform, some ten yards away. When she looks at Wolfe again, he is licking some invisible substance off the tip of his thumb. She doesn't think he's taken his eyes off her.

'Is that how you did it?' she says.

'I'm guessing, not confessing.' He leans forward again, more than matching her faint-hearted retreat, reducing the distance between them. 'The first blow would be unlikely to kill her, so he has to strike again. If he has some medical knowledge – again, I'm just speculating – he'll know that a hard object, like solid rock, slamming repeatedly into the temporal lobe would kill someone pretty quickly.'

If she becomes his lawyer she'll be able to record their conversations. For now, she has to remember as best she can. But storing information away is hard when your body has become too hot. When you can feel bubbles of sweat forming on the underside of your skin.

'There was significant head damage referenced on one of the post-mortem reports.' She wishes she could take off her jacket, but that would send all the wrong signals. 'Jessie, from memory. But you'd know that, wouldn't you? You'll have read it. And the pathologist couldn't say conclusively whether the damage was incurred post- or ante-mortem. So, given that Jessie's body was found at the bottom of a fairly steep slope, her skull could have sustained that damage when her body was thrown down it.'

He nods. 'True. So how would you have done it?'

'How would I kill three women?'

'Yeah. Say you want to kill three women, who are bigger and probably stronger than you. You want to lure them into a cave and then kill them, how would you do it?'

'Firstly, it would be impossible. Second, I wouldn't want to. And third, I'm not here to entertain you.'

He grins properly, showing those white, rather sharp teeth of his. 'Doesn't it strike you, Maggie, that it would take some awesome powers of persuasion to get a woman you hardly know into a cave?' he says. 'Even with the promise of mythological jewellery.'

'I agree. It would take someone exceptionally personable and persuasive. In that sense, you were a gift for the prosecution.'

The grin had been fading, it widens again now. 'You flatter me.'

'It's also possible they were dead when they were taken into the caves. No charm would be needed then. Just brute strength.' She lets her eyes drop, noticeably, to his forearms. Even in the loose prison sweatshirt, their bulk is noticeable.

His head is shaking. 'Maggie, when you and the prosecution talk about my good looks and charm, I'll happily go along with it. When you leap to my ability to manoeuvre dead bodies in confined spaces using ropes and pulleys, you're slipping into fantasy land.'

'How so?'

'The lightest of those three women was one hundred and seventy pounds. Myrtle Reid substantially heavier. The closest you can get a vehicle to Rill Cavern – and my car is not an off-road model, by the way – is twenty metres. So I'm supposed to have carried nearly two hundred pounds of dead weight up a one in four gradient and manoeuvred it down two hundred metres of tunnel. There isn't a rope-and-pulley system in the world that could pull that one off. And a wheelbarrow, trolley or wheelchair couldn't make the trip either – the police tried it. I promise you, if we're talking about a lone killer here, those women went into the caves alive.'

'Interesting point,' she says. 'Is it possible we're looking for a killing gang?'

'A cult of fat haters?'

'Or fat obsessives. Which again might point to you as ring leader.'

'Rubbish. I have no strong feelings on the subject of obesity, other than a general opinion that it's not terribly good for a person's health. You, on the other hand, are too skinny. What size are you? Six? Eight? Have you had eating disorders in the past?'

174

'We're not talking about me. Let's get back to how they were killed. The other two victims had no sign of head trauma, either before or after death, so the same method couldn't have been used for all three.'

He rubs a hand across his jaw, as though the skin there might still be sore from shaving. His hands are square, his fingers long. Dark hairs cluster between his knuckles. His nails are cut short, are clean. She's not listening to him, she realizes, has to think hard to remember what he's just said. Something about how Chloe died.

'I'd say he definitely used the wedding ring heist for this one,' he's saying. 'She wouldn't have been able to resist it, but this time he told her the rings were bound in stone in one of the rock pools.'

Maggie thinks back to her research. Most of the caves in the area have water in the form of underground lakes, ponds and dozens of small pools.

'They get to the pool in question. Its surface is around waist height and it's deep, maybe four feet. They lean over together; he's standing behind her, and in the cold cave she's glad of his body warmth pressing against her.'

'Chloe Wood wasn't on a date. It was a business meeting.'

His index finger jabs the air. 'You're right. Forget the subterranean cuddle. He shines the torch, points, she can't see it, he says, "Stand on tiptoe, lean over a bit more." She does, he puts a hand to the back of her head and dunks her under.'

Maggie looks steadily back, determined to let nothing show on her face.

When he doesn't get a reaction, he moves on. 'She's going to fight, obviously, and she's a big girl, so keeping her head under for the four or five minutes that drowning requires wouldn't have been easy. This killer has to be a big or fit bloke, wouldn't you say, Maggie? Someone who knows how the human body works, what pressure to apply and to where. He'd know all the weak spots, possibly be trained in combat techniques. How's Detective Sergeant Weston looking these days? He was pretty fit when I knew him.'

The mention of Pete's name bothers her, as though he has no place in this discussion. 'I'm not going to dignify that with a response. So you think the killer had a different mode of attack for each woman?'

175

'I think he had several methods up his sleeve. He'd have wanted a plan B, possibly plans C and D. Shall I tell you what I think he did with Myrtle?'

'Oh, please.'

'He let her take her chances. I think he led her into the cave, took her way down deep, and then, when she was transfixed upon something – probably the mythical wedding rings again – he quietly backed away, switched off the light and scarpered.'

'Not possible.'

'Why?'

'How would he have found his way out? Once he switched the torch back on, she'd see it and follow him.'

'Fluorescent rocks.'

'Excuse me?'

'Certain minerals have fluorescent properties, meaning they glow in ultraviolet light. I'd say he dropped a short trail, just enough to get him safely round the bend and out of sight. And that his torch had a normal setting and a UV one. Completely unseen, he followed the rocks out, ignoring or possibly enjoying the sound of Myrtle's screaming.'

'Too much of a risk. She could have got out. Someone could have found her.'

'Without light, Myrtle wouldn't have had a clue which way was up. The chances of her crawling in the right direction were practically non-existent. She'd have drowned, if she were lucky.'

'Stumbling around in the dark, getting bruised and sore won't kill someone,' she says. 'And nobody ever died of fear.'

'But even if she got out, all she could do was describe him. I doubt he was simple enough to give her his name.'

'That probably rules Pete Weston off the list of suspects. Any victim who survived would be bound to come into contact with the lead detective on the case.'

'Ah well, I'm just tossing ideas around. Having a bit of fun.'

And that was the problem. Men in his position weren't supposed to have fun. 'Hamish, I brought the papers that will officially appoint me as your lawyer. But what you're doing is making me question the wisdom of that.'

He isn't fazed. 'Oh, Maggie, you're not that easily spooked. All I'm doing is what every officer on the case will have done a dozen times over. I'm trying to work out how our man did it.'

'But you seem to take such pleasure in it.'

He looks, unblinking, into her eyes. 'No, the pleasure is in your company, I promise you. You are such a refreshing change from my mother.'

'You don't see anyone else?' she asks him.

He frowns. 'My dad, sometimes, but his health isn't great. And visits are restricted, as you know, for anyone other than my legal team and the police still working on the unresolved part of the case. Detective Pete is coming on Monday.'

She hadn't known that. The thought of the two of them talking makes her uncomfortable. 'Do you know what about?'

'Other than the whereabouts of Zoe Sykes, I haven't a clue. Actually, I'm quite looking forward to talking about you.'

'OK, we're running out of time and there are some other areas I need to cover.' She looks at her notes. 'One of the women I met at your mother's little support group, a homeless woman called Odi, claims to have seen someone entering Rill Cavern one night in April 2014. While you were on remand.'

The news hasn't surprised him. 'Mum told me. She was practically spitting feathers. I can't get too excited though. This Odi woman sounds like a pretty unreliable witness. Plus it was dark and she was some distance away.'

'I'm going to talk to her again. Away from the group.'

He looks troubled. 'From what Mum's told me, Odi's away with the fairies.'

'Ten minutes, everyone.' The guard's voice cuts above the general conversation. 'Ten minutes more.'

Maggie pulls on her gloves and puts her coat around her shoulders, conscious of his eyes on her. He's broken into a sweat in the last few seconds. In spite of his glib words and easy smile, she can feel his anxiety. His heart will be beating fast and hard.

'Time's up, Maggie,' he says. 'So, million-dollar question – do you believe me?'

It is the hardest thing to look him directly in the eyes. 'No,' she tells him. 'But I think I can get you out of here.'

He is silent. His shoulders are rising and falling with an accelerated breathing that he is no longer able to control.

'Isn't that what you want?' she asks.

'Of course. But I'd rather it be on the basis of my innocence than your cleverness.'

'Only one of those is in my control.' She waits.

He pulls himself together. 'OK. Let's find out exactly how clever you are. Here's what I want you to do. Feel free to take notes.'

For a second she can only stare. 'What you want me to do?'

'Of course. You're my lawyer now, or you will be when I sign the papers. That means I instruct you.'

Well, technically he is right, but—

'Time please, ladies and gentlemen. Can all visitors start making their way to the door.'

'OK, in the interest of speed, tell me what you want me to do.'

'Shouldn't I sign those papers first?'

Around them, people are getting up. Couples are embracing. Some are already making their way to the door. She fishes in her bag and finds the contract copies.

'I hope you brought a pen,' he says.

She rummages some more. 'Just a cheap one. I didn't want to risk anything decent.'

He scribbles his name at the bottom of two of the documents and hands back the black ink biro.

'My first job is to talk to Odi, the homeless woman, again,' she says, in an attempt to establish that she is the one in control here.

He gives a quick, sharp shake of the head. 'You're barking up the wrong tree with her. I think you should find out what happened to Zoe. Find her body, link her conclusively to the other three women and I'm in the clear, because Mum gives me an alibi for the night she went missing.'

'The police don't accept that alibi. They can't just take the word of your mother.'

'Then, you track down the other people who were in the restaurant that night. Someone will remember me.'

178

He's probably right. 'That won't be easy.'

'Of course it won't. If it were easy, the police would have done it.'

She gets to her feet. 'I'll serve you better, I think, by finding the computer the killer used to cyber-stalk those women.'

His eyebrows lift. 'How would you even begin?'

She takes a step away from the table, just to show willing to the hovering guard. 'I already have,' she says, as she turns on her heels.

After a few more seconds, he calls her back. 'Another thing.'

She stops. 'What?'

He raises his voice, to reach her across the distance she's travelled. 'I need you to find Daisy.'

Chapter 48

From the office of

MAGGIE ROSE

The Rectory, Norton Stown, Somerset

Friday, 18 December 2015

Dear Hamish,

Thank you for your time today. As soon as I can tidy away a few ongoing jobs, I'll put resources into a) Zoe, b) your alibi in the restaurant, c) the computer and d) Odi.

None of these tasks will be easy, and naturally I'll report back anything concrete. In the meantime, we should establish a correspondence and I will visit from time to time. Getting to know you, as a person, is an important part of what I do.

In the interest of complete honesty, I can see no point in looking for Daisy. It will take up an enormous amount of time and serve no purpose.

One other thing. Please don't, again, indulge in speculation about how the three women were lured into caves. Others might take it seriously. Others might not spot, as I did, that two of the victims thought they were meeting other women, rendering your romantic notions of being lured to see ancient wedding rings by a handsome man so much nonsense.

I appreciate your confidence in me. Do please let me know if there is anything you need.

Best wishes,

Maggie

Chapter 49

HMP Isle of Wight - Parkhurst
Clissold Road
Newport

Friday, 18 December 2015

Dear Maggie,

Good to see you today.

The computer? Seriously? Anyone remotely PC literate can wipe a hard drive of all incriminating data. I know I can – probably not what you want to hear right now – and this guy was savvy enough to build a firewall that the police and BT couldn't get through.

And if he wasn't confident in his cleaning skills, he'll have dumped it. Please don't waste your time, and mine, on wild goose chases.

Seeing you, getting letters from you will be a pleasure, even though I'm perfectly aware that any time you spend with me will be driven by self-interest on your part. You need lots of juicy material on me for your book.

I'll go with that, but I want something in return. When you write to me, tell me something of the world outside. I cannot tell you how much its absence hurts.

Sincerely yours,

Hamish

Chapter 50

From the office of

MAGGIE ROSE

The Rectory, Norton Stown, Somerset

Sunday, 20 December 2015

Dear Hamish,

Something of the world outside?

This morning, I walked by the Bristol Channel, on the beach where I first met your dog. (And your mother!) I went early, shortly after sunrise. Snow clouds hung heavy and low (they made their way north-west to Wales and missed us completely) and as the sun got higher they seemed almost to burst with gold light, while the sky behind them was the deepest and most perfect shade of violet. The tide was high, the waves were rapid and noisy. Along the length of the beach these little waves were breaking on the pebbles several hundred times a second and all the while the colour of the rising sun was spreading out across the world.

Usually, I walk up the cliff but today, something made me find the shelter of a bank and sit and watch the sun coming up. It was beautiful. And yet . . . I think I know now why you have a dog. And why you miss her so much. There are times when the need for another beating heart is hard to bear.

Maggie

PS. Don't dismiss the computer. Killers keep trophies. Maybe our killer still scrolls through the conversations he had with his victims, reliving the moments he knew he'd reeled them in.

PPS. I'm really not happy about your seeing DS Weston without me. I just hope you're very careful about what you say to him.

Chapter 51

THE WIND IS NEVER still here. Even on the hottest of days, sea-scented breezes will wash over the moor, soothing the burnt grasses. On cooler days, the wind on Black Down, the tallest hill in the Mendips, will dance like a dervish, whirling around walkers, racing alongside runners.

Wolfe is a runner, a lone one, because it's early in the day and the shadows are still long, throwing black stripes across the bracken. Later, a steady stream of ramblers will make their way up to the Bronze Age site that sits on the very peak of the Down but for now, it is just him, the plovers, the grouse and the occasional hare. He treads on a bramble and the sweet smell of crushed blackberry just manages to catch him before he moves out of reach.

As he reaches Beacon Batch the whispers of the long-entombed dead call up to him.

Faster, Hamish, faster. Something's coming and you need to run now.

Run, Hamish, run, it's hard on your heels.

'Wolfe! Visitor.'

Wolfe opens his eyes. Phil lies on his bunk, half-heartedly making a blue-and-gold paper chain. Soon he will sink back into the half-sleeping, half-waking doze in which so many offenders spend most of their hours inside. When he's not watching repeats of *Grange Hill*, that is. He has long since grown bored of Wolfe's workouts.

The door to the cell is open and an officer is looking in with no surprise on his face. Wolfe slows to a jog and looks at the clock. He has been running for forty minutes. He aims for an hour, each day. Then twenty minutes of press-ups, sit-ups, chins and squats.

'Wolfe! I won't tell you again.'

'Who is it, guv?' He says this to be annoying. He knows perfectly well who has come to see him.

'I'm not your frigging secretary, Wolfe. Get out here now.'

'Have I got time for a bit of a wash, guv? Maybe a change of clothes?' This too, is a wind-up. They both know he will go as he is, red-faced and sweat-stained.

'State of you.' His guard shakes his head as Wolfe meets him in the doorway. 'Cuffs.' Wolfe holds out his hands. They walk the length of the floor and descend the first flight of steps. Then the second.

'Good news for you, Wolfe. You're being transferred to the library.'

This is not good news as far as Wolfe is concerned. He has been working in the metal fabrication workshop every day for six months. It suits him. He has no wish to transfer to the library.

'Why's that, guv?'

They reach the bottom of the steps and head towards the private meeting rooms.

'Governor thinks it's better if staff in the library can read.' There is no suggestion of humour in the guard's face, but it's hard to tell for sure. 'And it's against prison policy for convicted murderers to work in metal fabrication. Access to all those potential weapons, you see?'

'Hadn't occurred to me, guv. When is this going to happen?'

'Couple of weeks. Start of next year. Suit you, sir?'

Wolfe smiles to himself. 'Suits me just fine, thanks.'

'Weston! How you doing, mate?'

Pete Weston is waiting for him in one of the visitors' rooms. He is intent on his mobile phone as Wolfe is led in and doesn't look up, doesn't acknowledge Wolfe's presence in any way. The accompanying officer, a dark-skinned, slightly portly young man, is not one whom Wolfe knows.

Wolfe sits and waits. The detective constable looks uncomfortable, his eyes flicking from Wolfe to Weston and back again. After a few seconds Wolfe glances back at the guard and makes a wanking gesture with his right hand. The guard pretends not to have seen.

Weston remains motionless, apart from the flick, flick, flick of his index finger. Wolfe whistles the first line of a tune, 'I Shot The Sheriff', and waits for the reaction that doesn't come.

'Take your time, mate. My schedule's pretty light today.'

Weston looks up, lets his eyes roam up and down Wolfe's body, in the way some of the cons checked him out when he first arrived. His nostrils twitch and he pushes his chair back an inch. 'Hamish.' He nods his head, as though solving some internal puzzle. 'You OK?' His eyes drift left. 'This is Detective Constable Sunday Sadik.'

Weston has aged. His hair is thinner on the temples, there's more grey than last time and his skin has a dryness and a pallor that probably isn't just the reaction to a cold winter. Wolfe sees the same thing happening to his mother, even though she visits fortnightly. In the outside world, people are ageing, time is passing in the normal fashion. In here, it stands still. Wolfe has a sudden vision of himself, being released in forty years' time, still a young man, going out to find everyone and everything he once knew has crumbled and gone.

The pain takes him by surprise and he grins, suddenly, stupidly, to hide it. 'Never better, mate. I see the quit-smoking resolution didn't last?'

Pure guesswork on his part, but the frown of annoyance on Weston's face tells him he's hit home. Weston has smoked for years. Every year he tries, and fails, to give up. He looks now at the guard. 'We'll be OK, thanks. I'll yell if I need you.'

The guard nods in response and turns to leave the room.

'Right then,' Weston says, as the door clangs shut and is locked from the outside. 'Let's talk.'

Chapter 52

IN HER OVER-HEATED, softly lit kitchen, at just after seven in the evening, Maggie sits and waits. The food is ready, wine and lager are in the fridge. She has a list of notes so that she will forget nothing. Two lists of notes. One for each visitor.

One of whom is twenty-four minutes late; the other due in six.

She almost, but not quite, checks her phone line. A telephone call booking system can't work to time. Not in prison.

Twenty-seven minutes and forty-two seconds later than the time arranged, the phone rings. She picks it up and walks to the window.

'Maggie Rose.'

'I hear you have dinner plans.'

She can't help glancing round at the ceramic pot on top of the Aga, at the loaf of bread she'd taken from the bread maker just ten minutes earlier, at the table, set for two people. Wolfe will have eaten two hours ago, the tasteless, formless slop that is so much of prison food.

'I went to that restaurant today and had a brief chat with the owner,' she says. 'I asked whether he'd be prepared to contact his customer base, asking anyone who can remember dining there on the night Zoe disappeared to come forward.'

'And?'

'He promised to think about it. Realistically, given how busy he was, it's unlikely to happen this side of Christmas. I can also put an ad in the local paper and instigate a social media campaign. It will take a lot of sorting through, though, and I can't help questioning how much good it will do. You weren't convicted of killing Zoe, remember?'

Hamish clears his throat. 'Speaking of Zoe, DS Weston asked me a question today. Will you answer him for me?'

'Of course.' She doesn't like that he knows Pete is coming round this evening. Doesn't like that the two of them have been discussing her, although she knows that it is inevitable.

'Please tell him the answer is no. I have no idea where the body of Zoe Sykes is. It makes no odds how many maps of Somerset's cave system I look at, I can't do more than scores of searches have already. And if, by some extreme coincidence, Zoe is found, no one will ever believe me innocent again. Which reminds me, how are you doing on that front?'

Wolfe will get ten minutes, at most, to call her. Already two of those minutes are gone.

'I don't need to believe in your innocence,' she says. 'Just to convince others of it.'

Outside, the wind is high and her garden is full of scurrying movement: the bending and swaying of trees, the shivering of bushes.

'Pity,' he is saying. 'It would be nice to have someone believe in me who isn't either my mother or bonkers. So, is he picking you up? If he's booked the Crown then not only is he a cheapskate but his intentions are unlikely to be honourable. He lives just upstairs, you know.'

'DS Weston is bringing round your files. He's going out of his way to be cooperative. But if you can't think of a better use of our time than juvenile banter, please carry on.'

From the street there is the sound of a car pulling up. Not quite seven o'clock. Why are the police always on time?

'Can you give him another message?' Wolfe says. 'Tell him no male over the age of fifteen wears Lynx.'

Footsteps are crunching along the gravel drive. She doesn't want to be caught talking to Wolfe.

'You must be out of time. If you can book the same slot tomorrow I can fill you in with any progress. Goodnight, Hamish.'

'Driving home for Christmas?' Pete slings his coat over the back of the nearest chair and looks across the table at the map of Bristol and the surrounding area. Maggie is over by the Aga. A cream-coloured apron is tied over her clothes and her hair has been swept up into a ponytail. The domesticity looks completely out of character. As does the fact that she is, quite clearly, flustered.

'Drink?' she offers.

'You're mellowing,' he tells her.

'Beer's easier than coffee.' She sidesteps to the tall fridge and stands in its light for a second. When she turns back, she has a bottle of Stella Artois in one hand, a glass in the other. 'Dinner's almost ready,' she says.

'Thanks, hope you didn't go to any trouble.'

'Least I could do. I really wasn't expecting to get the files so quickly.'

Pete's eyes fall back to the map. 'So, where are we going?'

'I'm glad you asked. I think we could work together on this one.'

'Unless I'm missing something, we're on opposite sides. How is our mutual friend, by the way?'

'You've seen him more recently than I. Which reminds me, as his lawyer, I'm entitled to be present at all future meetings. Please don't forget again.'

'I'll enjoy the company. Something I want to ask you, though. If you're not convinced of his innocence, why have you taken on his case?'

She pretends to think. Already he's learned when the thinking process is real, when it's faked. Pretend thinking involves a cute pout, a sideways glance. Real thinking is less pretty, a deep frown, a downward curve of the mouth, a blank stare into the middle distance. 'Maybe I'm falling for him,' she says, and the pout turns into that cat-like smile.

'You're far too smart.'

'We wouldn't be the first convicted murderer and representing lawyer to enter into a romantic relationship.'

'Is he coming on to you?'

'Are you?'

He looks at his coat. 'What am I doing here, Maggie? Why am I drinking your lager and getting increasingly enthusiastic about the lamb stew I can smell in your oven? And what's the map of Bristol for?'

She reaches behind for a glass of white wine. 'We're going to find the computer that the killer used to cyber-stalk the three women.'

'We are?'

'If you really believe Hamish is guilty, it's as much in your interest as it is in mine. You find the computer, there's some forensic evidence to link it to Hamish—'

'Fingerprints on the keyboard?'

'Exactly, and all doubt flies away. He stays in Parkhurst for the rest of his life, you're safely on track to make DI, and you get a transfer away from Portishead. You can start rebuilding your life properly and finally get over losing Annabelle to your boss.'

Why does everyone assume he is defined by Annabelle's having left him? 'And if we can't link it to Hamish? If it leads us to someone else?'

'Then it works even better for you. You're not only the man who caught a killer, you're the man who can admit his mistakes and put them right.'

If she thinks it works that way, she's an idiot.

'And even if it doesn't work that way, I don't think you could live with yourself if you knew for a fact that an innocent man was in prison.'

She comes close, leaning across the table, holding a pencil and compass. She puts its point into the street where Hamish Wolfe lived and draws a circle around it. 'It's somewhere in that circle,' she says. 'Probably in a small, rented office on a big, anonymous industrial estate.'

The circle encompasses a big area. It takes in the south side of Bristol, the western areas of Bath.

He shakes his head. 'It's somewhere at the bottom of the Bristol Channel.'

'Put yourself in his shoes.'

'Wolfe's shoes?'

She points a finger. 'The killer's shoes. You need a computer to start your cyber-stalking, but you can't use one that has any traceable connection to you. What do you do?'

'Buy one. Most basic model available. With cash, or a fake credit card.'

'And where do you put it?'

'Doesn't matter.'

'Yes, it does. You need it to be somewhere it can't be found, in case everything goes pear-shaped. Its location, like the computer itself, can't be traced to you.'

'I'm listening.'

'At the same time you buy the computer, you hire a space to put it in. Renting a house or a flat would be too expensive. A room in a house wouldn't work, because the other people who live there would notice.

190

Not a room in a cheap hotel either, because hotel staff spend a lot of time bored and they like to customer-watch. I think our man rented an office.'

'An office?'

'A small, basic office in a large, out-of-town industrial complex would be cheap and almost completely anonymous.'

'Seems a bit overkill, but I'll go with it. So you think that somewhere in this circle is the space our killer rented solely for the purpose of cyber-stalking victims. Maggie, do you have any idea how many—'

'Twenty-five industrial estates of a sufficiently large size to make them likely. You and your team could check them in a couple of days.'

'I can't put police resources into this,' he says, knowing that, actually, there is a good chance Latimer will agree.

'Didn't think so. Just you and me, then?'

He almost laughs. 'No. Just you. That computer is slowly rusting under ten fathoms of seawater and I am not wasting any of my—'

'Another beer?'

His glass is empty. He hasn't realized quite how quickly he is drinking. 'Thanks, and that's my limit, or I'll be phoning for a cab. You're reaching, Maggie. Even if Wolfe didn't tip it over the back of a fishing boat, this is a wild guess. It could be in a hay-barn, his granny's attic, the equipment store at his old surgery . . .'

'It's nowhere that can be traced to him. And it's nowhere it can be found by accident. The killer, who is not Hamish, paid for a safe environment and protection. He took the lease out sometime early in 2013, round about the time he first made contact with Jessie, Chloe and Myrtle. All we have to do is contact the letting agents for these estates and ask about modest, single units that have been occupied since 2013. It will be easier for you. I'll have to use a bit of subterfuge, but it won't be the first time.'

'Before I waste another second thinking about this, please convince me this computer is not slowly making its way out into the Atlantic Ocean?'

'If Hamish is the cyber-stalker, he didn't have a chance. You'd picked him up for questioning before he knew you were on to him. He was charged almost immediately and not granted bail. He could not have hidden or destroyed the computer.'

Annoyingly, that does make sense.

'And if it wasn't Hamish, the real killer will have destroyed it by now.'

'Unless he's planning to resume business.'

Pete laughs. 'It's two years since Myrtle was killed.'

'He's biding his time. He knows if he acts too quickly, the game's up. He also knows he might have to change his methods a bit. Find somewhere else to leave the bodies, maybe.'

'This is fantasy-land. Hamish Wolfe is our killer and that stew smells fantastic.'

She gets up and pulls on oven gloves. 'Would you fold the map up? Carefully, we'll be needing it.'

As she bends to the oven, he puts the map away.

'So are you here for Christmas?' he says. 'Got family coming?'

She smiles as though she knows he's fishing. 'I don't have a family. And Christmas is when I get most of my work done. I'll probably have Hamish's case cracked by the new year.'

She puts a casserole dish on top of the Aga and takes plates from a second oven. 'There's a list on the dresser behind you,' she tells him.

He turns around. The list is typewritten. Industrial estates. Beside each name are the contact details of a letting agent.

'Not sure what you want me to do with this.' He puts it back on the dresser.

'You know exactly what I want you to do with it. Phone the letting agents. Ask the questions. Produce a second list of possibilities and consult with me.'

'Since when did I become your unpaid gofer?'

She says, 'Are we just haggling about money now?'

'No. No money. No dogsbodying. I'm not doing it.' Even as he speaks he reflects that, come mid morning tomorrow, after he's filled Latimer in, he could easily be doing it.

'No big deal. I'll get through them all myself. Shall I let you know when I'm ready to start viewing? We're probably talking after Christmas now, of course.'

The new idea makes him smile. 'That's why you need me onside with this. Anything you find won't be admissible. You need me to carry out an official search.'

The house phone starts ringing. At first Maggie looks up, startled, telling him she doesn't normally receive phone calls at this hour. Before she can pick up, the answerphone kicks in. They both recognize the voice instantly. Deep, educated but bruised, somehow, and with a faint hint of the West Country.

'Maggie, it's Hamish. I need you to pick up right now.'

Chapter 53

'MAGGIE, PICK UP. Pete, I know you're there. Come on, you both need to hear this.'

Maggie feels her face drain. 'He's messing with us. Leave it.'

'Pete, I have less than four minutes to make this call, I've jumped a queue of a dozen other guys and I really don't want to dwell on what that's going to cost me. Now fucking well pick up.'

Pete stands, grabs the phone and switches on the loudspeaker. 'What do you want, Wolfe?'

Wolfe says, 'My cellmate just got back from computer class. There is a Facebook page you need to look at. Search for Hamish Wolfe. Come on, do it.'

Maggie spins her laptop around and types in the password.

'It's a community page,' Wolfe is saying. 'That support group my mother belongs to set it up. Someone posted about Maggie being appointed my lawyer and the abuse is piling up.'

'Hardly a first,' Maggie opens up Facebook. 'It happens every time I take on a new client.'

'Yeah, well, when was the last time someone posted your address and a photograph of your house on there?'

'Shit.' Pete comes to join her at the table.

The page appears, showing the usual pictures of Hamish looking like a Hollywood actor hired to play a serial killer. There is a series of posts from the public and, right at the top, a photograph of Maggie under the headline *Top Lawyer Takes on Wolfe Case.*

'Where did they get that photograph? No one has my photograph.' It is a snapshot. Maggie can't place the location. Her face is half in profile but her hair is unmistakable, both the colour and length it is now. This picture is less than a year old.

'I haven't seen it yet.' Wolfe is still on the line. 'But I understand there's another group called Vengeance for Myrtle. Started by Myrtle

194

Reid's stepfather and a couple of her brothers. Their aim is to get me castrated and blinded while they come up with something that will really teach me a lesson. From what Phil tells me, Vengeance for Myrtle published Maggie's address on this page and they claim they have her phone number too. They've been posting threats all evening. My group are taking them down and blocking the trolls as soon as posts appear but the one with her address was shared several times before anyone spotted it. The information's out there. Yeah, OK, mate, I'm coming. Just back off, will you? Fucking—!'

There is the sound of slamming, a breathless grunt. Maggie grabs the phone from Pete. 'Hamish?'

The line has gone dead.

Somewhere in the room is the pinging sound of a text message being received.

Pete takes the receiver from her and replaces it. 'He can look after himself. Go and lock the back door, check the others and then it would be really great if we could eat.' He nods at her laptop screen. 'I'll have a look through this.'

It doesn't take Maggie long to check security on her house. When she's done, she carries the casserole dish to the table. Without looking up, Pete moves the laptop to free up a mat and she wonders at his ability to always be in the right place at the right time, to know what is needed and to do it, without being asked.

She cannot imagine this man being in the way. Or ever being irritated by his presence.

'We see this sort of thing all the time.' He is flicking down the screen, reading some posts, dismissing others with hardly a glance. She leans across so that she can see them too.

Kenneth Kill Boy declares his intention of throwing firebombs through Maggie's windows this very night. Sten-Man plans to get a few friends together, break in and rape her up the arse, see how she likes what that bastard Wolfe did to other women. Both men know her address. Seconds after the posts appear they are deleted, someone is managing the page, but the damage has been done. Her safety has been compromised.

Pete closes down the laptop as another text arrives in a phone's inbox

195

somewhere. 'Your address being out there is something we have to take seriously.'

'I suppose.'

'I can have uniform swing by here more often over the next few days and nights. I might even get someone outside tonight. Long term though—'

'Please do nothing. I'm not worried. I may get a few unpleasant parcels in the mail. Nothing I can't deal with.'

'Maybe you should go home for Christmas after all.'

'This is my home. I have no other.' This is something she has known for years, its sadness never struck her before.

'I'm sure the Crown can find you a room. Even if just for tonight.'

She picks up a fork. 'Please eat. And everything is fine. I get abuse from time to time. It's inevitable in my line of work. I make enemies and social media gives them a voice.'

She's not sure she's convinced him. She's wondering what to say next, when a third pinging sounds. She gets up and reaches her mobile before the message fades.

'Anything we need to worry about?' She hears Pete's voice from a distance. She turns. 'My agent,' she lies, because she needs time to think. 'Routine stuff.'

Still puzzled, Pete forks a cube of lamb into his mouth, tears off bread and dips it into the gravy. He is hungry. She is not. It is getting increasingly difficult to put food of any kind into her mouth and her physical presence is lessened by the day. As the line on the bathroom scales creeps ever lower, so she has a sense of there being less of her. There may come a time when she ceases to exist altogether, when she melts away, like ice in a glass, like a stock cube slowly dissolving in gravy, like a rainbow when the sun shines a little stronger, and maybe that will be no bad thing.

'Maggie. Maggie! Are you OK? Let me see those texts.'

'They're private.' Her fork spears something that sends purple juice across the white plate and on to the table. Her fork goes down. She can't do this.

Pete has found a handkerchief – she forgot napkins – and is wiping the sauce from the tabletop. 'Who is sending you texts?' he asks.

'I don't know.' She shakes her head. There is no point in even discussing it. This man cannot help her. 'I don't recognize the number.'

'Wolfe? Does he have your number?'

'He can't text me. He doesn't have a mobile phone.'

'He's not supposed to have one. Lots of prisoners do.'

Pete gets up, still chewing, and comes around behind her. He picks up her phone and then resumes both his seat and his meal, but the phone is by his side, out of her reach. He can't access the texts, the phone is passcode protected, but if another comes in, he may see it before it fades.

She has to get a hold of herself. 'Pete, I wanted to ask you about that homeless couple, Odi and Broon. I need to talk to Odi. Can you put me in touch with any homeless charities who might be able to help?'

'I can probably tell you where she is right now.'

'She's in custody?'

'I wish she were. Given the temperature outside, she probably does too, but we can't arrest people for having nowhere else to go.'

'So where is she?'

'Porticoed entrance to the Town Hall in Wells. They've both been sleeping there the last few nights.'

'They're sleeping in the square?' She thinks back to Market Square in Wells, to the Regency Town Hall. 'That entrance is open to the elements on three sides, it isn't possible.'

'You do understand what's meant by the term, *homeless,* don't you?'

'I'll come with you when you go. See if I can find her.'

Ping.

Too fast for her, he picks up the phone but his eyesight isn't good enough to focus on the small type. She sees him frown, hold it further away, a flicker of frustration as the message fades. Then he taps on the keypad and she watches in disbelief as the menu appears.

'How did you do that?'

'Four. Nine. Seven. Seven. Most people use birthdays as their key codes. You're a cautious type, Maggie, you wouldn't use anything as obvious as your own birthday. Nor would you keep the same one all the time. I'm guessing you change codes on your phone every time you take on a new case. Four nine seven seven is Hamish Wolfe's birth date. Now, let's see . . .'

His eyebrows grow closer. He holds the phone a little further from his eyes. '*He loves me.*' He glances up. 'That's the same thing that was written underneath this table. You're getting text messages from the person who broke into your house. Why the hell wouldn't you tell me that?'

She's telling him now. Or rather, he's dragging the information out of her. She thinks about the words that were scrawled on the underside of the table they are sitting at, and fights back a temptation to crawl beneath it, to check they haven't mysteriously reappeared.

'Have you had them before today?'

'No.' She can see he doesn't believe her. 'No.'

His eyes go back to the phone. He needs reading glasses, is too vain to admit it. His hesitation gives her a split second to think.

'*He loves me.*' Pete reads out the first message again and moves on to the second. '*He loves me not.* Then we've got *He loves me* again. Hang on, this is—'

'A game lovers play with daisies. They count the petals, pulling them off one by one.'

'If there's an odd number, it's good, an even number and he loves her not?' he tries.

'Exactly.'

'When you had that break-in, did whoever it was have access to your phone?'

'I sometimes leave it downstairs, but it's passcode protected.'

She sees his raised eyebrows, his slightly pitying look. He got through her phone's passcode in an instant. Someone else could have done exactly the same thing. 'I've been an idiot,' she says.

He doesn't argue. 'Please tell me you changed the locks,' he says.

She nods. 'And improved them. No one's getting in here again.'

'All the same, it might be time to bring that Sirocco Silverwood character in for a chat. If you still think she's the most likely candidate?'

'She's the only one I've met who's claimed undying love for Hamish.'

'It does seem odd, though, that anyone from the Wolfe Pack would threaten you. They might all be an apple short of a barrel of scrumpy, but if they're genuine, it's very much in their interest to keep you on side.'

'Maybe they aren't all. Don't killers like to stay close to the investigation? They enjoy being at the centre of things, all the time having a big secret.'

'Anyone you suspect, apart from Sirocco?'

'How can I say? I spent very little time with them. They all looked pretty weird to me.'

'Says the lady with blue hair.'

Ping.

They both jump. He gets to the phone first. He looks at the screen and pulls a face. He hands it over.

'Dental appointment reminder for tomorrow,' he says. 'Sorry.'

She's had enough. She stands up. 'I need to get out of here. You can stay and finish your dinner, or you can come with me. Your call.'

Chapter 54

'THEY'RE NOT THERE,' Pete calls across Market Square as Maggie is getting out of her car. 'Their stuff's all there. They're probably in a pub somewhere, although I don't think they're exactly welcome in most of them.'

Maggie looks round at the smart shops, the medieval buildings, the soft golden glow of the cathedral tower.

'If you're still determined to talk to them tonight,' Pete says, 'come inside and wait an hour or so. I can do coffee, or we can sit in the bar downstairs.'

'I'm going to have a wander round,' she tells him. 'If I don't find them, I'll come and find you. Fair enough?'

'I'll come with you,' he says.

So very gallant. Always determined to do the right thing. A born police officer.

'Odi won't talk to me if she sees me with the police. You know that. I'll phone you in half an hour, I promise.'

He gives up and turns back to the pub. Ignoring the main entrance, he disappears around the side, into a private car park.

Maggie pulls the collar of her coat a little tighter and walks away from the main part of the town, towards the cathedral. The homeless are not welcome in pubs, there are no official shelters in the town, but the church will rarely turn away the needy.

She finds them in the nave, towards the rear, as far from the door as they can sit. To Maggie, it feels cold in the cathedral, but all things are relative and shelter of any kind must be welcome to those who have none they can call their own. Broon has removed his hat, out of respect to his surroundings, but his shabby red coat is as she remembers it. His hair is thick, salt-and-pepper grey, in need of washing. Odi's multi-badged cap is still on her head. She sits close to Broon, the two of them sharing body warmth.

The cathedral will close in less than ten minutes. Already, its staff are asking people to leave, their tone low and regretful. *So sorry to lose you, but only for now. Do come back again soon.*

Maggie sinks into the shadows outside the west door and waits, listening to the chatter as a group of Japanese visitors leave, followed by an American family, then a middle-aged couple from Yorkshire.

Broon and Odi are the last, as she knew they would be, and unlike all those who left before, there is no sense of purpose to their movements. They hover on the steps before descending carefully, like elderly people who have learned to fear stairs. Neither notice her as they step out of the lee of the building into the full force of the cold air. Odi is clutching a supermarket carrier bag.

Maggie expects them to make their way out into the main part of town, where lights offer a glimpse of cheerfulness and the narrow streets some shelter from the elements. Instead they go through the dark archway and Maggie slips along in their wake. They turn again immediately, away from the town, through a second dark tunnel towards the Bishop's Palace and Maggie loses sight of them.

The square is almost empty now. No one wants to linger on such a night. Through the windows of the Crown she can see people who are warm and fed, among friends. She sends a smile up to the man she has no way of knowing is watching her, and follows Broon and Odi.

There is something portal-like about the tunnel, because to step through it is to leave the town behind and enter a medieval world of walled gardens, moated defences and impenetrable stone walls. The moon has risen and she can see its reflection in the gently rippling black waters of the moat.

A sudden flurry on the water catches her attention. The moat attracts water birds, gulls from the nearby coast and moorhens that fly in over the meadows. There is also a resident population of swans who are fed from the gatehouse daily, summoned by the ringing of a bell.

The homeless pair are feeding the swans from the contents of Odi's carrier bag.

'Hello, Odi. Good evening, Broon.'

They turn slowly, as though their reactions have been dulled by the cold. She steps closer, wanting to ask them how they can spare food to feed animals, who are far from starving, but knows it will seem impertinent. She holds up a canvas shopping bag that she filled after persuading Pete to leave the house before her.

'I brought you some food. I hope you don't mind, but I cooked and I made too much for myself. It's lamb stew and home-made bread. It's still warm. I put it in a flask.'

Neither of them speaks.

'Odi, I really need to talk to you. Just for a few minutes. Would that be all right?'

'What about?' It is Broon who answers, placing himself fractionally in front of his partner.

'I want to suggest something. Odi, I know you say you remember very little about the person you saw going into the cave that night.'

Odi shuffles closer to Broon. 'I don't. It was too dark. I'm not even sure now that I saw anyone.'

Maggie is careful to keep her distance. 'I understand that. But if you really want to help Hamish, then I know you'll do your best to remember anything that could be useful to his case.'

She will have to take the absence of denial as all the encouragement she is going to get.

'What I want to suggest, Odi, is that you and I, and Broon too if that will make you feel more comfortable, go to see a hypnotist. We'll find a good one, someone highly recommended.'

'Hypnotist?' Odi says the word experimentally, stretching out the syllables, as though trying how the sound of it feels and tastes in her mouth.

'Yes. They can be very good at helping people find lost memories. What she would do is put you in a sort of trance. You wouldn't be asleep, exactly, just a bit detached from what's going on, and she'd ask you questions about that night. It's just possible that, in a state of trance, you would remember more than you've told us already.'

'I don't want you messing with my lady's mind.'

'Nobody wants to do that, Broon, of course not. Think of it this way. In everybody's head, there are stacks of memories, most of them filed away so carefully that we can't bring them to mind without some help. But they're still there. Odi, you could be the only person who saw the real killer, who has a chance of telling us who he is.'

202

Odi seems to shrink further away from her. 'I've told you everything already and I'm not seeing any hypnotist.'

'Odi, I—'

'No! Tell her, Broon. Tell her I won't. I don't know anything.'

Broon seems to swell, facing off against Maggie. 'We're leaving, Odi and me. First thing in the morning. We've said our goodbyes and we're off.'

'Where? Broon, this is really important, you can't just leave.'

'We haven't told anyone where we're going and we don't intend to. We've got nothing more to say.'

'She's frightened, Pete. She knows more than she's saying but I have no idea how to get it out of her. She completely freaked when I mentioned hypnosis.'

'I don't blame her.'

'Oh, don't be so ignorant. How can you live so close to Glastonbury and have such a closed mind?'

'Are you coming up? I've got the kettle on.'

From the driver's seat of her car, Maggie looks into the passenger-side wing mirror. 'No, they're watching me now. Waiting for me to leave. I think I've upset them enough for one night.'

'I spoke to the landlord, by the way. They have a very nice double room on the second floor, a long way from mine, and the locks on the door are solid. You really should not be going back to that big spooky house on your own. Especially not tonight, not with all that palaver on Facebook.'

In the distance, Odi and Broon move out of sight. They are heading in the direction of the Town Hall portico.

'Look, keep an eye on them, will you? It really is very cold.'

'If you're hinting I should offer them a bed for the night and buy them dinner, you can forget it.'

'Oh, very compassionate. But they already have dinner. I put the stew you didn't eat into a thermos flask.'

She cuts him off mid curse, starts the engine and drives home. If she feels a sliver of regret at leaving behind the promise of something new, she ignores it. The time for weakness has passed.

Chapter 55

'MAGGIE, LOOK AT ME.'

'I can't. You don't exist any more.'

'I'll exist as long as you do. Look at me.'

'No.'

Ignoring the voice behind her, Maggie lets the bedroom curtain fall back into place. Since the central heating switched off five hours ago, the house has grown a mid-winter chill. She lifts her dressing gown from the back of the bedroom door and wraps it around herself as she goes downstairs. On the front door the chain is in place.

She can't see the street from here. She doesn't need to. She's already seen the car in the road.

It has become instinctive to head to the kitchen on nights that she can't sleep. Maybe it's the last trace of warmth that clings to the Aga that she is seeking. She places her hands flat on its hob lids, and thinks of Broon and Odi in the icy chill of the Town Hall portico. When her hands have warmed a little, she picks up the phone.

An indrawn sigh answers. 'Hi, Maggie.'

'I told you I didn't need protecting,' she tells Pete.

'I've had to send someone over. A female constable. She'll sit in the car outside if she must, but since you're awake, I'd really prefer it if you let her in, allow her to check your doors and windows, and then sit downstairs for the rest of the night.'

'What's going on?'

'I'd come over myself but there's no way I can get away right now. I'll explain everything in the morning, OK?'

'No, explain it now.'

'Maggie, I really have to—'

'Now, or I come to find you. I'm guessing that won't be strictly convenient.'

She hears a sharp intake of breath. 'I'm in Wells, just outside the Crown. I got a call-out forty minutes ago.'

She closes her eyes and can see him, seeking the pale light of a streetlamp to make his call. He isn't outside the Crown, strictly, he's outside the Town Hall. Behind him, she can see the dark arches of the portico, concealing something unspeakable.

'Broon and Odi.' She means it as a question, it doesn't come out quite that way.

'They're both dead. Killed in their sleep, from what we can tell. Or possibly in a drunken stupor, they both reek of booze.'

She needs time, to let the words sink in, for them to become real. 'Well, they would, wouldn't they? It's how they keep the cold out. What happened to them?'

'I'm not at liberty to give out details. I'll come and see you in the morning. As soon as I can get away.'

The doorbell ringing makes her jump. If it is meant to reassure her, it does the opposite.

'I think your friend's at the door.'

'OK, listen to me. Stay on the line until you can see her. She's in her early forties, heavy build, short brown hair. Her name is Janet Owen. Open the door on the chain. Maggie, are you listening to me? Do not open the door to anyone but a female police officer.'

'I'm sorry, Pete. Sorry for what you have to go through right now.'

He doesn't answer. He is already getting on with his job.

Chapter 56

Daily Mail Online, Tuesday, 22 December 2015

TWO SLAIN IN WELLS

A brutal double murder of two homeless people has thrown doubt on the conviction of one of Britain's most notorious serial killers, according to the support group set up to clear his name.

The discovery, in the early hours of this morning, of two bodies in the medieval cathedral town of Wells in Somerset has led to calls for a fresh look at the evidence that convicted Hamish Wolfe, in 2014, of the abduction and murders of three women. Mike Shiven, 54, chairman of the so-called Wolfe Pack, said, 'The savage slaying of two of our own members, people very close to the investigation, who had fresh information that could have been invaluable, proves what we've been arguing all along. The police took the easy way out with this case. The real killer is still out there and now two of our own have paid the ultimate price.'

At the time of going to press, police were refusing to comment on alleged similarities between the manner in which the two travellers, currently known only as Odi and Broon, were killed and the means used by the killer of Jessie Tout, Chloe Wood and Myrtle Reid in 2013. They refused to deny, however, that the combination of head injury and throat wound could have been the modus operandi used to kill the three young women.

Wolfe's mother, Sandra, is in no doubt. 'Odi and Broon were killed for what they know,' she told our reporter at her £750k home in Somerset. 'If they'd gone to the police when I told them to, they'd probably be alive today. As it is, even the most incompetent member of the police force has to see now that the monster who framed Hamish is still out there.'

First detective on the scene of this morning's murders, Pete Weston, was also one of the lead detectives in the Hamish Wolfe investigation. He was unavailable for comment today.

Chapter 57

BROON AND ODI LIE SIDE BY SIDE. The post-mortem examinations are over and the bodies have been covered, for decency's sake, leaving just their heads and their feet visible.

The only lights are the powerful, surgical ones above the gurneys; the corners and edges of the examination room blur into darkness. Modern equipment aside, the scene reminds Pete of old paintings of surgeons at work, of shadowy figures thronging a central point, the surgeon holding a lantern in one hand, a sharp knife in the other. The pathologist, an Asian woman in her mid forties, likes to work in a darkened room, with light focused only on the corpse.

'It's all about the patients,' she explained once to Pete. 'I find it concentrates the mind upon them.' Privately, he suspects a different motive entirely.

Somewhere, in the gloom that is the rest of the lab, technicians are clearing away instruments, washing dishes, recording notes with the aid of pen torches. They move around unnoticed, nothing more than undulations in the shadows. Odi and Broon lie in stark relief, like museum exhibits.

'Can we get some lights on?' Latimer has just arrived, has already phoned ahead to request the pathologist doesn't start the briefing without him. Pete has been waiting for nearly an hour. Dr Mukerji ignores Latimer. She has her back to the viewing gallery, is finishing some notes.

'Not sure she's turned the intercom on yet,' says Pete, although he knows she has. They've just had a conversation about how much longer his boss is going to be, and doesn't he realize she has five other cases to get to today?

Latimer peers down at the gurneys and their occupants. 'And this happened just outside your bedroom window?'

Down in the examination room, Dr Mukerji turns to face them. 'Is this DCI Latimer, finally?' she asks Pete.

207

'Tim Latimer. Good morning. I don't have a lot of time. What have you got for us?'

Mukerji walks back to her notes. After over a minute, when even Pete thinks she's pushing it, she comes back. She stands in between the two gurneys, directly in the light, her hands behind her back. She looks at Odi, then up at the gallery.

'We have a white female, aged somewhere between thirty and forty – difficult to be more precise, given the conditions she's been living in over the past few years – in relatively poor health for her age. She is known locally as Odi.'

Mukerji's head turns. 'Her companion is known as Broon. He's slightly older, somewhere between forty-five and fifty-five, and like Odi, showing signs of his lifestyle impacting adversely on his health.'

Latimer pulls out his phone and starts flicking through text messages. Mukerji remains silent until he looks up again.

'Neither victim carried ID of any sort,' she continues, 'so it may be some time before we have complete identification.'

'We're working on it.' Pete meets the doctor's eyes briefly. Getting a complete ID, tracing next of kin, won't be easy. When people become homeless it is often for good reason. They cut all ties with the lives they leave behind.

'I didn't attend the scene.' Mukerji steps forward, so that her face and head fall into shadow. 'But my colleague who did estimated time of death as sometime between zero hundred and zero four hundred hours. The outside temperature last night was minus four, I understand, which, combined with the blood loss, would have hastened the loss of basal body temperature in both subjects.'

Pete wonders how long before she realizes she no longer has the limelight. 'Rina,' he says, 'there were people in and around the square until well after midnight last night. I checked with the landlord of the Crown. He went to bed at about twelve thirty, and he could still hear people milling around, getting into cars. It seems unlikely they were killed much before one o'clock.'

Mukerji doesn't disagree.

'And the milk float arrived a few minutes after four,' says Pete. 'I was down there twenty minutes later. They were stone cold by that point.'

'As I say, their bodies would have lost temperature very quickly last night, but I agree, twenty minutes would seem unusually fast. If you want to work to a tighter time frame, between 1 a.m. and 3 a.m. wouldn't be far out.'

The pathologist takes a step back and light floods her face once more. 'Both patients suffered from malnutrition,' she says.

'Seriously? She looks pretty well fed to me.' Latimer is looking at Odi's ample curves, covered but not hidden by the sheet.

'She may have consumed a lot of calories, but they would have been in the form of cheap, fast food, with very little nutritional value. Chips, burgers, pies, pastries. Addictive food, food that made her feel better, gave her a bit of an energy boost, and all but lacking in essential nutrients. Her internal organs were not healthy. Her companion was less obese, but his lungs and liver were in a bad way. These weren't healthy people.'

'Not really in a position to fight back, you mean?'

'Probably not, although just about everyone will put up a fight when their life is threatened. I mention it because, somewhat unusually, they did eat very well within a few hours of their death.'

'They ate lamb stew,' says Pete. 'Maggie Rose gave it to them. She wanted to talk to them about a possible sighting of someone going into Rill Cavern last April.'

'What?' Latimer's head shoots round to face Pete. 'Why do I not know about this?'

'It only came up recently, and as an eye-witness account, it holds very little credibility.'

'I think that's for me to decide, don't you?'

Down in the examination room, Mukerji speaks up. 'They also drank quite a lot of alcohol. Rum, at a guess, but tests will confirm that.'

'It was rum,' says Pete. 'We found an empty half-bottle amongst their stuff.'

'They probably drank all of it. They were quite inebriated. Would have been very difficult to rouse.'

'But very easy to kill?'

Mukerji's lips purse. 'Odi died from exsanguination, after her throat was slashed twice with a sharp, smooth-edged blade about seven inches

209

long. The first incision was deepest, severing the right carotid artery and the jugular vein. The second cut through the left carotid artery and the minor veins.'

As she speaks, Mukerji mimes the slashing of Odi's throat, standing behind the corpse, but to one side, enabling the two police officers to see what she is doing. She makes a big, bold movement, twice, from Odi's left ear to her right. Then she steps quickly to the other gurney. 'Broon, on the other hand, choked to death on his own blood. His throat was slashed at least four, possibly five, times and his trachea was cut open.' More miming. Pete thinks of the shower scene in *Psycho*, the repeated stabbings seen through a shower curtain.

'I'm not sure this could have been done by one person,' says Latimer. 'Even if they were incapacitated.'

'Possibly not. But you do have to take into account the head wounds.' Mukerji moves to the top of the gurneys. 'Both victims were struck over the head, just once in each case, but very heavily.' She moves Broon's hair to show them the mat of dried blood. 'The wounds to each victim are similar and smooth in nature. I'd say they were struck with a hammer, some sort of instrument, rather than a rock or a stone. Probably one of those large club hammers. It was wielded with great force, again suggesting a hammer, something that enabled the perpetrator to get a bit of swing on.'

She demonstrates, swinging her arm back and up, bringing it down swiftly towards Broon's head. 'The blow didn't kill either of them, there's some evidence of bleeding in both cases, but it would have been enough, especially given the alcohol they'd drunk, and the fact that they were asleep, also very cold, to incapacitate them for long enough for the perpetrator to take a firm hold on their hair and slash their throats.'

'Still feels like quite a task for one person,' says Latimer. 'Are we looking for someone with considerable physical strength?'

'That would certainly be an advantage, but what strikes me is the slick nature of it. Think about it.'

She mimes the hammer blow again, bringing her imaginary weapon down hard on Broon's head. Hardly has it made contact before she moves on, arm swinging back again, smiting down on Odi.

Pete can't help flinching.

210

'And now I step back, I put my hammer down and pick up my knife. I take hold of his hair in my left hand, I'm right-handed, by the way, and with my right, I slash deep into his throat. My first slash is pretty deep, would almost certainly have killed him, but even so I slash again, and again, making sure. When I'm confident I can leave him, I move on to my next victim.'

She sidesteps left, taking up position at Odi's head.

'Is it just me?' Latimer mumbles.

Pete steps back, away from the intercom microphone. 'No, she always does this. Totally freaked us out at first. Apparently she directs the pantomime every year at her children's primary school.'

'Fuck me, bet that's something to see.'

'The female victim was almost certainly conscious at this stage.' Mukerji hasn't finished. 'Dizzy, in pain, weak, but knowing she's under threat. She wasn't found where she was sleeping, was she?'

Pete thinks back to the scene that met him just before dawn. Broon hadn't moved, was still tucked up in his sleeping bag. Odi, on the other hand, wasn't by his side.

'We think she managed to crawl away a couple of feet before she had the same treatment as Broon,' Pete says.

'This victim is active.' Mukerji takes two slow deliberate steps away from the gurney, her eyes fixed on something only she can see. 'While her partner is being killed, she is dragging herself away, but I go after her.'

'Should have brought popcorn,' Latimer mutters.

'I catch her, take her hair in one hand and bring down the knife.' Mukerji mimes as she talks. 'Two slashes and it's over. I can steal away.'

She backs up, leaving imaginary Odi on the ground, sidestepping around real Odi on the gurney. 'No defence wounds. No sign of a struggle, other than her failed attempt to escape. Nothing under the fingernails. My job is done. It could hardly have gone more smoothly. I slip away, into the night.'

Latimer clears his throat. 'Thank you, Dr Mukerji, that was very—'

'Helpful,' interrupts Pete.

Chapter 58

HMP Isle of Wight – Parkhurst

Clissold Rd

Newport

Dearest,

When we choose to practise medicine, we accept that death will follow us around like a needy, timid puppy, forever at our heels, never quite coming close.

In the last few years, death came very close to me. I was responsible for the deaths of Jessie Tout, Chloe Wood, Myrtle Reid and probably Zoe Sykes too. They didn't die by my hand (he adds quickly in case this letter is seen by the wrong eyes!) but they are my responsibility all the same.

I'm saddened by the news of Odi and Broon's murders. I did not spill hot blood on the cold stone of Wells Market Square, but the blame lies with me.

They were two of life's innocents, a little too childlike to thrive in a world that has consequences and compulsions that would forever have been beyond their grasp. Odi and Broon were out of their depth, and they drowned that cold December night, in their own blood.

This cannot go on. You, my clever one, must see to that. It is time for the truth to be heard.

Hamish

PROPERTY OF AVON AND SOMERSET POLICE. Ref: 544/45.2
Hamish Wolfe.

Chapter 59

THE ARTIFICIAL CHRISTMAS TREE in the interview room is looking the worse for wear. Someone has been pulling the nylon threads so that now, with two more days to go, it has the look of a tree blighted by serious disease or nuclear winter.

Pete sits, as he's been told to do, as he's been doing for nearly fifteen minutes, and tells himself that he will wait two minutes longer and that is it. He has things to be getting on with. He reaches out for the Christmas tree and starts plucking it of nylon needles.

The door opens and Latimer, back from showing Maggie to her car, comes in. 'Wouldn't tell me where she's going. Don't suppose she mentioned it to you?'

Pete shakes his head. He has no idea what Maggie is up to. When she'd finished giving her statement – as one of the last people to see Broon and Odi alive, she'd naturally been one of the first they had to speak to – he'd offered to put a car outside her house for the day. She'd told him it would be a waste of time. She wasn't going to be there.

'Pete, I need to ask you this.' Latimer leans back against the door. 'Did you speak to those two characters, Odi and Broon, about the Wolfe investigation? In the last couple of days?'

Pete looks down at the carpet tiles. 'Who says I did?'

'Maggie Rose does. She's been talking to people in the square, market traders, street cleaners. You were seen talking to the two of them last Thursday.'

Pete sighs. 'Maggie herself told me about a possible sighting of someone going into Rill Cavern not long after the last victim disappeared. Odi and Broon were the witnesses in question. I had no choice but to follow it up.'

'And?'

He looks up. 'Waste of time. Broon was inebriated, Odi was denying she knew anything. I gave up after five minutes and, to answer your next question, I didn't tell Maggie about it at the time. In spite of what she likes to pretend, she and I are not working together and I don't owe her any information.'

Latimer gives an understanding nod. Then, 'Pete, I'm going to ask you to give her a wide berth for a week or two, maybe longer.'

'Come again?' Pete gets to his feet, still holding on to the tree.

'I know you've been getting a bit chummy with her, and I wasn't happy in the first place, not since there's been a chance of her taking on Wolfe's case, but after what happened last night, it really can't be a good idea for one of the lead detectives on a murder case to be cosying up to—'

'To what, exactly?'

'She thinks there's a connection between the Wolfe case and what happened last night. She thinks her taking an interest in that couple of walkabouts could be what got them killed and, frankly, I think she has a point. Who else would want to hurt them?'

Pete looks at his nails. They need cleaning. One of the tree's needles might do the trick.

'OK, well, if there's nothing else.' Latimer turns and puts his hand on the door.

'Actually, there is. I don't agree that the murder last night is connected to Hamish Wolfe, but if you're right and I'm wrong, there's one thing you're all forgetting. If Odi and Broon were killed for what they knew, whoever killed them will know they talked to Maggie hours before they died. She could be next. We need to keep an eye on her.'

Latimer nods. 'I'll see what I can do. Course, we'll have to find her first. Are you sure she didn't say where she was going?'

Chapter 60

THERE IS DOUBT about whether the plane will take off, more about whether it will be able to land. The cold spell gripping the UK seems to tighten its hold the further north she flies. Maggie spends almost the entire eighty-five minute flight staring out at a frozen, grey ocean of cloud. More than once, she wishes the plane need never have to land, that she can continue flying north, into the vast white emptiness with its promise of oblivion, but sooner than she feels ready for, a tightness in her ears tells her the plane has begun its descent.

Hamish Wolfe, who is now in a position to give her instructions, wants her to find Daisy. He wants her to track down a woman who disappeared years ago and who may not even be alive any more and he wants this, not because it will help his case, particularly. It won't. He wants it because he and Daisy have unfinished business. For some reason, even though his entire future is on the line, he is fixating on a woman who hasn't been in his life for nearly twenty years.

Thirty minutes late, the plane touches down on to tarmac slick with de-icing fluid before taxiing to the gate.

She can do it. Probably. She has before, more than once. The trick is to approach the problem in the right way, to ask the right questions, and the first question isn't: how would you find someone who has disappeared? It is: how would you disappear?

The Maggie Rose step-by-step guide to disappearing:

Step one: physically remove yourself. Move away from the place you are known, from where you have friends, family, a history. Choose a new home at random, this is most important, somewhere no one will think to look for you. Move there and keep your head down, because you never know who is looking.

Aberdeen, the most northerly of important British cities, is snowbound, but the road from the airport has been cleared. The city centre, when Maggie catches glimpses of it, looks like a silver city from

215

childhood dreams, as the famous mica crystals of the granite buildings gleam in the clear, northern light. She has never been to Aberdeen before, never been this far north. She reaches the ring road and heads towards a residential district on the city's southern edge. It is already late afternoon and the light is fading.

Step two: choose a new name and change it by deed poll. The good news is that this is easier, and much less official, than you might imagine. Most people envisage a court appearance, solicitors, the sign-ing of a formal document, inclusion on an official register, with both new name and old viewable by anyone so inclined. Whilst the change can be done with this level of formality, most people simply don't bother.

The reality is that only around one name change in two hundred is 'enrolled' and thus available to searches and inspections. Most people make their own deed polls, comprising very simple forms, completed and signed by them, witnessed by two adults. Once in possession of a 'deed poll', official documents, such as driving licences and passports, can then be changed to your chosen new name. Of course, the Passport Office, the DVLA, the administrators of any other official documents will keep records of your old name, and if requested to do so by a court, would almost certainly reveal these details. But lay people searching for the 'old you' will first of all have to know the new name you are going by. And they won't.

Maggie pulls up in a street of large, grey-stone Edwardian houses. Number 20 is two houses away on the opposite side of the road and flat 6 is probably on the first floor. She isn't in the least bit surprised when nobody answers the doorbell. She gets back into the car.

Step three: change your job, if you can. This is particularly import-ant for people working in the professions, which nearly all maintain registers of those entitled to practise. A professional body will allow for a change of name, but will keep records of that name change. Anyone staying in the same profession will be traceable through their profes-sional body, even if they choose to work overseas.

Starting the engine again, Maggie drives around the corner and parks near to a row of shops. McDonald's always has free Wi-Fi.

Step four: change your appearance. It's a small world, wherever in it you choose to move. Changing your hairstyle and colour, swapping spectacles for contact lenses, dressing differently, can all reduce the chances of an unexpected recognition.

On her second cup of McDonald's coffee, Maggie has finally finished her search. She checks the car can be left in its current parking spot and sets off walking.

The first place she stops at is a dead end. So is the second, and the third. The fourth is bigger, smarter, decorated in retro-Regency style with elaborate, white-painted wooden furniture and pink tasselled lampshades. The reception desk has a stencilled portrait of Audrey Hepburn, her cigarette holder held gingerly between highly manicured nails. Each nail is a different colour and pattern. This salon offers very sophisticated manicures.

Step five: keep a low profile. Especially avoid activity that will attract the attention of the media. Staying away from social media is probably a good idea too. Remember, it's a small world.

'Good afternoon, that is great hair.' The woman behind the counter is young with polished red lips and shiny black hair cut short. The very sharpness of her is at odds with the soft, feminine lines of the rest of the salon. 'How can I help you?'

'I'd like to book an appointment for next Saturday.'

The woman opens up a screen on her desktop computer and Maggie edges around the desk so that she can see the names that appear. Becca, Sophie, Rikki, Ashlyn. Others too. The salon employs a lot of people. All women. She sees the name she is looking for. Finally.

'Eleven fifteen OK?'

'That would be fine. Can I have a card in case I need to change anything?'

Step six: you have an Achilles' heel and you mustn't forget it. Your National Insurance number. Consisting of two prefix letters, six digits and one suffix letter, a National Insurance number is allocated at birth to every UK citizen and mailed to them shortly before their sixteenth birthday.

NI numbers are changed in only the most exceptional circumstances, which means your old name and your new will always be linked by your NI number.

Take heart, though. The existence of the link is one thing, being able to access it quite another. No ordinary citizen has the right to request the NI number of another. If you're hiding from an abusive husband, for example, he cannot request that HM Revenue and Customs reveal your new identity. The police might have more success, but only in exceptional circumstances after gaining a court order. So, unless you're wanted in connection with a serious criminal offence, it is highly unlikely that a court order would be given.

The bottom line is, if you work legally, in the UK, you can always be traced, but not easily, and not without good reason.

So, that's how you disappear. Finding the disappeared? Well, that follows on naturally.

Back in the car, now parked outside the salon, Maggie waits. Using her phone, and claiming a forgotten meeting, she cancels all four manicure appointments that she has just made.

Finding the disappeared depends upon how successfully they've adhered to the six-step plan. Where do most of them fall? At the first hurdle, of course. Finding the disappeared depends upon their failure to adhere to step one.

Five o'clock comes and goes, two of the employees exit the salon and walk hurriedly off to nearby bus stops or parked cars. The clock ticks round to five thirty and one more young woman leaves. Six o'clock, half past six. A tall, well-built woman with dark, shiny hair and a prominent nose leaves the building. She is wearing an emerald green coat and shiny black boots. Her make-up is perfect, but a little too heavy, as though it, too, must play a part in keeping out the northern chill. She walks with confidence, looks smart and well kept, but Aberdeen employers pay well.

The failure of step one. Most people, when forced to choose a new place to live, simply cannot do so at random. Try it. Imagine you have to leave, suddenly, without explanation or planning. Think of where you might go. You'll almost certainly zero in on a place of significance: the home of a friend or relative, the town where your mother was born, the seaside resort you stayed in as a child. We are homing animals. We flock to the familiar, and almost everyone who disappears deliberately, and who doesn't have the professional help of a witness protection programme, will be traceable through their location. Of course, some will be easier to find than others.

The dark-haired woman's face is pinched against the cold as she strides off down the street. Maggie leaves her car and crosses the road. She walks towards the young woman, who won't know her, will have no reason to be alarmed, and only at the very last moment does she side-step to bring them both on to a collision course. The woman, whose eyes have been down on the pavement, looks up. Those eyes are not hostile at first, certainly not scared. Just puzzled.

'Hello, Zoe,' says Maggie.

Now she looks scared.

Chapter 61

'AND NOBODY'S RECOGNIZED HER? Seriously? Her face was all over the news for weeks.' Hamish pushes his chair back and gets to his feet. In the small private interview room he seems taller than ever.

'She's lost a lot of weight,' Maggie says. 'Grown her hair, darkened it. She looks quite a lot like her older sister, Stacey, now. And you need to sit down, or the next time someone looks through the window, you'll be cuffed again. If they don't terminate the interview.'

He glances round at the door and rubs his wrist.

'Zoe is a very different young woman now,' Maggie says. 'I liked her.'

Hamish is still standing. 'Was it mutual?'

'Both she and Stacey were pretty hostile at first. Wanting to know who'd sent me, what I was going to do.'

He folds his arms and leans back against the door. 'And what are you going to do?'

It is the first time he has properly challenged her. 'I'm going to think about it,' she says. 'Talk to you about it. I told them I'm working on your case. That you're my priority, not them, or the police hunt for Zoe. Now, come and sit down, calmly, or I will bring this to a close and in future we go back to meeting in the hall during normal visiting hours.'

He takes a step towards her. 'So what's the story? Why did she run? Abusive boyfriend?'

'Abusive mother.' Maggie thinks back to Brenda's controlling behaviour, the jumpy youngest daughter. The unmistakable signs of OCD in the house. This woman, though, wouldn't be happy with controlling her house. She'd need to control her daughters too. 'All three girls suffered, but Zoe always got the brunt of it.'

Hamish leans on the table towards her. 'They didn't think of something less extreme, like, I don't know, reporting her to the authorities?'

She gives him a second. 'They didn't want to see her in prison. She's their mum.'

He nods, reluctantly. As a doctor, he'll have come across abuse of all forms. And the thousands of excuses the victims make for their abusers. *Mum's a bit of a bully. Mum has a bit of a temper. She doesn't mean it, she just doesn't always think. She doesn't know her own strength.*

'And you guessed this, when you met her?' he asks.

She points at the still-vacant chair. 'When I saw the police photographs of the red boots I knew something didn't add up. The blood spots were exactly where women get blisters if their shoes are too tight. I never saw the blood as necessarily sinister and when I looked in Zoe's wardrobe and realized her feet were actually nearly two sizes larger than the boots, I realized that they were probably a gift from her mother and that Zoe herself hated them.'

He sits back down, and the chair creaks beneath his weight. 'Why would Zoe's mother buy her boots two sizes too small?' His face is baffled. He has no idea what women obsessed with size do to themselves. To each other. Size five boots squeezed on to size six and a half feet. Of course they were going to hurt, but Zoe was going to wear them all the same, because her domineering, controlling mother had paid good money for them, money she could ill afford, and for heaven's sake, if Zoe lost a bit of weight then maybe the swelling in her feet would go down and they would fit.

'There were lots of clothes in Zoe's wardrobe that were far too small. Her mother was always bullying her to lose weight.'

Maggie closes her eyes and, for a few seconds, is back in the coffee bar in Aberdeen. 'She didn't like me because I was fat,' Zoe is saying as she clings to her older sister's hand. 'I let her down. Embarrassed her in front of the neighbours. She was always trying to get me to lose weight but somehow, when someone's on at you all the time, it just makes it worse.'

Maggie wants to hold her hand too.

'She used to weigh me before I went out. If I was over what she felt I should be, she wouldn't let me go. She phoned Kevin to say I was ill. Some days, she just wouldn't give me food.'

'She made her sit at the table and watch us eat.' Stacey says. 'Kimberly and I sneaked food to her as often as we could, but it wasn't always easy.'

221

'Zoe met Stacey the night she disappeared,' Maggie tells Hamish. 'Stacey borrowed her boyfriend's car and drove down from Aberdeen. Zoe threw the boots out of the car window, as they were driving through Cheddar Gorge. They realized it was stupid and went back for them, but only found one.'

'And how are your two new best friends feeling about my serving time for killing one of them?' says Hamish.

'They feel bad.' Maggie thinks a bit more, knows she has to be honest with him. 'But as Stacey was quick to point out, you'd have been sent to prison just the same, if Zoe had still been living at home.'

'If you knew this, if you guessed it before you got on a plane, why did you even bother going? I'm not paying you to swan round the country on wild goose hunts.'

She doesn't point out that, for the moment, he isn't paying her at all. 'Two reasons. One, I had to be sure. I have very little to work with here and I can't leave a stone unturned.'

He waits.

'Two, I need you to trust me.'

He wasn't expecting that. She can tell from the slight start of his head, the narrowing of his eyes.

'I am very good at what I do, Hamish. A woman who has hidden, successfully, from the police for years, I found in a matter of days. I needed you to know that, so that you do what I tell you to and keep nothing from me.'

His head sways in what might be a grudging nod. 'The trouble is, my one and only alibi vanishes like hot air when everyone realizes that Zoe's disappearance was in no way connected to the murders of the other three.'

He's right. 'I'm sorry,' she says.

'So, what happens? Zoe stays in Aberdeen and I continue to get petitioned by her family to tell the world where her body is?'

'If the time comes when the truth will help you, I won't hesitate to tell it. In the meantime, I'm hoping they'll tell it themselves. They're planning to wait until the younger sister is old enough to move north and live with them, before they come clean.'

'In the meantime, Zoe stays dead.'

'I'm sorry, Hamish. It's a setback, I can't deny that.'

'Actually, I'm encouraged. You're right, it is very impressive that you found Zoe so quickly. It gives me every hope for—'

'I'm not looking for Daisy.' She checks her watch. 'I have to go. I'm sorry I couldn't bring you better news.'

She gets up without looking at him, picks up her bag, fastens her coat. Only when she is turning to knock on the door for release does she look back. Hamish is staring at the tabletop. The lines of his face have fallen. He looks older, beaten. For the first time, she realizes, he has let the mask slip.

He lifts his head a fraction and their eyes meet. Eyes gleam. A tear starts to fall, then another. Then too many to stop.

She turns, bangs on the door and sets off along the corridor. Only when she is back in the cold, salt air, does she slow down. Still the tears flow.

They are hers, not his.

Chapter 62

From: Maggie Rose
To: Hamish Wolfe
Date: 23.12.2015
Subject: Daisy

I simply do not understand, given everything else facing you, why you are fixating on a woman who hasn't been in your life for nearly twenty years.

Daisy is an irrelevance, Hamish. If you can't see that, I'm not sure I can help you.

I'm sorry I left abruptly just now. When I say I hope you have a good Christmas, please believe I mean it sincerely. I'll be in touch after the weekend.

Best wishes,
Maggie
Sent from my iPhone

Chapter 63

HMP Isle of Wight - Parkhurst
Clissold Road
Newport

Wednesday, 23 December 2015

Dear Maggie,

Let me tell you something about Daisy.

She loved to dance. When music was played, music of just about any sort, she could not keep still. Her shoulders, her hips, her toes and her fingertips started jigging and bouncing and shaking in time. I teased her, she tried so hard to stop. She failed completely.

No dance style was beyond her. She dragged me to modern jive classes. I was close to hopeless but it was worth it to see the joy in her eyes when we, occasionally, got a movement right. It was worth it for the passion she brought to our lovemaking afterwards, as though the hour's dance class had been a sweaty, exhausting session of foreplay. Dancing turned Daisy on so much. She fucked like a rabbit afterwards.

She and I used to critique each other's written work. She was merciless with me, picking me up on every error, however minor, and yet went into a major sulk if I pulled her up on anything. She was a stickler for grammar, but not the expert she considered herself to be.

She also had the funniest, dirtiest laugh imaginable, like a donkey on speed. She was very self-conscious of it, tried so hard not to laugh out loud, but there were times when she simply couldn't stop. It was a badge of honour, in class, to make Daisy laugh and whoever managed it didn't have to buy drinks that evening.

She was one of the cleverest women I ever met, but so shy. She'd been to a small, all-girls school in the North and I think felt out of her depth at Oxford. She was one of the best, the brightest there, but she was the only one who couldn't see it.

You ask why I want to see Daisy again. I want to tell her that she was quietly wonderful. That she deserved better. And that I'm sorry.

Hamish

Chapter 64

From the office of

MAGGIE ROSE

The Rectory, Norton Stown, Somerset

Thursday, 24 December 2015

No, Hamish, let me tell you something about Daisy.

She was eighteen, little more than a child, away from home for the very first time, at a university where the pressure to succeed is enormous. She was a young woman seriously self-conscious about her weight (fat women always are), a woman who'd been teased and bullied and despised from the age she first became conscious that body-size was even a thing.

She would not have believed her luck when she attracted the attention of a man like you. At the same time that she fell completely in love with you, she told herself it was too good to be true. She braced herself for the inevitable rejection. She steeled herself to deal with the sight of you moving on to prettier, worthier girls. She never imagined how bad it was going to be.

You took this innocent, trusting, nice girl and you broke her.

I think you taped something that should have remained forever private and you showed it to your mates. Then I think you duplicated that video and sold copies to sad, seedy little men all over the UK.

And you know what else I think? I think you let her find out. You didn't even have the common sense and courtesy to keep the video well hidden. I think that's why she left. You drove her from the university she'd won a place in, from her new friends, from the career she'd longed for since being a child.

That's the kind interpretation of what you did to Daisy, Hamish. Others are making different, far darker, assumptions about what happened.

Tell me the truth about what happened that night, and then, maybe, I'll look for her.

M

Maggie seals the letter. The last postal collection on Christmas Eve is 10.30 a.m. and she has missed that by a couple of hours, but she doesn't want her letter to Hamish sitting in the house over the holiday weekend. She might be tempted to burn it. She opens the front door just as a delivery van is pulling up in the road outside.

A woman wearing a green gilet swings open the gate and crunches her way up the path. Her hands are red, dirty and cracked around the tips and nails, but there is an expectant smile on her face. Florists expect to be welcomed – how can someone get a delivery of flowers and not be pleased? – but this woman's smile is fading as she gets close enough to see the expression on Maggie's face.

'Christmas delivery for you,' she says when she's within earshot, because she hasn't quite lost hope that all will be as it should be, that Maggie will break out of whatever stressed daydream is keeping her in thrall and say what's she's supposed to say – *Flowers, how lovely, thank you, so sorry to bring you out in the cold.*

'No card,' the florist goes on. 'Apparently you'll know who they're from. The sender was very specific about the arrangement, though.'

Maggie has no choice but to take the cellophane-wrapped cluster of blooms. 'Everything all right?' the florist asks, although clearly it is not.

'Yes, thank you,' says Maggie, knowing that asking questions about who sent them will get her nowhere.

The florist turns and half runs back down the path as Maggie stares at the flowers that someone has sent her for Christmas.

A single rose, fat, pink and perfect. Surrounded by daisies.

Chapter 65

MAGGIE WAKES, sometime in the early hours of Christmas morning.

'He was pretty fit when I knew him.'

When has she heard that? Hamish's voice, but when exactly?

She switches on the light. Yes, definitely his voice, not something he wrote in a letter or an email.

Pretty fit when I knew him.

'And this is only occurring to you now?'

Is she never to have any peace? 'I've had a lot on my mind.'

Hamish had been talking about Pete and she'd assumed he'd been referring to the time of his arrest. The two men, inevitably, would have seen a lot of each other.

'That feel right to you?'

'No.' Not any more, it doesn't.

He was pretty fit when I knew him.

'It suggests an intimacy, somehow, don't you think? Something more than would come from sitting across a table in an interview room?'

'Maybe.'

'How can you judge someone's fitness just by how they sit, stand, enter and leave the room?'

You can't. You'll see weight, percentage of body fat. 'A medical doctor would be more in tune with what bodies are saying than a layman.'

'Even so.'

Is it possible Pete and Hamish knew each other? Properly knew each other, before the arrest?

From close by in the room comes a soft, low laugh. 'Maggie, Maggie, what are you not being told?'

Chapter 66

THE THIRD CRACKER in a row fails to snap and a heaviness sinks into the group of six people that has nothing to do with the amount of food they've eaten. 'Cheap Poundland rubbish,' Liz says, Yuletide exhaustion making her face seem thinner and paler than normal. Even her hair has lost some of its usual springiness. 'Tell you what, we could pile them all up in the middle of the table and set fire to them. They'd spark then.'

The younger of her two sons looks up from his new tablet. 'Yeah, Mum, can we?'

Liz glances towards the head of the table. 'Or failing that, stick the lot down Pete's trousers, followed by a lighted match. Might just get his attention.'

Pete starts. 'Sorry,' he says, 'miles away.'

He spoons the last piece of soggy sponge into his mouth. There is still half of the giant sherry trifle left in the bowl and he has a horrible feeling second helpings are about to be forced upon him. 'Delicious,' he says, to head off the attack at the pass. 'I now officially cannot eat another thing until New Year's.'

Liz's mother fiddles with her waistband. 'I always say Christmas pudding is too heavy after a big meal.'

Christmas pudding is Pete's favourite dessert. He hasn't eaten a mouthful since Annabelle left him.

Liz's dad nods at Pete, his pale blue eyes going from his daughter's last-minute guest to the remains of the meal. 'What do you say to that, young man?'

'Delicious,' Pete repeats, thinking next year, he doesn't care how many invitations from well-meaning colleagues and mates he gets, he is not spending Christmas Day in someone else's house. Minding his manners all day isn't too bad, but the endless expectations of gratitude are soul-destroying. And having to drive himself home means he can't even get drunk. He sneaks a look at his watch. Another two hours, at least, before he can make his excuses.

'Do you know who killed the tramps yet?' Liz's dad asks.

'Brian, that's enough,' says her mum. 'Now, I suppose—'

Liz jumps up. 'Stay where you are, Mum. You too, Dad. Pete and I will wash up. Kids, take your grandparents into the other room and entertain them.'

There is a subdued moan from one of the kids.

'And they do not consider watching you on your iPads to be entertainment.'

Pete gathers an armful of dishes and follows Liz into the kitchen. They run water, scrape food into bins, load the dishwasher and try to organize the chaos that is a Christmas kitchen. Pete looks at the closed door. 'This room soundproof?' he asks.

Liz shakes her head. 'Not remotely.' She drops her voice. 'And little pigs have very big ears – not to mention their grandparents.'

'Understood.'

They work without speaking for several minutes, listening to the sounds of the TV and the boys on their iPads.

'You could phone her.' Liz is at the sink, her back to him, when she breaks the silence.

'Tricky. Latimer has told me to stay away.'

She gives him a quizzical look over her shoulder.

'Give Maggie Rose a wide berth for a week or two, maybe longer, were his exact words. He's probably said the same thing to her.'

Liz frowns and smiles at the same time, one of the expressions he likes most to see on her face. 'How's she holding up, do you think?'

Pete lifts a stack of plates. 'Keeping busy, from what I hear. Not often at home. When she is, she rarely comes out. Situation normal.'

'She'll be used to pressure. She won't scare easily.'

'I know.'

Something in his voice makes Liz give him a good long look. She wrinkles her nose before turning back to the sink. 'What happened to Odi and Broon wasn't your fault, Pete,' she says.

231

Pete joins her at the sink and picks up a clean tea towel.

'It wasn't your fault, it wasn't mine, it wasn't anyone's fault except the psycho who held the knife.'

Pete glances round. 'They were practically under my window, Liz. If I'd cranked it open a notch I could have heard them snoring.'

She gives him a sharp look. 'You could not have anticipated that. No one could.'

'We should have done.'

'Rubbish.' She gives him another smile. 'Come on,' she says. 'Enough shop talk. Let's finish this lot and get drunk.'

Chapter 67

MAGGIE GETS OUT of her car into air so icy it feels like she's walking through knives. She pulls the collar of her coat up as high as it will go and sets off across the square. As she circumvents the enormous Norwegian spruce tree, that smells more of drunken men's urine than it does Scandinavian pine forests, she glances up at the window of the Crown that she has come to think of as Pete's window. She has no idea of whether it is or it isn't, but it comforts her a little to look up at a friend's window.

Or the window of someone who might have been a friend, had circumstances been very different.

She walks on, as the slow, sad melody of the cathedral's organ finds its way across the crisp square and into her heart. In front of the Georgian facade of Wells Town Hall a group of people are standing silently. Some of them hold lanterns. There are tea lights on the stone flags. The flickering of the candle flames, the stronger, more garish lights of the pub are reflected on the ripples of cellophane that have been left where Odi and Broon breathed their last.

She keeps her eyes down as she gets closer to Odi and Broon's shrine. Slipping to the front, she lays the roses down on the cold stone.

The tall male figure, walking down her drive, might have alarmed her, had she not already seen and recognized his car.

'What are you doing here, Pete?' She finds a key, fits it into the lock.

He reaches the bottom of the drive but keeps his distance. 'Where have you been? You shouldn't be going out on your own in the dark. Not while that Facebook crap is going on.'

'I've been to the square in Wells. I left some flowers in the Town Hall entrance. Again, what are you doing here?'

Slowly, he draws nearer. 'Making sure you're OK.'

She opens the door and turns. On the step, she is almost his height.

233

'I'm OK. But you can't just come round here. It's a conflict of interest. You must see that.'

His eyes seem darker than she remembers them. 'Did Latimer talk to you?' he asks.

'He did, actually, a few hours after Odi and Broon were killed, but it was hardly necessary. I'm working to get Hamish out of prison, you have a vested interest in keeping him where he is. If there's ever another court case, our being friends could jeopardize it. We can't be friends any more.'

'Is that all we were, friends?'

She knows exactly what he's asking her and also that she owes him something more than a curt dismissal.

'I've enjoyed getting to know you, but the timing didn't work. I'm sorry, Pete.' She turns away before she can weaken.

You'll regret that, says the voice that welcomes her home.

Chapter 68

'ARE YOU GOING to be writing all night?'

Phil is pacing again. He has spent the day doing it, stopping every ten minutes or so to smoke a cigarette. The air in the cell is thick with fumes and Wolfe thinks, not for the first time, that there is a good chance that if he ever does leave this place alive, he will be riddled with lung cancer.

He looks up. 'Nope, I'm nearly done.' There is another half-hour until lights out. 'Want to play cards?'

The two of them often play poker when they are locked up. Wolfe learned the game from his cellmate, but soon outstripped him. Roughly 60 per cent of the time, he lets Phil win.

Phil stops at the door and looks out. 'It's doing my head in,' he complains.

Wolfe has been at Parkhurst long enough to know that, of the three hundred and sixty-five days that make up the prison year, Christmas Day is by far the hardest to get through.

On Christmas Day, everyone is thinking about what their families are doing without them. Christmas Day is when the missing and the loneliness tip the scales and come down hard on the unbearable side.

Visitors are not allowed on Christmas Day. Prisoners can neither send nor receive gifts from outside. The queue for the telephone is less good-natured than usual. Squabbles are more or less continual. The suicide rate in UK prisons peaks over Christmas.

'Didn't even get to talk to Sal,' Phil moans. 'Who you writing to, anyway? Your mum again?'

He comes close, as though he might be about to peer over Wolfe's shoulder. Wolfe signs his name at the bottom and folds the single sheet of paper in two.

'Wouldn't you like to know?' he says.

Chapter 69

HMP Isle of Wight – Parkhurst
Clissold Road
Newport

My darling,

On the first day of Christmas, my true love gave to me . . .
a sigh, that spoke of sadness, and longing, and constancy.

On the second day . . . a hand, a fingernail's width from
mine, always.

On the third day . . . a fairytale, in which she is the
princess in the tower, and I the knight who must rescue her.

On the fourth day . . . a glimpse of black lace, as delicate
as cobweb on a winter's morning.

On the fifth day . . . the story of her first love, and the
assurance that I am her last.

On the sixth day . . . a letter, on ivory parchment, on which
she has squeezed the essence of her heart.

On the seventh day . . . a row of burning kisses, from the
nape of my neck to the base of my spine.

On the eighth day . . . a heart, beating in time with my own
as we lie together in the rose dawn.

On the ninth day . . . a promise, that she will be mine, ever true.

On the tenth day . . . forgiveness, for all that is past.

On the eleventh day . . . the full force of her rage, that
she and I are kept apart by those who are beneath us.

On the twelfth day . . . a plan, of brilliant, shining simplicity.

All the gifts I ever want from you, my love. Happy Christmas,

Hamish

Chapter 70

THIS MORNING, three days after Christmas, Wolfe looks tired. He is freshly shaved and the faint smell of soap he's brought into the interview room suggests he's washed, but his skin looks pale, the lines on his temples deeper, and there are purple smudges running diagonally from the corner of his eyes to the centre of his cheeks. He is yawning as he's led into the interview room and tries, unsuccessfully, to stifle it.

'Sorry. Bad night.' He holds his hands out to be uncuffed. 'Did you have a good Christmas?'

She hasn't come to exchange social pleasantries. 'Did you know Pete Weston before he arrested you?'

The door closes behind the guard and they are alone. Wolfe sinks into the other chair and unfolds his long, lazy grin. 'I was wondering when you'd work that one out.'

Today, his self-possession is annoying. A man in his position has no business being smug. 'I have quite enough exercising my brain, thank you, without your withholding information.'

The amusement leaves his mouth, not his eyes.

'How?' she asks. 'How did you know him?'

'First answer me this. Is he trying to get close to you? Personally, I mean.'

'He's asked me much the same thing about you.'

Wolfe looks around, at the small, square, dull room, empty apart from the table and chairs. 'He has a little more room to manoeuvre than I do.'

'Yes, I think he's interested. But he's not long gone through a bad break-up. I think he's vulnerable to any half-decent woman who'll talk to him right now.'

Somewhere, not too far away, is the sound of someone yelling. It has an authoritative ring about it, she thinks it's probably a guard.

'Are you pretending to like him to get information? Because if you are, I'm fine with it.'

'Maybe I'm not pretending. Maybe I do like him.'

Wolfe laughs, and this line of conversation has gone far enough.
'How do you know him?'

Now he looks almost bored. 'Perfectly commonplace circumstances. We played football for Keynsham Athletic first team for three seasons. I played left midfield, he was centre back. Sports teams usually socialize after matches, so I got to know him.'

Wolfe and Weston had practically been mates. That made a massive difference. 'He should have told me that,' she admits.

'Of course he should. Sports teams. Shared changing rooms. Skin and hair left lying around on towels. The opportunities to collect someone else's DNA are multitude. All he had to do was find a towel the same as mine and swap them.'

He has been building up to this for some time, she realizes now. Waiting for the right moment.

'Daisy the Dalmatian went to matches with me sometimes. Lots of the guys used to pet her.'

Daisy's hairs on one of the bodies. How easy would it be, to run a hand over a friendly dog's head and then later, when you were alone, to look down at the short, fine, black and white hairs on the sleeve of your coat?

'We gave each other lifts to away matches. I can't specifically remember Pete being in my car, but it has to be a possibility.'

The car carpet fibres, also found on Jessie's body. *Can I stick my bag in your boot, Hamish?*

'Hold on, wait a minute. He wouldn't be allowed to work on the case if you and he were friends. He'd have been taken off it immediately.'

Hamish gives her a slow, single nod. 'Which is exactly what happened. After the arrest, he took a back seat while all the evidence was gathered and sorted. I'm sure he was still involved, but he and I didn't come into contact. I didn't see him from the night of the arrest to my first day in court. A woman called Liz Nuttall took the lead on interviewing me.'

'Could he have got into your house?' She says it without thinking, because this is nonsense.

'Somebody did. Somebody accessed my computer and borrowed my car.'

At the end of the corridor a heavy metal door slams shut. Footsteps are heard hurrying towards them.

'Did this come up at the time? I can't remember seeing anything on the file.'

'Of course I mentioned it. But the reaction I got was the same one you're about to give me.'

'Why?'

'Exactly. What possible motive could Weston have for wanting to frame me?'

Actually, that was the easy bit. 'He was panicking. The case was going nowhere. He needed an arrest. Because of everything you'd just told me, he homed in on his football team and, for reasons that are probably only apparent to him, you fitted the bill.'

Wolfe nods at her to go on, like a school teacher guiding a slow pupil. 'And the problem with that theory is . . .'

'Too risky. Once the killer struck again, it would be obvious he'd arrested the wrong man.'

'Unless . . .?'

Unless, Pete himself is the kill—

'That's ridiculous. Why on earth would—'

Wolfe lifts up his hands. 'Why would I? Why would anyone?'

The footsteps in the corridor slow and then stop. There is a brief conversation between the guard outside and the newcomer. Then a new pair of eyes peer in at them.

'You have a history with fat women.' Maggie doesn't look up. She is used to prison guards coming to gawp at her.

Wolfe, who hasn't turned around, waits until he hears the window in the door closing again. 'My ex-fiancée is one of the skinniest women you'll ever meet. Ask my mother for photographs of me with Nancy, who I was seeing for nearly five years before I met Claire. She'd be drowned by size twelve clothes. I like my women lean.'

'Daisy?'

Again, that closed, reluctant look on his face when Daisy Baron's name comes up. 'Daisy was the exception. I fell in love with Daisy in spite of how she looked, not because of it. Had we carried on seeing each other, I'd probably have been on at her to slim down a bit, like the jerk I was in those days.'

'You never told her that, did you?'

'What, that I wanted her to lose weight? Christ, no. You didn't mess with Daisy. I'd have been a bit more—'

'That you were in love with her. You never told her that.'

That look again. Closed. Sad. Secret. 'No. I should have done. Maybe if I had, things would have turned out differently.'

There is more noise outside.

'Maggie?'

'Sorry. This racket is distracting. Is there something going on outside?'

'Something will be kicking off somewhere. It happens. Don't worry. The cons can't get down here without keys. You may have to wait a while before they let you out.'

There is movement on the floor above them as well and she is being too easily distracted. 'Where were we?'

'I was giving you the best alternative suspect you could hope for and you were worryingly unmoved by it.'

She makes herself focus. 'OK, I get that Pete could have framed you, and I get that it could just have been a combination of circumstance and chance that he chose you out of the whole football team, but what you haven't told me is why Pete killed three women. Especially given that he's killed no others in the two years since you were arrested.'

'None that you know of.'

'What's that supposed to mean?'

'Maybe he got a bit cleverer. Maybe he targeted women who weren't so easily missed. Lot of homeless women in and around Bristol. Maybe he got better at hiding the bodies as well.'

'And what was his motive?'

'Ah, glad you mentioned it. Has he told you when his marriage broke up?'

She has to think about that. 'Not specifically. Long enough for him to have moved out, not long enough for the divorce to be close to finalizing.'

'He found out Annabelle was shagging one of his colleagues in January 2013, six months before Jessie disappeared. Two months before the Facebook conversation with the fictional Harry began. The whole team knew about it, Maggie. Pete wears his heart on his sleeve. Especially when he's had a few.'

Is that true? She remembers Pete's outburst at the police station about his daughter. His coming round to her house half drunk on Christmas Day. 'Lots of marriages break up. Especially police marriages.'

'True, but this was a nasty one. He lost his wife, his daughter, his home, and he has to see the bloke who took them away every day and he has to call him sir. That kind of shit would mess with anyone's head.'

It would, wouldn't it? 'I still don't—'

'I've got a theory on how the bodies got into the caves, by the way. Are you interested?'

She holds up her hands in mock despair. 'Oh, please.'

'Everyone more or less believes the girls must have gone into the caves voluntarily, while they were still alive. Agreed?'

'Because it would be next to impossible to carry dead bodies that size up the gorge cliffs and into caves?'

Wolfe points an index finger at her. 'Exactly. But only if the bodies were moved as fresh corpses.'

She is conscious of her body tensing up. 'What are you saying?'

'I don't think the bodies were taken to the caves until some time after the girls died. I think they were kept somewhere and left to decompose.'

He stops, lets her think about it. She nods for him to go on.

'Body tissue breaks down very quickly,' he says. 'Especially in summer, or in hot rooms. Insect activity starts to eat away at flesh, at the same time the internal decomposition kicks in. Give it a few months, and you'd be left with not much more than skin and bones.'

'Which anyone could bundle into a big bag and carry to the caves quite easily.'

He leans back, stretches his legs. 'And if that's the way it was done, I'm in the clear, because I was taken into custody days after Myrtle went missing. Her body was still quite sizeable when I was taken out of the picture.'

'If we can prove that—'

'If you can prove that, Maggie Rose, I will be forever in your debt.'

There is a look in his eye that she doesn't want to dwell upon. 'I can look at the pathology reports again. See if there's anything at all that would fit that theory.'

'Thank you. And let's get back to Detective Pete. Odi may have

241

recognized him. She may have been too frightened to say something because who would take the word of a homeless woman against that of a . . .' He pauses, waiting for her to finish his sentence.

'Of a detective sergeant.'

'Once she'd said something, once she'd accused him, it would have been all over for her. A detective, especially a senior one, could track her down. She'd be looking over her shoulder the rest of her life. What would have frightened Odi more than knowing the killer she'd witnessed was a police officer?'

'If this is true, her death is my fault. I'm the one who told Pete Weston about Odi and the possible sighting at Rill Cavern.'

'Weston lives a hundred yards away from where Odi and Broon were killed. He knew they were there, knew they'd spoken to you. His windows probably overlook that Town Hall entrance. He could have sat quietly in his room for hours, waiting for his chance.'

She has no idea which of the Crown windows is Pete's. It could easily overlook the Town Hall.

'And if he left any trace behind, well, he was first detective on the scene, there'd been a bit of accidental site contamination. Maggie, do you really believe the murders of Odi and Broon were coincidence?'

She doesn't. Of course, she doesn't. 'Hamish, I know how desperate you are for another credible suspect – and I really think you could be on to something with the decomposition idea – but I know this man—'

'I'd tell you to ask him for a photograph of his wife, but if I'm right, that could be a dangerous thing to do. You should try and see her, though, discreetly.'

The door opens.

'Sorry to interrupt, Miss Rose. We're having some trouble on the wing. We need to get Hamish back to his cell.'

Hamish stands as the officers move to handcuff him.

'Find a photograph of Weston's wife, Maggie, will you do that?'

'Why, what on—'

'You need to look at Annabelle.'

Chapter 71

Email

Sent via the emailaprisoner service

From: Maggie Rose
To: Hamish Wolfe
Date: 28.12.2015

OK, I've had a look at Annabelle Weston. I found her on Facebook. Her privacy settings are tight but there is a publicly available photograph. She's a little overweight, I grant you, but really?

I don't see it, to be honest, but we can keep it in the armoury. I'm going to be on the road for the next few days, looking up a few of your old college friends. I'll keep you posted, of course. Take care of yourself.

M

Chapter 72

Email

From: Avon and Somerset Police, Detective Sergeant Peter Weston
To: Maggie Rose
Date: 29.12.2015

Dear Maggie,

Sorry about Xmas Day. Probably is a good idea if we give each other some space. Just until you stop flogging the dead horse that is Hamish Wolfe, then I'd love to take you out to dinner. LOL as the youngsters say! ☺

I'm going to be out of circulation for a few days. DCI Latimer is on at me to 'tie up every loophole in the Wolfe case'. The poor lamb is seriously rattled (be flattered). I don't share his anxiety, obvs, but I'm going to have to do something to keep his blood pressure at manageable levels.

So – wait for it – I'm going to track down Daisy Baron, Wolfe's girlfriend from college. I'm banking on her not giving up on her medical degree completely, so I've been checking medical school admissions in 1997 and 1998. Got a couple of possibles, both up north.

I'm sure it goes without saying I'm not exactly expecting to find a shallow grave with a bag of old bones in it, but it would open up a whole new dimension on the case if I did, don't you think?

Speaking of dead horses, Latimer has agreed to put some resources into finding that computer you and Wolfe are fixated on. If you send over that list you drew up, with an update on where you got with it, we might be able to help out. I still think it's a very long shot, but you never know.

A couple of other things. I've spoken to Sarah Smith, aka Sirocco

Silverwood. Talk about mad as a box of frogs! She denies going anywhere near your house and declined to submit fingerprints. She
could have been the one to leak your personal details to Facebook
but, without good reason, we can't haul her computer off for examination. Tricky one, but we'll keep an eye on her.

Oh, and I found the flowers by your bin. Daisies? What's going on,
Maggie? When and how did they arrive? They're currently rotting
slowly in the back of my car, just in case you go looking for them.

I'll be in touch. Dare I say, Happy New Year?

Pete

Chapter 73

Guardian, Saturday, 13 September 2014

HAMISH WOLFE TRIAL: DAY 5

A dramatic development in the Hamish Wolfe trial yesterday saw the judge ruling the evidence of a key prosecution witness as inadmissible and instructing the jury to disregard his entire testimony. Legal experts described it as a severe blow to the prosecution's case, as the witness had been expected to testify that Wolfe's dangerous, predatory tendencies could be traced back over two decades.

James Laurence, 39, a GP in Rawtenstall in Lancashire, and a university contemporary of Wolfe, had been giving evidence for nearly an hour when the judge, Mr Justice Peters, intervened and called into question the relevance and reliability of everything Laurence had told the court. Under UK law, he reminded the jury, evidence presented in criminal cases must be 'relevant, without being prejudicial, and reliable'.

'Your testimony is based on half-remembered anecdotes and groundless rumours,' the judge said to Laurence. 'Your memory of the facts, by your own admission and the testimony of others, is vague and unsubstantiated. The defence has been right to call your evidence repeatedly into question. It adds nothing to the prosecution's case, it would be dangerous to rely upon it further and I hereby instruct the jury to disregard it.'

Like Wolfe, Laurence studied medicine at Oxford and was a member, albeit on the periphery, of Wolfe's social circle. He'd been called as a prosecution witness to give the court an insight into the character of his former friend and, in particular, Wolfe's predilection for a certain type of female.

During questioning by the Crown prosecution barrister, Miles Richardson QC, Laurence spoke of an inner circle of five of the brightest medical students, all of them white men from professional or upper-class backgrounds, with Wolfe as their acknowledged leader. The five men, three of whom we are not permitted to name for legal reasons, studied together, socialized and, crucially, formed a secret club that was to lead, in the opinion of the police investigating team, to the death of at least one young woman.

'I knew something had gone on that night,' Laurence said from the witness box, referring to the death of young Oxford woman Ellie Holmes. 'The others all clammed up, but I knew it was something very serious. When we heard that a girl had died, I knew there was more to it than we were being told.'

The judge gave it as his opinion that, although Ellie Holmes had died whilst in the company of one of Wolfe's friends, there was no reason to challenge the Coroner's verdict of death by misadventure, and no reason to suppose that Wolfe had been involved in any way. As such, he said, it was not relevant to the current case.

'Eighteen years ago, the Coroner went out of his way to praise the efforts of medical student Warwick Hespe,' Mr Justice Peters said, 'whose vigorous efforts at resuscitation, sadly, failed to have the desired result and save Miss Holmes's life. There is no reason to think this was anything other than the unfortunate death of a young woman following her own reckless behaviour. Most significantly, though, the prosecution have presented no evidence to link Mr Wolfe to the incident.'

Nor, the judge went on to say, did he attach any credence to the rumours of a soft-porn mail order company which, according to the prosecution, the five men had set up to sell illicitly shot videos of young women having sex.

'There is no evidence that this business ever existed,' he remarked. 'It seems highly unlikely that a group of students would have found the wherewithal to set up such a company. Even its supposed name, which I will not test the court's patience by repeating again, strikes me as highly unlikely for a group of Oxford University students. The police have several times interviewed the five men in question, including Mr Wolfe, and each has claimed to have no knowledge of it. None of the footage supposedly shot still exists. We have the testimony of no women who were filmed against their will and made into unwitting porn stars. The prosecution have not thought fit to call any of the other men whom you claim were involved.

'Your evidence, Mr Laurence,' the judge concluded, 'strikes me as nothing more than envious rumour-mongering and poorly remembered tittle-tattle. Given that nearly twenty years have passed between the alleged events that you describe, and the murders that we are now dealing with, I cannot suppose them relevant in any way. Furthermore, your testimony, hostile as it is to Mr Wolfe, could be seen as unfairly prejudicial. I therefore instruct the jury to disregard your entire testimony as evidence. You may stand down.'

None of the detectives on the case were prepared to comment. The case continues on Monday.

(*Maggie Rose: case file 00326/8 Hamish Wolfe*)

Chapter 74

DRAFT

THE BIG, BAD WOLFE?

By Maggie Rose

CHAPTER 5, IS HE BANGED UP? OR DID HE SMARTEN UP?

One cast-iron test of whether the right man has been imprisoned bang to rights in cases of serial murder is whether or not the killings cease after conviction. Anyone daring to suggest Hamish Wolfe was wrongly convicted is met with the rapid retort that no other plus-sized young woman has been found in a Somerset cave since Wolfe's arrest.

Maybe not. But is it equally true to say that no other women have vanished? A quick search on the site of the UK Missing Persons Bureau throws up some serious concerns.

Lynsey Osbourne, twenty-two, last seen at her bedsit in the Filton area of Bristol on 12 February 2014.

Kelsey Benson, fifteen, vanished from local authority care in Honiton, Devon in May 2013.

(*NB: Actually, Benson wasn't that big, will probably need to find an alternative*)

Janice Robinson, forty-six, of Stroud, left her council house on the night of 16 September 2014 and hasn't been seen since.

These are only three. There are others.

Of course it would be fanciful to suggest that all these women fell victim to the same killer who ended the lives of Jessie Tout, Chloe Wood and Myrtle Reid, but even the most cursory glance at the list of our missing casts serious doubt on the assurance that the killer who targets large women is no longer at liberty.

He may just have got smarter.

(Will need updating just before going to press.)

Chapter 75

THE SMALL, black-fronted establishment, just off the main road through Rawtenstall in Lancashire, is perhaps a little too cheerful in its demeanour to be a magic shop from a fairy story, but its draughts, elixirs and cordials give something of the same impression. There are tinctures, restoratives and stimulants in here that are not of the commonplace. Blackbeer and raisin? Blood beer? Sarsaparilla?

The rows of jars stacked high on wooden shelves have colourfully intriguing contents and mysterious-sounding labels. The packets on the counter rustle with dark promise. The oak floor is highly polished, but stained in places where substances, too powerful ever to be properly cleaned away, have spilled over the years. There are three small tables, each spread with an embroidered linen cloth. This is Fitzpatrick's, the last remaining temperance bar in England, and Maggie is being asked to choose between a rhubarb and rosehip cordial and an iron brew tonic.

'Which do you recommend?' she asks the jovial, grey-haired man behind the counter.

'You look cold to me. Why don't I warm you up a toddy?'

Conscious of the day outside getting dark and not wanting to be driving over the moors too late at night, she agrees and takes her seat opposite the man she has come to meet.

'The Temperance movement started in Lancashire.' His accent is Northern, his voice pitched surprisingly low for such a small, thin man. 'Back in the nineteenth century. Suddenly, working people had more money and alcohol took off in a big way. By 1880 there was a temperance bar in every Northern town. Now, this is the only one left.'

There are red veins in James Laurence's cheeks and eyes. His face has the saggy appearance of someone for whom bloating has been a problem in the past. He is forty years old, looks considerably older.

'James, why do you think the judge didn't take you seriously?'

Laurence's hand rests on the half-pint glass of black liquid. He lifts it continually, taking minuscule sips. 'I was stitched up in court. They made me look a fool.'

'The defence barristers?'

A begrudged nod. 'I mean, everyone's a twat at university, aren't they? They found pictures of me wasted at parties. They kept asking me how much I used to drink. Whether I took drugs. They implied I'd been out of my head all the time I was there, so how could I be relied upon? As if you can't get a medical degree at Oxford if you have a drink problem.'

Maggie avoids looking at his hands, which she already knows have a tremor more pronounced than normal. 'I've looked at the court reports,' she says. 'I don't think it was so much that you were deemed unreliable, as that there was no supporting evidence. No trace of the porn business you talked about, and none of the sex tapes you described have ever been seen.'

He makes a scoffing noise in the back of his throat. 'Oh, they've been seen all right. Just not by anyone who's prepared to admit it.'

'Of Hamish Wolfe's social circle at Oxford, you were the only person called to testify against him. Any idea why?'

'The others couldn't shop Wolfe without dropping themselves in it. So, by default, it was my word against that of all five of them. What with that, and the defence barrister trying to discredit everything I said, I was on a hiding to nothing. In the end, the judge practically told the court I'd been lying.'

As hot, spiced steam wafts through the small room, the bartender brings a clear plastic beaker in a silver-coloured cup to the table. Maggie can smell lemon and ginger. He waits for her first sip and she gives the expected nod of approval, even though the brew tastes like something she'd take for a cold.

'Do you think Hamish was guilty?' she asks Laurence.

A shrug. 'The evidence was there. And it fits with what I remember from college days. They were a nasty bunch.'

In court, James Laurence had claimed to have been one of the group. A close friend. 'How much do you know about what they were up to? The so-called Fat Club. The porn business.'

'Quite a lot. I was on the same floor as Chris Easton, that first year. He and I used to study together sometimes.'

'It would really help if you could tell me what you know.'

Laurence shrugs as though it makes no difference, one way or another. 'I think, in fairness, it started as a bit of a laugh. Hamish was keen on this girl on the course. She was a real chubster, and the other four kept on at him. You know the sort of thing: What do you see in her? Is there any room in the bed? Then Oliver Pearson decided he was going to shag a fat bird too – his words not mine – and it went from there. Turned into a sort of competition. They'd go out into Oxford town centre in the evenings, to the sort of clubs and pubs where the townies went, not the students, on the hunt for bigger women. Then Simon—'

'Simon Doggett?'

'Yeah, that's him. He and Hamish were on our floor one evening, they came into the kitchen to find Chris, and Simon announced he'd videotaped his session the previous night with a girl he'd picked up. He asked who wanted to see it. So the three of them set off for Simon's room. They said something about going to find Warwick and Oliver too.'

'Did you go?'

His face tightens. 'I wasn't asked. I didn't really come on to their radar screen, except when I could be useful. Took me a long time to see that. Anyway, a few days later, Chris needed some help setting up a hidden camera in his bedroom. He'd made a complete mess of it. Wanted me to sort it out.'

The bartender is still in the room. Maggie drops her voice. 'Did he tell you what he was doing with the films?'

'Nope. He was very tight-lipped.'

'So how did you know about the business? The one that was mentioned in court?'

Now it is Laurence who is conscious of their one-man audience. He lowers his voice. 'I needed to borrow one of Chris's textbooks one day. He wasn't in. I think he was in the bathroom, because his clothes were on the floor, but his computer was switched on.'

Maggie nods her head, knowing that appearing judgemental at this stage will make him clam up.

'He was using some sort of graphics package to design labels for the videos. As soon as I saw the branding, Fat Girls Get Fucked, it all made sense. Next time he was out, I let myself into his room and looked round. There was a cardboard box under the bed, full of videotapes. More than a dozen different films. All the guys had kept their faces from the camera, but I recognized the backs of their heads, and their rooms. Warwick, Oliver, Simon, Hamish. They were all at it.'

'How many tapes did Hamish feature in?'

'I only saw one, but there could have been others.'

'The girl he was with, was it the one you mentioned, the one on the course?'

He thinks for a moment, and shakes his head. 'No. This was a blonde girl, even bigger than Daisy.'

'Daisy?'

'Yeah, Hamish's girlfriend. Well, sort of. They obviously weren't exclusive.'

'Did any of the tapes feature Daisy?'

'Not that I saw, but I do remember hearing the others talking about a tape with Daisy in. They described it as a bit special.'

The door opens and a rush of cold air comes in, along with a middle-aged couple. It is completely dark outside now, the lights of the town stretching up and over the moors.

'What happened to Daisy?' Maggie asks.

'She disappeared. When it all kicked off.'

'What kicked off?'

'The business I tried to testify about. It happened one night in Hilary term. That's between Christmas and Easter.'

'Thank you, I know. Go on.'

'Simon and Oliver came banging on Chris's door. They woke me up. I went outside, asked them what was up, and they told me, "Nothing, go back to bed."'

'Your room was next door to Chris's?'

'That's right. I couldn't hear much of what they were saying and they left quickly, but I did hear them talking about picking up Hamish. I assumed that they were on their way to Warwick's house.'

'What did you do?'

'I went back to bed. What else could I do? But next day, there were rumours going round about the police being called to Warwick's house. That someone had died there in the night. The university kept it quiet.

There was a small piece in the *Oxford Mail* about an unnamed girl being found dead in a Magdalen College house, but then nothing more was heard until the inquest.'

'Did you ask them about it?'

'I asked Chris. But he said they hadn't gone to Warwick's, and they knew nothing about what happened there. He said they'd gone to Hamish's because he'd drunk too much and they were worried about him.'

'Did you believe them?'

'No. I saw Hamish that day. He didn't look to me like he was nursing a hangover. He looked like he was shitting himself.'

'Did you say anything to the authorities?'

'What was I supposed to say? That three guys had gone somewhere in the night and I'd just assumed they were going to Warwick's?'

'So, what do you think happened?'

'I think Warwick took a girl home with him, planning to make a video. I think something went wrong. Maybe he was trying something a bit more adventurous than normal. Maybe it wasn't just him, maybe Oliver and Simon were involved too. Something went wrong and the girl died. The gang got together and made it look like she'd died accidentally.'

'Not as easy as it sounds, surely?'

He gives her a pitying look. 'They were medical students. They knew about causes of death and what post-mortem examinations look for. If nothing else, they would have stripped the room of the recording equipment, removed any signs of kinky sex. At worst, Warwick killed that girl and the others helped to cover it up. At best, they conspired to pervert the course of justice. And they got away with it.'

Laurence's hands are shaking noticeably now.

'You're angry about it, aren't you?' she says.

'Yeah, I'm angry. I'm angry that some people believe themselves to be a cut above the rest of us. I'm angry that the rule of law doesn't apply to all of us equally, and I'm seriously pissed off that my word, when set against that of five upper-class, over-privileged twats, wasn't believed.'

She gives him a moment. 'Tell me about Daisy.'

'What's to tell? Nobody saw her again after that night.'

'Do you think they killed Daisy too?'

'Oh, I wouldn't be a bit surprised.'

255

Chapter 76

NEW YEAR'S EVE is arguably one of the most depressing shifts to work in a police station. The 0600–1400 hours crew had practically congaed their way out to the nearest pub when their shift ended, but the 1400–2200 bunch are having to make do with soft drinks and snacks. Halfway through the shift, the cola is warm, the crisps are soft and the team are feeling the party might have passed them by already.

Liz comes back from the loo, makes a quick detour to her own desk and then leans over Pete's. 'Fifteen possibilities,' she says, putting the file down in front of him.

Pete reaches across and sees a printed list of industrial estates. Liz has followed Maggie's instructions to the letter: look for modest-sized units, rented out in January 2013, due for renewal in 2018. 'We can get round them all in the next week or so,' she says.

Pete nods. 'I suspect Maggie is working on it as well. She could find it before we do. If it exists. Which I seriously doubt. Did I mention that?'

Liz smiles, starts to walk away, then turns back again. 'If Hamish gets out, it won't be good for you,' she says. 'Not in the short term.'

Pete wonders if he can sneak a beer out of the Asda carrier bag under his desk. The chances of a call-out at this hour on New Year's Eve are slim, but you never know. 'I guess at the end of the day, all we can do is the right thing,' he tells her.

What Liz does next is completely out of character. She bends over, and kisses him on the temple. 'I kind of love you,' she says.

Christ, he needs a beer. 'Get out of here,' he tells her.

Chapter 77

HMP Isle of Wight – Parkhurst
Clissold Road
Newport

Thursday, 31 December 2015

Dear Maggie,

The old year is groaning it's last and this will be the third New Year's Eve I've spent in prison.

On 31 December 2013, fired up with self-righteous anger, I made a page full of resolutions. I was going to find the best lawyer, have private eyes combing the country for fresh evidence, I was going to keep a diary that I could publish and make my fortune, get fitter and stronger, learn a language to give my time in here some meaning. That first year, I had so much energy, so much hope. I need hardly tell you how well all those resolutions worked out.

Last year I tried again, but it was harder, knowing how slim were the chances of any of them coming to anything.

Tonight I find it almost impossible. Resolutions are about taking action, making changes, having control; and yet I have no control, can take no real action, have no power to make changes. The worst part of being in prison, I've realized, is having so little influence over my own life. Resolutions seem beyond me now; all I can do is wish.

It's coming up to midnight. So here are my three wishes:

1. I want to make love to a woman again. I want to feel her soft, warm skin next to mine, to know that perfect meeting of mind and body.

2. I want to run, with the rain in my face, making footprints in the ground. I want to run faster than the wind, like the animal I'm named after, safe in the knowledge that no one will ever catch me again.

3. I want to walk on that beach with you, the beach where you saved my dog. I want to watch the sun come up with you by my side, to wrap my coat around you to keep you from the chill and I want to kiss your cold lips and whisper 'Thank you'.

Happy New Year, my beautiful, clever lawyer. Thank you for saving Daisy. Thank you for giving me back hope.

Yours truly,

Hamish

Chapter 78

THE BASEMENT BENEATH Maggie's house is large and high-ceilinged, with several interconnected rooms. The first, at the bottom of the staircase, is the biggest. In this room, there are narrow, horizontally configured windows, very high in the walls, that allow in weak beams of dusty light, but even in daytime the single, low-watt electric bulbs – just one in each room – are needed.

Close to midnight, in winter, the subterranean rooms are full of shadows, but Maggie knows what lurks in each. Every time she comes down here, she thinks about ghosts, but she hasn't seen one yet.

'Bit early for spring cleaning,' says the voice that is never silent for long, and that always has plenty to say for itself below ground.

'Technically, late.' Maggie carries a box to the bottom of the stairs. 'Still a few more minutes of 2015 left to run.' The box joins several others stretching up the wooden staircase. Before the night is out, Maggie will carry them upstairs and put them in the back of her car. She has already identified four household-waste disposal sites, none of them too close to home, where she will drop them off in the next couple of days.

There is stuff in these boxes, old books, souvenirs, with which she is loath to part, and yet there are no memories here that aren't replicated perfectly inside her head. She has forgotten nothing. Probably never will.

'We're on the move again, then?'

'Probably,' she says, knowing it is more than probable, it is certain. One way or another, her time here is coming to an end. Will she miss this house, she wonders. Unlikely. It will be nice, if anything, to find somewhere smaller, without cavernous rooms and draughty corners. A cottage, she thinks, with thick, stone walls, a dense, thatched roof, and open fires in every room. A cottage with no hallways, or corridors, or basements. A cottage in which one room leads to another and the garden is tiny, and the neighbouring houses are close by, possibly even linked.

It might be nice to be among people again. She has already started checking available property on the Isle of Wight.

She takes one last look around.

The high shelving units around the room are empty now. She has never been a hoarder and it hasn't taken long to clear the room completely. The second, smaller room holds nothing but the furniture she inherited when she bought this house. That can stay where it is. And the third room. She needs to check the third room.

From somewhere upstairs she can hear a clock chiming.

'Happy New Year, Maggie,' says the voice that has been her companion for nearly twenty years. She doubts, now, that it will ever leave her.

'Happy New Year, Daisy,' she replies.

Chapter 79

31 December 2015

Dear Hamish,

This time next year, my love, we will walk on sands of powdered gold and swim in waters that have the power to wash away the past.

This time next year, my love, we will eat food and drink wine beneath stars that will be dust, long before I cease to adore you.

This time next year, my love, we will fall asleep at dawn, having spent the hours of darkness in a tangle of hot limbs, spinning ecstasy from starlight and building castles from moonbeams.

This time next year, my love . . .

Me

PROPERTY OF AVON AND SOMERSET POLICE. Ref: 544/45.2
Hamish Wolfe.

Chapter 80

Monday, 4 January 2015

Dear Hamish,

Here's a little something of the world outside.

On the fourth Saturday of every month, there is a farmers' market in Glastonbury. Maybe you know it? As you spotted for yourself, I eat very little, but I love to look at fresh food, skilfully made and beautifully laid out, and farmers' markets fascinate me.

I try to get there early, before the crowds, and just wander around, admiring the colours of the fruit and vegetable stalls, the artistry of the artisan bakers, smelling the cheeses, marvelling at the sheer inventiveness of the makers of cordials, pickles and preserves. So much summer goodness captured within glass.

I never buy anything, but it would be nice to, I think, if I could be sure it would be eaten. Can I get something for you when I go next? I need to check what I'm allowed to bring into Parkhurst, but maybe some clementines with their waxy green leaves? Or maybe your taste veers more towards passion fruit and pomegranate? Some Cheddar cheese, perhaps, with a rich dark pickle? I'm being cruel, aren't I? I really must check the regulations before I torture your taste buds any more. I wouldn't be allowed to bring glass into a prison anyway.

I had a very interesting chat with James Laurence last week and I'm heading to Bristol later today. Your old friend Oliver Pearson has agreed to see me when he gets home from work. I'll stay over tonight and fill you in when I visit tomorrow.

I received your last letter. I'm touched, but no need to thank me as yet. I am acting out of self-interest, remember?

Best wishes,

Maggie

Chapter 81

CLIFTON OCCUPIES THE HIGH GROUND – geographically speaking, if not morally. It stands on the east of Avon Gorge, overlooking the river and much of the city, but its grand Georgian terraced houses were built on the profits of tobacco and slavery. Number 12 Goldney Road is a four-storey, end-of-terrace property, occupied by Oliver Pearson, his wife Lisa and their two young children.

Like her husband, Lisa Pearson is a registrar at the Bristol Royal Infirmary. She has been on maternity leave since her oldest child, a three-year-old daughter, was born. The couple admit Maggie into their home without enthusiasm.

'Hamish is wasting your time,' Oliver Pearson is telling her now. 'Chablis?' Without waiting for an answer he pours wine into a glass the size of a goldfish bowl. It isn't intended for her, though. He raises it to his lips in the manner of someone who has been looking forward to his first drink for some time.

'Thank you, but I came by car.'

'Lisa?' He holds the bottle up as his wife, all honey-blonde hair, hockey thighs and active breasts comes back into the room. She holds a baby against one shoulder and barely looks at her husband. 'It would be quicker to put it in a bottle and give it straight to Ludo.'

She empties the last few drops from a toddler's cup into the sink. 'Coco wants you to kiss her goodnight, by the way. If you can remember where her bedroom is.'

Pearson's face tightens. He hasn't offered Maggie a seat, or to take her coat, and she is hovering, uncomfortably, in the middle of the room.

'Hamish was best man at your wedding,' she says.

A surly nod. 'That's right.'

'And godfather to Coco,' Lisa says. 'I can't tell you how that goes down at mother and toddler groups.'

'You must have good reason to believe your former best friend guilty of three murders, Mr Pearson.'

'Four murders.' Lisa Pearson's eyes go from Maggie to her husband.

'Mr Pearson?'

'Justice in this country is weighted in favour of the guilty.' Apart from the glass in his hand, Pearson looks like a pontificating school teacher. 'Far more guilty people go free than innocent people are wrongly convicted. If Hamish was found guilty, it would have been for good reason.'

'That's an argument I would expect from a perfect stranger. You were his friend.'

'So?'

'So you would have an informed opinion on whether or not your former friend is capable of killing three women.'

'Four.' Lisa, on the periphery of the conversation, is not going to be left out of it entirely.

'So was he?'

Pearson sniffs loudly. 'What do you want me to say?'

'I want you to tell me why you think Hamish Wolfe capable of killing three women.'

There comes an audible exhalation from the far side of the room. 'Am I the only one in this room who can count?'

'Does he have a history of violence? Did you see him mistreat women? Was he abused as a child? Did he show any signs of a mental disorder? You're a doctor, you'd spot a problem in someone you knew well. Was he on medication? Did he seek counselling? Did he ever say or do anything that made you question, in any way, his mental stability?'

'Whoa!' Pearson puts his glass down and holds up both hands. 'You're not in a court now, love. You're in my house. Have you spoken to the others? Warwick? Chris? Simon?'

'No, you were the only one who would take my call.'

'More fool you,' snaps his wife. 'Anything for a bit of attention.'

Pearson's head whips round as though someone has slapped him. 'Well, I get precious little in this house.'

Maggie speaks quickly to get their focus back on her. 'I intend to get Hamish's conviction overturned and my best chance of doing that is to find alternative suspects. I have four in mind, so far, Mr Pearson, and you're one of them. Let me tell you what I think happened in Hilary term, in the year 1996.'

Pearson seems to hunch down, like a fighter getting ready to charge. 'I think I want you out of my house.'

'I think the videotapes you were making to supplement your beer fund got a little bit too adventurous. I think—'

'Videotapes? What the hell is she talking about?'

'You're leaving. Now.'

Maggie stands her ground. 'I don't know how much you know about IT, Oliver, but nothing ever disappears from the internet, not completely. If any of those videos were ever posted, even decades ago, there are companies who can trace them. They're not cheap, but I'm not working to a budget.'

'Out.' He strides ahead, making for the front door.

She follows, nodding a goodbye to Lisa Pearson and the baby, neither of whom respond, and leaving her card on the side table by the door. 'I'm staying at the Hotel du Vin in the town centre. I'll be here till eleven o'clock tomorrow.'

Chapter 82

THE ENGLISH CHAIN, Hotel du Vin, specializes in contemporary design in quirky old buildings. The Bristol hotel, in an old sugar warehouse, is three floors of rigid leather furniture, roll-top baths and bed linen so crisp and white it could be made from freshly milled paper. Wine bottles, all of them empty, are everywhere, as though the hotels are permanently recovering from the best party ever.

Maggie has been awake for several hours, has taken a walk around the waking city and breakfasted on salty, creamy eggs Benedict that made her feel slightly ill. She will leave in an hour. Until then – the phone is ringing.

'Good morning, Miss Rose, this is the front desk. There are three gentlemen here to see you.'

She didn't expect them quite so soon. Nor that three of them would come. Feeling that frisson of excitement that tells her a plan is going better than anticipated, she checks the room and carries her overnight bag down to reception. They are in an alcove of the lounge area, drinking coffee. She has a second to study them before they spot her.

'Good morning, Oliver.'

The three men stand as she approaches. Not out of politeness, the looks on their faces tell her that, but in a rather feeble male attempt at intimidation. No one offers to shake her hand.

The smell of successful male is very strong, a combination of expensive aftershave, coffee and last night's alcohol. One of them is very tall, his dark hair more than half silver now. The other is shorter, making up for his lack of height with extra girth. She ignores Pearson and speaks to the other two. 'Simon, Chris, good to see you. Is Warwick running late?'

'Warwick's in Scotland.' Pearson looks down his nose at her. 'We didn't even bother calling him.'

They think they can bully her with nothing more than physical

267

presence, these men. They think an extra few stone in bone, fat and muscle will be all it takes. 'Whereas you just had a fairly easy drive over the Severn Bridge.' She deals with Simon Doggett first. He still plays rugby, she sees, but he favours his right leg when he stands. Repeatedly turning out as front row, bearing the weight of several large blokes, has done some serious damage to his left knee.

'And you're in Gloucester, I believe, Chris?' The tall man is in better shape. 'You picked a good field. Orthopaedics is a growth area.'

She sits in the nearest armchair and they do the same. They look like a business meeting. She could be the slightly quirky sales rep, trying to persuade three senior doctors to buy a new and expensive drug.

'Oh, don't look so wary, boys. I checked the medical register to find out where you're all based. And I found your photographs in a Magdalen College yearbook. None of you have changed so much as to be unrecognizable. I'm not a witch, just a good investigator. Now, who'd like to start?'

'This is the only time we're going to talk to you without lawyers present,' Pearson tells her.

This makes her smile. 'A lawyer is present. Me.'

'What do you want from us, exactly?' asks Doggett.

'I want to know where you all were on 6 July 2013, 11 September 2013, and 4 November of that year. Those were the dates the three women disappeared. Oh, and better let me know where you were on 8 June 2012, when Zoe Sykes vanished. Just until we rule her out.'

All three stare at her. Pearson voices their thoughts. 'Are you insane?'

It is possible she might actually enjoy this. 'When I've found evidence of the business you set up all those years ago, James Laurence's testimony about you will suddenly become much more credible. Then we have five potentially dangerous, predatory men, not just one. It seems a little far-fetched to imagine you worked together to kill Zoe, Jessie, Chloe and Myrtle, so your alibis, or lack of them, should point me in the right direction.'

Simon Doggett stands up and practically spits his last mouthful of coffee at Oliver. 'She's an absolute fruitcake. I can't believe you dragged me from Newport for this.'

'Which of you killed Daisy?' Maggie looks from one to the next, seeing the sweat break out on Easton's temples, the red veins in Pearson's cheeks glow a little brighter. 'Because I don't believe it was Hamish. He was fond of her. And he was with her that night, wasn't he? She was there when you came to his house in the middle of the night. You probably didn't know, Hamish thought she was asleep, but she heard what you were saying. She knew what happened to the girl in Warwick's room. I think she threatened to go to the police and you had to shut her up.'

They are staring at her the way they might watch a dog tear apart a rabbit, the way they might look after slowing down to pass a road traffic accident, repulsed but fascinated at the same time. She has become the human equivalent of roadkill.

'But you knew you'd never get away with two dead women in one night, so Daisy had to disappear. The only thing I'm not sure about is whether you were all involved, or just some of you. I'm certain Hamish wasn't, though, because he thinks she's still alive. He wants me to find her.'

While she's been talking, they've risen, one by one. They want to hurt her. They won't, though, not here. The veneer of civilization clings to them like burnt jam to the side of a saucepan.

'Seeing as how you're a lawyer, Miss Rose, you'll understand about restraining orders,' says Easton.

Maggie smiles.

'I shall be applying for one and I advise the others to do the same. And I'll be lodging a complaint against you at the bar.'

'I wouldn't have the reputation I have without a few complaints and restraining orders, Mr Easton. Have a good trip back to Gloucester. I'll be seeing you.'

Maggie doesn't watch the three men leave. She just hears the swish of the door and feels the rush of cold air as the front door of the hotel closes behind them.

All things considered, that went rather well.

Chapter 83

FOR ONCE HAMISH hasn't shaved. Dark stubble, almost a beard, covers his jaw and neck and lines his upper lip. He hasn't showered either. He smells like the Lycra-clad men who run past her in the street, and of clothes that need washing. This is the first time he hasn't made an effort for her and Maggie isn't sure how she feels about it. But if he's starting to take her for granted then maybe it's time to remind him how much he needs her. She starts speaking almost before his cuffs have been removed, before the guard has closed the door, shutting them in together.

'No more lies, no more evasions. I want to know what happened the night Ellie Holmes died and Daisy Baron disappeared. I will know if you're not telling me the truth.'

He rubs one wrist, flexes and bends his fingers. 'Did the guys lie to you?'

She thinks back to the three men who tried to bully her in the Bristol hotel. 'Not as such. They rather cleverly avoided telling me anything too much. They blustered. Poured outrage over each other and themselves. They're hiding something, though. They're frightened.'

He scratches the side of his neck and inserts his little finger into his ear. 'Even so, I really can't believe any of them framed me for three murders. I know these guys. They don't have it in them.'

She glares. 'That's interesting. Because they all think you're more than capable.'

He looks surprised, then a little hurt. His hands fall back on to the table. 'Really?'

'They all think you're guilty. Oliver Pearson especially, and his wife. There was awe in their voices when they spoke of you.'

He thinks about this for a moment. 'If they believe me guilty, they can't be.'

'No, you're right. I don't think any of them are guilty of killing Jessie, et al. I never did.'

A rare flash of frustration clouds his face for a second. 'Then we're no further forward. Especially as you seem determined not to think of Pete Weston as a possible suspect.'

Oddly, his annoyance helps to calm her. She takes it as a sign that he is, in spite of the front he puts on, struggling. 'Hamish, we don't need to present the Crown with the real killer, even an alternative one. All we have to do is throw enough doubt on your conviction. And those three were guilty of something. Which brings me back to the question you're trying to avoid. What happened that night?'

His eyes drop to the table. 'You're not going to like it.'

'I like nothing about this whole sorry business. Get talking.'

He peers up at her through his eyelashes. 'I love it when you're bossy.'

'I'm not playing games with you, Hamish.'

He scratches the side of his head. 'OK, everything James Laurence testified in court was true. My defence did a bloody good job of discrediting him, but he was telling the truth.'

'There was a Fat Club?'

'There was. And my seeing Daisy is what started it. I took a lot of banter over her. It's not always easy, seeing a woman you actually want to spend time with, as opposed to the sort of girl your peers think you should be with. Especially when you're young and a bit unsure of yourself.'

'My heart bleeds.'

He pushes himself back on the chair and fixes her with a stare. 'As my lawyer, you're really not supposed to be judgemental. You sound more like a pissed-off girlfriend.'

'Get over yourself. And keep talking.'

For a second he looks uncertain – whether to fight back or do as she says. 'The other guys started picking up fat girls in bars,' he says. 'We went into town, away from the usual student hang-outs. We were looking for women who weren't necessarily looking for a relationship.'

'Or who didn't expect to be taken out to dinner a few times before they put out?'

He gives her a pitying look. 'We were students. We didn't do much fine dining. A girl was lucky if we paid for her drinks. Anyway, at first it was just a bit of a laugh.'

'You were involved too? Even though you had a girlfriend?'

'I was nineteen, Maggie. I was a good-looking bloke. Sorry to sound conceited, but there it is. Yes, I liked Daisy, but I wasn't ready to settle down.'

'So this was a competition? A prize for the most bedpost notches.'

'Nothing as formal as that. It was just a bunch of dickhead guys pissing around.'

'Until someone had the idea of recording the encounters for posterity? Who was that? You?'

'No. It was Simon, from memory. He made a tape. We all watched it. Found it a bit of a turn-on, if I'm being absolutely honest, and that became the next stage. We all bought surveillance cameras, fitted them in our rooms and went into the movie business.'

'How many films were made?'

He shrugs. 'I lost track. A few dozen. More, maybe.'

'Who thought of selling them?'

He is silent. His eyes slip away from her.

'Was it you?'

'That's what the others will tell you. And, yes, it probably was me who said, Hey, guys, you know what, we can make a fucking fortune out of these babies. But setting up the business involved all of us.'

'How much money did you make?'

'Enough. Our student finances became a lot more manageable.'

'And nobody spotted it? Nobody recognized themselves?'

'Women tend not to watch porn. And we didn't exactly promote it around the university. We used shops in other towns to sell them. Most of our viewers probably had no connection with Oxford.'

'How many tapes featured you?'

His eyes leave her face again. 'Three, maybe four.'

He is still lying. There were more than four.

'Was Daisy in any of them?'

'No. That one was private.'

'What happened to Ellie Holmes?'

He looks down, washes his hands over his face. When he looks up again she sees creases around his temples. This is how he will look first thing in the morning, she thinks. Tired, a bit crumpled.

'Death by misadventure,' he says. 'The Coroner got that right. She'd drunk a lot over the course of the evening. Warwick encouraged it, of course, it was always a lot easier when they'd had several drinks, but he didn't know she was taking anything else.'

'Taking what, exactly?'

'Ecstasy. A bad dose. Contaminated with methyl diethanolamine. Sent her into primary cardiac arrest. If Warwick had taken her straight from the club to A & E, she'd probably still have died.'

Maggie has read the post-mortem report into Ellie Holmes. This is all true. Just not the whole truth. 'Go on,' she tells him.

Hamish takes a deep breath, as though about to dive into a cold swimming pool. 'When she lost consciousness, Warwick panicked. He tried to resuscitate her and failed. Then he phoned Oliver.'

'Who phoned Simon, and then went to collect first Chris and then you?'

He examines his fingernails for a second before looking up. 'I guess James was a lot smarter than we gave him credit for.'

'You were alone at home?'

'I shared a house with three other guys. They were all there, but they didn't wake up. Daisy was there too, that night. It was the last time I saw her.'

'We'll get back to Daisy. So, the four of you were roused from your beds. What happened?'

'We went to Warwick's house. The girl was dead. She was starting to go cold by this time. There was nothing we could do for her.'

'So you did what you could for yourselves?'

'I said you wouldn't like it.'

'Good call. Go on.'

'We washed her. Got all traces of Warwick off her body and dressed her again. We put her in the bed, making it look as though she'd passed out from alcohol and Ecstasy. While three of us were doing that, the other two were clearing the room. We took away the camera, Warwick's various props. And we wiped his computer clean of anything to do with Fat Club or the business. We knew the police might take it away. We had to do it there and then.'

'This must all have taken some time. Didn't the medical examiner realize she'd been dead too long?'

A swift headshake. 'It's really not that easy to pinpoint time of death.

The most anyone can usually do is give a window of a few hours. Warwick claimed he'd been asleep beside her and wasn't sure what time she'd died.'

'Warwick called the emergency services?'

'That's right. After we left.'

Maggie is silent.

'I know what you're thinking. And I don't necessarily disagree. But we didn't kill her. Even Warwick had no idea what she'd taken.'

'He was a medical student. He could have spotted the signs.'

'There's not a single symptom of Ecstasy use that can't be mistaken for inebriation.'

True or not true? She needs time to think. Hamish doesn't appear to be lying. The girl died, as young people do every year, from a dodgy dose of Ecstasy, and a group of friends conspired to keep their unsavoury behaviour from coming to light. The discovery of a porn business that exploited unknowing subjects would have had them sent down from Oxford, ended their medical careers before they'd even begun. Admission even now might see them struck off. It's understandable that Pearson, Doggett, Hespe and Easton are concerned.

On the other hand, it doesn't make them murderers.

'OK, now tell me what happened to Daisy.'

Hamish yawns, giving her a full view of the fillings in his teeth, the fur on his tongue. 'I wish I could,' he says. 'She was gone when I got home. I went round to her room the next day, but she'd cleared out. Taken most of her stuff and vanished. The university knew nothing about it. They got in touch with her family, who just told them she wouldn't be returning.'

'Did you look for her?'

'I went to see her parents during the Easter break. I hadn't met them before but I knew where she lived in Leeds. They told me she'd gone travelling. That they weren't expecting her home for at least a year and then she'd be enrolling in a different medical school. One they weren't prepared to disclose to me.' His face clouds over at the unpleasant memory. 'They weren't welcoming.'

'Maybe they knew you'd made their daughter a porn star. Parents tend to frown on that sort of thing.'

'Daisy wasn't part of that. Did I not already make that clear? No one saw the tape of me and Daisy. It was private.'

'Rumour has it, and I quote, it was some weird shit. Bondage, is the best guess. Sadism.'

Hamish pulls a face. 'Fantasy.'

'Why was it called *Daisy in Chains*? Was she? In chains, I mean?'

'I don't tie women up.' He gives her an unpleasant smile. 'Unless they ask very nicely.'

'So, why would she just disappear?'

'My best guess? She heard enough of what we were saying to know something serious had gone down. Then she found the tape of her and me.'

'You left it lying around?'

'I'm not a complete fool. I knew she'd found it, though, because it was missing. It wasn't where it should have been. And I checked my browser history on the computer. In the middle of the night, someone – and it can only have been Daisy – found the folder for the business and looked at several pages. I'm guessing she realized what we'd been up to, saw the tape that she was on, and put two and two together, making a whole bigger number than four.'

'Daisy thought you'd been using her. That you'd only been seeing her to get salacious video footage. She thought dirty old men the world over had seen the two of you having sex.'

'Yeah, it's possible she thought that. But it wasn't true.' He pushes his chair back and claps his hands together, effectively signalling he's had enough of this particular line of conversation. 'So, where does this leave us?'

'I have to go.' Maggie checks her watch. 'Did I mention I'm seeing your mother and that support group again tomorrow night?' She starts to check her bag for keys, phone. 'And where we are is, we have four alternative suspects – five, if we decide to count James Laurence.'

He grins. 'Six if we include Pete Weston. Give my love to Mum, won't you?'

'More significantly, we have a fresh double murder, which everyone including the media is saying could be linked to your case.'

'And that happened right outside Pete Weston's bedroom window.'

'I've also made some progress in tracking down that computer, in that I've ruled out several possible sites.'

'If I'm right about Weston, he'll have moved it.'

'You're not. And I need to run if I'm to make my ferry.'

He shakes his head, looking sad and amused at the same time. 'That's all great, Maggie, but actually, I wasn't asking for an update on the case. I was talking about you. Do you believe me yet?'

Chapter 84

THE PHONE IS RINGING as Maggie opens the back door several hours later. She runs across the room to catch it.

'So did you catch the boat?'

Hamish, but sounding different somehow, as though he is talking through a mesh filter.

'Just barely, thank you.' She is out of breath, hasn't even closed the back door. 'I had to take the ramp at speed.'

'I've been thinking about you pretty much non-stop since you left.'

She is walking back towards the door but stops in the middle of the kitchen. 'Oh?'

'Those two men whose sentences you got overturned, did you believe in their innocence? Or did you just not care? Does a man's innocence or guilt make any actual difference to you?' He is almost shouting at her down the line. 'Or is it all about proving to the world how clever you are? Because if it's the latter, I'm just not sure any more.'

There is a cold draught blowing through the house. She sets off again for the hallway. 'Hamish, have you been—'

'I'm not drunk, although the illegal hooch is doing the rounds again. Just curious.'

Even allowing for the background noise he is still speaking loudly. She isn't sure she believes in his sobriety. 'Well, then you need to think about what you're actually asking me.' She pushes the door shut, turns the key and leans against it. 'Do I really need to rehearse the time-honoured reasons why everyone, innocent or guilty, is entitled to legal representation?'

She gives him a moment to respond. He doesn't, but she can hear his breathing. 'You're feeling sorry for yourself, Hamish. I don't blame you, but I don't have time for it, I'm afraid.'

The kitchen has grown cold during the day. She will need to crank up the heating.

'So what do you have time for, Maggie? What do you do, all by yourself in that big house of yours, other than play God with other people's lives? Come to think of it, why do you even do it? What makes a clever young woman say to herself, I will walk among murderers and liars and thieves, and I will succour them?'

How does he know she lives in a big house? 'Hamish—'

'Why? Why don't you want a normal career? Why don't you want friends, a partner, children? Have you ever even been in love, Maggie Rose?'

His mother. Of course. His mother has seen her house, will have told him about it. 'I'm sorry, Hamish,' she says. 'I won't be dragged into this sort of nonsense. I understand that you're upset, but it's late and things always look better in the morning. Goodnight.'

She puts the phone down before he has the chance to respond. She is trembling.

Email

Sent via the emailaprisoner service

From: Maggie Rose
To: Hamish Wolfe
Date: 5. 1. 2016
Subject: Why?

I can find just one question worthy of an answer in that self-indulgent diatribe. I do this job because it is rewarding (financially and in other ways) and because it is needed. It doesn't matter to me whether the people whose convictions I overturn are innocent or guilty, just that their convictions are unsafe. No one should be convicted on the strength of a flawed case. The best, strongest, soundest system of justice in the world is the one that allows itself to be scrutinized and challenged. I scrutinize. I challenge.

In common with many people I fell into my specific career by accident. I became interested in the case of Steve Lampton, sufficiently

278

so that I met with his wife. I saw the weaknesses in his conviction and I made the decision to do something about it, if I could. I never liked the man. I never particularly believed in his innocence. For all that, he should never have been convicted.

One more thought, before I go to bed. It's late and I'm tired. Are you familiar with the expression: Don't look a gift horse in the mouth?

Maggie

Chapter 85

HMP Isle of Wight – Parkhurst
Clissold Road
Newport

Wednesday, 6 January 2016

Dear Maggie,

When I climbed, or caved, I did it with a team. Often a small one, just me and a buddy, but I relied upon 100 per cent trust between us. Before I could allow myself to dangle 100 feet up a rock face, I had to trust my buddy with my life. I am trusting you with my life and yet you do not trust me back. I find this hard. Close to impossible. That is all.

Thanks for your email. It made sense, but you left a question unanswered.

Have you ever been in love?

Hamish

Chapter 86

Email

From: Avon and Somerset Police, Detective Sergeant Peter Weston
To: Maggie Rose
Date: 6.1.2016
Subject: Result!

Daisy Baron enrolled at Newcastle University in 1997 and graduated in 2001. Four years instead of the usual five, but she was given credits for having done her first year at another medical school, according to the very nice Mrs George in the records office.

So, if she's dead, Wolfe didn't kill her. Not at Oxford anyway.

You're welcome!

P

'Listen! Can you hear that?'

Maggie closes down her email program and gets up from her desk. The house is silent. As is the street outside. 'What?' she says, with ill-disguised impatience.

'The baying of hounds.'

'Oh, very funny.' She walks into the next room, although she knows by now that she will be followed wherever she goes.

'Detective Pete is not a man to be underestimated.'

'The trail will go cold. Daisy didn't leave Newcastle.'

'He won't give up.'

'He's gone as far as he can. He has to operate within the law.'

Maggie hears a soft laugh.

'Unlike us.'

Chapter 87

'WHY?' PETE ALMOST MOANS down the line. 'Why on earth are you seeing that lot again?'

Maggie turns off the main road. The huge, wire-meshed gates of the caravan park are closed, but Bear, in a quilted coat that makes him look even bigger, is waiting to open them.

Maggie says, 'What part of "we can't see each other any more" did you not understand? Oh, how extraordinary.'

Where there should be the unrelenting blackness of the winter night sky, there is colour, movement, neon lights racing in wild, abandoned shapes and leaving glowing, rainbow trails behind them.

'I'm not seeing you, I'm talking to you on the phone. What's extraordinary? And you haven't answered my first question.'

She drives into the park and pulls up at the barrier. In the rear-view mirror, she can see Bear closing the gates again behind her. He ambles back towards the car and she wonders whether she need offer him a lift to the clubhouse. It would be rude to make him walk in her wake, but she doesn't want the huge, unsavoury mass of him in her car, breathing the same air, leaving behind traces that she will never be able to see, let alone clean away. He draws level with the driver's door and she cannot avoid lowering the window a few inches.

'Treats tonight.' He leers down at her, like the oil-secreting uncle who thinks cheap sweets will make up for his unseemly presence.

'Do you need a lift down?' Politeness, social conventions are surely the heaviest chains of all.

'Waiting for Mike. I'll see you down there.'

Pete is still on the line. 'Maggie, what's going on? Why are you there and what's extraordinary?'

'They've got the fairground going.' She drives along the road that runs parallel to the beach, the one that takes her through the painted fences, the flimsy chalets, the sturdier caravans, and sees none of them.

They are thrown into shadow by the baubles whirling and spinning ahead of her. The fairground, eerie and empty on her last visit, is lit and active. The Ferris wheel is turning, as is a merry-go-round. She can see the impaled horses like plaster kebabs rising and falling. Lights flash from the waltzer, from the dodgem cars, from the side-stalls. The crashing of the waves is drowned by several different tracks of rock music. If there are people on the rides, she can't see them. Everything seems to be taking place without human participation.

'In this weather? In the dark? Seriously, Maggie, why are you there?'

'Three reasons.' The spinning lights have become a little mesmerizing. 'One: you lot have failed, dismally, to find out who broke into my house before Christmas, so I'm going to ask a few questions of my own.'

'Look, I'm at least an hour away. Can you just sit in your car and do a crossword puzzle till I get there?'

'They won't talk to me if you're here. And it's years since I've been on a carousel.'

'Jesus wept. And the other reasons?'

'Sorry?' She is distracted by the sight of Sandra Wolfe, bundled up against the cold in the doorway of the social building.

'You said you had three reasons.'

'Oh yes. Well, there's a chance Odi confided in somebody in this group about what she saw in the Gorge that night. Also, I think whoever killed her and Broon will be here. And that could well be the person who framed Hamish.'

'Oh, give me strength. Maggie—'

'Think about it. Serial murderers are notoriously narcissistic. While the hunt is on, they're completely at the centre of things, but once someone else is caught, all that excitement goes away. Whoever framed Hamish can't kill again without giving the game away, so the only way of keeping the buzz going is to get involved with the group that's trying to free him.'

'I don't believe I'm hearing this.'

'And an added bonus is that they can keep an eye on any developments, spot any threats. Odi knew more than she was letting on. I want to find out who she was close to, who she spoke to, other than Broon.'

'No, no, no.' Pete's voice is climbing. 'If there is even the remotest chance you're right, I've rarely seen anything as callous as what happened to Odi and Broon. This is not someone you want to mess with. Forty-five minutes – and I'm risking death and mutilation in an RTA.'

'I wouldn't want that. Why don't I meet you in the Crown when I'm done? It can't hurt for once. I'll fill you in then.'

'Somebody will be filling in your shallow grave, you daft cow.'

There is a sudden silence on the line, the silence of a man who knows he has gone too far, has overstepped the bounds of the fragile friendship.

'I'm touched.' Far from being offended, she finds his concern oddly moving. 'Come if you must, but don't rush. I need time to talk to these people.'

'Bear does this occasionally.' Sandra strides ahead as the two women make for the fairground. 'He's not supposed to, but the owners live abroad in the winter.'

They step under the illuminated, painted arch into the realm of enforced, motor-driven jollity and can almost smell last season's candyfloss and stale cooking oil. The rides aren't empty after all. There are people on the waltzer. Rowland is driving a solitary dodgem car around the track, weaving in and out of the other stationary cars with a look of fierce concentration on his face.

'He lost his driving licence a couple of years ago.' Sandra is standing close, her taller form keeping some of the wind off Maggie.

'Sandra, was there anyone in the group that Odi seemed particularly close to? Apart from Broon, I mean. Anyone you saw her talking to?'

Sandra thinks for a few seconds. 'Not really, just Broon. Oh, and Sirocco sometimes, I suppose.'

Right on cue, Sirocco herself emerges from the darkness, her loose, black clothes giving her the appearance of a crow with an injured wing. 'I've been waiting for you,' she says to Maggie. 'Come on the big wheel.'

Maggie shakes her head. 'I don't think so. I'm not great with heights.'

Sirocco actually takes hold of her arm. 'It's perfectly safe. I want to talk to you about Odi. And I don't want anyone else listening in.'

'What? What is it?' Sandra isn't going to be left out.

'Just her.' Sirocco takes Maggie's arm and pulls her along towards the now stationary Ferris wheel.

'Who operates it?' Close up, Maggie can see that several of its lights are missing. It looks bruised, as though it has narrowly escaped from a fight.

'Bear. It's his job in the summer. It's fine, come on.'

The wheel appears decades old. The chairs seem flimsy, nothing more than double swing-seats with fold-up footrests and slot-in-place bars to protect the occupants. Bear is standing beside a red chair. There is a metal hood, which may offer some protection from a downpour, but nothing to guard them from the wind.

'Ladies.'

Maggie opens her mouth to ask about maintenance and realizes that Bear is the sort of man who feeds off the fear of women. She does not want him to see that she is nervous. 'Just once round, I think,' she says, because it will sound as though it is she who is in charge. 'It's going to be cold up at the top.'

She climbs in first. Sirocco gets in after her and the chair rocks. Only Maggie and Sirocco will be riding the wheel, because Bear pulls down the safety bar, locks it in place and goes back to the control cab. The wheel starts to turn and they move forward before swooping up. Almost immediately, the wind gets stronger.

'Odi knew something, didn't she? What did she know?' Barely is their seat a dozen feet from the ground before Sirocco twists round to face her. She is hatless, and her long black hair is flying up and around her head. She smells of patchouli oil.

'Why don't I ask the questions?' They will have to shout the entire conversation. Already, this is feeling like a ridiculous idea. 'A few weeks ago, someone entered my house without permission. Any idea who?'

Sirocco frowns. Her eyebrows are artificially dark, shaped to be two arched wings above her black eyes. They do not match.

'They left a paper rose behind,' Maggie goes on, 'which I'm guessing they stole from Sandra, because I know it originated with Hamish, and they wrote something on the underside of my kitchen table.'

A sly smile creeps over Sirocco's face. 'Did it freak you out, knowing they'd been in your house while you were asleep?'

285

'Oh, I'm used to dealing with crazy people. I'm just not sure what the purpose was.'

They are high above the ground. When Maggie looks directly ahead, she can see nothing of the fairground, just the black sky and some darker shadows where clouds might be. She is beginning to doubt that this woman has anything useful to say to her, and the strain of shouting is starting to tell in her throat. 'Sirocco, I know this group is a bit unorthodox, and frankly I don't care as long as you do no harm, but coming on to my property is harming me and I want to know why it's happening.'

'If it was Odi and Broon, it can't happen any more, can it? They're dead.'

This is going nowhere. If Sirocco was the intruder, she isn't about to admit it. 'I don't think it was them. But it's quite possible that Odi and Broon knew something, or that someone thought they did. Either way, it could have got them killed.'

'Exactly. So what was it?'

The wind is getting stronger. 'I have no idea.' Maggie is beginning to wonder who is doing the interrogating. 'She didn't tell me.'

'You saw her, just before she was killed. You were probably the last person to see her alive.'

An alarm bell is ringing. Not a real one. An alarm in her head. 'How do you know that?' she asks.

'She told you something, didn't she?'

'She told me nothing. I was trying to persuade her to see a hypnotist, but she refused point-blank. I thought she was scared. Sirocco, I thought you had something to tell me. This is just wasting my time and it's freezing up here.'

Maggie twists around, to see that just one chair is higher than theirs. She catches a glimpse of the ground and is surprised by a wave of nausea. She has never suffered from vertigo, in spite of what she told Sirocco earlier, but there is something about being so high, surrounded by so much dark wind, that is throwing her off-kilter.

'I was talking to her,' Sirocco shouts, 'trying to get her confidence. I knew there was something she wasn't telling us. She'd have told me in the end, I know she would.'

'Sirocco, you are neither the police, Hamish's lawyer or a member of his family, it really isn't your place to be interfering like this.'

'What are you saying, that I got Odi and Broon killed?'

'No, of course not.' But how did she know that Maggie and Odi had spoken? Had Sirocco been in Wells that night?

'Maybe you got them killed? Maybe someone saw you talking to them, figured she'd told you too much, so they had to be got rid of.'

'If that's the case, whoever did it will have to kill me too, and I'm still alive.'

Sirocco's black stare deepens and Maggie can practically hear the thoughts behind them. Still alive but at the top of a Ferris wheel, on a dark night. The wind is buffeting this flimsy seat and she is suddenly very conscious of all the joints and rivets, the nuts, bolts and screws that hold this steel seat together. Salt air, sea spray, rain – all have a corrosive effect on metal. How sound is this seat, the structure beneath it? How stupid has she been, agreeing to get on board?

'Maybe you killed them,' Sirocco hisses. 'Maybe you're the killer, and you realized they knew too much. You were the last person to see them alive. You knew where they were. You gave them food, maybe it was drugged. Maybe you didn't go home, maybe you waited till they were asleep and slit their throats.'

This woman may not be entirely sane. Even more alarming is the fact that the wheel seems to have stopped turning. Maggie finds a fixed point on the horizon, the light on a radio mast. She is right. They aren't moving any more.

'I was at home, nearly forty miles away, when the bodies were discovered. I called Detective Sergeant Pete Weston on my landline, so there will be a trace of that call. A woman police constable knocked on my door while I was talking to Sergeant Weston.'

'You had time to get back. They were killed hours before they were found.'

How does she know this?

'The contents of their stomachs were examined during the postmortems,' Maggie says. 'Traces of any drugs would have been present. The pathologist found nothing but alcohol – and they bought that themselves. The police found a Tesco receipt in Odi's purse.'

This last is a lie. The last she heard, the police have no idea where the rum came from, but the wheel has definitely stopped moving and this woman is growing increasingly agitated.

'Sirocco, if you really care about getting Hamish released, then we have to work together. Cooperating with me will achieve much more than flinging wild accusations around. Why has this ride stopped?' Maggie peers over the side, trying to see something below that can explain the cessation of the ride. The boarding platform, some fifty feet below, is empty.

The seat, which is almost certainly not designed for strong winter winds, rocks on its axis. There is a reason why fairgrounds and amusement parks close in winter. Wind and ice play merry hell with safety. When she looks back at Sirocco the woman has another of her maddening smiles plastered across her face.

'Bear stopped it,' she says. 'He won't start it again until he sees my signal.'

'Whatever the signal is, give it now,' Maggie says. 'I won't ask you again.'

She waits. Three, five seconds. Enough. Forcing herself to move, because movement of any sort at this height feels unwise, she tugs off one glove and finds her phone.

Sirocco lunges towards her. Maggie pulls back and the seat swings. She feels a moment of paralysing fear when she realizes she is staring directly at the ground, then the seat rights itself and her phone is tugged from her hand.

'Give me that back.'

Sirocco stretches out her right arm, dangling the phone in mid-air. Her mismatched eyebrows lift as she opens her fingers.

Maggie grips the seat and peers down. There is no one on the ground close enough to hear her shout, and shouting will make her look as though she is panicking.

'Every second we are up here increases the trouble you will be in when we get down,' she says. 'Tell Bear to start the wheel again now.'

'What do you really want with Hamish?'

'We can talk when we're back on the ground.'

'He's in love with me, you know. When he gets out, we're going to be together.'

'Good for you. In which case, you should be doing everything you can to cooperate with his lawyer, instead of putting her life at risk like this.'

'That stupid woman, his mother, she doesn't know anything. I visit him all the time. He writes to me.'

'Then you should know that the only chance he has of getting out of prison alive is if I can find new evidence. I cannot do that stuck at the top of a Ferris wheel. You are being very foolish and making me extremely angry.'

'You say you're his lawyer.'

'I am his lawyer. Get us down from here now.'

'You say that, but you've done nothing. He's no closer to getting out than he was before. You can't do it, can you? You're just stringing him along, making him like you, keeping him to yourself.'

'Be reasonable. I've only been working on his case for a few weeks. The police had months and months.'

'Tell me what you've done. Tell me what you've found out.'

'Absolutely not. That is confidential to my client. Ask him about it, if you're so close.'

'I will. I'll ask him next time I see him.'

'Good. I'm glad that's settled. Can we go down now?'

Sirocco takes hold of the safety bar with one hand and, for a split second, Maggie thinks she is going to force it open. Instead, she keeps her other hand on the back of the seat and starts swinging.

The chairs are designed to rock, it is part of the thrill of the ride, but usually on a warm summer's day. Rocking in the dead of night, in the midst of a strong wind and on equipment that might not be entirely sound, is another matter altogether.

'What did Odi tell you?'

This again? It is hard to speak, rather than gasp. 'Nothing. I wanted her to try hypnosis. She refused and became frightened.'

Not as frightened as Maggie is right now.

'I think you're right,' Maggie says. 'I think she did know something, but she didn't tell me.'

'Who then? Who did she tell?'

'Broon, possibly, but he's dead too.'

'Who else?'

'There was no one else.'

The wheel is moving again. Is she sure? Yes. Oh, thank God. They are no longer at the crest of the wheel, but coming back down the other side. Several people, including one large figure wearing a reflective coat are gathered on the platform below. The seat descends further and she can see the shiny white stripes on a uniformed peaked cap. A police officer is looking up at them.

At her side, Sirocco actually growls with frustration.

'I bloody well told you. That lot are mental.' Pete is waiting for her when she has given her statement. He takes her arm and she thinks other people seem to be deciding her movements this evening. Sirocco persuading her, against her better judgement, to get on to the Ferris wheel, the police constable sent by Pete leading her to a patrol car, the detective who took her statement. And now Pete, steering her out of the back door of the police station. If they keep it up, she may lose the ability to direct her own actions.

'What will happen to her?'

'Sirocco, aka, Sarah Smith?' Pete holds open the door and she steps outside. His car is parked near by. 'We'll probably charge her with assault under the Offences Against the Person Act. That would mean magistrates' court tomorrow, probably Minehead. There's a good chance she'll be released on bail, though, so you might want to think about a restraining order. In you jump.'

'I need to find my own car. I expect it's still at the fairground.'

'It's at your house. I had someone drive it round. Are you going to keep me out here all night?'

She sinks down. The driver's seat groans as he joins her and starts the engine.

'What if I need to talk to her again?'

'You don't.' He is intent on the road, driving too fast, the way police officers invariably do. 'We ran her fingerprints as a matter of course. Turns out they were the ones on that paper rose that we couldn't trace before. Looks like she was the one who came into your house that night, leaving billets-doux under the table.'

290

This is not good news. 'Her fingerprints on the rose establish a link between her and Hamish. They both touched it.'

'She may have stolen it from Sandra Wolfe, but that seems less likely. I'm going to contact Parkhurst in the morning, see if there's any record of Sirocco visiting Wolfe.'

'You think she killed Odi and Broon, don't you?'

'It's not impossible. How would she know you'd spoken to them unless she was in Wells that night?'

'Could a woman have done that? She isn't particularly big or strong.'

'She took them by surprise, in the middle of the night. They'd have been dopey, sluggish, even without the rum they'd drunk. Sneak up behind, grab Broon by his hair. Odi would have been easier. Yeah, I'd say it was possible.'

'Why, though? If she's on Hamish's side, why get rid of the one person who could testify in his favour?'

'There was no way Odi could testify for Wolfe. She was a completely unreliable witness, a good distance away, on a dark night. Wolfe, being guilty, would know her testimony counted for nothing, but thought he could use it to his advantage. By having her killed, he suddenly makes her much more important. Now, we're all asking what she knew.'

'Sounds a bit far-fetched to me.'

He wouldn't be the first dangerous prisoner to use someone on the outside to construct an elaborate defence though, would he?'

'Who are you thinking of?'

'Keith Bellucci and Vanessa Carlton.'

Before his execution, Bellucci was one of the Woodland Stranglers, two brothers who abducted, raped and murdered young women in woods above St Louis in the 1970s.

'Remind me,' she says.

'Carlton met Bellucci while he was on death row. He persuaded her to kill another woman, in the same way he'd killed several, and sprinkle her dead body with his sperm. This was before DNA, so only his blood type could be identified.'

'The plan being that the police would find a fresh body, killed in exactly the same way, apparently by the same perpetrator and conclude they'd got the wrong man locked up. Did it work?'

'Fortunately not. Carlton made a mess of it, the victim got away and she got caught. The romance didn't survive her imprisonment.'

Maggie is still reeling from the news that Sirocco might have been telling the truth when she claimed she was in contact with Hamish. And yet he has denied knowing her. Which of them is lying?

Pete says, 'If Wolfe's defence team – which I guess is you – can establish a connection between the Wolfe murders and what happened to Odi and Broon, then doubt has to be cast on his conviction. You don't need me to tell you that, and Wolfe certainly doesn't.'

'So are you going to charge Sirocco with murder?'

'No evidence as yet. We're searching her flat as we speak. I'm going round there after I drop you off.'

'Can I come?'

'No, you bloody well can't. Oh, while I think of it: Daisy Baron is not on the medical register, so she's not currently practising as a doctor in the UK. Tracking her further isn't going to be that easy after all.'

'I'm honestly not sure why people are fixating on Daisy. It was twenty years ago. She's irrelevant.'

They drive in silence for some seconds.

'Hold on,' Maggie says, 'if Sirocco killed Odi and Broon at Hamish's instigation, what was all that about tonight? I'm on his side. Why would she attack me?'

'That engine is not firing on all cylinders. She doesn't necessarily see you as someone essential to Hamish. In her twisted brain, she's all he needs. No, you're the opposition, with your wacky blue hair and your cute-as-a-china-doll face, and your unlimited access to him in prison. You're the love rival.'

'*He loves me*, scrawled in fake blood under my kitchen table?'

'Exactly.'

'I can't believe Hamish had Odi and Broon killed. I just can't.'

He shakes his head. 'Oh, Maggie. I really hoped you were smarter than that.'

Chapter 88

NEXT MORNING, the phone wakes her. Maggie knows it is Pete before she looks at the screen.

'Don't say I never give you good news.'

'What?'

'I got through to Parkhurst first thing. Deputy Governor did me a favour. There is no record of a Sirocco Silverwood or Sarah Smith ever visiting Wolfe in prison. He checked phone logs as well, and email traffic. He mainly contacts you and his mum, never Ms Smith. The relationship is a fantasy on Sirocco's part. That doesn't make her any less dangerous, by the way.'

A weight has fallen away. 'So she didn't get the rose from him?'

'Can't see how. The other partial prints on it could be his, but not conclusively. She could have nicked it from his mum. Hell, she could be into origami herself.'

'Thank you, Pete. Did you find anything at her flat?'

'Yep. We found her mobile phone. She was the one texting you that night – you know, the old *he loves me, he loves me not* malarkey. And she has use of a mate's car from time to time, so she could, in theory, have followed us all to Wells. Nothing to tie her to the Odi and Broon murders yet, but we'll keep looking. We can keep her inside for today, at least.'

'Pete, I didn't thank you for last night. For sending that constable round to the fairground.'

'I won't do it again.'

She is smiling. 'Yes, you will.'

'No, I won't.'

'Thank you.' She puts the phone down gently. 'You will,' she says to herself.

Chapter 89

HAMISH SAYS, 'I'm glad you're OK, but I don't want you taking any more risks for me.'

'I think I can safely promise you to avoid poorly maintained fairground rides in the middle of winter. And, who knows, your favourite detective might find something at Sarah Smith's flat that links her to Odi and Broon's murders.' Maggie stops, wondering what could realistically be found by the police at Sirocco's flat. And whether she might be a possible suspect in the Wolfe murders. 'You might want to tell your parents to steer clear of her, though,' she says. 'Just in case she gets bail.'

He reaches down below the table.

'Something I thought you might be interested in.' Hamish is holding out a soft-covered book, A4 size, about a centimetre thick. 'I had Mum bring it in. It's our yearbook from Magdalen College. Here you go.'

He turns it to face her. She is looking at a photograph of students gathered for the Commem Ball. It is early in the evening, because the sky is still light and the revellers pristine and fresh. It is the same photograph that, cropped down, was used by the media during Hamish's trial. Hamish is in white tie, the most formal of evening dress, and is with a group of similarly dressed men and glamorous young women. The woman on his arm, though, is different from the others.

Her hair is dark and thick, swept up on to the top of her head. It will curl down past her shoulders when loose. Her eyes are big and brown. Her nose large and angular, her teeth slightly overlapping. Her skin is lily pale. She's wearing black, as large women often do, but the fine fabric flows over her limbs and torso like a silk waterfall. The neckline is a deep V-shape, drawing attention to her large breasts and cleavage. The sleeves are long and slim, made from black lace. Tucked behind one ear is a large, white flower.

'Daisy,' Maggie says, feeling a pang of deep sadness. 'She was gorgeous.'

Hamish sounds a little defensive. 'Yes, she was.'

She looks him in the eye. 'You were a fool.'

He doesn't disagree. 'So many times, I've asked myself, is it too late for Daisy and me. If I were to find her again. What do you think?'

She opens her mouth to say that she has no opinion on the subject, that she couldn't care less about Daisy, but can't do it. His eyes are holding her. They are locked in some weird staring competition. She is trying to look away, just can't quite—

The door shakes in its frame as something hard and heavy slams against it. Wolfe is faster than she, jumping immediately to his feet. He takes the two strides that bring him to the door and peers through the inset window. The door is banged again. Directly outside, someone is swearing.

'Fuck!' Wolfe spins round. 'Get in the corner. Now!'

She hears the words, but they don't quite make it to the part of her brain that directs movement, because nothing happens.

There is a fight going on outside. She can hear punches, grunts, the rasp of breath. In the distance, maybe on another floor, there is more noise. Wolfe is pressed right up against the window, as though trying to block the view out. Or the view in.

'Maggie.' Wolfe is whispering, low and urgent. 'Get out of sight, now.'

'What's happening?' It is a stupid question. She knows what is happening, can hear it. The guard outside is being beaten up. She can hear the grunts and gasps of someone in pain, the solid thud of heavy bodies crashing around. She has no idea how many are out there. It could be two, or a dozen. She and Hamish are locked in though, aren't they? They are safe? She pushes her chair back.

One last loud exclamation outside and silence falls. Hamish gestures again for her to move and this time she does, darting to the corner of the room.

Three loud bangs on the door and a shout. 'Who's in there?'

Hamish's grip tightens on the handle. The door is locked. She is repeating it to herself like a mantra. The door is always locked. It's standard procedure. When she's ready to leave, she always hears the guard slide back the bolts and turn the key.

The same bolts that are being slid open now.

The door is still locked. The door is still locked.

With the key held by a guard who is likely unconscious or even dead.

'Wolfe! Is that you in there?'

Move on, she is praying, wreak your havoc elsewhere. Above all, do not search the guard's unconscious body. Don't find the—

The key is being turned. The door pushes open a fraction. Wolfe shoves it closed and leans against it. The colour of his face turns quickly from near white to bright pink. He is breathing in short, angry bursts. She should help, surely? Her strength is better than nothing.

'Maggie, get on the phone.'

Angry that she didn't think of this sooner, she finds her phone and makes the call. Someone is kicking the door now and Wolfe is losing ground.

A voice on the phone tells her that the situation is known to the police and a response is under way. 'How long? How long before you get here?'

She doesn't hear the answer. She has dropped her phone at the sight of Wolfe's boot-clad feet sliding along the floor. The door is opening and she can see a bent knee behind it, straining forward.

With a sudden change of tack, Wolfe leaps from the door and it crashes open. She darts from her corner and stands behind him.

'Who've you got in here, Hamish?' The voice is South London, a white man, she thinks, somewhere in his thirties or forties. Not old, not young.

'Somebody in here smells a fuck of a lot nicer than you do, Wolfe.' Midlands accent. Older.

Someone hawks and spits. She can see the bloody gob of spittle on the tiled floor. Three pairs of feet.

'Turn around, gentlemen. Walk away.' Wolfe does not sound terrified, but he wouldn't, would he? He is one of them. She is the prey.

On either side of Wolfe, the jackals come into view.

'Hello, Bluey.' The Londoner grins at her with the sunken jaw of a mouth that has few remaining teeth. He is smaller, thinner, older than Wolfe and alone might not be a threat. The other two, leering at her from the other side, are younger and bigger.

'Out you go, Hamish. We'll look after your visitor for you.'

'Not happening, guys.'

The smell of them is stronger and their voices louder. It is as though they are leaning in towards her. One of them keeps sucking in air, noisily, as though he is feeding on the smell of her.

'I spoke to the police before you broke in.' Years of practice keeps her voice steady in difficult situations. 'They know what's going on here. I wouldn't be surprised if they're already in the building.'

'Oh, I think we've got a bit of time.' The man is actually unfastening the top button of his jeans.

'Hang on.' This from one of the others. 'Who says you go first?'

'Nobody's going first,' says Wolfe. 'The man who touches my lawyer, who puts my appeal at risk, I will come for with a razor. I will slice open his abdomen and I will pull out his intestinal tract. I will do this at night, so that no one finds him till morning, after he has spent several hours dying in agony. I will do this to each and every one who jeopardizes my chance of getting out of here. Now, does anyone think I'm bluffing?'

No answer, but she has a sense of the pack being less sure of itself. Hamish thrusts out his hand.

'Keys.' He steps forward, taking the fight to them. 'Who's got them?'

'Come on, Wolfe, ten minutes?' The man from the Midlands is wheedling now, like a kid trying to negotiate a bedtime reprieve. 'We'll let you go first.'

'Give me the keys and fuck off out of here.'

There is an unspoken signal between them, then the leader mutters something. They turn. One of them has left. Two are out of the door. They are going, they are actually going. Maggie stares at the doorway, willing it to be empty. The third leaves, with one last obscene gesture, a thrusting of the hips in her direction and a wiggling of a fur-covered tongue.

Elsewhere in the prison, the fighting is still going on. Overhead, along the corridor she can hear yelling, swearing.

'Hold up, you're not going anywhere.' She has been making for the door, Hamish is holding her back. 'Listen to me. Maggie, are you listening?'

297

'I have to get out.' She twists round, grasps his arms. 'Listen, they're everywhere. That lot could come back. They'll tell others. I'm not safe here.'

'This is the only place you're safe. I'm going to lock you in.'

'No!' She can see no logic in this. Lock her in here with these animals? She will fight him if she has to. She tries to pull away, he holds her fast.

'Maggie, until this calms down, you need to be where no one can get at you. I'll lock you in and nobody will get the key from me, I promise you.'

She is shaking her head.

'I swear you'll be safe.' He is pulling away from her now. He leaves her in the centre of the room and makes for the door.

'Hamish, don't leave me.' Maggie has never imagined anything so pathetic could come out of her mouth.

He turns, one hand on the door. 'I can't lock the door from the inside. We're sitting ducks here. I can't fight them off for ever.'

'I know. I still don't want you to go.'

She sees him unsure of himself, doubtful. Then he seems to step forward. Except he hasn't moved, she is the one who crossed the distance between them.

'Thank you,' she says.

Doors are slamming. Something hard and heavy is being banged against metal. People are coming.

She feels his face reaching down towards hers. She tells herself that he is taking advantage, as all male prisoners would, of a few minutes alone with a woman and that she is allowing it because she might just owe him her life. She tells herself this, as his arms wrap around her, and every muscle in his body seems to tense, and all the while she knows she is a fraud, that she is the one who will kiss him.

She stands on tiptoe as their lips meet.

Her arms cup themselves around his shoulders and she loves the hard play of muscle she can feel under the cotton fabric. Her fingers play with the rough cotton, clutching it into fists, stretching it out like elastic and she knows she is grasping at his clothing because she doesn't quite dare to do it to his flesh.

In another universe, someone screams.

'Aw, Christ almighty.' Wolfe has let her go, stepped back away from her. She is trembling. The reaction of her body to the threat of rape was nothing compared to this.

He bends forward and kisses her one last time. 'Keep out of sight. Keep quiet. Someone will come.'

She is alone. She hears the door close, the key turn, then Hamish's footsteps run lightly away down the corridor. She walks to the corner of the room, the one that cannot be seen from the door and sinks to the floor. She waits.

Chapter 90

PETE WALKS INTO THE CID ROOM to find a group of detectives gathered around Liz's computer screen.

'What've I missed?' he asks, heading to his own desk.

'Riot at Parkhurst,' Sunday tells him.

The coffee Pete has brought with him overspills as he puts the cup down too quickly. 'What are you looking at?' he calls over.

Sunday names the police intranet site but it takes several seconds to load up. 'Someone fill me in?' he says.

'Kicked off about noon,' Sunday tells him. 'Outside normal visiting hours. The place is still in lockdown. No one going in or out.'

Pete double-checks the date, although he hardly needs to. He knows that Maggie is visiting Wolfe today. As a lawyer, she won't need to stick to visiting hours.

The site loads and he keys in *HMP Parkhurst*.

'Can anyone give me an update on Parkhurst?' Latimer has joined them now. 'Nobody there's answering the phones.'

'It's saying here the prison staff have regained control, sir,' Sunday says. 'The Governor's quoted as saying it couldn't be described as a riot, just an hour or so of disturbance, and that's under control now.'

The page Pete is looking at has been assembled in a hurry. The header tells him it is the official intranet page of HMP Isle of Wight. Side menu bars list procedures, staff members, contact telephone numbers, publicly available documents and others that are confidential to the police. The main item on the home page, though, is a news feature.

Fighting broke out on H wing of Parkhurst Barracks at 1157 hours today and quickly escalated to spread to B and D wings. The prison is still low-staffed after the Christmas break and staff were momentarily caught off guard.

A state of emergency was declared and assistance from the local police service requested. Order was restored at 1323 hours.

Several inmates and three prison staff have required medical treatment. One officer and two inmates have been taken to the local hospital. The ringleaders have been placed in solitary confinement.

Several visitors were on the premises when the disturbances broke out. None of them were affected and all have since been escorted away from the prison.

Prison management are working on the theory that the disturbance was deliberately orchestrated, and that it could even have been intended as some form of distraction. All prisoners, though, have been accounted for.

Pete taps out a phone text.

You OK? You at Parkhurst?

Maggie's response takes four minutes.

I'm fine. Just been allowed to leave. Trying to catch the next ferry. Were any of the inmates hurt, do you know?

Liz has left her own desk and wandered over to join him. Pete holds up his phone to let her read the exchange. She does so, then turns away without a word and goes back to her own computer. Pete passes on the information he has to Maggie. She doesn't reply.

Chapter 91

WHEN MAGGIE UNLOCKS her door her hands are still shaking, just as they have been for hours now. The day just gone exists for her in a series of freeze-frames: the door of the interview room opening to admit armed police; being escorted out of Parkhurst while looking around every corner for one face; giving a statement at the Isle of Wight police station; declining medical attention; insisting on leaving as soon as she could; steering her car on to the ferry.

In the hours since Wolfe locked her in the interview room, she has existed in a mental vacuum. She cannot think about what has happened. Or where she goes from here.

Another text message arrives. Pete is trying to get in touch with her, has been all afternoon and evening. She types out a reply:

Going straight to bed. I'll be in touch.

Later that evening, the phone rings. For several seconds she stares at it from across the room. It will say, *number withheld,* because calls from prison always do.

'It's me,' he says.

'I know.' She sighs down the line.

'Are you OK?'

'I'm fine.' She is not. She has never been further from fine and she knows that he knows it.

'Good. When will I see you again?'

'I'm not sure.' She struggles for something appropriate to say. 'I'm getting to the end of my search of the industrial estates. Just a few more to check. If I find anything, I'll be in touch right away.'

'Then I'll have to hope you do.'

Silence falls again.

'What happened today, Maggie?' he asks her.

He isn't talking about the riot. 'It was the shock,' she says. 'I wasn't thinking straight.'

'I wasn't thinking at all. That's the effect you have on me.'

A lump is solidifying in her throat. She feels an urge to slam down the receiver, to end the call. At the same time, she wants it to go on for ever.

'It can't happen again,' she manages. 'I am not one of your prison groupies. I can't be your lawyer and some sort of screwed-up girlfriend.'

His voice drops to a whisper. 'So be my lawyer. Get me out of here. Then we'll talk.'

She presses the receiver close to her mouth and remembers the warm, plump lips she held there just hours earlier. She longs for him to say something more. Just one more thing. And then he does.

'There is no room in my head for anything but you, Maggie Rose.'

Wolfe gets just four minutes. Everyone needs the phone tonight. Families will have seen reports about the riot on the news and will be anxious to talk to loved ones. The queue stretches down the corridor. He hands the receiver over to the next man in line and makes his way back to his room. Crusher is waiting for him, his narrow grey eyes gleaming.

Wolfe looks him in the eye. 'So, did anybody get hurt?'

'Couple of bruises. Split lips. Some guys will be in solitary for a few days but they'll live. Work all right?'

Wolfe thinks back to the terrified woman in his arms. He remembers her arms going round his neck, her lips pressing against his. He holds up a hand to high-five the other bloke and grins. 'Yeah. Good job, mate. I owe you.'

Chapter 92

The Sunday Times Magazine, Sunday, 17 August 2014

ONE DAY, ONE LIFETIME

Solicitor Rebecca Singer, who married her client, convicted murderer Jonathan Evans, in 2012, describes her typical day.

I get up early, and go out running before my son wakes at about 6 a.m. I find I need this regular discipline now that so much of my life is out of my control. I'm home in time to fix myself a fresh juice breakfast and then Jack, two, is up and it's non-stop until I drop him off at nursery.

Jonathan tries to ring in the mornings. A lot of the other inmates sleep late, or just don't get moving too quickly, so early in the day is when he has most chance of getting to a phone. We talk for ten to fifteen minutes and I always make sure he and Jack exchange at least a couple of words. Jack needs to know the sound of his father's voice.

I keep a list of topics by the phone, on a small blackboard. These might be TV programmes I've watched, books I've read, current affairs that have interested me, even the spat I had with a woman in Waitrose. When you know you only have ten minutes to talk, the pressure to think of something to say can be enormous. I find I do most of the talking – I guess my life is so much more varied than his – but I make a point of being interested in the minutiae of his day, too.

Jack goes to nursery at 9 a.m. and then it's a short drive to my offices in town. I get involved in most areas of criminal law – filing cases, investigation, visiting police stations, taking witness statements, liaising with the court, etc. – but most of my time is spent on appeals and that involves a lot of paperwork and research. I visit prisons from time to time, but never HMP Wandsworth where Jonathan is currently. That would be a potential conflict of interest. Most of my clients know nothing about my private life and I like to keep it that way.

Jack and I get home at about six and he's usually very tired, so we just watch a bit of TV before it's time for his bath and bed. There is a photograph beside his bed of his dad and me on our wedding day. I had a friend Photoshop it so that you can't really tell it was taken inside a prison. I always sit with Jack until he falls asleep. Friends tell me I'm creating problems for myself down the line doing this, but Jonathan sits and looks at our photograph at exactly this time too. It is our time together as a family.

People often assume that Jack was conceived before Jonathan was convicted, but Jonathan and I met and married before we thought about having a family. HMP Wandsworth doesn't allow conjugal visits, but as Jonathan's solicitor I'm allowed time alone with him. We try not to take advantage of the system, but at the end of the day, we're two people in love.

Evening is when I work for Jonathan. I manage his website, answer mail on his behalf, post blogs and Facebook stories, and of course I'm working on his appeal all the time. I write to him, too, putting down my thoughts, dreams, memories, both good and bad. I've discovered the incredible emotional punch that can be packed inside a good letter. It is important for me to find ways in which our unusual relationship works better than more conventional ones, and in this regard I feel we have the edge. Communicating via written correspondence really intensifies the level of our connection. There are couples that spend hours together every day who don't have the intimacy that Jonathan and I share.

People ask me how I do this, how long I can carry on with this half-life but, knowing Jonathan, there can be no alternative for me. And it's really not so bad. I speak to him, write to him, most days. I see him every couple of weeks. He's not there to carry out the rubbish or take the lid off the marmalade jar, but I know I'm in his thoughts every waking hour. He thinks of no other woman but me. I'm as sure of his love as any woman can be.

People ask me if I feel my life is on hold. I understand them thinking that way but the answer is no. My life might be unconventional, my family certainly is, and of course I hope things will be different in future. For now, though, I wouldn't have it any other way.

(*Maggie Rose: case file 64/701 Hamish Wolfe*)

Chapter 93

'PETE, MAGGIE ROSE on the phone for you.'

Pete is on his way back from the loo, having stopped off at the coffee machine. It's two days since the Parkhurst riot, and this will be the first time he's spoken to her.

'Hi, Maggie.'

'I think I've found the office the killer used. The computer is still in it. I'm there now.'

It takes a second for the news to sink in, then he's looking around to see who else is in the room. 'Where? Where are you?'

She names a small industrial estate on the outskirts of Bristol's south side.

'Maggie, I can't just – what makes you think you've got the right place?'

'It's a one-room office with private toilet and kitchen. Taken in the name of a company called PCG Ltd, which doesn't exist. I checked. The rent's paid up until the middle of next year, but nobody's been near the place for months. We know that because a load of junk mail's built up just inside the door. I'm with the caretaker of the site. He has a spare set of keys, but we haven't been inside yet.'

He's trying to think. And to get Liz's attention. 'OK, I'll try and have someone pop round in the next few days.'

'I thought you'd say that. The security system on the gate involves the guard keeping a record of people going in and out of the estate. It's in case of an emergency evacuation. They need to know which units are occupied and who's in each one.'

'And?'

'They don't keep CCTV footage for more than three months, and they don't take car registrations, but the logbooks go back three years. The office was used regularly, right up until the middle of November 2013. That's two weeks before Wolfe was arrested. No one has been near it since.'

306

Pete sits a little more upright on the desk. The telltale symptoms of excitement are kicking in. Elevated heartbeat? Check. Damp under-arms? Check. Tight feeling in his chest? All present and correct. 'If that's true, it points to Wolfe being the tenant.'

Her voice hardens. 'No, it points to someone making it look as though Hamish was the tenant. Are you coming down?'

He fakes a sigh. 'I suppose so.'

It takes nearly two hours to assemble a team, but Maggie is waiting in her car when he pulls up outside Unit 14 on the Wynchwood Estate. Two hours in the cold have taken their toll on her appearance. Her face is pinched, and almost seems to be reflecting the blue of her hair. She gets out and stands by her car, expecting him to approach her. He doesn't. He concentrates on the building. Everything he's looking at, she'll already have checked out. He can't afford to miss anything.

Unit 14 is in a block of red-brick offices. There is just one door, on the front of the building; 14a is on the ground floor, with an identical room, 14b, above it. There are windows at ground level, but blinds cover them.

From somewhere nearby, a thin, dark-haired man appears. Maggie joins him and they approach.

'This is Hector,' Maggie says. 'He manages the estate.'

Pete stretches out his hand, shows his warrant card with the other. 'Good to meet you, Hector. Do you have an office where we can talk?' He turns around to see the crime scene investigators have arrived and are unloading equipment from their van. 'Maggie, I'd like you to stay in your car, please. Guys, no one goes in there but you.'

Turning his back on Maggie, Pete follows Hector to a nearby build-ing, where the manager has made a small, windowless room his home. He examines the visitors' log and double-checks what Maggie has already told him about CCTV footage.

'What about bills? Electricity? Internet connection?'

Hector has a foreign accent, but his grasp of English suggests a bet-ter education than his job requires. 'Electricity is included in the rent, up to a certain amount. Phone lines, internet, all that sort of thing is the tenant's responsibility.'

That means there could be bills. A paper trace. Although someone going to this amount of trouble will probably have planned for that. 'Did you ever see anyone going in there?'

Hector thinks for a moment. 'A lot of people come and go. You could ask security, but the lady already did and the guard wasn't with us this time last year.'

'Have you been in the room in question? Recently?'

Hector shakes his head. 'I've never been in it. I offered to show it to the lady, but she said we should wait for you. What do you think is in there?'

The look on the manager's face suggests he's hoping for a body, a stash of stolen goods at the very least.

'Probably nothing.' His radio crackles into life. 'Weston.'

'You need to get down here, Pete.' It is the head of the investigation team. 'I think your colourful friend could be on to something.'

Hector's ears are visibly flapping. Pete steps outside. 'What?'

'First up, no fingerprints anywhere in the room. Not a one that we've found so far, which is suspicious in itself. More than that, though, we fired up the computer. Maggie suggested we use the password *Daisy*.'

Pete swears under his breath. 'She's there? Why is she in there?'

'She isn't. She's hovering in the doorway. Anyway, it worked. This is it, Pete. The computer that was used to stalk those women. There's a Facebook account, email, the lot. We're packing it up.'

Pete sits in his car, facing the building where a one-room industrial unit has become a crime scene. He is on the phone.

'They're taking the computer out now.' He watches it being carried out to a waiting van on its way to a facility where geniuses who look like teenagers will strip it bare. Back inside the building, the investigators continue to comb the small, square room and the smaller kitchen and lavatory.

Several yards down the road, Maggie sits in her car. She is taking photographs, occasionally making notes on a laptop.

'We're going to have to tell Latimer,' says Liz.

'Soon as we know anything for sure.' The last thing he needs is Latimer poncing up here like some bloody great drama queen, demanding answers that nobody can give him. 'It still points to Wolfe, Liz. It's in the right location. The password. And anyone else would have closed it down by now.'

Liz doesn't argue.

Pete looks over at Maggie's car. For a second, they seem to make eye contact. Then the investigators appear in the doorway once more, this time carrying the office desk, wrapped in a protective covering. It goes into the van, as does the chair. The carpet will come next, anything moveable from the kitchen and toilet, even the light fittings and blinds.

'We have to talk to Latimer,' Liz says again. 'As soon as you get back.'

'I know. We will.'

Pete is momentarily distracted by the sight of the grey carpet being carried out. Then the head of the investigation team heads over and Pete winds down the window, letting in a blast of cold air. The technician holds up a clear plastic evidence bag. 'Little bonus surprise for you, Pete.'

In the bag is a pen. A cheap, plastic biro, without its lid. Blue ink. The technician leans in, as though trying to soak up some of the warmth from the car.

'Tucked between the edge of the carpet and the skirting board,' he says. 'Of course, it might be nothing to do with the last occupant. It could have been there for years. But pens tend to have fingerprints. Especially ones that have been forgotten about.'

Chapter 94

LATIMER NODS HIS HEAD, his eyes on the neatly written notes in front of him. He points a pencil at Pete. 'So, if I understand it correctly, we have a city the size of Bristol, not to mention Bath and their various suburbs, small towns and villages, and this woman homes in on a crucial piece of evidence on the strength of a hunch? Did Wolfe tell her where to look?'

'Well, whoever rented and furnished the office in the first place would have a head start when it comes to finding it again,' says Pete.

'No fingerprints, hairs on the carpet? Anything to tie it to Wolfe?'

'Not so far, sir,' Liz tells him. 'But the team are still looking.'

Latimer sighs, then spins his computer screen round so that Pete and Liz can see it. 'Guys,' he says. 'Do you ever think there's maybe something not quite right about this Maggie Rose character?'

Pete glances sideways at Liz as he pulls his chair closer. Latimer has been looking at Maggie's website. 'What do you mean?' he asks.

'The whole blue hair business, for one thing. I mean, who dyes their hair blue?'

'What women do with their hair is a mystery to me,' says Pete. 'I think it's a mystery to most blokes, to be honest.'

'Exactly. So you're not asking the questions you should be asking. Liz, on the other hand, I would have expected more from.'

Liz opens her eyes a little wider. 'OK, sir,' she says. 'What should we be asking?'

'When people dye their hair unnatural colours, it's for a reason, usually a desire to be noticed. I mean, everyone notices bright turquoise hair, don't they?'

'I guess.' Pete can't look at Liz any more.

'And yet Maggie Rose is a recluse. She doesn't do interviews, she never appears in court. No pictures on her website. Hardly anybody meets her unless she's working directly with them. Why would someone who makes a point of avoiding attention dye her hair such a noticeable colour?'

'I give up, sir,' says Liz. 'Why?'

In response, Latimer stands up and walks to the window. 'When I was a kid, I was fascinated by magicians,' he says. 'Even the cheesy, crap ones you get at parties. I really wanted to know how they did their tricks and I could never spot it. And then, when I got older, I read books about magic. No real magician will reveal his secrets, but what they all seem to have in common is the use of distraction.'

A short silence.

'Distraction is the magician's way of diverting the audience's attention from what he doesn't want them to see,' Liz says.

Latimer turns back to them. 'Exactly. So, what I'm asking myself is, if the wacky hair and the sapphire eyes and the bright-coloured clothes are a distraction, what is it that she doesn't want us to see?'

Liz and Pete look at each other. She gives him a small, almost imperceptible nod. He turns back to his boss.

'Sir,' he says, 'we've got something to tell you.'

Chapter 95

My darling Hamish,

Sometimes I feel that this winter will go on for ever. That I will never see blue sky again, that the world will forever be cloaked in dull, damp cloud.

Sometimes I feel that I will be cold for ever. That my limbs will quiver with chill, that my skin will shrink from the frozen air and that my hair will hang, dull and dank, down my rigid neck.

My bones ache with cold. My heart bleeds from the wounds of a thousand icy needles. The corpse that will claim me one day is hard upon my heels, is snapping at me, hungry before its time.

I'm dying slowly, here. Only you. Only your skin, your body, your kiss, can bring me back.

I need you, Hamish. And I'm running out of time.

Me

PROPERTY OF AVON AND SOMERSET POLICE. Ref: 544/45.2 Hamish Wolfe.

Chapter 96

WOLFE IS RELAXING, lowering his heartbeat, settling his breathing, the way he once did before a difficult operation, before a long run, before taking the plane up. He has a towel around his neck, so anyone glancing in will think he's just finished one of his exercise sessions. He glances at his watch, even though he's told himself he mustn't and swears that he won't do it again. He knows exactly what the time is. Calm is what he needs to be right now.

A shadow blocks the doorway. One of the guards is looking in.

'Guv.' Wolfe nods his head, once. Just enough for politeness.

'Dismantling the grotto are we, lads?'

The paper chains have all been taken down and lie in coiled heaps like copulating snakes on Phil's bunk.

'Twelfth night, Guv,' Wolfe says. 'Unlucky to keep them up any longer.'

'Twelve what?'

'Twelfth of January,' Phil pipes up. 'The date you're supposed to take your Christmas decorations down or the bad pixies will come and get you. Or something like that.'

Wolfe doesn't let himself smile. The screws don't like smiling inmates. It always makes them think they're missing something. Which, of course, they usually are.

'Yeah, well. Make sure they go in the bin. Frigging things are a fire hazard.'

The guard leaves, his footsteps clipping down the corridor, the door closing in his wake. Wolfe gets up and opens it again before pressing one hand against his trouser pocket to feel the reassuring hard lump of steel in there.

Across the corridor Mr Sahid is watching him. Sahid looks at his watch. His eyebrows rise. Wolfe lets his head drop, maintaining eye contact, then lifts it again.

Sahid throws back his head and yells something in Arabic.

A second later, two men appear from nearby cells. In a movement so slick, so coordinated, it looks rehearsed, they vault over the rail and drop. Immediately a whistle blows and shouts are heard. A guard comes racing. Inmates crowd out of their cells.

Wolfe turns to find Phil directly behind him. He bends his head to let his cellmate hang several coils of paper chain around his neck.

'Good luck, mate,' Phil tells him.

The two men, who are young and very fit, who have never drunk alcohol in their lives and who have trained at a special gym for Muslim men since they were sixteen years old, haven't dropped far. Landing on the net that prevents the upper corridors from being used as suicide launching pads, they are now using it to stage an impromptu circus act.

Wolfe, still draped in paper chains, makes his way along the corridor, peering over the railing, as though seeking a vantage point for the entertainment below. Men are yelling encouragement, guards are insisting that everyone goes back to their cells right now. The men ignore them. This is fun enough to risk a cuff on the back of the head.

The two men are holding hands and leaping high into the air. One of them somersaults over the other. As he lands, one foot goes through the net and the crowd applauds as though it's just seen the best stunt ever.

Wolfe reaches the door. Men are pouring in from the next hallway and it will be locked soon. Already the cry of 'lockdown' is sounding along the block and that is the signal for the fighting to start. Wolfe picks up his pace. He is running by the time he gets to the end of the second corridor. This door is locked but Wolfe hasn't wasted his time in the metal fabrication workshop. The key he's fashioned over several weeks won't win any design prizes but it's been tried and tested and doesn't fail him now.

When he arrives at the gym Wolfe throws the towel over the security camera just as he does every time fight club takes place. Any guard seeing the camera black out at this time of day will assume a malfunction. He will investigate, but not while a full-scale riot is taking place in one of the blocks. Wolfe has about five minutes, by his own calculation, and that should be enough.

Time enough to cut through the black masking tape holding together the steel frame of the five-a-side goalposts, so that the pieces fall apart where Wolfe has previously sawn through them; also in the metal fabrication workshop. He now has six, six-feet-long tubes and three shorter tubes of just over a foot long. The longer tubes have small, black eyelets screwed into them at eighteen-inch intervals. Wolfe took a risk, attaching the eyelets in advance, but it has paid off. No one has spotted them and their being pre-attached will save valuable time. When he gets outside he will slot the long poles together, using four clamps made from doubled-over aluminium cans. These he has been storing in the canvas bag that, even in the dim light of the gym, is still the blue of Maggie's hair.

Also in the bag are the nuts and bolts that will fix the three shorter poles to the two, assembled, longer ones and hold them in position.

The steps of the ladder are made from reinforced wire netting, cut from the football nets that Wolfe found in the canvas bag. Alone in their cell at night, he and Phil have cut and twisted the netting into ten, very strong, lengths of wire rope and these he will fasten on to the eyelets of the poles to form steps. For the past two weeks, the 'steps' have been hidden inside the paper chains that have adorned their cell. The discarded paper lies scattered around the gym floor now like a snowstorm seen by someone on psychedelic drugs.

With Phil's help, and with a number of other prisoners and guards who owe him favours turning a blind eye, Wolfe has fashioned a ladder capable of getting him to the top of the outer fence and down the other side. His heart is pumping hard now, but this happens a lot to a man who is in peak physical condition and he needs the rush of adrenalin he knows it will bring.

He runs from the gym.

Chapter 97

'WHAT IS THIS, a movie trailer?' Latimer leans closer to Sunday's laptop. At the windows, Liz is pulling down blinds so that the four officers can better see the frozen image that has appeared on the screen. 'A home movie?' There is something about the photography, maybe the lack of light, the positioning of the furniture in the room, that has an amateurish feel to it.

'We found the videotape under her bath in the en suite,' says Sunday. 'Given that we were there, at her invitation, investigating a trespass, it should be admissible. I copied it there and then, which wasn't easy, but I managed to get the right equipment biked over. The cover is a copy too, but pretty close to the original. Once I got back to the station, I transferred it on to our hard drive.'

Latimer lifts the fake video cassette that Sunday has mocked up. It is plain, the sort bought in multi-packs to store home movies. The date on it is 15 January 1996. A title has been handwritten.

Daisy in Chains.

'Where's the original?' Latimer asks.

'Back under the bath,' Pete tells him.

'So, how did she get hold of it?' Latimer says.

'Just what we asked ourselves,' Pete says. 'One possibility is that Wolfe told her where to find it.'

'Except Hamish has always insisted there was only ever one copy made,' says Liz, 'and that Daisy took it with her when she left Oxford.'

'He's a liar, we know that already,' says Latimer, but his face says he is less sure of himself. 'Play it,' he says.

Sunday clicks on the Play arrow and Latimer, Pete, Sunday and Liz are looking at a small, simply furnished room. The desk and computer, the books on the shelves, the single bed, all suggest a student bedroom. The lights are kept low, but there must be a dozen or more candles dotted around the room. The counterpane on the bed is dark red, speckled

316

with something white. Petals. There are flowers in the room, several vases of them, all containing the same flower.

In the centre of the picture stand a man and a woman, kissing. The woman's hands are on the man's shoulders, one drifts lower to rest on the small of his back. The man is wearing jeans and has his back to the camera. He appears tall, broad shouldered, with dark hair that curls down past the nape of his neck. He holds the woman by the head, his hands tangling in long, dark hair. The woman is naked.

'That's Wolfe,' whispers Latimer.

Wolfe, a much younger Wolfe, has moved behind the woman now. A good head taller, he nuzzles the side of her hair as he runs his hands the length of her ample body, over her large breasts, her pillow of a stomach.

'And Daisy Baron,' says Pete. 'We found her in yearbook photographs of Hamish and his Magdalen set.'

'He's positioning her for the camera,' Latimer says.

Pete nods. The woman – Daisy – a girl really, hardly more than eighteen, doesn't know the camera is there. There is no hint of self-consciousness about the way she leans into her boyfriend, parts her thighs to let him touch her.

'What's she got on her head?' Latimer asks.

'Flowers,' says Liz, whose face is looking pinched. 'He's made her a daisy chain.'

Pete can see the thought process taking place in Latimer's head, the same that went through his own when he first saw the video. *Daisy in Chains.* Daisy chains.

'Shit,' Latimer says. He looks at his watch. 'We haven't time for this. Fast-forward it.'

As the computer flicks through the frames, the four officers see an odd, speeded-up version of a couple having sex. It reminds Pete of 'What the Butler Saw' machines on the pier when he was a kid. Cards attached to a circular frame, shown quickly to give the impression of movement. They watch Wolfe put a garland of flowers, another frigging daisy chain, around the girl's neck, see him leading her to the bed, bending over her, lying on top of her. They see her plump thighs wrap around his waist.

The footage, run at normal speed, might last twenty-five, thirty minutes. This is no fervent, soon-over student fumbling, Wolfe is putting on a show for the camera. The team flick through it in five minutes.

It's over. Wolfe lies flat on the narrow bed, Daisy by his side, cuddled up against him. The flowers, crumpled and bruised, are on Wolfe's head. He's grinning, one arm flung up over the pillow, the other around his girlfriend.

'Not what we've been led to believe,' says Latimer.

'Nope,' says Pete. 'No chains. No S & M. Nobody dies. Just a young couple in love.'

'You'd be very pissed off, though, if you thought your boyfriend had shared it with the world,' says Liz. 'If you thought he'd just been using you.'

Latimer nods his head. 'OK, what else?'

Chapter 98

MAGGIE WANDERS FROM ROOM to room, checking door and window locks, thinking of the signs that precede a great storm. The swell on the ocean gets higher, the waves more rapid. At the same time, clouds flee from the sky, barometers hold steady and the wind drops.

Nothing has happened for hours now. This is the calm before.

The house is empty. Even the voice in her head has fallen silent. She can feel the other's presence though, knows she is close, just out of sight. The doorbell clangs. The sound scares her, even though she has been expecting it.

Pete isn't alone. They will probably never be alone again. The brief friendship bloomed like a day-lily, a flash of colour in a dull yard, shrivelled and dead by the time the sun came up again. At his side is the young male constable that she has seen before. Sunny, she thinks; maybe Sydney. She doesn't care and won't ask. The time for pretending is over.

They follow her down the hall to her study. She has already placed two chairs in front of her desk.

The younger man is excited, but nervous too. This young police officer is slightly afraid of her. Pete looks sad. Maggie wishes she could tell him that, to an extent, she shares his sadness but that would hardly be appropriate any more.

'We wanted to share this with you as soon as possible,' he says. 'We agreed there's nothing to be gained by you not having the information as soon as us.'

They have found something in the abandoned office. 'Thank you,' she says.

'The computer is definitely the one used to make contact with the three victims.'

She has rarely heard Pete speak so formally, so like a police spokesman on the evening news.

'Our investigators found the conversations that Hamish Wolfe had with Jessie Tout, Chloe Wood and Myrtle Reid. They're double-checking times and dates, IP addresses, all the technical stuff, but there seems little doubt.'

'We'd really love to know how you managed to find it so quickly when we couldn't.' The constable has a stain on the collar of his shirt. He looks tired.

'I looked.' Maggie returns the young man's stare. 'You didn't. Not really.'

The constable's face says he's registered Maggie's aggression, and is up for a fight – to a point. He says, 'We wondered if perhaps your client gave you some idea where to look.'

'Why on earth would he do something so stupid? And all you've found is the computer that was used to make contact with the women. You haven't found anything to link it to Hamish.'

'Actually, we have,' the constable begins, before Pete silences him with a look.

'There was a pen,' Pete says. 'A biro, hidden away beneath the carpet. It has Hamish's prints on it.'

Maggie stares back at him for a second. 'It proves nothing,' she says, although she knows that, in the eyes of the world, it will prove a great deal. 'If someone broke into Hamish's house to steal evidence, they could easily have found a pen.'

The constable sneers. Maggie's hand reaches out for a paperweight and clasps it tight. The sneer fades.

'Just three women?' asks Maggie.

Pete frowns. 'You mean, did we find any trace of Zoe?'

'Yes, that's what I mean.'

'Nothing,' says the constable. 'In fact, the first activity we found dates to after Zoe's disappearance.'

'I thought so. I don't think Zoe's disappearance had anything to do with the three murders,' Maggie says. 'I think it may have been entirely unconnected, except that it gave the killer the idea. A fat girl vanished, presumed dead. Hamish supposedly had a history with fat girls. The real killer decided to make other fat girls disappear, and direct the blame towards him by planting evidence.'

Pete sighs. 'Maggie, this conspiracy theory is going nowhere.'

'Why didn't you tell me that you and Hamish were friends before his arrest?'

He flushes. 'We weren't friends.'

'Why didn't you tell me that your ex-wife, who left you for your boss, just six months before Jessie was murdered, is a very similar size to Hamish's supposed three victims?'

He gives an odd, twisted smile. 'Are you serious?'

Maggie turns to the constable. 'If anything happens to me, Detective, if I vanish suddenly, or have a freakish accident, I do hope you'll remember this conversation.'

The man laughs, but glances sideways at his sergeant. Pete reaches into his coat pocket. He pulls out a clear plastic wallet, with several loose sheets of notepaper inside and puts them on the desk in front of Maggie.

'They're just copies,' he says. 'The originals are at the station.'

'What are they?' Maggie sees the heading on the stationery and can feel fibres in her body start to tighten. *HMP Isle of Wight.*

'Please read them. They're in date order. We'll wait.'

She wants to refuse, to tell them to leave the letters, that she'll get to them in her own time. She knows they won't agree.

Aware that she has no choice, she unfolds the first letter.

My love,

When I think of the moments in my life that have given me greatest pleasure: the scaling of an impossible rock face, watching the moon over the ocean on Christmas morning . . .

Hamish's handwriting. She reads it through to the end. The second letter talks about how the world sees him as a monster and how only the woman he loves can redeem him. The third is more whimsical, poetic even, deeply moving in its sadness. She recognizes his turn of phrase, his sense of humour, his imagination. The raw eroticism of the Christmas letter stabs her in the gut. There is no doubt that he wrote these letters. Five of them in total, the most recent sent just a week or so ago. Hamish has been writing love letters. And not to her.

321

She has a sense of a great weight above her head, a weight that will fall soon, crushing her entirely.

'Who is the recipient?' She hears her own voice sounding old and worn out. Hamish sees no one but his mother and herself. He told her that. She believed him.

Pete says, 'I suggest you read the replies.'

There are more letters. The next batch is in a different handwriting, harder to read. No address.

My darling,

I was sleeping when we met. I've been sleeping my whole life. You woke me. Not with a kiss - oh, if only! - but with the knowledge that there is another in the world like me.

She can't read this drivel. She skips to the end.

Yours, always,
Me

There are more. One is enough. 'Are these genuine?' she asks, although she knows they must be. 'Who sent them?'

'All letters sent into and out of Parkhurst are copied,' Pete explains. 'We applied for a warrant to examine Wolfe's correspondence – after we found the originals from him in Sarah Smith's flat. Remember Sarah Smith? You know her as Sirocco.'

'These letters were sent to Sirocco?' Maggie manages. 'To and from Sirocco?'

'That's right.'

Sirocco? That weird, needy, clingy girl? Hamish in love with Sirocco?

'Are you OK, Miss Rose?' the constable says. 'Can I get you a glass of water?'

If that man speaks to her again, she will hit him. 'You told me she never visited. You checked. She was lying.'

'Actually, she wasn't,' Pete says. 'She just didn't give her own name. She used the name Sophie Wolfe, pretending to be Hamish's sister.'

322

'That's impossible. She'd need ID.'

'She had it,' Pete tells her. 'She used Sophie's old passport and had a new one issued with her photograph. She looked sufficiently like her for the Passport Office to be fooled. We spotted it the minute we checked the visitor's schedule. We'll add it to the charges she's facing, of course.'

'She would have needed Wolfe's help to do that,' says the constable. 'He probably told her where she'd find the passport, how to sneak in to his parents' house. They've been conspiring together.'

Maggie has an urge to get up, to bang her fists against a hard surface. She clasps the seat with one hand. 'Sirocco killed Odi and Broon. She tried to kill me.'

'Yes, that's another thing,' says Pete. 'We have absolutely no evidence to connect her with the murder in Wells Market Square. Which means we can't charge her. The only charge that will stick at the moment is that of threatening behaviour towards you. I'm afraid she was granted bail this afternoon.'

'You're kidding me?'

They get to their feet.

'She's been told to come nowhere near you,' says Pete. 'But as we know, she is a bit unstable. You might want to keep your doors locked. Obviously, if you're concerned at any time, you should dial 999.'

Pete glances back as he leaves the room and his eyes settle on the pile of letters. 'You can keep those.'

Chapter 99

'HE DOESN'T LOVE HER.'

'If you say so.'

'He can't love her. Have you seen her? He's been using her.'

'So he loves you, but he's using her, is that right? And yet, she's the one who got the letters.'

Maggie pulls herself out of the bath and feels cold again immediately. She finds a gown and slippers. She is shaking, she is so cold. She leaves the steam-drenched bathroom and the temperature drops by a degree or more.

'He loves me. He said so.'

'Actually, that's not what he said. He said, he *loved* – note the use of the past tense—'

'Enough!'

'Look at me.'

'I don't want to.'

'It's time. Look at me.'

Her feet dragging like a sulky child, Maggie steps across the carpet to the full-length, free-standing mirror in the corner. The lights in her bedroom are always kept low, and the steam has stolen out from the bathroom to coat the surface of the mirror. She can see nothing of her reflection but a hazy shape.

In spite of the cold, Maggie lets her robe slip to the carpet. She can just about make out her tiny frame in the steamed-up mirror. She hasn't weighed more than nine stone for years, but in recent weeks the weight has fallen off her. She was eight stone six pounds this morning. She'll have gained two pounds, roughly, during the course of the day. She always knows, to half a pound, how much she weighs.

She pulls loose her hair and fluffs it up around her head. She can just about see the pale blue curls and the paler face.

A slender body, a perfect oval face, and bright blue hair. That is the reflection hiding itself from her right now.

'I'm still here.'

'I know.'

'I'll always be here.'

'I know.'

As the mirror clears Maggie's reflection gains substance. She can see the pale, pale skin on long, slim limbs. She can see loose and saggy skin, that she can never reveal to the light of day, because its folds and wrinkles are revolting, in spite of the relentless surgery she once endured. She can see the long, angry red scars, on the insides of her arms and legs. Disfigured limbs, that must always be clothed in long sleeves and trousers or opaque tights, that have never known the soft stroke of a lover's hand. Never felt warm, damp kisses.

As the steam fades completely, so do Maggie's scars, until they vanish and her flesh blossoms. She is growing, blooming, swelling. All the pounds she once lost by walking endless miles day after day, by existing on near-starvation levels of food, are coming back. She is getting plumper, riper, regaining the former self she once gloried in. She feels the weight of her breasts, the silky slide of her thighs as they brush together, the jiggling of her ass as she moves.

The last trace of steam leaves the mirror and Maggie can see her face again. It is the same face, but looking so very different with so much added flesh, and before the surgery removed the hook of her prominent nose. Before expensive dentistry corrected the crooked teeth. Her hair isn't blue any more. It is longer, thicker, curlier, dark as polished jet. Her eyes are conker brown. She has become the woman she used to be, before a broken heart and the shame of public humiliation forced her to flee, to change herself completely. She has become, once again, the woman she will always be inside; and the voice in her head breathes a long, satisfied sigh, happy at last.

She is Daisy.

Chapter 100

BBC News Homepage, Tuesday, 12 January 2016, 2000 hours

CONVICTED MURDERER AT LARGE AS PARKHURST WALLS BREACHED

Killer of three, Hamish Wolfe (pictured), could be on the run tonight after escaping from Parkhurst Prison on the Isle of Wight. While the prison has made no official statement, and the Governor remains unavailable for comment, it is thought that Wolfe has already left the island.

According to unconfirmed reports that have reached the outside world through contraband mobile phones, Wolfe, 38, convicted in 2014 of the abduction and murder of three women, made a bid for freedom late this afternoon, slipping away during a disturbance and using a home-made ladder (pictured below) to scale the perimeter fence. Our correspondent has been unable to confirm that police dogs tracked him ten miles across open country to Sandown Airport (pictured), but has seen heightened police activity around the site.

Airport staff have confirmed that a two-seater Cessna has been reported missing from the airfield. It is understood that the plane's owner is not currently in residence on the island and that the airport's control room was given no details of a planned flight.

Wolfe is a qualified and experienced pilot and authorities are concluding that he escaped in the plane.

A spokesman for Avon and Somerset police refused to deny that the force is working on the assumption that Wolfe will head back to his home and that they are compiling a list of places and people that he might head for.

While no specific warning has yet been issued by police, Wolfe is considered a very dangerous man and the public should not approach him.

Screenshot placed in Avon and Somerset police files.

Chapter 101

MAGGIE ROSE, who started life as Margaret Rose Baron, nicknamed Daisy by her parents, is reading and re-reading the item on the BBC website about Hamish's escape. When she feels she knows it by heart, she flicks to Twitter, to the stream of misspelled tweets supposedly sent from contraband mobile phones inside the prison, that have been retweeted several thousand times already.

She can find nothing else on the internet to bear out the escape story but knows that Pete has been trying to get in touch with her for nearly an hour now. She has ignored his phone calls, and his texts, but the email from his colleague with the odd name caught her attention. The message contained a link to the BBC site.

She has tried to telephone Parkhurst but the phones are not being answered. She has tried to contact the Isle of Wight police but gets voicemail messages. Somehow she found the energy to get dressed, although she hardly knows why.

She tries to work out how long it would take a fit man to run ten miles. How long it would take a light aircraft to fly from the Isle of Wight to Somerset.

Will he come to her?

She remembers Sirocco's words on the night the two of them met. 'He has a plan. You're part of it.' If Maggie has played a role in this, she cannot see it. Everything Hamish has said to her, about relying upon her, about trusting her, has been a lie. He has been stringing her along, while all the time planning to escape.

Is he with Sirocco right now? Are they fleeing together?

Unable to keep still, even to stay in one room, she gets up, descends two flights of steps into the cellar and flicks on the dim lights.

Dead flies litter the floor of the first, largest room and crunch underfoot. No matter how many she sweeps away, there always seem to be more. Most are houseflies, but there are others too, moths, crane flies, huge great bluebottles. She has no idea where they come from in the middle of winter but they appear with a worrying regularity. As though there is something down here that attracts them. Which is impossible, of course. She cleans down here often. It is the most frequently swept, dusted, bleached and polished basement in the West Country.

And still, the flies.

She looks around for the broom, not sure whether she left it down here after her last visit or took it back upstairs to the kitchen cupboard. As her eyes fall on the dark walls, the now empty shelves, the flagged flooring, she has a sense that this may be the last time she ever comes to the cellar.

She should check, one last time, make sure there is nothing she missed.

Three storage heaters line one wall. A fourth stands beneath the high narrow windows. This room, like the rest of the house, is never cold when she is in it. For several years her heating bills have been huge. A faint smear of dust has settled on the heaters but she needn't worry about that. Not any more.

The high, narrow, horizontally figured windows, alone in the room, are never cleaned. They are beyond dirty, filthy even, as though someone has smeared mud across them, making it impossible for anyone outside to see in. The windows are the one big disadvantage to this house and yet they are necessary all the same. The windows let in the flies.

Maggie walks past them, catching a scent of the chill night air, towards the back of the cellar. The smallest basement room appears to be a bathroom but the plumbing has been disconnected long ago. Turning on the taps would produce nothing but a few splutters of dank air. Any liquid poured into the Victorian-style roll-top bath would drain, not to waste pipes, but into a large, shallow tray that lies immediately beneath the plug. Several large buckets stand to one side.

The bath is spotless. So is the drain tray. So are the buckets.

By the side of the bath is a large plastic container of household bleach. More out of habit than because she knows it is necessary, Maggie opens it and pours it around the rim of the bath. Bleach is thick and it takes time to run down the enamel sides of the bath, gathering in the bottom, draining out into the tray. Slowly, the tray fills. She will empty it tomorrow, on the land at the bottom of her garden, because pouring that amount of bleach down the drain would be traceable.

The sudden banging makes her jump. Someone is upstairs, hammering on her back door. Knowing she has no choice now but to move with events, she makes her way up, expecting to see Pete. He will want to make sure she knows about the escape, that she is taking sensible precautions. He will think she needs to fear Wolfe. She sensed a new and unsettling coldness in him earlier, but Pete is a good man. He will no doubt offer, once again, to find a room for her at the Crown in Wells.

The very air seems to be thickening around her, making it harder to move freely. Every step she takes upstairs increases the heaviness in her chest. Is it possible, really, that she might never see Hamish again?

Silently she opens the door to the back hallway. She has disconnected the security lights at the back of her house and can only see a dark silhouette through the glass of the door. She doesn't think whoever is out there is tall enough to be Pete. Her heart leaps momentarily, but too small to be Pete is too small to be Hamish and it settles back down again. She unlocks the door and opens it.

Sirocco.

'He's out,' Sirocco steps forward, as though Maggie will simply invite her in, take her coat and put the kettle on. 'He's escaped. Have you heard?'

Sirocco seems to be wearing even more loose, flowing clothing than usual. On her head, clamping down her unruly black hair, is a tight-fitting beanie-style cap. She looks dressed to travel and the sight sends another pang into Maggie's heart.

There is some hope, though, in her being here. She isn't with Hamish yet.

'I saw it on the news,' says Maggie, wondering how to take this forward. The last time she saw Sirocco she'd been afraid for her life. This isn't the top of a Ferris wheel, though, here she is on home ground.

'Read this.' Sirocco has fumbled in her coat pocket and is holding out a sheet of pale blue paper. 'Read this and tell me what it means.'

Maggie glances down and sees handwriting that she recognizes. Suddenly, the heaviness inside her seems more manageable. Her heart, that has been fighting to keep beating, picks up its pace.

'Come in,' she says, stepping back from the doorway. In the kitchen she will have room to move. In the kitchen there will be enough light. She will be able to see what's coming.

'There isn't time. He's on his way. You need to read it now.' Agitated though she may be, Sirocco seems strangely reluctant to come any closer to Maggie. This time, it seems to be she who is afraid.

He's on his way. Maggie can hear a drumming in her ears as she backs into the kitchen. 'Why should I be able to understand it?' she asks. 'If you can't, what makes you think I can?'

Sirocco approaches cautiously. The letter – Hamish's last love letter? – dangles in the air between them. Then it is in Maggie's hand. It is damp. Maggie glances down, then back up again.

'I can't I'm afraid. I need my reading glasses.'

'I'll read it to you. Give it back.'

Still holding the letter, Maggie walks past her, out of the room, heading once again for the basement. 'I left them downstairs just now. I won't be a second.'

'Get back here.'

The stairs are seconds away and Sirocco is following her. 'Where are you going?' Her voice has risen, become shrill. 'Is that the cellar? Are you going in there?'

'You can wait up here,' Maggie reaches the cellar door and pulls it open. 'What did you mean when you said, "He's on his way"? Why on earth would Hamish come here? This is the first place the police will look.'

She looks back when she is halfway down the steps. Sirocco is hovering, uncertain, at the top.

'He's coming for me,' Sirocco says. 'He's been planning it for ages. I've been helping. He wrote to me, telling me where to meet him.' She points to the letter in Maggie's hand.

'So why am I involved?' asks Maggie.

'He said to ask you. He said he had to write in code, so the prison staff wouldn't know what he was telling me. If there was anything I didn't understand, I had to ask you. Let me just read it to you, please. We don't need to go downstairs. I have to meet him now.'

Maggie's heart, which has been accelerating for some time now, is

330

starting to beat painfully. She climbs back up four steps. 'I may still need to read it for myself,' she says. 'But OK.'

Sirocco pulls the letter open and leans back, to catch the overhead light.

My darling, Sirocco begins, and then looks up, almost triumphantly at Maggie. Maggie nods at her to go on.

I've been thinking about lovers of old, those who were real, and those who lived only in the hearts of those who knew the stories. Dido and Aeneas, Antony and Cleopatra, Henry VIII and Anne Boleyn, Arthur and Guinevere.

Sirocco stumbles a little over the names, as though they are unfamiliar to her. Maggie wants to tell her to get on with it.

'They rarely end well.' I can just hear you saying it, my little glass-half-empty girl!

There is a tiny, annoying smile on her face now.

But what of those we never hear about? The couples who fall in love in their twenties, who raise children and dote on their children's children, who face life's triumphs and tragedies together and who, at the end of a long and largely happy life of blissful anonymity say to each other, 'I wouldn't have had it any other way, my dear.' Aren't they love's true heroes?

Sirocco's voice has fallen lower. Maggie takes a step up, so as not to miss a word.

Blissful anonymity isn't within our grasp, of course. If you and I are to be together, you will share my notoriety. We will be the new Bonnie and Clyde, as talked of as Fred and Rose West, as hated as Hindley and Brady. You will be tainted, my sweet girl, a monster by proxy.

331

I cannot ask it. And yet I know that, were our positions reversed, I would give up my good name, my guarantee of freedom for you in a heartbeat. Believe this, my darling, if you never believed anything good of me before. I would give up my chance of redemption, to spend my life with you.

You know where to find me, my Guinevere. Arthur will be waiting. All my love,

Hamish

Sirocco's eyes lift and meet Maggie's again. 'What does he mean?' she asks. 'I don't know where to find him. He's never called me Guinevere before.'

The world can transform in a matter of seconds, Maggie discovers. It just has. She turns away, so that Sirocco will not see her smiling, will not guess that her heart is racing, her head singing.

'What?' Sirocco says, suddenly confused. 'What is it? Do you understand it? Where are you going? Come back up.'

'Of course I understand it,' Maggie takes the last step down. She turns the corner, but hears with satisfaction the sound of the other woman's footsteps.

'You know what he means?' Sirocco is calling out as she follows. 'You know where he'll be?'

'Oh yes.'

Maggie hears the softer footstep that tells her Sirocco has reached the stone floor at the bottom of the steps.

One of the most surprising aspects of this whole business, Maggie thinks, as she takes up position in the centre of the room, is how easy it can be to persuade women to do the dumbest things. Like stepping down into the basement of someone they do not know.

With Jessie, she'd faked an injury. Jessie had been the most challenging, in fairness, because Jessie had stepped out that bright Saturday believing she was to meet a handsome doctor. She'd almost refused to go with the smartly dressed young woman who'd claimed she was Harry's PA, and that he'd been unavoidably delayed in theatre, but would meet her later at his house.

Chloe, on the other hand had been easy. Chloe hadn't thought to question that the quirky jewellery tycoon had both workshop and office in her basement. Myrtle had never doubted the need to waddle below ground to view the Disney collection, or that the slender, blue-haired woman leading the way was Anita Radcliffe's daughter. And now this deluded woman is proving as stupid as the rest.

Sirocco's flowing black form appears in the doorway as she looks nervously around. The basement is empty now, apart from the flies. The boxes of souvenirs – the women's clothes and possessions – have long since been disposed of. Maggie is nothing if not a very careful killer. More recently, her old medical textbooks, her childhood things, have likewise been taken away. She will leave behind nothing that will link her to her former life. Or to what she has done in this one.

There is nothing in this basement room that should alarm Sirocco. From where she is standing, she cannot see the disconnected bathtub in which the bodies of three large women decomposed and drained away until their remains weighed practically nothing. Hamish had been bang on about that.

The two women stand and face each other. Sirocco looks on the verge of tears. 'How? How come you know where Hamish is going and I don't?'

As Maggie steps forward she feels a fleeting moment of pity for what the girl has lost. She holds out her left hand, ostensibly for the letter, really as a distraction, so that Sirocco won't see, until too late, what Maggie has in her right hand.

The club hammer, identical to the one that killed Odi and Broon, cuts its way through the air and connects with the side of Sirocco's head. The hard resistance of bone is more solid than Maggie expected and her arm feels a jolt of pain as Sirocco sways.

Maggie swings her arm back, ready to strike again, but Sirocco sinks to the floor, her black clothes spreading around her like a stagnant puddle. She is unlikely to be dead, not after one strike, but Maggie can waste no more time. She has somewhere else to be.

'How do I know where Hamish is going?' she says to the motionless form on the cellar floor. 'I know because these letters were never meant for you, I'm afraid. You were just the postman.'

Chapter 102

HE HAS LEFT A TRAIL FOR HER. The fluorescent stones start at the cave entrance and lead her, breadcrumb style, into its depths. She doesn't need them. She has been this way so many times, she thinks she can do it in the dark. She steps into the cave, leaving light behind – or maybe she did that a long time ago. Either way, her path is clear.

After a few yards, she picks up his scent. Not the one she remembers from so long ago, that heady mix of aftershave and shower gel and something that was so essentially male, so completely Hamish, but the new smell, the one born of prison and violence and frustration.

She likes them both.

The trickling of the water over the rocks sounds like music. The first time he brought her here, there really was music. He'd carried a battery-operated CD player in his backpack, along with a padded mat and blanket, cold champagne and glasses, and lots of candles.

'I don't like caves. They make me claustrophobic,' Daisy had complained, when what she really meant was that she didn't like climbing up the sides of steep hills to get to them. She didn't like the constricted feeling of squeezing her too large body through tiny gaps in the walls.

'You'll like this one,' he promised. 'There's a pool where Arthur and Guinevere's wedding rings were thrown hundreds of years ago. The rock grew around them and all you can see now are two small rings of gold in the rock face.'

She'd gone willingly, after that, because who can resist a tale of enduring love. Or heartless betrayal. The legend could be read both ways.

Twenty years ago, he turned the cave into a fairy grotto with dozens of tiny, sparkling lights. She'd sat on the rug and watched in wonder as this beautiful man went to so much trouble for her. She'd known in that moment, for better or worse, she would love him until the day she died.

She hadn't known then, of course, that it was going to be so very much for the worse.

The narrow rock passage sweeps down low and she must too, but she knows he is waiting on the other side.

The vaulted chamber is much darker than she remembers from that first time. He has had neither the time, nor the opportunity, to collect tea lights. All he has is a small torch and a travel rug, both of which are probably from the plane.

He is sitting, his back to the river, watching her approach.

'Hey, gorgeous,' he says.

She draws closer, reaches the rug and sinks down beside him. He is too pale, even in this weird absence of light, too thin. So much older than the boy she fell in love with, and yet so completely the man who has been in her head every waking moment for two decades. Only the sadness is different. The sadness at what she has become.

'How long have you known?' She asks the question, and yet knows the answer before he gives it.

'Almost from the first,' he says. 'Someone planted that evidence. It didn't take me long to realize you were the only one clever enough.'

Of course. He'd known that Maggie Rose and Daisy Baron were one and the same, long before that first Parkhurst visit. She would have seen any gleam of recognition in his eyes, any sudden, sharp realization of the truth. He has been playing the game for as long as she. Only he has been playing it better.

He tries to smile, doesn't quite make it. It will cost him dear, this knowledge of what he has turned her into.

'And the only one who hated you enough,' she says.

He is so very, very sad. 'Still?' he asks her.

She shakes her head. 'No.'

'Well, that's something, I guess.'

Twenty years ago, on this very spot, he'd barely been able to keep his hands off her. Now, he sits apart. She reaches out and traces her index finger along the back of his hand. He glances down at it.

'Seriously?' she says. 'I was the first person you thought of? After all this time?'

His hand turns and, after a moment's hesitation, takes hold of hers. 'The whole cave business more or less convinced me.' He looks around. 'Especially when Myrtle was found in here. Then you sent my mother

335

those books. Did you think I'd forgotten you were called Margaret? That I never knew your middle name? The books clinched it. You never did get the hang of participles, did you? And it's not, "*too young an age*", it's "*too early an age*". How many times did I tell you that?'

She edges closer. 'Don't tell me you're still a grammar fascist.'

'What happened to Sirocco?' he asks her.

She doesn't reply and he sees what has happened to Sirocco.

'You knew that,' she says quickly. 'You knew when you chose to involve her. When you sent her with that last letter.'

He doesn't argue. The darkness that seeped into her all those years ago has found its way into him too.

'The police will get to my house soon. They'll find her. They'll work out that I killed the other three. They'll know you're innocent.'

'Jessie, Chloe, Myrtle,' he says, as though their names are seldom off his tongue. 'Did there need to be three?'

'Two could be coincidence,' she says. 'Three makes a serial killer.'

He nods slowly and she thinks she will have to work hard to chase that sadness away. But that's OK. They have plenty of time.

'Odi and Broon? Did she see you coming in here? Is that why?'

Maggie is getting bored, talking about dead people. This isn't why she came. 'Who knows? Odi was scared of me, but then again she was scared of everything. I just don't like loose ends.'

'Looks like I'm a free man.' His face brightens, but the look of levity is forced and false. 'Although, technically, I could still be charged with stealing a plane.'

She smiles too. 'Can't help you with that one, I'm afraid.'

'So, what was the plan? Leave me there to rot? When the police found that office you hired, that computer, that frigging pen with my fingerprints on it – how did you do that, by the way? – I thought that was it. That I'd have one last visit, you'd smile your little cat-like smile and I'd never see you again.'

His gaze holds hers and doesn't falter.

'It was the pen you signed my contract with,' she says. 'I just changed the ink and removed the cap. And, no, I would never have left you to rot. I thought perhaps we'd fall in love, that I'd become a prison wife, devoted, loyal, working tirelessly for your release but never quite managing it.'

'Keeping me exactly where you wanted me. Totally in your power.'

'Something like that. Of course I also have enough evidence hidden away to have got you out at any time, should my mind have changed.'

'Victims' hair? Clothes? In a safety deposit box somewhere? Ready to plant on some unsuspecting patsy?'

She smiles.

'So what happens now?'

She shrugs, feigns carelessness, even though her heart has never beaten faster. 'You're a free man. The dead woman at my house will ensure that. I'll be the killer of six people, you'll be the innocent man, wrongly accused. You'll be a national hero. You can return to your profession, make a fortune from public appearances, start a family, have the life you used to dream about.'

'And you'll be behind bars?'

'Oh, I didn't say that.'

He looks long into her eyes and she knows he has guessed her intentions. If Hamish turns his back on her tonight, she will climb to the highest point of the Gorge. She won't be the first wronged woman to seek solace on its cold, high edge.

She makes a show of looking at her watch, although from the moment she entered the cave she has known exactly what the time is. 'They'll be hot on our heels, my long-lost lover. Which is it to be?'

He breathes out a sigh so long, so heavy, that she half expects to see him deflating. Then, awkwardly, as though he has been sitting too long, he gets to his feet. He reaches down, takes her hand and pulls her up. For one, heart-stopping moment, she thinks he will kiss her. Then he takes a long step back.

'I'm truly sorry about what I did to you at Oxford.' His eyes lift, go over her shoulder and fix on something behind. 'But you should have gotten over it.'

Maggie spins round to see dim pools of light immediately in front of the rocky overhang. She can just about make out two forms. Pete.

And Sirocco.

Chapter 103

'MAGGIE ROSE, I am arresting you for the murders of Jessie Tout, Chloe Wood, Myrtle Reid, Odi Smith and Broon Richards.' As he speaks, Pete is thinking fast, measuring the distances between the four people in the cave, reminding himself where the dangerous places are, because he's seen the look in Maggie's eyes and he knows this could still go very badly wrong. She will almost certainly have a weapon and she is very close to Hamish. 'You do not—'

'Shut the hell up!' It is Pete at whom she yells, but her eyes haven't left the woman at his side. 'Who the hell are you?' For the moment she is ignoring both Pete and Hamish, but that won't last long. Soon the full force of her rage will be directed at the lover who spurned her. A second time.

The woman Maggie knows as Sirocco Silverwood opens her mouth to speak but Pete catches hold of her arm and stops her.

'This is Detective Constable Liz Nuttall,' he says. 'Hamish's liaison officer. You didn't hurt her just now, you'll be relieved to know, but she was wired up and we heard everything that went on in your house. Hamish is wired too, by the way.'

Out of the corner of his eye, Pete sees Liz allow her huge coat to gape open, to let Maggie see the body armour that was meant to protect her from knife wounds. All the same, he will never again send a constable into such a situation. The fifteen minutes that Liz was in Maggie's house were the longest in his life. Especially when she went into the cellar and they lost comms.

Maggie spins round to look at Hamish.

'You knew? You were part of this?'

Hamish bows his head once. His eyes leave her and settle on Liz. 'It took me a while to persuade Liz, but I got there in the end.'

'And Liz convinced me,' says Pete. 'It's over, Maggie. I need you to come with me now.'

He moves forward again, trying to block Maggie's view of Liz, because he really doesn't like the way the two women are looking at each other. Liz, though, is not about to be intimidated by the woman she's worked for months to bring to justice. She lifts up both hands and takes off first the beanie cap, then the long black wig.

'This is a gel skullcap.' She is speaking directly to Maggie. 'Skateboarders use them for the more dangerous stunts. I know you meant to knock my brains out, but you've just given me a nasty headache.'

Hamish seems about to move.

'Stay where you are, please, Hamish,' Pete says. 'Maggie, I want you down on your knees with your hands in the air. I'll make this as quick and as comfortable as possible, but we have to get you out of here.'

In response she backs away. 'Are you mad? Do you imagine for one moment that you'll convict me? Think about what you've been doing. Illegal searches of my house, breaking and entering, threatening me on that Ferris wheel. Not to mention springing a convicted murderer from prison. Any confession of mine that you taped was made under duress, when I was in fear of my life. There is more chance of the two of you going to prison than me.' She turns to Hamish. 'As for you, you're going to rot.'

'Officially, we've only ever been in your house with your permission,' says Pete. 'The break-in – or, strictly, trespass, because your door was unlocked – is likely to remain an unsolved crime. There is nothing to suggest that the origami rose, the writing under the table, the daisies delivered on Christmas Day were anything to do with us.'

'I know they were.' She's practically spitting at him. 'You staged that break-in so I'd agree to the crime scene people coming in. You released my personal information to Facebook too. You were trying to frighten me, to intimidate me into making a false confession.'

'Prove it,' says Pete. 'Prove that the three of us had anything to do with that.'

'As for the Ferris wheel incident,' says Liz, 'I remember it quite differently. It was your idea. You frightened me when we were at the top. Sandra and Bear will back me up on that, by the way.'

Maggie is getting angrier by the second and Pete knows he needs to wrap this up. But she has turned on Hamish now. 'You escaped from prison and stole a plane. That is a serious crime, and if these two jerks helped you, then that alone is enough—'

'Actually, he didn't.' The new voice cuts through the cold air of the cave. Pete should have known Latimer wouldn't be able to keep out of it for long. Keeping him in the dark about the unofficial undercover operation he and Liz instigated is probably still something he'll have to answer for. Oddly, though, he finds himself quite relieved to see the boss. Especially as he hasn't come alone. At least two of the uniformed officers they left outside have made their way in with the DCI. Sunday is with them too.

Latimer glances around the cave and addresses Maggie. 'There was no ten-mile hike across the Isle of Wight, no James Bond style escape in a light aircraft,' he tells her. 'The ladder and the handmade key were only to provide some photographs that Sunday here used to create a very convincing fake BBC website. And to provide a bit of noise on Twitter. Hamish left Parkhurst in a police car and came here via the Isle of Wight ferry and the M5. Technically, he is still in police custody and no crimes have been committed by my team.' He glances over at Pete and drops his voice. 'Although God knows they came close.'

'Maggie,' says Hamish, 'you need to go with Pete now.'

Maggie turns back to Hamish and shakes her head. Her eyes don't leave his, although she must surely be able to sense, if not see, that Pete, Latimer, Sunday and Liz are all making their way towards her. God knows how they'll get her out of here uninjured if she fights, but they have to bring this to an end. Behind them, more uniformed constables are entering the cave.

'You love me,' Maggie tells Hamish. 'I know you do.'

'No.' Liz speaks up, her voice echoing through the cave. 'He loves me. That part was true.'

Hamish takes the last step that will bring him up to Maggie.

'And that dog isn't called Daisy,' Liz shouts. 'She's called Cruella.'

Maggie seems to sway but she's still looking at Hamish. Pete doesn't think either of them have blinked for the better part of a minute. Hamish reaches out and puts his hands on her shoulders, bends down and kisses her cheek, whispers something in her ear. She seems to slump against him. Hamish looks over her shoulder at Pete and nods.

340

With a sudden, painful screech, Maggie rears up and strikes out at Hamish. Taken by surprise, he loses his balance. Liz rushes forward. Maggie darts away. She cannot leave the cave, there are too many officers blocking her way, but she isn't heading for the exit. She stumbles across the last few stretches of damp limestone to the edge of the river.

'Daisy!' yells Hamish, as she throws herself into the water.

The current reaches up and grabs a hold of her. Every police officer in the cave runs to the river's edge and shines his torch on the water. In Latimer's beam they think they catch a glimpse of a pale hand as the water rushes underground. Then nothing.

Chapter 104

The Times Online, Thursday, 14 January 2016

'CONVICTED' MURDERER FREED PENDING APPEAL

Hamish Wolfe was released from prison yesterday by a High Court judge pending a fresh appeal into his conviction. 'It would appear, from what I have learned this morning,' said Lord Justice Robinson, 'that new evidence in this case has come to light. If substantiated it may, in the fullness of time, lead to a quashing of Mr Wolfe's conviction. In the meantime, I see no reason why Mr Wolfe should not rejoin his family.'

Police have, this morning, named thirty-eight-year-old lawyer and true-crime author Maggie Rose as their new prime suspect in the murders of Jessie Tout, Chloe Wood and Myrtle Reid. Rose fled police custody during an attempted arrest two days ago and is believed to have died. A police search for her body is currently under way.

Hamish Wolfe, thirty-eight, was given a whole life tariff in 2014 and has served fifteen months of his sentence, primarily in HMP Isle of Wight. While family and friends campaigned energetically for his release, the turning point came when he secured the confidence and support of his police liaison officer, Detective Constable Elizabeth Nuttall, thirty-four.

The divorced mother-of-two confirmed to reporters this morning that she and Wolfe are romantically involved and expect to marry shortly after his release has been formalized.

Nuttall is not the only woman to fall prey to the handsome former surgeon's dark charm (he received, allegedly, over a hundred letters a week in prison), but in her case, the infatuation might cost her dear. A spokesman for Avon and Somerset police confirmed this morning that she has been suspended from her CID job and is expected to face misconduct charges for entering into a relationship with a convicted prisoner without informing her superiors. If it is found that she acted incorrectly, she may be dismissed from the police service.

At a press conference this morning, senior officer DCI Tim Latimer refused to condemn DC Nuttall. He said, 'Clearly there needs to be a full investigation, but at this stage I'm proud that my officers, in particular Detective Sergeant Pete Weston and Detective Constable Liz Nuttall, were prepared to put the pursuit of justice before personal considerations.'

Hamish Wolfe has been unavailable for comment today and is believed to be with his parents at an undisclosed location, but Ms Nuttall told us that she couldn't be happier that her fiancé's innocence has been proven and that they can look forward to a normal life together. 'I started to believe Hamish shortly after I became his liaison officer,' she told us. 'After that it was a question of finding proof, and of convincing my colleagues that there'd been a miscarriage of justice.'

The couple have not yet set a date for their wedding. 'Soon,' Ms Nuttall told us. 'Very soon. Hamish needs some time, obviously, to get used to being in the outside world again. I'm going to need to be patient with him, cut him some slack but, yes, it's going to happen soon. No, I haven't spoken to him for a couple of days, but that's fine. He needs some space.'

When I ask what would have happened if proof hadn't been forthcoming, if she'd remained convinced of his guilt, she doesn't have a ready response to hand. I decide to push a little and ask which came first, the belief in his innocence, or a dangerously irresistible attraction.

'I fell in love,' she says. 'Obviously I'm much happier to love an innocent man, but if he'd been guilty?' She pauses for a few seconds before giving me her answer: 'I would have loved him just the same.'

Acknowledgements

My grateful thanks to:

My family, including my mother-in-law, who gets dragged on research trips during the coldest months of the year and who never seems to mind. My dog, Lupe, for being beautifully behaved during our stay at the Crown in Wells and for not killing the cathedral cat. Peter Warner, for advice on what lawyers can and can't get up to with convicted felons. Adrian Summons for the detecting stuff. Brian Snell of the Mendip Caving Group, for help with disposing of bodies beneath the Mendip Hills. (Sidcot Swallet and Goatchurch Cavern are real caves, but Rill Cavern and Gossam Cave are my inventions.) Any remaining mistakes are my own.

My two UK editors, Sarah Adams and Frankie Gray, both of whom worked exceptionally hard to get *Daisy* to the publishable stage. A cheery wave, also, to Kelley Ragland at St Martin's Press in the US, Andrea Best at Goldmann in Germany and all my lovely overseas publishers.

As ever, the Transworld team: Alison Barrow, Tom Chicken, Elspeth Dougall, Christina Ellicott, Larry Finlay, Giulia Giordano, Gary Hartley, Becky Hunter, Louise Jones, Naomi Mantin, Deirdre O'Connell, Gareth Pottle, Bradley Rose, Kate Samano, Bill Scott-Kerr and Nicola Wright.

By no means least, my agent, Anne-Marie Doulton, and her colleagues, the Buckmans.